One More Breath

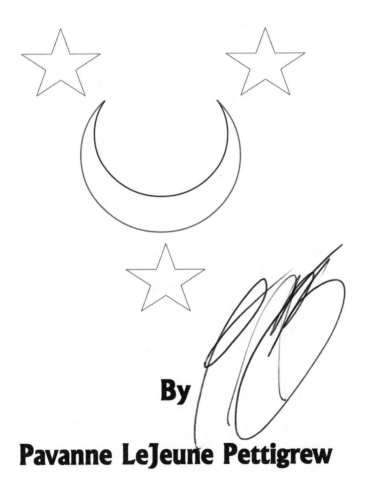

By

Pavanne LeJeune Pettigrew

ONE MORE BREATH

By

Pavanne LeJeune Pettigrew

To order additional copies of this book or for book publishing information, or to contact the author:

Publisher Page
P.O. Box 52
Terra Alta, WV 26764
www.publisherpage.com

Tel/Fax: 800-570-5951 or 304-789-3001
Email: ppettigrew@headlinebooks.com

Publisher Page is an imprint of Headline Books & Co,

ISBN 9780929915395

Library of Congress Control Number: 2006901169

*Cover Map from: Heritage Map Museum. WWW.Carto.com
Cartographer: G. Blaeu.
Date of map: 1636.
Title: Insulae Americanae In Oceano Septentrionali.*

Public domain illustrations from Howard Pyle's Book of Pirates.

Jack Bellamie's Flag by Carol Rogers, Artist
—Owner of Buffington Studios of Photography, Clarksburg, WV

PRINTED IN THE UNITED STATES OF AMERICA

Acknowledgments

This book exists due to the indispensable contributions of certain key people.

First, I wish to thank two prime movers: Maddy Gourevitch, for breaking me out of my self-imposed cocoon, and her mom, Sheri Greenawald, who pushed me to "Write! Write!" as only Sheri can push. Mads, your sometimes-annoying persistence in dragging me to "that movie" that summer struck the spark and puts the lie to the "wisdom of age." And, Sheri, I probably wouldn't have taken this project seriously, but for your nagging me from across an entire continent. Thank you both for the dragging and nagging.

Special thanks go to my friends and co-conspirators, Jon Cavendish, Anita Chapman, and Lori Derrick, who were so patient and generous with suggestions, editing, and material assistance as the story unfolded. You guys rule!

An additional and unique boon was Jon's most generous loan of his fictitious butler, Emerson Bentley, who has since returned to his duties at Cavendish Hall.

In the book's early incarnations, I relied heavily on the valued opinions and input of my erudite and learned readers, Debbie Davis, Karen Fisher, Julie Robinson, and Sarah Shaver. Thank you so much.

That I had the confidence necessary to produce this book is due to unfailing encouragement from certain wonderful aunts, uncles, and cousins during the years of soul-crushing struggle. Uncle Don and Aunt Garnet "Tommie" Pettigrew, Aunt Joan (Pettigrew) and Uncle Jimmy Watson, Uncle Dick and Aunt Dovie Pettigrew, Uncle Bud and Aunt Barb Shaffer, Aunt Joy Arco, and Aunt Pat (Sheaffer) and Uncle Jack Weaver and Cousins Jackie and David J. Weaver, I love you all and am forever grateful. One cousin, Joy Lynn Reed, is a modern-day Betsy Ross who made Blackjack's flag a beautiful reality. Joy, thank you so much.

Of course, the generosity of all of these dear ones would have come to nothing without the courage and insight of my publisher, Cathy Teets. Thank you, Cathy, for considering *One More Breath* and making it happen.

Finally, I would be remiss if I didn't acknowledge the influence of a certain person whom I've never met. JCD, your genius brought light and life to a dark, dead world and inspired more than just this story. *Nais tuke! Nais tuke! Nais tuke!*

Table of Contents

PART ONE

PART TWO

PART THREE

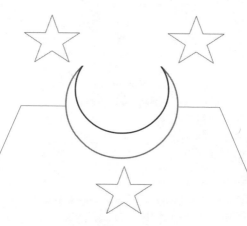

Dedication

To the memory of my parents,
Harry Jackson and
Mildred Viola Sheaffer Pettigrew

Part One

1—Bellamie's Blunder

He knew he should never have remained with a ship that was bound for Jamaica. Better to have stayed near the *Sinecure* while she was hauled out for repairs in Vestal Cay. Being land bound for three months was a miserable prospect, to be sure, but at least he wouldn't have found himself trapped in an alley with bloody Rothwell and his lackeys closing in for the kill—or the capture prior to the kill. His hanging tomorrow would be Port Royal's social event of the season. Furthermore, it would redeem Rothwell's stature within the Royal Navy after having lost his prize quarry at the very hour of dispatch four years before.

His own nature warred within him: to make a stand here and now, likely forcing Rothwell to kill him on the spot, thereby robbing the martinet of his big day, or to submit to arrest and gamble that the phenomenal luck of Captain Blackjack Bellamie would extend to one more narrow escape from the executioner. Not much time to ponder such a momentous decision: he could hear soldiers closing in, Rothwell shouting orders.

The alley meandered to a dead end surmounted by buildings and walls. No barrels or crates were available for climbing; no low branches or convenient ropes dangled hope of escape. But ultimately, he simply could not surrender without an attempt, however hopeless, to save his own life.

Leaping onto the lowest wall, he clawed frantically at the crumbling masonry, dislodging a brick and tearing the flesh on his hands. He fell back and in desperation attacked again, this time sheer momentum carrying him to a tenuous, one-handed grip on the capstones. Losing his black tricorne, he scrabbled to get a boot into the hole left by the loosed brick as Rothwell and his men rounded the last turn in the alleyway, spied his frantic clambering, and surged forward.

His boot found purchase and he propelled himself to the top of the wall, hurling himself up and over, but not before Rothwell's pistol roared.

Scarcely hearing the weapon's report, he realized he was wounded as he felt a white-hot stab of agony pierce his left flank just as he hurtled over the wall. Crashing to the ground on the other side, he grabbed at the injury with both hands and instinctively bit down hard on the scream that tried to break from his lungs, as he staggered to his feet to take flight once more. Rothwell would soon be upon him to claim his prey.

He ran, driven onward by pure force of will as his lifeblood soaked through his clothing and dripped from his hands pressed over his ravaged side. He could not stem the blood that would surely lead his pursuers to him, nor could he be certain of retaining his grip on consciousness much longer.

Ahead lay a freshwater rivulet from the surrounding hills and he hurtled toward it, angling his path downstream away from the road until he reached the water's edge, where he waded in.

Instead of crossing to the other side and continuing his hopeless retreat, he struggled against the moderate current, making his painful way upstream, beyond the ford, around a bend, and then up the low bank in the direction from which he had come, into a thicket of sheltering trees. He sank down on the soft forest floor, his breath tearing from his throat as the agony in his side pulled down a black curtain of blessed nothingness. He didn't hear the excited shouts of his tormentors as they spotted his blood trail that ended at the creek bank; neither did he see them racing downstream like stupid, baying hounds looking for his drowned or exsanguinated corpse to grace their gibbet.

The spotty moonlight illuminated a small, wan figure crumpled on the ground under the trees, lying too still, scarcely breathing. The forest was astir with the noisy, important business of the creatures of the night, but their hapless visitor remained insensate, alive and nothing more. Only God and the denizens of the thicket knew where the sparrow had fallen.

After a time, he began the slow climb back to consciousness, first by simply being aware of his own existence, then by trying to make sense of his world. *Where am I? No rocking, so I'm not on a ship; a lot of noise, but not human. What's wrong with me? Oh, God, the PAIN! Wet and cold, and so thirsty!*

Then it came back to him: putting aboard the frigate at Vestal Cay, going ashore in Port Royal, fleeing Rothwell, the wall, the shot, the *pain*. He remembered backtracking upstream to this place. Then, through his misery and confusion, Captain Blackjack Bellamie smiled, snowy teeth glinting in the pale moonlight. Alone, badly injured and suffering, he nevertheless had thwarted Rothwell once again. The mental picture of his old adversary's frustration was a comfort second only to drink. He knew that he must somehow get himself to safety, recover, and return to the *Sinecure* to complete this triumph.

Assessing his situation, he quickly eliminated the most attractive option: to turn back toward town, where rum was abundant and ships sailed with the tide, outbound from this hellhole. He was not exactly in top form, physically, and the raging fire in his flank would eventually overpower his normally sharp mental acuities. He was in no condition to run into authority figures, deal with drunken, belligerent seamen, or seek passage on anything that floats.

No, unappealing as it was, his best hope lay in the countryside, away from town, away from people. He needed fresh water and a safe, dry place to sleep where nature could take her course. A barn...yes, soft straw in a quiet loft and plenty of water for the beasts. He was a beast; Suzette had said so, as had Gertrude...and Fleur. It must be so. *How much blood does a beast have? Seems to be a lot missing. And that ball is still in there; have to get that out soon. Probably be rather painful.*

Thus, his fevered brain played out disjointed thoughts as he limped toward a speck of light, likely a farmhouse. Farmhouses meant barns nearby.

The moon had set, or maybe it was just darkened by clouds, and the wind was picking up, threatening rain. He was trembling with cold, fear, weakness. The little light still glowed before him, though, and he seemed to be getting closer.

Moving onward, he closed his aching eyes, just for a moment, and was knocked to the ground by something very large. Shaking his head to clear it, he looked up at his attacker: a stone wall, no, a stone house. He had walked blindly into the side of a manor house, the source of the light.

No human could have heard the tiny sound of a small, dark pirate walking into the side of a large, stone mansion, but in a barn behind the house an elkhound heard it and sent out an uproar, waking the horses and the stableman. Jack's hope of climbing into a safe, quiet loft was quickly dashed and supplanted by an urgent need to hide before man and dog bore down upon him.

The light was coming from French doors off a second floor balcony farther along the side of the building. Beside it, a lattice with thick vines ascended from the ground to the roof. He grasped onto this and dragged himself upward and over the balustrade, collapsing on the floor in the shadows beside the doorframe just as the stableman and his hysterical dog rounded the corner below.

The dog halted at the lattice, leaping and snarling and spinning in frantic circles as Jack froze in the darkness, scarcely daring to breathe. He heard the stableman shouting toward the balcony, calling to someone named "Señora Caruthers."

After a moment, the French doors opened and a woman about his own age emerged, fastening her dressing gown as she looked down to the stableman.

"What is it, Rodrigo? Why all this racket?"

"Are you all right, Señora? Beowulf heard something; he is saying it is up there."

"Of course I'm all right, Rodrigo. The wretched dog hears the storm coming, is all. Take him back to the barn."

"But—your light; are you certain you are all right?"

"I'm fine, Rodrigo. Just couldn't sleep, so I'm reading awhile. Go back to bed. And take that infernal noise with you."

"Very well, Señora." With that, the stableman dragged the protesting animal back to the barn and the lady of the manor closed the door and returned to her book, leaving the exhausted pirate to catch his breath in the gathering storm.

Jack lay back against the stones of the house, afraid to attempt standing until his vertigo had passed. He was still bleeding, growing weaker, and possessed of a raging thirst. If he tried to continue running, the intrepid Beowulf would surely drink what remained of his blood. It appeared he would have to take his chances inside the manor house and hope that the milk of human kindness and the luck of Captain Blackjack Bellamie would converge to spare his life once more.

He peered through the door glass and saw the lady of the house sitting at a little table, reading by the light of an oil lamp. She was a small woman and obviously genteel and privileged. However, without the element of surprise she could probably overpower him, considering his present state...best to wait for the advantage, get the drop on her. He sat back to bide his time. *Time and blood, both runnin' out.*

The rain began in earnest, soaking the shivering pirate and multiplying his desperation.

After what seemed an eternity, he saw a shadow slide across the balustrade, indicating movement within. A look inside showed the room to now be empty, the lamp gone, with only the faintest light glowing from the hall beyond. He tried the latch and found it unlocked.

Chloe Smyth Caruthers returned to her room carrying the lamp in one hand and a pitcher of water in the other. If it weren't so late she'd have rung for Maria, but there was no need to wake her faithful maid for such a trifle.

Over the five years of her widowhood, Chloe had begun to think of Maria and the butler, Emerson, as family. Even the stableman, Rodrigo, Maria's husband, had proven his devotion to their little world in ways small and large, until the household had evolved into a cooperative domicile of four thoroughly civilized adults. She seldom needed to "pull rank" and disliked ever having to do so.

After Lieutenant Governor Caruthers died, she had quickly extricated herself from the social scene that had been *de rigueur* while her husband still lived. She and her small staff had settled into the routine of daily life, taking their pleasures from the agreeable surroundings of the estate, the comfort of peace and plenty, their mutual respect and dignified friendship. Any sadness or disillusionment she kept in her heart, expressing it to no one, including herself, dismissing the feelings when they attempted to surface. So many people were much worse off than she.

Her husband had been a good man and she had cared for him, she supposed. She had certainly respected him and was grateful for his generosity toward her, but she had found marriage to be a massive disappointment, a sentiment she had never dared voice to anyone.

Hers had been a smart match at the time, engaged to the newest Member of Parliament. But after the excitement of the ceremony at the cathedral in Canterbury, any hope for girlish dreams of romance and grand passion was gone. She longed to warn younger women to curtail their expectations, but squelched that desire, along with many others, as being unseemly in the wife of an M.P.

Then came her husband's appointment as lieutenant governor, the excitement of preparations for the move to the Caribbean, the farewells, the long sea journey, the new people, and the new home with all the strange and exotic sights, sounds, and smells. That had been an enjoyable time for her.

Shortly thereafter came the biggest excitement of all , the news that promised to revive her hopes for the future: she was with child. Her husband purchased the estate, moving them from the lieutenant governor's manse, so that his little heir would be born in his own home and have property to inherit in the New World. Her husband's parents had sent Emerson, Maria, and Rodrigo from their own household in Cuba to provide comfort to the new family, unwilling to trust local help.

But some time before the completion of her sixth month, she had awakened with a terrifying backache that was quickly followed by savage cramps, bleeding and the eventual delivery of a dead child. Rodrigo's furious dash to fetch the midwife had been in vain.

Maria had not left her side, cooing and fussing over her, then murmuring the rosary and weeping quietly. No one would let Chloe see her baby and it was three more days before her husband reluctantly told her that it had been a little girl. At her insistence, he admitted that the child was perfectly formed, just so very small. In her heart, she resented not being allowed to say goodbye. She bitterly questioned the general wisdom that she would have been so traumatized by the sight of the little thing that she would never conceive again. She began to sense that much of what she had been told about life and love was conveniently incorrect.

After a brief period of mourning, Lieutenant Governor Caruthers had returned to work, and soon was behaving as if nothing had happened. Chloe tried to go back to the way she had been six months previously, but something was profoundly different with her. She found that she longed for her husband's rare visits to her room at night instead of dreading them as before. She so ached for physical, human contact that she would have welcomed the fleeting, darkness-hidden coupling just for the few moments of closeness.

But, likely out of mistaken consideration for her feelings, he had not returned to her bedchamber since she had become pregnant. She dared not reveal such longings to him, as the disgrace would have been more than she could bear. He might even think she had gone mad with grief and have her put away. She pushed her feelings down, down to the depths of her heart and carried on as a well-bred English lady.

A year later, she received word from England that her parents and both brothers were dead of the fever. She was still wearing black when her husband set sail for Cuba and was lost at sea in a violent storm.

Chloe Smyth Caruthers was utterly alone for the first time in her life and made the shocking discovery that having no one left to lose is an unanticipated, and not insignificant, comfort.

Chloe noticed the door onto the balcony standing ajar and concluded that the wind had blown it open. She placed the lamp and pitcher on the little reading table and turned toward the door to close it.

Just as she passed a tall, japanned armoire, she was seized from behind, the icy blade of a dagger pressed to her throat and a hand reeking of blood covered her mouth. She could feel the man's lean body against her, hear his labored breathing as he spoke softly into her ear, "Don't mean t' hurt ye, Ducks. Just a stranger in yer gates needin' a bit of water and a—" He abruptly went silent as the dagger clattered to the floor and his hands seemed to float downward. A second later, her attacker lay unconscious on the carpet. She stared, rooted to the spot, unable to fully process the deluge of events.

Typically stoic, she didn't scream. She wanted to hurry out of the room and call for Emerson, but she was riveted by the fascinating incongruity lying like a large, broken doll on her Oriental rug. Whoever he was, he was certainly no danger to her at the moment.

The cannon fuses and shark teeth braided into his long, black hair, the faded black bandanna around his head, the once-flamboyant, red, fringed sash (now sodden with water and blood), the deeply tanned skin, huge gold hoops in his ears and a ring on every finger and both thumbs—the man was clearly a pirate of some exotic sort and obviously in serious trouble. All that blood! He was injured, perhaps shot by the authorities or a rival pirate, and a long way from a ship, crew, or friend.

Despite his deplorable profession, the pirate's face held a look of intelligence, at least in repose. His words came back to her, "Don't mean t' hurt ye, Ducks." He must have meant it, as he could have cut her throat without a word and helped himself to anything he wanted.

She bent a little closer to peer at this beguiling intruder into her tidy little world just as a single tear drew from under his soft, black lashes and trailed down his cheek. Something in her heart wrenched at the sight and her terror dissolved into pity for this fragile creature for whom she was the last hope.

But she wasn't stupid. She gingerly removed his belt with the pistol and sword, picked up the dagger, and stashed them behind the armoire. Then she knelt beside him and set about locating the source of his bleeding. With the sash removed and his shirt pulled up, she soon found the evil little hole that was slowly leaking away a human life. She lightly touched the edge of it with her fingertip, having no idea what to do next.

The pirate moaned and she jerked back. She wiped the blood from her finger onto the hem of her gown and, when she looked back at him, his eyes were open, obsidian pools focused on her face. For a moment neither spoke. Then she told him, "Don't be afraid. I'm going to help you."

The pirate placed his open hands together and lowered his chin, attempting a feeble bow of gratitude. The effort was too much; his hands fell back at his sides and his eyes closed again. Chloe took a blanket from her bed and covered him to his shoulders, then went to Maria's room—to pull rank, if necessary.

Maria sat up with a start, shocked to find her mistress standing beside her bed, patting her hand insistently, and calling her name.

"What is it, Señora? What is wrong?"

"Maria, listen carefully. Something has happened and I need your help. I need you to remain calm and quiet."

"Of course, Señora, but what is so urgent?"

Chloe proceeded to tell her of the events of recent moments; Maria listened with wide-eyed astonishment and then followed her mistress into the bedroom where the pirate lay shivering under the light coverlet. As soon as Maria laid eyes on him she crossed herself and gasped.

"*Madre*—! It is Jack Bellamie!"

("*Black*jack. *Black*jack Bellamie," came the faint correction from the Oriental rug.)

"The pirate who escaped the noose four years ago with the help of Jenny Hunter?"

"*Sí.* I would recognize him anywhere!" Maria had seen Jack at his hanging.

Chloe never attended executions, finding government-issued death just as depressing as any other, regardless of the criminal's guilt; furthermore, the blood lust of the supposedly enlightened observers filled her with deep despair for the whole human race. Emerson clearly shared her distaste and would busy himself at the estate with any absorbing task that would occupy him throughout the morning of the spectacle.

Maria, on the other hand, never missed a hanging, not that her sensibilities were coarser than those of her mistress, but because she felt it her Christian duty to go and pray without ceasing for the immortal soul of the condemned. Rodrigo, of course, accompanied her, driving her to the fort and back in the dogcart. Upon returning home, neither ever mentioned the horrible affair except to bring news and greetings from friends and acquaintances.

She and Rodrigo had been at the fort four years earlier for the hanging of Blackjack Bellamie and his henchmen. The whole of Port Royal had been buzzing with gossip about how the battered little skiff with its cargo of seventeen half-dead buccaneers had drifted ashore near the gubernatorial estate where they were discovered by the governor's headstrong daughter, Jenny, who proceeded to secrete them in an abandoned boat shed.

To sustain them, she had been smuggling food and drink from the mansion for several days before her godfather, Commodore Rothwell, became suspicious and followed her. He returned to the fort and promptly sent a squad of marines to arrest the rovers, whereupon they were swiftly tried, found guilty of piracy, and sentenced to hang the following day.

Jenny's strident protests at the trial only served to fuel the already rampant gossip about her relationship with the bizarre captain of the outlaws, as everyone assumed that such a highborn young woman could never be so fiercely attracted to anyone less than an officer, however great the age difference and however spurious his commission. Her deeply embarrassed father had had her forcibly removed from the courtroom, but wild Jenny wasn't so easily defeated.

On the day of the execution, the convicts were on the scaffold, each bound and hooded and in a noose, as the formalities advanced toward their imminent demise. Jenny was unusually well behaved and no one paid any attention to her as she meandered her way to the outer edge of the crowd.

Suddenly, the lugubrious dignity of the moment was shattered as she snatched a loaded pistol from an officer and placed the muzzle to her own head.

"Free them! Free every one of them! Free them now or you'll have another corpse to carry from this place! Now!"

Above the noise of the thunderstruck crowd, Governor Hunter was screaming for someone to stop her, disarm her.

But when three soldiers moved toward her, she drew back the hammer and they halted. Her mother dropped to the ground in a faint and all went breathlessly quiet.

She had situated herself such that no one could approach her without being seen, so disarming her by physical force was not possible. In the silence, she spoke to Rothwell, calmly, but with a steely resolve.

"Now that I have your attention, Uncle, please release each of the prisoners immediately." Her godfather appeared frozen, his mouth agape. "Give the order, Uncle, NOW! Do it or you will see me die before your eyes."

The commodore's love for his goddaughter now in grand conflict with his lifetime of military discipline, he could not seem to make a move or a sound. The distraught governor, however, was in no such quandary and he bellowed out the orders to save his only child.

"Release the prisoners! Cut them free! Hurry!"

The executioner, now assisted by several guards, began removing the nooses and hoods and cutting the ropes that bound the men's hands. Jenny did not relax her position.

"Now, move aside and let them pass."

The pirates trekked down from the scaffold as the crowd parted before them like a lightning-struck tree. Typical of their kind, some of them made lewd, arrogant remarks and gestures as they passed through, taking care to make certain that Rothwell received the most and the worst. Captain Bellamie went so far as to reach out and tip the commodore's hat off of his head. Rothwell appeared to be on the brink of madness.

Jenny had more business to conduct. Before the troupe had left the arena, she called one out.

"Everson! Hold up!"

A young pirate halted, paled and swallowed hard; his compatriots continued on without him. Jenny continued to watch her father as she summoned the boy, the erstwhile ship's carpenter.

The youth moved through the citizens and soldiers toward his rescuer as she instructed him to arm himself. He helped himself to a musket and two pistols as their rightful owners looked on in impotent fury. Jenny never took her eyes off her father who had been rejoined by his shaken wife.

Lady Hunter's pleas were not to her daughter, as she was well aware they would be ignored; she begged her husband to accede to the girl's demands, anything to spare her child's life.

With Everson by her side, Jenny laid out her ultimatums.

"Someone fetch my father's scribe and bring paper, pen and ink—and his official seal." A nod from the stunned commodore and a soldier ran to carry out the order.

She addressed the chaplain.

"Reverend Lawson, you will perform a marriage before these proceedings adjourn, so please open your prayer book to that particular page and close it to the benediction for the dead."

When the scribe arrived, she made her father dictate a full pardon for one Daniel Everson, affix his seal, and then do the same for a certificate of matrimony joining herself and the newly pardoned.

The nuptials were indeed performed as the girl ordered. Reverend Lawson had to stand with his back to the throng so that the bride could keep an eye on things and, despite the pleading from her parents and the chaplain, she resolutely continued to hold the gun to her head throughout the service.

When the nervous preacher pronounced them husband and wife and informed Mr. Everson that he may kiss the new Mrs. Everson, Jenny just snorted.

"That can wait till later. First, I want both of those documents given into my hands immediately. Second, my husband and I will be permitted to leave this fort unmolested. Third, if these papers ever vanish from my personal possession or if my husband is harmed in any manner whatsoever, I cannot be prevented from ending my own life and, with it, the life of the child I am carrying."

At this, her poor mother fainted again, the crowd gasped, and the groom whirled to look at his bride in astonishment. Her safety and that of her husband now assured by her bogus pregnancy, she lowered the weapon, tucked the precious papers into her bodice, and swept through the opening crowd with Daniel in tow, pausing briefly before the governor to inform him of her intentions.

"Father, you may expect the two of us to join you and Mother at dinner this evening, at which time you will become better acquainted with your new son-in-law. Until then, we shall be in seclusion celebrating our marriage."

By the time the newlyweds had departed, the other sixteen convicts had made good their escape, commandeering a schooner and forcing its crew to make way with all speed. No one ashore was aware that the ship's departure was anything but routine until three days later when the sailors rowed ashore in the launch to tell the tale, having been released by their captors precisely for that purpose.

And now, Captain Blackjack Bellamie had returned to the sands of Port Royal. Why?

It didn't matter. If Chloe and Maria didn't do something soon, he would remain forever *under* the sands of Port Royal.

Chloe showed Maria the wound in his side, as he looked on in a semi-stupor. But despite her best attempts to be gentle, Maria necessarily caused him still more pain as she carefully examined the damage. He bore it stoically, the sucking in of his breath the only sign that he was hurting and, each time, she apologized. Chloe watched and stood by to assist when needed. Twice he asked for water and they readily complied.

Maria determined that there was no exit wound, so the ball was almost certainly still in him. She feared the thing had penetrated to his gut, in which case he was done for, but she didn't speak of this. *If* it were merely lodged in the flesh of his side, however deeply, and *if* she could retrieve it without causing him to bleed to death, and *if* he didn't then get infected, he would survive. The odds were not in his favor, but he had a chance.

She had to locate the horrid thing and remove it. She sent Chloe to get a bottle of the strongest alcohol they had, an Irish whiskey Rodrigo loved. Chloe kept it in a locked cabinet in the larder and allowed him to have a little of it on special occasions. Rodrigo was not an alcoholic, but this particular commodity was hard to come by and packed a punch to boot.

She was also to bring Emerson to help get Captain Bellamie onto the bed so Maria could work on him more easily and he would be off the hard floor. She retrieved the whiskey and then apprised the butler of the situation as he trailed her upstairs. If he was shocked he didn't show it. Typical Emerson.

When they entered the bedroom, Maria had already removed the pirate's vest, shirt and boots and had put several sheets onto Chloe's bed to protect the fine linens. He gazed at his benefactors with deceptively calm eyes and said nothing.

Then the three of them set about trying to lift him while causing him a minimum of discomfort, but despite their good intentions he howled in pain and grasped Emerson's arm and the side of Maria's shift in his fists.

In a moment it was over and he rested on the softest bed he'd ever felt. Through a haze, he saw bustling movement, heard conversations he couldn't discern, smelled clean linen.

Chloe was tearing strips of cloth into bandages. Emerson had left the room and returned with a basin and was pouring some of the whiskey into it. Maria had fetched a sharp knife, a needle and stout silk thread, and a large, bone crochet hook. These items went into the bowl with the whiskey, but Jack was largely oblivious to such details.

Maria directed them to give him whiskey, all he could drink. Emerson held Jack's head while Chloe placed the bottle to the pirate's lips. He drank gratefully, choking once on the burning fluid. Rum was so much better, but this was not bad. Then, blessedly, he became even less lucid.

Maria cleaned the wound as best she could with the whiskey as Jack moaned piteously.

Emerson and Chloe had little to do but watch until Maria said, "Hold him, arms and legs." Chloe held his wrists against the pillows, while Emerson went to the foot of the bed and grasped the pirate's ankles.

With her patient thus immobilized, Maria took the crochet hook and probed into the bullet hole, digging for the ball, whereupon Jack loosed a scream that bore no resemblance to any human sound and passed out. The three felt relief that he wasn't suffering any longer, but Emerson and Chloe kept looking away from Maria's gory investigation, which seemed to them to take forever.

Suddenly she cried, "I have it!" and began trying to work the crochet hook under the ball to bring it out. It moved upward about a centimeter and refused to budge further. He was not gut-shot, but the ball was lodged deep within a muscle: not the worst case, but bad nonetheless. Perspiring in the cool room, she used the knife to widen the wound and soon had the innocuous-looking sphere of metal in her blood-soaked fingers. She spent little time admiring her work, though, quickly taking the needle and thread in hand to begin closing the damage.

They took turns pressing folded cloths against the wound, hoping to see the crimson flow begin to abate. Gradually, it did, and they bandaged the area as tightly as they could, winding strips of linen around his slim torso and tying them with stout knots. Some red still came through, but it wasn't copious.

Maria made the sign of the cross over Jack and placed him in God's hands.

"Now, we wait."

The day had dawned bleak, dark, and rainy. Chloe welcomed the gloom, as it would make it easier to rest and she was now utterly exhausted. Maria had offered to turn down the bed in the guestroom for her, but Chloe wanted to stay with their patient during this critical period. He had not awakened throughout his surgery and remained asleep—or unconscious—still. She lay down beside him on top of the counterpane, pulled an afghan over herself and went straightaway to sleep.

2—Curiosity

The rain had stopped and the day slid past with the three dutiful servants tending to the routine functions of the household with an air of unusual solemnity. Their mistress and their strange guest continued to sleep, both requiring, above all else, pure restorative slumber to mitigate the events of the previous night.

Maria had, of course, told Rodrigo, who recalled the episode with Beowulf, now understanding the dog's fury. Otherwise, little was said until they all had gathered in the kitchen for the evening meal.

Emerson inquired of Maria if Madam should be taken a tray.

"I looked in on them again just a few moments ago. They are both still asleep."

Rodrigo looked up. "Are you sure Captain Bellamie still lives?"

"*Sí*. He was breathing. But he felt too warm when I touched his forehead."

Emerson frowned. "That is indeed unfortunate. Do you think fever will take him after all of your work to save him?"

"It is in God's hands."

The three ate in silence for a while. Finally, Emerson spoke.

"We don't know who shot him or why. It is unlikely that a sailor or another pirate would have chased him so far inland. Most probably it was Commodore Rothwell's men, which means they will not give up the search until they are convinced he is dead or off the island. If it is discovered that Madam assisted him, she will surely join him on the scaffold."

Maria gave a little cry and covered her mouth, staring at the butler with terrified eyes.

Rodrigo voiced the obvious question. "And what of us,

then? No one will believe she did it on her own, without our knowing. We will hang, too!"

Ever rational and controlled, Emerson pointed out that the staff could truthfully plead obedience to their mistress. However, without Lady Caruthers to work for in Port Royal, they would surely be returned to Havana where they would tend the household of the late lieutenant governor's younger brother.

Rodrigo mock-spat at the mention of that person. "*Pah*! I would rather go to the scaffold with Señora Caruthers and the pirate."

Maria was in tears. "What to *do*? What to *do*?"

"Listen to me, both of you." Emerson rose from his chair and leaned on the table with both hands, looking intently from one face to the other before resuming.

"We are going to keep our wits about us and not let emotions lead us to destruction. We will keep this secret at all costs and do nothing to rouse the suspicions of the authorities. We will go about our business as if nothing is changed, but keep ever vigilant for visitors from the fort. A plan for such eventuality is certainly in order. If Captain Bellamie survives his injuries, we will do all that is necessary to get him on a ship and away from here. Perhaps by then the Eversons will have returned from their journey to England and will be able to assist us. If he dies, we will bury him deeply in an unmarked grave and take this secret with us to our own respective graves. Do I make myself clear?"

The other two readily agreed, grateful that Emerson was taking charge and remaining clear-headed as ever. They spent the remainder of their meal imagining possible scenarios and devising plans accordingly. They were relieved to feel the situation under their control once more and know that they were working in accord.

Rodrigo went to feed the animals and settle them in for the night, Emerson cleared the kitchen of their meal, and Maria went upstairs to look in on the sleepers for the tenth time since morning.

Chloe lay supine; her head turned toward Jack, as sleep left her. She opened her eyes and was momentarily startled to be looking at a stranger in her bed, but quickly recalled who he was and why he was there. She pulled her hand from under the afghan and touched his temple with the backs of her fingers; *too warm.*

Her heart sank, but she reminded herself that some fever was natural after what he had been through (or so she hoped) and that he really wasn't terribly hot. She supported herself on one elbow, leaning to study his face, to look for any clue as to his condition. He seemed a little flushed, but that would be the fever, and he was breathing regularly and deeply.

Just then her maid entered the room.

"Maria, he's feverish!"

Maria felt him. "He is no worse than an hour ago." It was meant to be encouraging, but her worried countenance betrayed her.

Chloe stood and the two women turned back the counterpane to look at his wound. The bandages were bloodier than before, but not greatly so, and what was there had dried and darkened. It was a small but positive sign. He didn't respond to the disturbances and Chloe silently wondered if he ever would again.

Maria stayed with him while Chloe went into her dressing room to perform her ablutions and dress for the day. When she emerged, she found that she was ravenous and sent Maria to bring a tray. Jack must be needing sustenance far worse than she, but there was nothing to do about it unless—*until! until!*—he awakened.

When Maria returned, Chloe sat at the little table to eat her first meal in twenty-four hours and, after it was finished, she realized she could not have told anyone of what it consisted. She was partly amused, partly alarmed at her distracted state of mind. She tried to settle back into reading her absorbing book to reclaim some sense of normality, but after four pages she had to face that she couldn't recall a single word. She tried again, redoubling her effort to concentrate, and once again she failed.

With a resigned sigh she closed the book with the marker

still on the same page she'd put it on the previous night when she had left the room to get a pitcher of water. She needed to be practical. The situation was most assuredly not normal, so why should she expect to behave as though it were? There was a gravely injured pirate in her bed and she would be in danger of her own life should the situation be revealed to the wrong people.

If Captain Bellamie were to die, her troubles in this regard would be over. It would not be difficult to dispose of his body, and dead men tell no tales. Nevertheless, she was disturbed to find that she fervently wanted the man to live, and she couldn't discern why. *Well, after all, no one should lose his life while still in his prime, not even a pirate*, she thought. Death was so final, wasn't it? Perhaps, if he were to live, he could rehabilitate himself and become a God-fearing, worthwhile citizen, do some good in the world like his former shipmate, Everson, and avoid eternal damnation. Yes, that was the reason her heart sank at the thought of his dying.

No, that was not the reason and she knew it. Something else was going on in her head that she simply could not sort out, and trying to do so was exhausting. She resolved to push it down into the depths with the rest of her inconvenient emotions. She went to her vanity and pinned up an errant lock of hair, smoothed her dress, and called for Maria to sit with their guest while she went down to the parlor to play the harpsichord. That never failed to calm and restore her.

As Chloe lowered the cover on the harpsichord's keyboard, Maria entered the parlor and asked if she wished the guestroom prepared for the night. Again, Chloe opted to stay in her own room and look after Jack. Besides, she was now the only one sufficiently rested to do so through the coming night. Maria nodded and set about her evening duties upstairs.

Chloe went outside to inhale the fragrance of the Caribbean night and deal with her conflicting feelings. Some of these thoughts were not obeying her mental command to leave, and such recalcitrance worried her.

After a bit, she returned to her room to find Maria pressing a moist cloth to Jack's forehead. Alarmed, she rushed to the bedside.

"Is he worse?"

"No, no worse. But no better."

"Thank you, Maria. I'll take over from here. Get some sleep."

"*Sì*, Señora. Tomorrow we must turn him or his lungs will begin to corrupt. And pray that it does not start him bleeding again."

Chloe sat on the bed beside Jack, continuing the ministration with the cloth, turning it when it grew warm, rewetting it as necessary, and allowing herself the luxury of an unhurried study of his face.

His features were nearly perfect: the soft dark eyebrows, lashes, and mustache, the lovely cheekbones, the smooth, honey-tan complexion with just a hint of a scar from his left ear to his sparse beard, the nose flawless in every dimension, the exquisite lips.

She wondered how many feminine mouths those lips had kissed. *Do pirates kiss their lovers at all?* Some were reputed to have mistresses sailing with them on their ships and some even to be married with families ashore. *Is Captain Bellamie married? Unlikely. Do pirate husbands kiss their wives more than do lieutenant governor husbands? Or is kissing, like unicorns, a lovely myth?*

She sighed. She was letting her imagination run away with her. *Just because a pirate has perfect features does not make him a tender lover...necessarily.* Maybe the only intimacy this one had ever known was with prostitutes, whatever it was they did—or perhaps that and the occasional rape. *Wonder what that would be like?* Did Jenny Hunter Everson know? No, Mrs. Everson had maintained staunchly that Captain Bellamie was a "fine man." *So*—but what had she meant by that?

Chloe lifted her chin, rose from the bed and walked to the balcony. *She* was in control and these ridiculous thoughts would simply have to go away. She was just momentarily off balance because of the extraordinary disruption of her otherwise well-ordered life. It was a natural reaction. And now it would vanish. *There.*

She looked down at the balcony beneath her feet. He must have climbed the trellis and hidden here to escape that monster, Beowulf. Imagine climbing in his condition! Well, he didn't weigh much, which would help. But even so, how it must have hurt, how frightened and lonely he must have felt. *Poor thing.* She'd best return to her charge and try to help him.

The pirate slept on, seemingly as much at peace as Chloe's thoughts were at war. She would focus on the task at hand since attention to duty was the best antidote for a disordered mind. She carefully turned back the covers to check his bandage once more.

Still no fresh blood. She felt like cheering! She started to replace the covers, but paused. In the urgency of saving his life, she had noted only minimally that his torso was a landscape of scars. Now, she could look more closely.

His left arm bore the only mark that appeared to be voluntarily inflicted, a tattoo of three stars and a crescent moon with upturned horns. The outer length of his right forearm bore a deep, fiery red scar, like a bloody furrow in a field of flesh. She recoiled at the thought of what must have caused that. On his left shoulder a long-healed spot the color of wine and the size of a doubloon was surely an old bullet wound. Numerous other, smaller marks on his chest and arms appeared to be less-serious injuries, most likely sword cuts.

How much physical pain this man must have endured! Chloe shuddered to imagine it. But had he endured heartache, too? Sometimes that could be far worse, even though the scars weren't so easily seen. Had he lost a dear one to death? Loved in vain? Mourned a lost home? Felt unwanted? Buried a child? Had he ever shed tears of pure sadness?

Stop it! she silently commanded herself. Whatever his life's disappointments and grief, if any, they were no concern of hers. *Back to task and stop dwelling on such things, Chloe Caruthers.*

Maria had said that his lungs might become diseased. Best to keep on top of that. She lowered her head and laid her ear on his nearly hairless chest. His breath coursed deeply within him, a clear, sighing sound she found oddly comforting, like the whispering voice of the sea on a calm night. She heard his heartbeat, strong and steady, a decidedly masculine sound that made her feel safe and happy. She lingered, drinking in the music of his body, feeling herself more peaceful and more alive than she could remember.

Suddenly, the door opened and Maria entered, carrying a freshly filled lamp. She halted and the two women stared at each other. Chloe jerked erect, felt herself go crimson to the roots of her hair, and stammered out, "Uh, um, I was just checking his lungs—you know, uh—no need to let them go bad, er, I mean, they're just fine, no rales or anything. Good sign, that, yes? Wanted to know. That's all." She could hear how flustered she sounded, but could not seem to gain mastery over her speech.

Maria nodded and gave her a strange look, then went to the table and put down the lamp, taking the nearly empty one with her as she departed.

"Good night, Maria," she called, too cheerfully.

"Good night, Señora."

"I'll see you in the morning." Why couldn't she just shut up?

"*Sì*, Señora."

Furious with herself, Chloe stalked to the table and snapped open her book. Settling into the chair, she attempted to read, but had no more success than the last time she tried.

Well, what's done was done; all she could do now was to behave as impeccably as ever and the incident would be forgotten soon enough. Perhaps she should go into the guestroom after all. Bellamie seemed stable enough to be alone for a few hours.

No, no, that would look guilty and call more attention to her, making it worse. Just remain an attentive, efficient nurse and her intentions would not be misconstrued. She should cover him up again and try to get some sleep herself. Perhaps she could get sleepy if she put her mind to it.

She started to lift the quilt back over him, but decided to take one more look at the wound, just in case. She had no personal motive for this, of course; no, it was merely for the reassurance that the lack of fresh blood was a hopeful indication that the man might live after all. A noble thought, to be sure.

She sat beside him again, replaced the moist cloth on his head, and leaned across him to examine the bandage. Still nothing new. *Superb*!

He would need a bath soon. Pirate hygiene was not exactly the gold standard, and he was rather grimy. When he had first arrived, the smell of frank blood had been overpowering, but now that the bleeding was stopped, she inhaled a different bouquet from him. A salty sea smell, pitch, hemp, and a kind of foreign spice she couldn't identify. And, of course, sweat. Man sweat, warm and cloying. That needed to be washed off, certainly. But it really wasn't a bad smell, actually…

She breathed him in and stared at his tanned chest, watching it rise and fall, remembering the sighs and heartbeats within. Her eyes trailed downward to a thin, vertical line of black hair beginning below his navel and disappearing under the top of his breeches. Even she knew where that led.

"Look at anything ye like, Ducks. I've no objection."

She leapt up and backward, nearly falling to the floor. She gaped with horror at his grinning face, his white teeth flashing, his dark eyes crinkled with amusement. Her cheeks burned, her mouth opened and closed, opened and closed, but no words would issue forth. In confusion, she turned to the balcony, then reversed and rushed to the door, wanting only to flee this unbearable humiliation.

But then she stopped. She stiffened her back, raised her chin, turned, and walked back to the bed, her face a haughty mask.

"I will thank you, Captain Bellamie—"

"It's Blackjack. Captain Blackjack Bellamie, Ducks."

"I will thank you, Captain Blackjack Bellamie, to keep a civil tongue in your head when addressing a lady."

"My apologies, M'lady. No offense intended."

His ready and unexpected civility undid her resolve and she found herself stammering for the second time that evening.

"Well, uh, accepted, and um, just be more careful in future. Please."

"Aye, M'lady. I have naught but respect f'r yer Ladyship and gratitude f'r yer kind hospitality, but if ye'll be so good as to hand me my belongings, I'll be takin' yer leave now." With that he tried to sit up, but was felled by a shot of pain that made him gasp, bite his lip and hiss, "Damn, that hurtsss!"

She rushed to him and bent to see if he had reopened his wound. Too soon to tell for certain.

"Captain Bellamie, you simply must cooperate until you are healed, at which time I will gladly restore your 'belongings' and bid you fond farewell. Until such time, please do me the courtesy of not making the task of keeping you alive more difficult than you already have." She examined the bandage again and thought she saw some brighter red. *Damn him!*

Duly chastened, more by the pain than by Chloe's little lecture, he lay back on the pillow and watched her pour a glass of water and bring it to him. She had not waited for his request, remembering her own nearly unquenchable thirst after losing so much blood during parturition.

She slid her arm under his shoulders and eased him upward ever so gently until he could drink without pouring it all over himself. He was so weak she had to help him hold it to his lips, but he drank deeply, inhaling and exhaling into the glass rather than stopping to breathe. She took it from him before he could finish and he flashed her a look of consternation.

"Not all at once, Captain Bellamie. You'll vomit and tear out your stitches. You may have all the water you wish, but in small allotments."

He pouted, but she pretended not to notice. They both knew she was right. While they waited for him to be able to receive the next drink, she tucked the sheet around him and then eased another pillow under him. A little more angle would help him keep the water down. Chloe was pleased at how much she had learned and remembered from her own accouchement.

After several long minutes, she let him drain the remainder of the water from the glass.

"More."

"Not yet. Soon."

Feeling more confident now, she put her hand on his head. Still fevered. Replacing the cloth on him, she pressed it onto his temples, feeling the heat soak through to her fingers as he closed his eyes, enjoying the comforting coolness and pressure.

And so went the next several hours, as the rest of the world slumbered. A few swallows of water, the cool cloth, a little more water, cloth again. Few words were spoken; few were required. The earlier prickly edge was gone from their interactions. Neither saw a need to "best" the other or to guard against real or imagined slights. Their goal was common between them: to get Jack well.

In his heart, Jack was immensely grateful for Chloe's tender ministrations; in her heart, Chloe was immensely grateful for Jack's improvement.

Eventually, he noticed her eyelids beginning to droop. He himself was exhausted from so much activity in such a weakened state.

"Do you have a name, M'lady?"

"I'm Mrs. Chloe Caruthers."

"Ye may call me Jack, Mrs. Caruthers."

"Chloe."

"Chloe. And where is Mister Caruthers, whilst his bride is diligently saving a black-hearted scalawag from the grim reaper?"

"I'm a widow, Jack. Five years now."

"Ah. Condolences. But, my dear Chloe, ye clearly need to

get some rest. Ye've done well by Ol' Blackjack fer tonight and I'm thankin' ye, but I'll live till morning if ye stop and get some shuteye."

She smiled and thanked him, blew out the lamp, and proceeded to lie down beside him as she had before. He stared at her, astonished.

3—Panic Times Two

The indigo sky was fading to azure as daybreak approached. All was quiet in the Caruthers house.

Suddenly, Jack's eyes flew open. He turned his head sharply to look at the sleeping woman beside him, then grabbed her arm and began shaking it.

"Chloe! Mrs. Caruthers! Come, Darling, wakey, wakey! Ol' Blackjack needs you. *Please* wake up, Chloe!"

She sat up in a panic. "What? What's wrong? Are you bleeding?"

"No, Ducks, but more urgent. All that water. I need a chamber pot. Now!"

Flabbergasted, Chloe rushed into her dressing room to fetch the one from behind the privacy screen. Blushing furiously and not meeting his eyes, she placed it on the bed beside him and ran for the door.

"Wait! Come back, Ducks. I can't even sit up without help. This does no good by me side."

"You'll have to manage." Again, she started for the door.

"Very well. It's your bed."

She came back, hating everyone from Adam and Eve on down. "I'll get you situated, but then you're on your own."

He smirked and watched her burning face as she moved him into a sitting position on the edge of the bed. All that movement hurt, but her discomfiture was so hilarious as to make it worthwhile. He reached to unbutton his breeches and she bolted like a spooked stallion.

"Wait! Chloe! This won't work."

"Why not?" she wailed. "What more do you want from me?"

"I'll answer the second question at another time, Ducks,

but for now, I can't balance me bloodless carcass on the side of the bed and hold everything I need to hold to get the job done. And time's a-wastin'."

Chloe thought she would die of mortification on the spot. If he were asking her to do what she thought he was, the bed would just have to be sacrificed.

In the end, she wound up sitting close beside him, twisted at the waist to face behind him, her left arm extended across his chest for him lean on and her right arm reaching across her own body to grasp the handle of the pot and steady it between his open thighs. She was beside herself with embarrassment and rage, made all the worse by the certainty that, although she couldn't see his face, she knew that he was wearing that infuriating smirk and thoroughly enjoying this. If Maria walked in just now, Chloe would leave and never come back.

After what seemed an hour, he finally gave a contented sigh. "Ye did good, Darling. That's much better."

With her eyes still resolutely averted, she lowered the noticeably heavier pot to the floor and steadied him while he did up his drawers. Then she eased him back onto the pillow, never once looking at him. But she knew that smug grin was there nonetheless.

She carried the chamber pot back into her dressing room, her gaze focused determinedly ahead. However, as she replaced the vessel in its commode, her curiosity got the better of her and she sneaked a peak at its contents. It wasn't that she actually thought a man's urine would look different from her own; she simply wanted to know what it did look like.

What she saw immediately cooled her unreasonable anger toward Jack and erased her humiliation. There was blood in his urine, never a good sign. It brought her back to the reality that he was far from healed. She decided not to discuss it with him; there was nothing he could do about it, anyway. She'd talk to Maria.

Returning to the bedroom, she met his eyes for the first time that morning.

"If ye ever want another occupation besides lady, ye'd have a great future as a contortionist. Always in demand." That suggestive smile.

She just looked at him blankly, probably the only response that would have softened him.

"Sorry, Ducks. I'm sure that was unpleasant for ye, but please know that I appreciate it. Believe that."

Jack dozed, tired from the morning's exertions. Chloe returned to her dressing room to prepare herself for the day. As she was walking back into the bedroom, there was a knock at her door. That was odd.

She went toward it and paused. "Yes? Who is it?"

"It is Maria, Señora." Maria never knocked. Well, after yesterday, that must have changed. Chloe told her to enter.

The maid was carrying a tray with tea and scones, her usual morning routine. Chloe was eager to report their patient's improvement.

"He woke up last night. He drank a lot of water and talked some. He's still pretty weak, though."

"Of course, Señora. How is his fever?"

Chloe had forgotten to check on that in the frenetic activities since she had awakened. Maria felt his head and Jack opened his eyes.

"Ah! Doctor Maria. Your patient has survived. What a good surgeon you are!"

She blushed a little. "You are not yet well, Captain. Do not try to do too much too soon."

"Not to worry, Ducks. Yer comely mistress keeps me in my place, don't ye, Darling?"

Chloe wanted to hit him. Why was he so exasperating!

Maria headed for the dressing room, telling Chloe that it would be good if he could eat something. She emerged carrying the covered chamber pot as she always did when she left the bedroom after bringing her morning tray, but this time Chloe followed her into the hall.

"Look in there, Maria."

The maid lifted the cover and looked inside, then back to Chloe.

"Yours, Señora?"

"His."

"We must be very careful with him. This might heal of its own, but we must be vigilant."

"Is there anything we can do?"

"Just keep him quiet and pray that the injury heals itself."

Chloe's day held more shocks for her. Thinking that the worst was surely behind her with the chamber pot fiasco, she decided to eat some breakfast and try to get some food into her patient. Perhaps a little nourishment would give him enough strength to manage his own bodily functions next time.

She poured tea into the two cups and sweetened it with a little honey. (She didn't ask or care whether he wanted honey in his tea; honey was good for him and what was good for Jack was good for her at this point.) Then she spread jam onto two pieces of scone, and carried the tray to the bed. She alternately ate and fed him, encouraging his lackluster appetite with glowing descriptions of how soon he would be healed and strong and able to return to his ship.

He fully understood that her concern was genuine and that it was because he was by no means out of danger of death from his wound, but he was unable to resist teasing this kindly woman who was her own jailer. Besides, it was such easy entertainment for a pirate with limited options.

"Ah, I can see I've overstayed me welcome, Ducks. Pass that tasty scone and Ol' Blackjack will be a bad memory before ye can say, 'Damned pirate!'"

"What! I didn't mean it that way! I'd never imply that you ... Of *course* you're welcome for as long as you need or like, I just thought you...I'm not that kind of...I didn't mean *that*!"

It was a benefit that it hurt to laugh, because Jack would have received his first slap from a well-bred English lady had he done so.

Just as they concluded their repast, they heard hoofbeats outside. Chloe rushed to the window and saw several red-coated horsemen cantering toward the manor.

"Soldiers!"

"Hand me my weapons, Ducks, and stay calm."

"Don't be ridicul—"

"*Now*, Chloe!"

She obeyed, fetching the items from the armoire. Then she started for the door, turned and came back to pin up her hair and don a shawl before going into the hall where she was met by a breathless Maria.

"Señora! Soldiers!"

"I know, Maria. Do not let them see that you're frightened. Close your eyes and take a deep breath." Maria did as she was told and crossed herself for good measure. "Stay up here unless I call for you. If you are questioned, pretend you have difficulty understanding their English and behave as if nothing has happened."

"Rodrigo!"

"Rodrigo will know how to handle them, Maria. Concentrate on your own conduct. We will get through this."

They heard the knock and then muffled voices from below when Emerson answered the door. What if the soldiers burst into the house? Chloe's heart was pounding so hard she feared it could be seen. She drew her shawl more securely around her and, putting on her most aristocratic air, descended the wide staircase.

"Who is it, Emerson?"

"Soldiers from the fort, Madam, looking for some escaped prisoner." Emerson, looking typically bland, had deliberately twisted their words, using the ploy of pretending to misunderstand due to having no knowledge of the event.

Lieutenant Howard spoke as she approached to stand

beside her butler. "Sorry to disturb you so early, Lady Caruthers. Not an escaped prisoner, exactly. We're looking for a fugitive pirate, Jack Bellamie, if you recall."

"I don't recall, as I never saw the man, although I've heard of him. All of Port Royal has. Surely, you don't think he is headed this way."

"We can't be sure, Madam. He's wounded, but Bellamie is capable of anything. We just wanted to know if you or any of your staff have seen anything—unusual—and to warn you to be careful. Mr. Bellamie is a savage marauder to whom life is cheap."

She had to stifle a sharp rebuttal. Rothwell's little toady had no idea that he was looking at a very-much-alive Chloe Caruthers because *Captain* Bellamie was most assuredly not the demon he had just described. Regally impassive, she played along.

"How alarming. But, speaking for myself and my staff, I'm sure we have seen nothing out of the ordinary and we shall certainly notify you the moment we do." Had she ever told so many lies in so few words?

Emerson closed the door, graciously accepted his employer's sincere compliments for his handling of the situation, and went about his business without so much as a raised eyebrow. Maria begged permission to go to the stables and tell Rodrigo, which, of course, Chloe granted. Rodrigo would be helpful in calming his wife and preparing her for the next visit—if there were another.

The immediate danger past, Chloe waited outside her bedroom door, composing herself and allowing the trembling to abate before dealing with Jack.

She opened the door, expecting to see Captain Blackjack Bellamie with his cutlass in one hand and pistol in the other, eyes blazing, ready for a futile fight to the death on her great feather bed. Instead, he was the very picture of bored relaxation, languidly picking his teeth with a fingernail.

"Guests leave already, Ducks?"

"They're gone." She picked up the weapons and carried them to the armoire.

"Have a care! Do not damage those."

"Why would I damage them? I didn't before."

"Easy, Ducks. I meant nothing by it. Why so testy?"

"It's been a very trying morning, Jack, can't you see? We all came within a hair's breadth of disaster and you act as if nothing has happened."

"Nothing has happened, M'lady. The soldiers came. The soldiers left. All is as it was."

"Jack, are you insane? This is a life and death situation. Such languor is simply not natural!"

"And ye think my becoming hysterical would change an iota?"

"But what if Rothwell's men had searched this house? What if they had come through that door instead of I?"

"In the first place, I'm not deaf. I heard them leave. In the second, while they were on the premises, I was on alert and prepared to make what would almost certainly be the final resistance. But I didn't have to do it, now did I?"

They looked at each other for a long moment, his words repeating in her mind as she tried to understand how such pragmatism could be possible. When she spoke, her voice was softer.

"Jack. You've been through such awful experiences. How can you not be devastated by it all?"

"Because, dear gentle Chloe, those awful experiences have taught me one thing: as long as ye can take one more breath, there is hope."

4—Reason to Hope, Reason to Weep

Maria returned from the barn feeling nearly euphoric after their deliverance. She prepared a midday meal that was especially varied and nutritious, partly from a sense of celebration and partly to provide the best nourishment to her patient. While it cooked she went up to her mistress' room to perform a task she was dreading.

She knocked and was told to enter, whereupon she found Lady Caruthers sitting beside Captain Bellamie, reading to him. His eyes were lightly closed, as he basked in the peaceful moment. Maria felt even worse about what she had to do.

"Señora. Captain Bellamie. The bandages must be changed. It would be well to do it now, if you please."

Chloe agreed and asked Jack if he were ready.

"Maria's the doctor," he chirped.

Pulling the old bandages off the wound was an ordeal, even after soaking them with whiskey to soften the dried blood. Chloe and Maria knew it had to be ghastly for him, but he merely clenched his teeth and made not a sound.

Once uncovered, the stitches proved to be intact. The area was angry red and swollen, naturally, but it appeared rather better than either of them had expected. A little fresh bleeding from the bandage removal was not excessive and stopped within minutes. Maria put clean bandages over the wound and declared his recovery to be preceding unusually well, much to their relief.

There was one more thing Maria had to do for him before she returned to the kitchen: he must lie on his right side awhile for the health of his lungs, as he had been on his back since the night he arrived. She leaned over him to pull him toward herself and Chloe knelt on the bed at his left to help lift him without pulling his stitches. Ever so slowly they went until he was nearly prone and

Maria tucked a pillow under his chest.

The maneuver had gone well and had not been unduly hurtful. Maria gathered the soiled bandages and departed to tend to the laundry and cooking. She was too absorbed in the success of her efforts and the relief that it was over to notice the look on her mistress' face.

Chloe walked to the window and pretended to stare out at the sky, turning away from Jack as she fought back tears. This was simply too much. She couldn't take any more! As she had rolled him from his supine position, she saw his back for the first time. Five thick, raised welts ran diagonally from his right shoulder blade to his left hip. Long healed, they were mute testimony that he had been savagely whipped.

She wanted to weep like a child. The appalling inhumanity! If she were Jack, she would bear a vendetta against all mankind. Yet, he seemed anything but bloodthirsty or bitter. She was awash with admiration and pity, respect and wonder—and tears that would not be contained.

Losing the battle to rein in her anguish, she remained at the window, fumbled in her sleeve for a handkerchief and surreptitiously dabbed her streaming eyes. She didn't fool Jack for a moment.

"Chloe."

She couldn't trust herself to speak.

"Chloe, Ducks, do ye know something Ol' Blackjack doesn't?"

She shook her head.

"Tell me why yer upset."

She shook her head.

"Come here and talk to me, lest I infer that ye and Doctor Maria have seen me impending demise and seek to keep it from me. Is that it?"

She shook her head.

"Chloe, come here. *Now*."

She turned and went to the bed. Sitting in front of him, her hands clasped in her lap, she hunched over into a veritable ball of misery as tears streamed down her cheeks. Jack watched her knowingly.

"Ye saw, didn't ye, Ducks."

This time she nodded.

"It was a long time ago, Chloe. I was young and full of meself. I crossed the line with the quartermaster on a barque out of Port-au-Prince and learned that rules apply to every member of a crew. Because of my youth, I was spared worse. I could have been keelhauled."

Moved by her empathy, Jack placed his hand on her back as he spoke. She flinched, unaccustomed to being touched, which he understood, but he didn't draw away. As she relaxed under his warm hand, he moved it in small circles, a discreet and gentle caress.

Thus they sat in silence for a while. Jack studied her as she calmed down, wondering why one with so much property, wealth, and position—and such pretty blue eyes and soft blond hair— was so bereft of humor and so fearful of human contact that a comforting touch made her respond like a head-shy mare. He wondered what her scars were and why.

When Maria entered with a tray (after knocking, of course), the two of them remained as they were, so the tableau that met the maid's eyes was that of a couple seemingly in the throes of some sort of angst. Maria found no surprise in this; she already knew that Chloe was in love with Jack and that Chloe, herself, didn't yet know. Sooner or later there had to be tears. She hoped her mistress was not on the threshold of more sadness.

She left the tray and quickly departed.

Slowly, like one waking from a dream, Chloe rose and prepared to serve the meal to Jack. It didn't occur to her to dine herself, although she'd had very little at breakfast and it was now well past midday. She placed another pillow behind him and eased him back onto it, poured the tea and broke the bread, not meeting his eyes. Unlike the morning's embarrassment, though, she now avoided his gaze because he would see too deeply into her soul and she wasn't ready for that, likely would never be.

Maria had prepared a fragrant ragout with freshly baked bread, plantain, and a fruit compote. The aroma was tantalizing, but Chloe scarcely noticed until Jack broke her trance.

"Eat up, Ducks. Must keep up yer strength to look after Ol' Blackjack, ye know."

She looked up at his twinkling eyes—and twinkled back.

They chatted companionably during their repast, laughing a little, commenting on the sumptuous fare. She told him that Maria's cooking skills were eclectic, English from Emerson, Spanish/Cuban from her homeland, Creole from the island, and something that seemed to defy identification with any region. She had been known to serve kidney pie, gumbo, Spanish rice, and toad-in-the-hole at the same meal, but it was always delicious.

Jack told how meager and unpleasant the meals could become after weeks at sea and how pirates were always just as eager to steal food and drink as silver and gold. For some reason, she found that amusing and Jack saw her laugh in unfeigned merriment. So, she wasn't humorless after all. Perhaps she had still more human qualities he had yet to discover.

5—A Threshold Is Crossed

After the meal, Jack seemed much
improved and, when Chloe checked, his
temperature was nearly normal. He expressed his deep gratitude
for her unflagging attention and urged her to take a break and get
some fresh air.

She called for Maria to help get him onto his side again and
to remove the dinner tray. Afterward, Maria was to remain nearby
and look in on him frequently, allowing Chloe to take a stroll
around the grounds and then return for a nice, relaxing soak in
the big copper tub.

Jack wasn't yet asleep when Chloe left, so Maria busied
herself doing small chores in and near the bedroom. At length,
she heard him call for her assistance.

Having tended to his need, Maria started to leave the room,
but he called her back. He requested a basin of water, a cloth,
and some soap. Maria nodded and left, returning with the
requested items moments later. She left them by the bed and
moved toward the door, then paused.

"Leave those breeches by the bed, Captain, and I'll take
them for laundering." She went out and closed the door.

When she returned later to retrieve the basin and clothing,
he was getting drowsy, but asked her when Chloe would
return. Maria hid her delight that he seemed eager to have her
mistress with him again. The two were deep in conversation when
Chloe arrived and asked that her bath be prepared.

By the time Chloe emerged, much refreshed, from her bath,
Jack was deeply asleep. Careful not to wake him, she felt his
forehead. Still no fever. Her heart sang.

In her dressing room, she sat at her vanity as Maria helped
with her hair.

"Señora, I have good news about the Captain."

"Oh, please tell me."

"While you were gone, he made his water again and already there was no blood."

Chloe's face darkened and she paused before speaking.

"Oh, that's—very good news, Maria." She had been spared an ordeal and the result was wonderful news, so why did she suddenly feel angry with both Maria and Jack? *Ridiculous!*

Oblivious, Maria went on. "He needs a bath, Señora. He wants you to do it."

Chloe turned from the mirror to look directly at her maid.

"Me? Why does he want me to do it?"

"He didn't say, Señora. Perhaps he feels more comfortable with you."

"Yes, perhaps. Well, when he awakens, I'll have you prepare one."

"Very good, Señora."

If Maria had an opinion on the subject, Chloe couldn't read it in her face. She decided that it was simply not an issue for anyone but herself.

Chloe watched Jack sleep. It was a relief to do so without fearing that each breath would be his last. She recalled their earlier conversation when she had broken down after seeing the scars on his back, remembering his kindness toward her. His had been the most extraordinarily comforting touch she had ever felt. Now she knew why Jenny had called him a fine man. And this fine man wanted her to bathe him.

She went out onto the balcony as the sun lowered in the western sky and the shadows lengthened. Night sounds drifted from the forest and fields as she reflected on this most remarkable day, which wasn't yet over. She wanted to think on what she was about to do, try to remember how Maria had partially bathed her when she was so weak after childbirth.

But, she was sure that Jack was weaker now than she had been then and would not be able to assist so much. She didn't want to behave as she had that morning, or try to do it with her eyes closed, or panic and call for Maria to take over. It would be degrading to lose control in front of him again since he was giving her a second chance to behave like an adult. She went inside.

He slept on. He looked mild for a pirate, his hand curled on the pillow under his chin. Chloe realized that she actually trusted this admitted outlaw. He certainly must have a fierce, dangerous side, but she had seen his compassion, his humor, and his wisdom. She sensed that he understood her, possibly better than she understood herself and she knew that that understanding would make him careful with her.

Chloe lit the lamp as the room grew dark, then sat by the bed to wait for Jack to awaken. She hoped it wouldn't be much longer for fear her mood of calm resolve wouldn't last, but she needn't have worried. A few moments later, he stretched out his hand, made a soft sound in his throat, and looked around for her. She came to him, smiling shyly.

"Hello, Sleepyhead. Are you feeling better?"

"Aye. All thanks to the Caribbean's finest nurse."

"You are welcome, Captain, I'm sure." More softly, "Maria says you want me to give you a bath."

"Do ye dispute that I need one? I can go another month or two, if ye like."

"No, no the time has come." Whereupon, she called for Maria.

The necessary items for the task appeared so quickly it seemed almost magical. Maria must have had a large pot of water heating and everything assembled in anticipation.

Chloe proceeded, following the plan she had rehearsed in her head.

Since he was already on his side, she began by washing his back. Her touch was so light he could hardly feel it.

"Chloe, Ducks, ye can't hurt me there. Put some muscle into it."

She scrubbed harder, encouraged by the contented sounds he made as she did so.

Moving downward, she was surprised to find that his breeches were no longer on him; she didn't mention it, though. She bravely washed down over his slim bottom and was pleased and a little surprised not to have been struck blind.

That finished, she eased the extra sheet from under him so that he would lie back on the clean one underneath.

Next, she washed his face, careful not to get soap in those haunting eyes. She thought that surely he must be able to do this himself, but resolved to say nothing if he didn't volunteer.

Neither said anything, yet the ambience between them was as if there were no world save the little sphere that encompassed them. She didn't have to avoid meeting his eyes nor play coy games with him and he would not tease her nor make her unnecessarily uncomfortable. She was unaware that it was a conscious decision on his part, but she was confident that he would not smirk or taunt her this time.

Unhurried, she bathed his chest, his arms and hands, his belly. He assisted by moving as necessary, but made no offer to take over from her at any time, although it was obvious that he could have washed his own arms and hands, at least. The agreement was that she would bathe him.

Next, she did his feet and legs up to mid-thigh. He was now completely naked and clean except for his pelvic area, which was covered by a corner of the sheet. She knew that he if were going to spare her this potential embarrassment, now was the moment. He said nothing, did nothing, neither releasing her nor pushing her. She realized that he was deliberately leaving control of the situation entirely with her and therefore, she had no fear.

She knew that she could break the silence and suggest he finish the job and he would do so without comment. But she didn't want to break the silence, didn't want to fail him, didn't want to fail herself. She was sure that he couldn't possibly know how momentous this was for her, couldn't know how she had lived all the years before this hour.

Without changing her demeanor, she slowly removed the sheet and gazed upon his manhood. For a moment she simply stared, transfixed. Unlike the rest of him, this was neither tan nor pale white, but a pallet of pink, purple, and burgundy, laced with blue veins, the thin, snug foreskin translucent. She dimly realized that this area was already clean, freshly washed, yet he had let her continue anyway. This part of the bath wasn't for him, it was for her, and he had made it so in the gentlest way possible.

She continued to gaze at this most personal part of him, unrushed, permitted to deal with her own thoughts, and she was deeply touched by this consideration. The beauty of the moment threw into sharp contrast the stifling life she had led, the constricted world she had always lived in, a world that approved of her eyes seeing the obscene marks of savagery inflicted upon him, yet would be scandalized by what she was now doing: looking at part of a living human being, the giver of new life, a normal, natural occurrence on half the population. The horror of this dichotomy, the weight of the terrible waste of her sterile life bore down on her and she dropped her chin to her chest and squeezed her eyes tightly shut, but the hot tears came anyway.

Jack had not expected this at all. Unsure what to do, he reached down and tentatively stroked her hair to comfort and reassure her. Her body shook with sobs, but she made no sound. He stared at her, confused.

Then, suddenly—he understood.

He moved his hand down to her back, gently urging her up toward him. She complied, melting willingly against his chest, her face pressed into the angle between his neck and shoulder. Not wanting to ever leave his encircling arms, she drew her legs up onto the bed beside him and gave herself over to her grief.

Taking his time, letting her spend the worst of her misery, he merely held her and didn't speak. Then, as she quieted, he moved his head a little, bringing his lips closer to her ear, and whispered, "Chloe. Ducks. Ye've never seen a man before, have ye?" Her silence was his answer, and he said nothing more. It was enough.

He reached for the coverlet and drew it across them both.

6—Two New Beginnings

Lieutenants Howard, Ambrose, and Ellsworth entered Commodore Rothwell's office still groggy with sleep, but were immediately aware that their commander was fully awake and agitated. Twice the previous day he had grilled them about their searches of the area, and twice he had received unwelcome reports. He could not shake the feeling that they were overlooking something.

"Gentlemen, I have called you here at this early hour because we cannot afford the luxury of quitting while Bellamie is still free and in our midst. It is my hope that a night's rest has refreshed your memories or brought additional insight as to who might be hiding him."

Wisely refraining from pointing out that their "night's rest" had been truncated by more than an hour, Howard spoke for the three.

"Sir, we found nothing suspicious at any of the domiciles or shops where we searched, nor did we locate any trace of his trail. If his body were to have washed up on shore, our men would certainly have noticed and reported it."

"So say the rest of you?"

"Yes, Sir," the two agreed.

"Then he is probably still alive and we must redouble our efforts. Let's review what we know. Bellamie was hit and has lost a great deal of blood, so he is not likely to have survived without assistance. His trail ended with his heading downstream, probably hoping to get to the shore and effect escape via water, but our troops were in force in the area and saw nothing. No further trail has been found nor has his body; therefore, it stands to reason that someone has voluntarily protected him since that evening. Our task is to locate that person."

Ambrose spoke up. "Sir, it might not have been voluntary. I mean, he could have threatened them."

"Considering the amount of blood he has lost, I doubt he has the strength to be terribly intimidating. No, one of our 'loyal citizens' is guilty of aiding and abetting a known arch criminal. When we find that person—and we will find him—he will be given a fair trial and hanged along with his pirate friend."

None of the three lieutenants dared voice the thought that, if the Eversons were on the island, no one would have to wonder where Bellamie was being cosseted. The subject of those two and their former relationship with the pirate captain still rankled Rothwell, though he tried to hide it.

Ellsworth looked doubtful. "With all respect, Sir, I fail to see what more we can do without additional information."

"Precisely, Lieutenant. Therefore we must garner that information for ourselves. We have no choice but to search every house, shop, barn, and outbuilding within the radius he conceivably could have traveled. It seems drastic, but milder steps have proven fruitless."

Gillette was frowning. "Sir, how do we cover everything in such a large area without seriously depleting the garrison of troops?"

"We begin in the immediate area of the waterfront at the mouth of the stream. The populace is more concentrated in that region and it is also near where his trail appears to have left off, so success will probably come in that area and the troops will quickly be able to return to the fort.

"Proceed with as little fanfare as possible to avoid alarming the people and forewarning his hosts, but leave no haymow, no cupboard, no cloak un-inspected. Do I make myself clear?"

At their affirmative, Rothwell unrolled three maps whereon he had designated each lieutenant's sector of responsibility and a proposed time frame for advancement of the search into the hinterlands, should it be necessary. Clearly, he had been working on this plan all night and gave the officers orders to begin immediately.

Jack saw the first blush of morning as it softly illuminated the woman sleeping in his arms. He had been unable to close his eyes all night. He was finally strong enough to think clearly and now he realized that his situation had just become more complicated.

Throughout the long night, he had reflected on his life and found that he was in a predicament he had successfully avoided until now. He had always had a lusty sex drive and had observed few restrictions in satisfying it. He drew the line at men, children, and animals; he didn't find them stimulating, anyway.

He thoroughly enjoyed women. In fact, after enough rum, any female from puberty on could be entertaining in a pinch, but entertaining was the most she could be. He couldn't imagine being "in love," nor had he ever desired such an encumbrance.

No, Blackjack Bellamie had resolved early on never to allow the physical need for sexual release to enslave or endanger him. As long as he had at least one good hand, he need not surrender control of his life to another person for such pleasures. He restricted his assignations to prostitutes or female pirates, women who were as cavalier about such activities as he. Virgins and other men's wives were far too dangerous to be worth the risk.

But now he had stumbled into unknown, indeed unimagined, territory. He had never meant to seduce his caregiver. In fact, in his debility, he had only minimally noticed her attractiveness, certainly had not intended staying at her estate long enough to expend any energy not necessary for escape.

Seeing that she was a mature adult and learning that she was a widow and had even given birth (according to Maria), he had taken her astonishing prudery as an artifice and found easy sport in teasing her because of it. Subconsciously, he felt that his causing her to take herself less seriously would be some recompense for her generosity in his time of great need. He would not have dreamed of harming her in any way.

But her revelation the night before had changed the entire picture for him. He had no precedent in which to cast it. She was as tenderhearted and unspotted as a young virgin, yet had suffered wholly adult sorrows. He sensed that he had acquired a responsibility he would never have willingly accepted.

Sometimes, on quiet nights at sea, he wondered if someday he might fall in love and accept the complication of being two instead of one. Just keeping the one alive and free had been sufficient trouble so far, but he knew pirates who had wives or mistresses and who seemed to fare well enough.

In truth, he couldn't imagine how he would ever meet someone who would be worth the effort, since a prostitute was obviously not wife material and a maiden would better belong to a younger man. Fleur would have been his choice among the lady pirates, but she would allow no man to touch her, preferring to go a-whoring right along with Jack and the crew. Besides, she was now a captain in her own right and no longer sailed on the *Sinecure*.

He wasn't old yet, but not young, either. When he learned of the apparent joy that love had brought to his former carpenter and Jenny Hunter, it had sewn a seed of longing in him that he hadn't begun to recognize until he had been back on the *Sinecure* for more than a year. It was that small sense that life was finite and that there should be something more...

A decision had to be made before she awoke: would he reverse course and take her no farther into the realm of *amour*, or would he continue dismantling her invisible prison and set her free? (There was a third choice, but it hadn't yet occurred to him.)

She stirred in his arms and he knew that he would not leave her imprisoned when she had saved his life; he must free her for them to be square.

When Maria brought the breakfast tray, she also brought Jack's clothing, his shirt, breeches, vest, and sash—all mended and washed and neatly folded. His dark eyes had shown with a spirit Chloe had not seen in him as he touched his garments.

He stated that he felt good enough to get dressed and try to walk a little. Maria agreed that he was probably ready to try at least and, with the usual warnings, brought him some willow bark tea to blunt the inevitable discomfort such activity would bring.

After Maria left, Chloe retreated to the dressing room to prepare for the day, after which she returned to help him into his clothes. Neither mentioned the emotional happenings of the previous evening and she performed her task with no indication that it was anything other than a routine matter. As she worked with him, he watched her placid face and felt a sense of accomplishment.

Propped up on the pillows, he shared their meal and waited for Maria to return to assist Chloe in getting him on his feet. He felt truly optimistic for the first time since he had been spotted by the marines on the street outside the pub.

While Chloe and Maria eased Jack to his feet and supported him as he walked his first tentative steps across the room and back, the three of them laughed and bantered with joy at his deliverance.

And Rothwell's three lieutenants began their intensified manhunt.

7—Jack's Story

Jack's recovery seemed to accelerate throughout the day. Although he frequently needed to lie down and rest after his exertions, by midday he was able to sit at the little table and dine with Chloe. Evening found him walking about the room and even into the hall with only Chloe or Maria beside him to steady him. He loudly attributed this remarkable ability to "getting me sea legs under me" again.

After dinner, Maria took a hard line and forbade any more strenuous activity until after a night's sleep. She changed his bandages once more and found the wound to be settling down and healing quite nicely. Chloe could scarcely contain her delight.

When the remnants of the meal had been cleared away and Jack and Chloe were again alone for the evening, they were unable to resist going out onto the balcony to bask in the sweetness of the tropical night. For a while they sat in silence, listening to the lovely sounds, but eventually she spoke.

"Jack, you speak like an Englishman, yet you seem to be from someplace more exotic. Were you born in England?"

He sighed and took a long time to answer. This was a subject he had shared with only a choice few and with no one for more than a decade now.

"Aye. I was born in England, but I do not consider myself to be a subject, nor does the Crown consider me such."

"Your parents were foreigners, then?"

"My parents were born on English soil, as were my grandparents."

"Then, why…?"

"Because the Roma are not of any nation. We are not accepted, nor do we wish to be."

"Roma. You're a—"

"Gypsy, Ducks. The word won't bite. *Tako kalo rat,* 'true black blood.' I was born the third of three, the only boy, as our caravan camped near Newcastle. I had a normal childhood: two loving parents, aunts, uncles, grandparents, sisters, cousins, friends. We played and grew and learned just like English children do. We weren't taught reading and writing and British history, but we learned horses and Romany tradition and human nature.

"We also learned that home was the wagon under us and the people around us and that we are despised and unwanted throughout the world. Constant movement is a necessity, but it's our nature to be free and that is the price we gladly pay."

"I've never met a Gypsy before, so please forgive my ignorance when I ask if your people possess real clairvoyance or if it's all a ruse."

"From infancy, Chloe, a Romany child learns to size up a situation in a single glance and to see the hidden secrets in a room or a face. We don't actually read minds or see the future; we simply see details that others miss. As a survival skill, it's unsurpassed."

"Why did you leave your caravan and turn pirate?"

Another long silence as Jack composed himself for the disclosure to come.

"When I was ten years old, we had made camp along a stream about fifty miles from London. It was normal for us to never spend more than one night in the same place, but heavy rains came and cut us off from the direction we were heading. Instead of simply turning back, we chose to wait one more day to move on.

"Fatal mistake. A band of soldiers and some ragtag locals set upon us after midnight. They burned the wagons and arrested most of the adults. Those who resisted too vigorously, including my parents, were slaughtered on the spot."

"Oh, Jack. How awful! And what became of the children?"

"We were taken away to be 'civilized', meaning to be pressed into labor on local farms or in shops. The younger ones were sent to orphanages until grown to decent working size. I was small for my age and was sent to an orphanage in Portsmouth.

"Never saw my sisters again. I hope they didn't experience what I did in the orphanage. But they were old enough to be of some use, so, who knows?

"I endured more than a year in that snake pit, growing sicker in mind and body than I would have thought possible. I could see the masts of the ships in the harbor and knew that they meant escape, meant freedom.

"One evening around dusk, I saw a cart emptying coal into our hopper. I scurried across the concourse and grabbed onto the harness of one of the horses, stretching myself under the animal's belly and holding on to the hame, my heels hooked in the near trace. The starvation rations I'd been given by my generous hosts had made me so nearly weightless the Percheron must have thought I was just some annoying fly. He hardly twitched.

"In the deepening gloom, neither the proctor nor the teamster noticed a small, dark Gypsy child clinging beneath a large, black horse.

"It wasn't safe for me to 'dismount' until the driver stopped at his stable and, when he alit to open the gate, I was off like a shot. Doubt he ever knew I was there. I ran through streets and fields until I got to the harbor.

"On the dock were several casks of water waiting to be loaded into the hold of an outbound ship. I drained one into the harbor and then hid in it until first light when the dock men came on duty and aboard I went.

"We were well at sea when I finally dared emerge from that cask and, even then, I hid in the hold until I was discovered the next evening by a sailor. I was hauled before the captain and his officers and made to believe my life was near ended. But once he had my undivided attention, he gave me food and drink, chores to do and a hammock to sleep in.

"I became a kind of apprentice cabin boy and was worked plenty hard for my passage, but I knew the sea would be my home from that day on. The rocking of the ship was like the swaying of a wagon, the crew seemed as the members of a caravan, and the work became my play."

"That wasn't a pirate ship, surely."

"No, she was a merchantman, the *Lady Estelle*, bound for the Mediterranean. We never made it to the Pillars of Hercules, though. Barely a week out and we were caught in a gale that snapped the rudder chain and broke off the foremast. We were riding at sea anchor when a corsair flying the black flag came upon us. After a nominal attempt at defense, we surrendered and were taken aboard.

"The ship was the *Archangel* and we were given the option of joining the crew or being marooned. Soon the ship's Articles filled with Xs and signatures and we began our lives as pirates.

"I knew from the first day that this was the life for me. Her captain taught me seamanship, sword fighting, and other piratical skills. Man by the name of Korsakov."

"Korsakov. I've heard that name. Who—?"

"Long story, Ducks. Ol' Blackjack's bent yer ear long enough fer one night. Tell ye all about it another time." At this, he stretched and tried to stand. Chloe went to his side to help and the two friends walked arm in arm back into the house.

At their evening meal, Maria told Emerson and Rodrigo how splendidly the Captain's recuperation had proceeded throughout the day. She didn't mention that she had ceased asking their mistress if she wished to use the guestroom, it being tacitly understood upstairs that Chloe would remain with their patient even though he no longer required round-the-clock nursing. Such matters did not concern the men, nor would they care.

The household seemed to have returned to a degree of normalcy, although the question of their secret guest was far from settled. The following day would be Thursday, Emerson's weekly respite from his duties, so conversation centered on mundane affairs to be dealt with in his absence and on what items Maria and Rodrigo would need to procure on Friday, their market day.

As the evening chores were completed downstairs and in the stables, Chloe came out of her dressing room wearing a sleeping gown. She was somewhat unsure what to do or expect after the day now past and the night that had come before, but she had placed her trust in Jack and wasn't worried.

She found him deeply asleep, exhausted after his busy day (and sleepless night), but he had folded back the counterpane on "her" side, mute invitation to her to actually get into the bed, rather than just sleep beside him under the afghan. She was touched by the sweet gesture, but she also felt an unfamiliar mixture of relief and disappointment.

8—Forewarned

Emerson Bentley was up before the sun, dressed in his riding habit, eager for a bracing gallop in the cool of the morning. Rodrigo would have Zeus, the big gray Arabian, already groomed and tacked up, ready for their day, and they would be off as soon as Maria prepared the small pouch with some biscuits and fruit.

A superb equestrian, Emerson typically spent his Thursdays riding and jumping until midmorning, then both man and mount would rest by a stream and enjoy the peace of the countryside. After a visit to the bazaar, he usually would go to the home of some friends where several like-minded individuals gathered to discuss philosophy and current events, enjoy chamber music, read poetry, or play bridge until evening.

Wonderfully refreshed after such pastimes, he would set out for home, unhurried, putting Zeus through dressage maneuvers along the way. Rarely did they return before the last streaks of color were fading from the western sky.

But this day was different. Shortly after midday, Rodrigo heard someone riding hard up the path behind the stables. He looked and saw Emerson and Zeus coming at full gallop, the horse lathered and breathing hard. Emerson leapt to the ground as the animal slid to a stop beside the stableman.

"Emerson! What is the matter?"

"I have disturbing news, Rodrigo. Go and bring Maria out here. Don't let Madam know."

Rodrigo went to the house to fetch his wife while Emerson unsaddled Zeus and led him in circles to cool him. Moments later the two Cubans arrived looking worried. Emerson drew them into a corner of the building out of sight of the house and wasted no time on preliminaries.

"While I was passing the bazaar, I overheard a conversation among some servants from households near the waterfront. It appears that soldiers from the fort are searching every home and building looking for Captain Bellamie. They are entering houses and leaving no corner unexamined, even into ladies' chambers. We must have him out of here before they come."

Maria looked as though she might faint. She sagged against Rodrigo who seemed to be dumbstruck. Emerson asked her the key question.

"Is he able to be moved?"

"No, no. He cannot. He will die. His stitches. He is too weak."

"Then pay careful attention. There is a way out of this, but we have to keep our heads. As thoroughly as the soldiers are searching, they are moving slowly. They appear to be proceeding methodically from the waterfront inland, so it will probably be two, maybe three days before they come this far. If his recovery continues at the pace you've described, Maria, he will be much stronger by then. The question is, will he be able to travel?"

"No, at least not alone. He is healing, *sì*, but it takes many weeks to restore so much blood. One of us must go with him. The Señora must choose."

"Very well. Here is our course: tomorrow the two of you will go to market as usual. You must behave as you normally do. Do not reveal any agitation, but listen to the gossip and try to determine the speed and direction of the search so that we may plan accordingly. Don't ask too many questions, but get the answers we need. For today, we would best keep this from Madam and the Captain. Such unpleasant news will only upset them unnecessarily since they cannot make decisions until we have more information.

"In the meantime, let each of us be thinking about ways to spirit him away from here and the details involved, for we will need as many ideas as possible tomorrow evening. Return rather earlier than usual, but not so much as to alarm Madam, and speak with me first."

Here the three parted, Rodrigo to tend to Zeus, Maria to the kitchen, and Emerson to retire to his quarters to think and prepare.

9—What Hath Jack Wrought?

Chloe and Jack were enjoying their day and Jack's new mobility, browsing through rooms, chatting, even preparing to go downstairs (but carefully) to the parlor where she would play music for him. Despite their apparent ingenuousness, they both knew that this was an oasis of tranquility that couldn't last forever and that made it so much the sweeter. Fortunately, they had heard nothing of the excitement at the stables.

Jack could not remember ever having been inside a mansion. Chloe was showing him a plunderer's vision of paradise: everywhere was silver, gold, crystal, fine tapestry, imported carpets, *objets d'art*, silk, china, exquisite furniture—enough to fill the hold of the *Sinecure* and more. She was explaining the special meaning or sentimental worth of this piece or that while he was doing a buccaneer's accounting in his head. The irony was not lost on him that this was booty he would never take nor allow to be taken by any of the Brethren that he commanded.

More revelations awaited him in the parlor as she led him to her most prized possession, an ornate harpsichord given to her as a wedding present from her husband. She showed him the intricate paintings on the case with their references to the Muse, to Pan, to the Psalmist, and on the soundboard inside with seraphic choirs in pearlescent clouds. She demonstrated the mechanism for him, how striking the keys made the plectra set the strings vibrating. At her urging, he tried a few keys for himself and was delighted with the result.

She opened a cabinet beside the instrument and produced a book that was tall and wide, but not thick, which she placed on the music rack and opened to the strangest writing he had ever seen: lots of parallel lines and black dots, but very few letters or words. Jack had never seen written music. There had always been music in the caravans, on board the ships, and in the taverns and brothels, but it seemed to spring fully formed from the performers' memories or imaginations.

He settled onto a chaise to watch her work. She sat at the keyboard and focused her attention on the book in front of her as her fingers produced the most evocative sounds he had ever heard. This music was nothing like the raucous accompaniment to working, drinking, or swiving to which he was accustomed; this music drew long-forgotten memories from deep within him. It was the emotional music of the Gypsies, at turns filled with driving fury or aching melancholy, then crisp, dancing, or fiery. His eyes moistened, even as his heart raced. He actually thought for a moment that he could smell his mother's hair.

Eventually she paused and turned to see if her audience were still there or perhaps had gone to sleep. To her surprise and delight, his face was radiant with the effect of the music and he rose from the chaise to come to her.

Wordlessly, he took her in his arms and held her closer than she had ever been held. She could feel his heart pounding against her own bosom. Then he inclined his head toward her and gradually closed the distance between them to kiss her.

Soft but insistent, the kiss lingered as they breathed each other's breath; after a moment he stopped, but continued to hold her. His hand pressed her head against his shoulder for a while; then he cupped her chin and kissed her again.

Chloe knew that if she died in the next instant, her life would have been worth all the pain that had come before.

Chloe had asked Maria to serve the evening meal on the veranda, as Jack was now strong enough to go anywhere around the house so long as Chloe stayed beside him as insurance.

They lingered over the dessert and wine until the countryside was in darkness. When Maria was finally summoned to clear the table, she asked her mistress if there were anything special that she and Rodrigo should bring back from market the next evening.

Jack seemed especially interested that Maria would be gone all day and asked Chloe if Emerson would be serving their meals and tending to their needs in her absence. He hid his pleasure at the revelation that the butler did not work upstairs except when requested by Chloe for special assignments. She assured him that Maria would leave food prepared so that they could eat whenever they wished and that she would attend to their morning requirements before leaving. She had completely misread his motives.

He hadn't fooled the worldly Maria, though. She hurried after them as they proceeded through the hall.

"Señora. Captain Bellamie. Before I leave tomorrow, we should remove those bandages and leave them off for air to begin drying the wound." She knew that no bandage at all would be better for him than a soggy, sweaty one.

Emerson's day off had been spent in intense work. He had maps rolled out, books open, pages of notes to himself spread about. Normally at this hour on a Thursday, he'd have had a light meal and a bath, and would be falling into peaceful slumber from a day well spent, but tonight he was still laboring by lamplight. Sleep, if it came at all, would be brief.

All three of the servants were restive with the same fear: what if their assumptions or Emerson's calculations were wrong? Would the morning light bring the hounds of hell to their doorstep and doom them all? Emerson alone was able to banish that unproductive thought from his mind long enough to make rational headway with the problem.

Such terrors were wonderfully absent from the imaginations of their mistress and her guest. Jack was formulating plans of an entirely different nature and Chloe was comfortable to follow whatever course he would set before her. In some ways that evening, Jack was the master of the estate; in other ways, it was

Emerson. Fortunately for Chloe, both men held her in high esteem and sought to protect her.

She and Jack slowly ascended the stairs and entered "their" room. They lit a lamp and she went into her dressing room straightaway to begin preparing for bed. He made his preparations by stripping off his shirt and breeches and throwing them over a chair.

He turned back the counterpane on the bed and lay down, then had a thought and scooted into the center of the bed. A second thought made him return to his usual place and sit on the edge. In a burst of modesty, he pulled the sheet across his lap.

Why is she taking so bloody long? He picked at his teeth, plumped a pillow and smoothed his moustache. He had a timeline in his head and it didn't include long waits doing nothing. If he were paying her, he'd just barge through the damned door and take his purchase or yell that he demanded a discount for wasted time.

But this was an entirely new situation for him. All those years that he had regarded himself as the very model of the experienced man of the world, he had conveniently disregarded the fact that he had never once taken a woman non-commercially. Well, there were the few female pirates, but even they had usually expected something material in return, if they weren't too drunk to think of it, in which case he left them something anyway to avoid making an enemy in the Trade. *Bloody hell! I'm near as innocent as she.*

Suddenly, he wasn't in such a hurry. So immersed in these thoughts was he that he didn't notice she had left the dressing room until she was walking to her side of the bed.

"Chloe!"

She stopped and looked questioningly at him. He merely beckoned her. As she approached him, he stood and embraced her, kissed her as he had downstairs. But this time, as she held him, her hands were touching his skin, including the lash marks on his poor back. It filled her with tenderness toward him, but her uncontrolled emotionalism had been spent and healed the night of the bath, so there were no tears now for his painful past or for hers.

He drew back from her a little, to study her face, to trace with his fingertip her brow, her nose, her lips. His eyes, black as Newcastle coal, were looking at her with such softness she felt as if she were falling into them, falling into heaven itself.

His attention dropped a little lower and he began to untie the laces of her sleeping gown. She continued to watch his face as he did so; had she looked at his hands, she'd have seen a barely perceptible tremor.

The gown dropped to the floor and now Chloe, too, was nude. The small strip of cloth holding his bandage in place was all that remained between them. She felt his arousal against her and began to tremble.

He whispered the first words she had said to him. "Don't be afraid...don't be afraid."

Still holding her, he took a step backward to the bed, lying down and pulling her beside him. He needed her to be on his right, as he still could not lie on his left side. He had planned this in advance; she had no plans at all except to follow his lead and continue to trust him.

He had resolved not to consummate their union tonight. There were many preliminaries he wanted to lead her through and he wanted them to be able to enjoy their greatest moment in total abandon, meaning privacy. Until tomorrow, there was naught but a door between themselves and Maria.

Lying facing each other, uncovered and unclothed, in a lighted room—even Chloe's girlish imagination had not thought such things ever happened. He was kissing her again and flicking his tongue across her lips, tenderly seeking admission. This she granted and then responded with her own tongue. Was a woman supposed to do this, too? She hoped she was doing it right. He seemed to like it. She was getting dizzy; if she weren't already lying down, she was certain she'd faint.

What he did next was even more astonishing. He left off kissing her mouth and trailed kisses down her neck, back and forth across her collarbones, then down to her breasts. Her nipples couldn't get any harder than they had been since he undressed her. She supposed he knew enough about women to know that they were soft most of the time. Was that even important? Probably not.

He took one in his mouth, sucked briefly, went to the other and did the same, then back to the first and settled into sucking deeply, his eyes closed in sheer pleasure.

I thought only babies did that! Surely, he doesn't think I have milk for him. Of course not, how absurd. Is this what they call "depravity?" Probably. Oh, it feels so wonderful! If it IS depravity, then I'm depraved. Jack and I are depraved. Depraved together. Depraved! Depraved! Oh, look at him. He IS a baby, MY baby. How could anyone ever, EVER wish to harm this? They'll not touch him, not hurt him again. I will kill them ALL with these two hands if they try to hurt him!

She encircled his head with her arms, protecting him from all the pain "out there" and kissed and nuzzled the top of his head.

She catches on pretty fast, he thought and switched back to the other breast. *Don't want it to feel neglected.*

She wondered what they would do for tallow. Her husband had always been thoughtful enough to prepare himself with tallow so that that big, dry rod wouldn't shred her delicate parts when he rammed it home. She was certain there was none in the room with them. Surely Jack knew better than to cause a lady such damage. He'd already demonstrated that he knew a thousand things more than she could have dreamed. *Trust him; he said not to be afraid.*

What is he doing? Why is his hand going there? His FINGER! She would have screamed, but Jack was faster and clamped his mouth over hers. He withdrew the offending digit and waited for her to calm down before he un-kissed her.

"Shhh, Ducks. No need to alert the staff. I didn't hurt ye, did I?" He hadn't expected such a response.

"No! No! Not hurt! Not at all! Don't stop!" She was strangling on her own breath. And she knew they'd never need tallow. Ever.

"We need to leave off for tonight, Darling. Tomorrow we'll have each other all day and need hide nothing. Take a deep breath, Chloe, Ducks. Yer turnin' blue."

"Please, Jack, just a little more, just a little!" She was winding her leg over and around his, pulling him into her.

He disengaged himself and held her shoulders. *Mother of God! She's actually begging. She has no idea what this means and she's NOT ACTING!*

"Chloe, Ducks? Darling? Sweetheart? There is no such thing as 'just a little more.' Maria can hear us. We don't want it like this. *Please* wait until tomorrow." She looked as if she were starving to death and he felt like an ogre.

When she finally regained some semblance of normal breathing, he cuddled her, whispering, "Think of patriotic songs or leftover eggplant or something." But the songs just twisted into paeans of praise for Jack and the eggplant looked really suggestive.

He got out of bed and went into the dressing room, behind the privacy screen, ostensibly to pass water before turning in for the night, but he efficiently and quietly solved another problem while there. Maybe tomorrow he could teach her such useful tricks for herself, but for tonight, he couldn't help her. He felt guilty about that for almost a minute before he began snoring.

Maria was up long before first light, making last minute preparations for their trip to market, arranging the food for the Señora and the Captain so that they wouldn't want for anything in her absence. Rodrigo had finished the morning feedings and was catching several fat hens to put into crates for transport to town. Eggs were packed in straw; melons and smoked meats had been put into nets and loaded onto the wagon.

Everything for breakfast was on the tray and she carried it upstairs to her mistress' room.

She knocked. No response. She knocked again. She could hear muffled voices, then Chloe, sounding blurred with sleep.

"One moment, Maria. One moment."

Finally, she was told to enter and, when she did, her mistress greeted her with a great deal of formal dignity despite the fact that her sleeping gown was on backward and inside out and her hair was falling across one eye. Maria pretended not to notice. The Captain was lying face down at the edge of the bed with one arm and one leg trailing off the side, part of the sheet draped across his middle, his braids splayed out in all directions and the stupid look of a pole-axed ox on his face.

If that was what they looked like after a quiet night, Maria didn't want to imagine what would greet her on her return from market. She left the tray, picked up the chamber pot and departed with the admonition that she would be returning sooner than usual to get the tray and remove the Captain's bandages.

Chloe tried to get Jack to eat, but he told her to go away, it was still night. She was sleepy, too, but she ate a little out of habit and set the tray aside. She lay back down and had just dozed off when Maria knocked again.

Chloe muttered, "Enter," and didn't bother to get up this time. Maria saw the uneaten breakfast.

"Señora—?"

"Leave it, Maria. Too early."

"I should still remove the bandages, Señora?"

"Oh, um, yes. Go ahead. Jack. Jack, wake up. Maria's going to remove your bandages."

He wrestled himself over onto his back, managing to tie himself up in the sheet in the process. Maria was nervous about what the day might reveal at the marketplace, the almost certain crisis ahead for their household, and had endured a night of poor sleep, so she was rapidly losing patience with these two great slugs who couldn't even wake up to eat her delicious breakfast. She yanked on the sheet rather too hard to get it out of the way and Jack's eyebrows went up.

"My apologies, Captain. Rodrigo and I are in a rush to be on our way."

"Quite all right, Doctor Maria. Give me a moment to wake up and I can help with the task at hand."

"Never mind, Captain. I just about have it." With that she

untied the strip and had the rest off of him a moment later. Her alacrity had made it less painful; one quick pull and it was over. "Let the air get to that today, perhaps even a little sunlight, and we can remove the stitches in about a week."

Jack thanked her and bade her safe journey; Chloe slept through it all, or pretended to. Certainly, it was uncharacteristic of her not to show interest in his newly exposed wound.

He heard the rattle of the harness and the crack of Rodrigo's buggy whip as the little cob moved them out onto the road. Then, all was quiet.

He lay there, uncertain how to proceed, eager to have this experience with Chloe, but not wanting to wake her. He assumed, correctly, that she hadn't slept well the night before. His imagination was filling him with tension and anticipation.

She was so quiet beside him, her head turned away from him, yet he sensed that she wasn't asleep. Something wasn't right with her. Was she waiting for him to make the first move? But, what if she had changed her mind? It even occurred to him to feign a relapse in order to get her attention and warmth. No, he had no choice but to wait and see. That relapse idea would be a good ploy to keep in mind should the situation deteriorate.

At last she stirred, rose, and walked to her dressing room without so much as looking at him. Not a good sign. He continued to fret as she took her time with her ablutions and clothing.

She must be angry with me.

When she finally emerged, she swept to the bedroom door and out into the hall without a backward glance. It happened so fast, he didn't even get a word out.

He frowned; she was fully dressed in pale green silk, not the garb of a woman about to romp with her man. He waited to see if she would return. She did not.

Finally, he decided he must take matters in hand, so he hurriedly dressed and left the room in search of her. The hall appeared empty and the house was silent. He literally didn't know which way to turn.

Chloe sat on a damask-upholstered bench in a small sitting area around the corner of the upstairs hall and looked out the window at the garden below. She was at an impasse; emotions that had lain dormant all of her life kept exploding forth in the presence of Jack Bellamie and she wasn't going to let it happen again.

She had wept rivers of tears (for herself and for him) and had shown her embarrassing naiveté. That was bad enough. But last night she had behaved like an animal, clawing at him and begging him for sex. She blushed to remember it.

He probably thought her some kind of lunatic. She was sickened at his certain loss of respect for her and of hers for herself. Worse, she would never feel his intoxicating kiss again.

That thought brought tears, but she forced them back. *No more!* No more uncontrolled emotional outbursts, alone or in his presence. What had she always been taught, "Control your hunger, control your thirst, control your emotions?" There was no excuse for a lady to do otherwise. She stiffened her back and inhaled deeply.

Jack was about to start down the stairs when he spied a few inches of pale green silk on the floor at the far corner of the hall. On bare feet he walked silently to it and saw her sitting at the window. He went to her and knelt by her side.

"Chloe, don't be angry with me."

She hadn't expected that. "I'm not angry with you."

"Then why are ye turning from me? I wanted us to have the day together."

"We appear to be together at the moment."

"Please, don't twist my words. I humbly apologize for any slight or insult ye perceived and assure ye none was intended."

She looked at his beloved face. He was hurt by her behavior and it wasn't his fault.

"Jack, it isn't you I'm angry with. It's me."

"Why? Why would ye be that?"

"I've behaved abominably since you arrived, have thoroughly disgraced myself, and I shan't do it anymore. I apologize to you for my bestial behavior last evening and pray that you will not think the less of me."

"Think the less of you? Chloe, I'm awestruck by the woman ye have revealed to me! Every good and desirable quality is met in ye."

"No, Jack. The feelings I betrayed to you last night were shameful and degrading. I wish I could remove it from your memory and from mine."

"Chloe, Lass, I'll be thankin' ye not to go removin' Ol' Blackjack's happiest moments from his memory, if ye please, especially if memory is all he'll have."

She studied his face, trying to resolve the clash of their views on the subject. Her perspective was from a lifetime of rigid inculcation; his was, at least, more humane. He held her gaze, not as a challenge, but in supplication. She remembered the night she had bathed him, her heartbreak at seeing her wasted life, and then his seemingly fathomless compassion for her.

If he truly felt repulsed by how she had behaved last night, he wouldn't be looking at her like this and trying to dissuade her from her self-effacement. She recalled that she had voluntarily placed her trust in him to lead her into this facet of life that she'd missed until now. If she gave over to him at this point, it would have to be total, no going back. Fear of the unknown battled with her trust and longing.

Suddenly, a realization hit her that nearly made her leap from her chair and—what? Embrace him? Run away? She was jolted by the absolute certainty that she was in love with Jack! Totally and completely in love with him. She had never known that feeling before, but she now realized that it had been there all along, almost from the moment she had first laid eyes on him. She loved him more than anything that existed on Earth. She would deny him nothing, hurt him never!

She didn't, couldn't, speak, but he read in her eyes that something profound had happened. He could not have put it into words, but he surely knew his next move: he took her into his arms and held her fiercely. He didn't kiss her, he held her as if she were a treasure he had just rescued from destruction. So they remained for several long moments.

When he finally eased his embrace, she looked up at him and received his kiss. He stroked her hair, "Chloe. Darling Chloe, please come back to bed. I want to make love to ye."

From the foyer below, Emerson looked up and saw the lovers returning to Chloe's room. He continued his daily duties without changing expression, but one question had been answered for him: whom his mistress would select to flee with the Captain when the time came.

In the bedroom, Jack held her and whispered, "Chloe, please don't ever turn from me again."

"Never, Jack. Never again."

He opened the French doors to allow a breeze into the room, then returned to her and slowly undressed her. He couldn't remember ever undressing a woman slowly before, but, he reminded himself, this was new territory for him.

He had been pondering a certain question most of his life. The subject received a lot of attention from groups of his mates when they were crowing about their conquests of the fairer sex and it sometimes erupted into heated arguments. The married pirates generally shunned the discussions out of respect for their wives and, ironically, if any of the men were to know the answer, it would likely be they.

The question was whether the female sexual crisis was real or a myth. Men like Jack, who consorted only with "professional" women, knew that the whores would do or say anything to get a gratuity or secure a return customer. They were well schooled in screaming with feigned ecstasy, sometimes even pretending to be in pain from the customer's "oversized" equipment. (The same slut might have been seen the previous evening taking on a pony, if the price were right.) He never fell for such ploys, merely taking them as part and parcel of the service being rendered. If the act were especially well done and energetic, he made it worth her while as he left her room.

To the obverse, he had found that telling the whore that she was beautiful, the best he'd ever had, that she had spoiled him for all others, usually got him a far superior ride than if he had been truthful or silent. Unfortunately, many of these women seemed to actually believe him and that earned him a slap the next time they met. He figured the slap was usually worth it and had little sympathy for them if they couldn't play the game.

The occasional female pirate he had plundered had been as drunk and as lewd and as noisy as he himself, so he really couldn't say what was happening with her except that she was enjoying it.

With Chloe, it would be different. She was utterly without guile and probably even more ignorant about the subject than was he, so whatever happened with her would be real. He felt somewhat guilty that he was using her as an experiment, but that benefit was incidental to his principal motivation.

In bed with her, he began as he had the previous night. He wanted to take his time, not just hop on her and ravish her as her late husband probably had done. He wanted to see how far he could take her. He talked with her, asking her if she liked this touch or that, telling her what to do for him.

This was another revelation for Chloe; she had thought talking was forbidden except for an embarrassed "Thank you" from the man as he left the room.

Her desire reignited as a firestorm, having gone unsatisfied the night before. Now, whatever Jack did that she liked, she could ask for more and he would accommodate her. She was aware that she was making a great deal of noise, but no one could hear her except Jack and he seemed to love it. She could let herself go free.

By the time he began to penetrate her she was wild with fever; she felt as if nothing of her existed except that which was receiving him. She clung to him with a tenacity he could scarcely believe from one so soft and refined and she sounded like an animal in agony. Her eyes were wide open and she stared at him with pupils so dilated those blue eyes looked as black as his own. He was glad she held her teeth tightly clenched, because, if she were to bite him in the state she was in, she would do him permanent damage.

It required a Herculean effort for him not to spend in the presence of such raging female lust, but he had to know! Surely her ferocity could not continue to climb much farther. There had to be a summit—and then what?

A moment later he found out. She arched her back and released a scream that began as a guttural, bestial growl, then rose in pitch and crescendo until he feared she would rend her throat.

She shrieked garbled words, some of which sounded like "Help me!" or "God!" or "Jack!" At that point he felt a powerfully convulsing, rhythmic pounding inside her that lasted for nearly a minute; then she gradually quieted.

He could hold back no longer. He poured himself into her as they gasped for breath through their triumphant kiss. He had his answer. He would never tell any of his mates how he knew, might never tell them *that* he knew, but he would never doubt again. And he would never be the same.

He lifted her hand to his lips for a kiss as he cascaded into post-orgasmic oblivion; she was too exhausted to do anything but catch her breath and ponder what had just happened to her. Nevertheless, she had already decided that, as soon as Jack awoke, she wanted more of the same.

10—The Lark Descending

Chloe learned more about herself and the male of our species that morning than she could have imagined possible. One important lesson was that Jack wouldn't be able to charge right back into the furious passion they had just experienced. He looked so precious, lying asleep beside her, drenched with perspiration from their ecstasy. This time as she studied his perfect features, she was looking at the greatest treasure life could give and it was given to her.

She simply could not wait to continue. She snuggled against him, trailed her fingertip down over his profile, leaned over to kiss those exquisite lips, pressed her breasts against his warm, damp chest. He opened his eyes, smiled at her, and tried to pull her close to him so that he could make her feel appreciated while still getting some rest.

She wanted him to wake up and she wouldn't leave him alone. She tickled and teased him and refused to settle down against his side.

Finally, he looked blearily at her.

"Chloe, Ducks, what is it ye be wantin'?"

"Wake up, Jack. Let's enjoy our day together."

"Seems like we've been enjoying it a great deal, or did I misread yer signals?"

"Is that all there's going to be? I thought we'd—you know—all day."

"Sweet Chloe, the day is far from over, but ye need to understand something. Ye can't fire a cannon again until it's been reloaded."

She didn't quite grasp the concept, so he had to be more graphic with her. She tried to understand and finally decided that it was mostly because he was still weakened from his injury. But by the time she had gotten to that point, Jack's "cannon" was nearly reloaded.

Since the urgency of the initial storm was past, they could take more time, become more experimental. He told her about some of the many positions that a couple could employ; she wanted to know how he knew such things. He didn't pretend to be innocent, but truthfully said that he had heard about them from Hindu sailors his crew had taken on near Madagascar. It seemed there was an ancient book that described such activities. She was amazed! What kind of person would put such things on paper?

Nevertheless, she was eager to try out a few with Jack. He had to draw the line at any that required his supporting both his weight and hers; he wasn't well enough for acrobatics, yet. Nothing would do but that he promise her that they would try them when he was stronger.

Her boundless enthusiasm simply astounded him. Was this the same prim lady who nearly fainted because a sick man had to pee?

They enjoyed each other until nearly midday when exhaustion, hunger, and the island's oppressive heat changed their perspective. The long-forgotten breakfast tray was rediscovered and cleaned off. Even the tepid tea was perfectly fine, as it took very little to comfort either of them.

After eating, they washed themselves and prepared to rest until late afternoon when the air was not so suffocating. She spread a quilt on the floor in front of the French doors and threw down a couple of pillows for their siesta, giving them the advantage of the slight breeze and the bed a chance to cool and dry. She drifted into sleep thinking that her heart could not possibly contain any more joy. Jack's happiness was great, also, but was tempered with the knowledge that he could not stay in this paradise with a price on his head and a ship needing her captain.

The sun's rays grew longer and the heat of day began to lessen. The lovers slept peacefully beside each other, their naked bodies kissed by the muted light and the scent of tropical flowers on the air. Jack awakened slowly, inhaled the fragrance and enjoyed a languid, cat-like stretch. A small pain in his flank reminded him that he wasn't quite whole yet. But he was so much better.

That he was alive at all was nearly miraculous. He looked at his sleeping lover, his salvation. He had hoped to set her free in repayment for her having restored his life at the risk of her own and he seemed to have succeeded beyond his wildest dreams, but soon he would have to leave her. The thought saddened him. It would hurt her so and he found the thought of her pain hurtful to himself.

He also knew that he would never feel the same about women, having experienced her. Oh, he would still enjoy the whores and female pirates when he was randy and had had enough rum. It was always a relief to unload into a woman, but he had never thought of one as much more than a receptacle. This person beside him was a—person. She had given him something she had given no one else, something that he had had with no one else. And, just as he knew that he would not experience it again with another, he realized that she wouldn't, either. Perhaps his setting her free had been the cruelest thing he could have done to her.

He was pondering these concerns when she turned and smiled at him. He suddenly clasped her to himself with more fervor than he intended. Chloe took this to mean that he was lusty and she happily responded.

But he held her away from himself and looked intently at her sweet, adoring face. His heart hurt seeing her so happy in the moment and she saw that something was wrong.

"What is it, Jack? Do I displease you?"

He quickly embraced her again so she wouldn't read his thoughts in his eyes.

"No, no. Mother of God, no! Chloe, ye couldn't displease any man."

Knowing that he still hadn't answered her concern, he had

an idea for something he could give her that might ease the pain of his absence.

"Chloe, have ye ever wondered how a sailor manages all those long nights at sea away from his bonny lass?"

She wasn't quite catching the gist, so, he had to explain about a man's recurring and compelling need. She was surprised to know that lust could occur without the object being present.

He repressed the urge to ask her if her husband had been impotent. He would have, if Maria hadn't told him about the baby. But, since Chloe hadn't mentioned it, he decided that discretion was the better part of valor on the subject of the late lieutenant governor's virility.

As he described what he and most other men did to relieve their "loneliness" she was simply fascinated. When the little minx wanted to see a demonstration, he was so flummoxed he couldn't begin. He finally had to enlist her assistance, so that what was normally a solo became a titillating duet. She was delighted.

But then he inadvertently took the wind from her sails.

"What I want ye to know is that ye can similarly comfort yerself after Ol' Blackjack has gone back to sea."

She looked as if he had punched her in the stomach! Joy vanished in an instant as she took in the weight of his words. The smile froze on her face and her eyes filled with horror.

Poor Jack realized too late what he had done and bitterly regretted it, but there was no undoing it now. He reached to hold her, but she pulled away, recoiling from him as if he were a leper.

"Chloe, Ducks, surely ye knew all along that I can't stay here forever. Rothwell wants to kill me and I have a ship and a crew what need me. I'm a pirate, Ducks, and this is not the sea." He hadn't mean for it to sound so dismissive, but he wasn't going to lie. Why did the truth have to be so damnable?

She pulled the edge of the quilt up to her chin, covering her nakedness, never taking her wide eyes off his face. He felt absolutely wretched.

"Please, Chloe, I don't wish to leave ye—" But she had bolted into her dressing room. He could hear her throwing things around and he heard a strangled sob. He went to her and found her furiously donning a dressing gown.

"Perhaps you should get dressed, too, Captain Bellamie. It's getting late."

He couldn't let this happen! For lack of a plan, he lunged at her and grabbed her in his arms. He tried to get to her face to kiss her, but she fought back with surprising strength, hitting him with her fists and struggling furiously. He held on and she clawed the side of his face and neck, drawing blood.

"Ow! Dammit, Chloe!"

He would not hit her, but he stopped trying to use as little force as possible. He wrestled her to the floor and straddled her, pinning her arms above her head as she had his the night of his surgery.

Unable to reach him with her hands, she tried to kick him, but he was out of range sitting on her like that, so in pure animal fury she sank her teeth into his left arm just above the tattoo. She tasted the metallic tang of blood and bit harder. He roared in pain and drew back his right hand to slap her.

They both saw that hand coming toward her face and he stopped just in time. For a moment they were frozen, Jack bruised and bleeding, Chloe with his blood on her lips and his rough hand just inches from her face. He was far more remorseful than she.

"Go ahead, Captain Bellamie. Why stop short of beating me? While you're at it, you may as well cut my throat and rob me, too! But, I must say, your style of *rape* is interesting, though. Go ahead, *damn* you! Get it over with!" She was quaking with rage and helpless sobs, but her eyes burned defiantly into his.

He dropped his raised hand, lifted it limply again to try to express something that he couldn't put into words, finally covered his own face with it to stop having to see what he was seeing in her eyes.

"Chloe, don't, don't…"

"How could you hate me so much, Jack Bellamie? What

have I done that you would want to strip me of my last shred of dignity? *What?*"

"I don't hate ye, Chloe. I could never hate ye."

"I loved you, Jack! Is that what you were wanting? Congratulations! Another successful raid for the legendary Captain Blackjack Bellamie. What a rousing tale for your precious buccaneer crew when you meet again."

"Chloe, please. Don't think such of me. I owe ye my life, why would I deliberately hurt ye? I love ye, Chloe Caruthers and I've never loved another."

When she didn't reply, he went on. "It breaks my heart to leave ye, but we both know I can't stay. Ye could never be a pirate, or I'd take ye as my mate on the *Sinecure*." Then, more softly, "Life is cruel, but this is how it has to be."

He felt something on his face and thought he must be bleeding again, but when he wiped his hand across it, there was no red. He was crying and he couldn't remember having done so since he was a child, after the murder of his parents cast him into a hostile world. He felt nearly as hopeless and as miserable as he had then, and now his misery was compounded by hers.

Chloe had stopped fighting and was staring at him, riveted by his tears and his words. She thought she might be dying, that it was all too unbearable and her heart could not endure it. It was easier to hate him and fight him than to see him cry.

His grip on her had loosened and she lifted her arms to cradle him. They wept and held each other wordlessly, for there was no solution to their dilemma and now they both knew it.

After a time, she cleaned and treated the wounds that she had inflicted, placing little kisses on his face, neck, and arm near the damages. She could not remember ever feeling more utterly bereft. While she tended to him their eyes frequently met, each seeing the immeasurable pain in the other. They spoke not at all.

The day was growing old as they returned to their bed and lay quietly in each other's arms. At length, he began whispering to her in a language she had never heard before. She knew that it must be Romany and she sensed that he hadn't spoken it for many years, possibly not since the night his little child's world was destroyed. Although she could not translate the words, she knew it to be poetry by the rhyme and meter and by the loving softness of his voice. Then he began to sing to her in the same language, slowly and tenderly, a sad melody filled with longing, until his voice broke hoarsely and he buried his face in her hair.

They made love sweetly, as quietly and gently as their first intimacies had been wild and frantic. In the afterglow, they continued to hold each other and tried to will time to stand still.

But time would not stand still and the sounds of the returning wagon heralded the end of their time together in the great feather bed in the room that had seen the flowering of their love.

11—A Matter of Hours

Emerson didn't wait for Maria and
Rodrigo to come into the house. He was outside waiting for them
by the time the wagon stopped rolling at the kitchen door.

"Rodrigo, did you learn about the search for Captain
Bellamie?"

"*Sì*, we think we have true information, but you should decide
after you hear it."

The three entered the kitchen where Emerson already had
his maps and notes spread out on one of the massive tables. He
listened to the sometimes-contradictory stories relayed to
him. Maria had gleaned certain information from the women who
gathered at the bazaar, while Rodrigo had heard from the men
other tales that seemed to negate Maria's. Some were too
outlandish to be considered, some versions seemed to corroborate
another, and some were worth considering only if Maria or
Rodrigo had considerable faith in the credibility of the teller.

Emerson had the towering onus of sorting all the gossip,
deciding what was to be discarded and what may be believed
and then devising the all-important plan based on that
information. The longer the Captain could stay at the manor, the
more strength he could regain for the horrific journey that lay
ahead. But, wait too long, and the soldiers would come and wreak
havoc on all five of them. He had to get it right.

Having extracted the information from the two, he allowed
them to return to their tasks of unloading the wagon and tending
the horse. Studying the papers in front of him, he measured and
counted and then repeated it all to make certain he hadn't missed
anything.

The result was not encouraging. Rothwell's men would arrive
at the estate no later than Monday morning, and possibly as early

as tomorrow afternoon. The fugitives would need to be on their way at dawn to avoid unacceptable risk. This very evening must be spent in preparations.

Next he had to decide whether to tell Chloe and Jack now, which would certainly alarm them but would give them the opportunity to make preparations of their own, or to wait until morning and have everything ready for them, thus giving them one more night of peaceful rest before their arduous trek. Emerson doubted that they were sleeping much, anyway, and knew that it would be foolish not to get the Captain involved in the decision-making.

He sensed that, in some fundamental way, he and Captain Bellamie had many qualities in common. He respected Jack for his worldly wisdom, his equanimity, and his courage. There was much more going on in the pirate's head than the casual observer would guess from the swaggering seaman's gait and the crude, outlandish speech. Each of them had cultivated a misleading exterior that served him well in his respective world.

Over an hour had passed before he felt that he had a sufficiently thorough plan to present to his mistress. By then, Maria had come into the kitchen to begin cooking as Rodrigo finished at the barn. Emerson didn't want to waste any time, so he began apprising Maria of what some of her responsibilities would be over the coming night.

"Maria, you said that Madam must decide which of us will accompany the Captain when he flees. Do you doubt who her choice will be?"

"No, I know how she will choose. You or Rodrigo should be the one, but the Señora will go herself." Maria looked resigned.

"You are correct. The situation is greatly compounded by Madam's lack of experience. The Captain will be of considerable help to her and she will certainly take the very best care of him, but we must accept that, if either dies, the other is not likely to survive."

Chloe had noticed the somewhat earlier than usual return of

her servants, but it held no meaning for her. She was absorbed, once more, with steeling herself for sadness and loss.

Jack wanted to tell her about the *Sinecure*, about the exhilaration he felt at her helm and the heady freedom of the Sweet Trade, thinking that, if she could understand the irresistible draw his chosen life held for him, she would perhaps feel less abandoned. He had attempted to do so, but saw that his words just cut her the more sorely. He hated that he seemed to keep hurting her, even as he tried to be kind.

When Maria knocked and entered with a supper tray, he was grateful for the distraction. But Chloe couldn't look at the food and he felt guilty again, this time for having a healthy appetite while she was too heartbroken to eat. He loved her, but he was beginning to want to go away to some place where his actions produced results he could control. Then he felt guilty for thinking that.

He encouraged her to eat, even tried to feed her, but she remained obdurate. He gave up and finished most of his own meal, then realized that he hadn't really tasted it.

When Maria came to retrieve the tray, she said something astonishing to them.

"Señora. Captain. Begging your pardon, but Emerson and Rodrigo and I request you to speak with us in the dining hall, if you please."

The servants were summoning her? Chloe had never heard of such a thing. She could imagine no scenario that would merit such effrontery.

Her tone was strident. "Maria, what is the meaning of this? My staff requests my presence? Who is the mis—"

Jack touched her arm to stop her before she said something he never wanted to hear from her. He despised the arrogance of the upper classes and had perceived Chloe as being somehow different.

She actually stopped and lowered her voice at the command of his touch. He was the master of the mistress, at least for the moment.

"Why this unusual request, Maria?"

"There is something we need to show you, both of you, and it is downstairs, Señora."

Jack and Chloe looked quizzically at each other and followed her from the room.

As they entered the dining hall, they saw Emerson and Rodrigo looking at papers spread on the table. Emerson looked up.

"Madam. Captain. I have news of great import that involves us all. Maria and Rodrigo have received indisputable information today that soldiers from the fort are entering every home, shop and building searching for Captain Bellamie. No privileged rank is being spared and no detail unexamined.

"Based upon their report, I have ascertained that their arrival here shall be possibly as early as tomorrow afternoon, although more likely the following morning. Captain, you must be far away from this estate when they approach."

Here he paused to let his words take effect. The three servants watched as their mistress sank down onto a chair, her face deathly white. The Captain's frightened expression was so brief that the three missed it, watching her; he quickly regained his composure and flashed his white-glinting smile.

"Ah, well, Ladies and Gents, it's been a pleasure, but it's time for Ol' Blackjack to weigh anchor. If I may just have me belongings…"

Emerson went on, ignoring his flippancy. "Captain, there is no area of the southern coast of this island that is not swarming with Rothwell's men, each dreaming of the bounty on your head. You cannot hope to escape to the south or to the east. Your only chance is to strike northwestward toward Montego Bay where you may more safely seek passage on any ship that will bring you to your own. However, the territory between here and there is fraught with dangers of all kinds and your survival is by no means guaranteed."

"Ah, but Mate, ye forget one thing: I'm Captain Blackjack Bellamie. Remember?"

"The enterprise will certainly benefit from the element of luck, Captain, but surviving will be the result of planning and preparation. I'd put my faith in more than the angels, if I were you."

"By the Powers, yer right! When the time for action is at hand, the time for preparation is past. Unless I miss my guess, Mate, I'd say those papers before ye indicate a plan in the works already."

"You guess correctly, Captain. I'm assuming that, as a mariner, you possess a compass?"

"Aye, and it's a fine one."

(Chloe was hearing all this from a very long distance, processing the words well after they had died away in the air. Her mind was turning dully, trying to keep up. It was dawning on her that Jack and Emerson were laying out plans for Jack's imminent departure.)

"Very good. And I know that you can read charts of the sea, but are you familiar with maps of the land?"

"Aye. I've seen a few."

"Very well. If you'll look at this one, Captain, you'll see that I have drawn—"

"No!" Chloe found her voice. Rising from the chair, she shouted, "I forbid it! He is still too weak. Sending him into the wilderness is a death sentence."

Emerson calmly pointed out that at least he had a chance on the run, that his remaining at the estate guaranteed his dying on the gallows and that they would all be implicated in aiding and abetting him.

She appealed to Maria. "Tell them it's true, Maria. Tell them that he can't stand such a journey in his condition!"

"*Sì*, it is true. He cannot travel alone. He still has stitches and his blood is not yet restored."

Rodrigo spoke up. "Señora, perhaps Emerson or I should accompany him to safety."

Chloe felt a like hare surrounded by hounds. "No! Not you. Not Emerson. I will go with him. I've cared for him all along and I can continue to do so until he is safe."

Jack wished to interject a note of reason at this point, as the party was getting out of hand. "If I may have a say in me own fate here, I need be escorted by no one, as I'm perfectly capable of—"

"Shut up! Jack, please just shut up. This decision is not yours, nor is it Emerson's. It is mine and I have made it. You and I are leaving at first light, so we need to be making ready instead of engaging in this ridiculous contention."

The servants had been fully expecting her to insist on going with him and were not shocked by her vehemence, but Jack was looking at her wide-eyed and slack-jawed, unable to hide his surprise. She had actually told him to shut up. And he knew he'd better do just that, so he sat down and let her take the helm.

Chloe was firmly in charge now. "Emerson, you have apparently thought this through in advance. How long is this journey and what are we going to be facing?"

"The journey will be approximately ninety miles and I would not count on making more than ten miles per day, if that. In other words, you will be traveling on foot and living off the land for nearly two weeks. The fields and forests are abundant with food and water, but I cannot overstate the prolific dangers that lurk at every turn in such surroundings.

"In addition to poisonous plants, insects and animals, you must beware of dehydration, exhaustion, infection, injuries and parasites. Also, the ranches you will be crossing and the hills you will be skirting are home to various types of people who will consider you as trespassers undeserving of life and will act accordingly.

"Compounding all of this is the fact that neither of you is in good enough physical condition for such a grueling venture. Captain, your limitations have been duly noted; but, Madam, with all due respect, your life has not been one of hard work and privation, which is what you will be facing every day on this trek. My greatest concern for both of you is that you will overestimate your abilities or stamina and meet with grave misfortune."

"We can do this, Emerson, because we must. The Captain

and I will certainly keep each other in check, even if we *are* overconfident of our own prowess." She gave Jack a stern look, indicating that it was he who would be overconfident of his prowess. He just shrugged and tried to look innocent.

Emerson turned to Jack. "Captain, you would ignore my advice at your peril. It is unlikely that either of you will reach the northern shore alone. If you cannot rein in your exuberance for the sake of your own safety, then please do so for Madam's.

"If the two of you will please remain for a few moments, I have detailed assignments for Maria and Rodrigo that should be begun immediately in order to be completed by morning."

He placed Maria in charge of initial food supplies, medical and first aid materials, hygiene, and clothing; Rodrigo was put over weapons, ammunition, rigging, and procurement of food. When they had departed to work, he returned to Chloe and Jack who were sitting close together and talking quietly and seriously. Emerson was glad that Jack was finally displaying the proper attitude.

"Madam. Captain. I have prepared maps for you showing the best and alternative routes. Please allow me to show you." He had their focused attention as he explained the direction they must follow, major landmarks to watch for, and where the going would be most or least difficult.

He was unsure of the Captain's literacy, so he had thoughtfully used symbols as much as possible to avoid embarrassing him. He was depending heavily on Jack to navigate using the maps and compass. He also suggested that they both memorize the maps as much as possible because the heat, humidity, and rigors of the excursion would soon render them unreadable.

He gave them an overview of how to obtain food once their initial rations were gone, how to avoid bad water, the importance of frequent rests, the use of walking sticks to aid balance and discourage curious (and possibly venomous) reptiles. Jack already knew some first aid from his experience with ships' surgeons, so Emerson did not have to spend precious time on that subject.

They learned that the English language would likely be a

detriment to their safety if they were set upon by some of the locals. Spanish (which Jack spoke minimally and then with an English accent, Rodrigo said) would be even worse, should they come cross any Maroons. It was agreed that, in the presence of others, Chloe would pretend to be mute and Jack would speak only Romany unless and until the strangers' sympathies could be ascertained. If any of them understood Romany, then he and Chloe would be among friends, Jack maintained.

Emerson stressed and stressed again the importance of frequent hydration, of drinking water even before feeling thirst. Equally important was the need to rest during the heat of the day, as dehydration and heat prostration would be their worst enemies.

It was settled that when they arrived at Montego Bay, Jack would book passage on any ship that would take him to the Bahamas, from which he could get to Vestal Cay; Chloe would board one bound for Port Royal and return home.

Finally, he told them to go to bed and get some rest, that he, Maria and Rodrigo would remain awake until morning preparing their necessities.

"I am certain that sleep will not come easily, but at least rest your bodies before beginning this undertaking. Your long and difficult expedition begins in a matter of hours."

12—Farewells, Troops, and Troupers

Throughout the too-short night the three servants worked. Emerson, having completed his principal contribution in devising the plan and briefing the travelers, was free to lend assistance to the other two as needed, helping Rodrigo make packs out of sailcloth and harness leather, baking hardtack while Maria sewed, ticking items off inventory lists he had created during the planning stage. Through the long and detailed process, he had remained as unruffled as ever, although Maria and Rodrigo were weeping more and more frequently.

At last all was in readiness and the faithful staff had time to gather for a cup of tea before Maria would have to summon the sojourners. Emerson had become the *de facto* master of the manor and would remain so for some time. His first act was to promise Rodrigo that he could have some of the whiskey he loved once the fugitives were on their way. Maria asked if she might have a glass of wine and Emerson agreed.

"I think we are all entitled to a little liquid comfort when this is completed."

At last Maria ascended the stairs, her heart so heavy she could scarcely lift her feet. She knocked and was told, after a long pause, to enter. She carried the breakfast tray, a flask of scented oil, and some articles of clothing.

"Señora. Captain. It is time. Emerson says for you to wash yourselves with this oil to keep insects from biting. And, Madam, he says you must not dress as a proper lady, but wear these breeches, vest and shirt. Your hat and boots are downstairs for when you leave."

"Pray, why must I dress as a man, Maria?"

"He says that you will be better able to travel over rough ground without a skirt impeding you, Señora; also, that two gentlemen traveling together will attract less attention than a man and a woman." Once again, Chloe couldn't fault Emerson's reasoning, but she had never worn breeches in her life and was not happy to start something so new and strange at this critical juncture.

"Please try to eat breakfast, as you will need the energy later. Just call when you are ready, Señora." Maria was leaving these last private moments completely with Chloe and Jack. She went out and they were alone once more.

They looked at each other with a mixture of dread and resignation. He tried to smile, but it wasn't convincing. They went into each other's arms and remained in silence, knowing that the minutes were ticking away.

"One last time in the feather bed, Ducks?"

She just nodded. If anything so joyous as the act of love can be performed in profound sadness, they did so.

Jack dressed in his full gear, including his vest, sash, boots, belt and weapons for the first time since his arrival. Chloe had never seen him in it except when he was wet, bleeding and comatose on the floor. When she emerged from her dressing room and saw him, her breath caught in her throat. Standing before her was, to the rest of the world, a fierce pirate captain, but, to her, he was her handsome Gypsy Rom, the love of her life. Her knees nearly buckled under her, but her mood of awe was cut short by Jack's derisive snicker.

"If yer a man, Ducks, I'm the bleedin' King of England." He was actually laughing out loud at her. Seeing that she took offence, he hugged her. "Chloe, yer too much a woman to fool even a blind man. No mystery I love ye so."

Well, it was difficult to maintain a fit of pique in the face of such a compliment, so she laughed with him. "I feel ridiculous. Worse, I feel naked."

"We can be naked later, Sweetheart, but fer now, yer plenty clothed. Ye'll find that Emerson is correct in this being better suited to travel by Shank's mare."

And so, their aspect somewhat lightened, the bizarre pair started to leave their room for the last time. As if on cue, they both paused and turned to look at the room and the bed. Jack's life had been spared there; Chloe's life had begun.

In the kitchen, they found their respective packs open on the table with the contents displayed alongside. As they watched, Emerson, Maria, and Rodrigo took turns placing the items into the packs and explaining what they were, how to use them, and other instructions. Rodrigo had produced not one but two pistols, one for Chloe and a spare for Jack. Extra powder and shot were supplied along with a vicious-looking dagger for Chloe. He told Jack to teach Chloe how to shoot during a rest period, as there was no time to do so now.

At last, the packs were buckled onto the travelers and nothing was left but to say goodbye. Emerson and Jack shook hands and bowed slightly to each other with great solemnity. Jack knew that if they survived this ordeal, it would be because of Emerson. "Please accept my deepest gratitude for all ye've done fer me. Captain Blackjack Bellamie is forever in yer debt."

"Godspeed, Captain Bellamie. Godspeed, Madam." He bowed to Chloe, who wanted to hug him, but refrained in the name of good taste and to avoid embarrassing him.

Maria was sobbing. She curtsied deeply before Jack, who lifted her by her shoulders, uncomfortable with expressions of class distinction. He kissed her on the cheek. "Doctor Maria, how do I thank ye for savin' me life? Yer truly an angel from Heaven's highest order. I'll never forget ye."

Chloe wouldn't allow Maria to lower herself before her, either. "Maria, my dear friend, I'll miss you. But don't be sad. I'll be back within the month."

Maria blessed both of them with the sign of the cross as they prepared to climb into the produce wagon where Rodrigo was sitting patiently holding the reins. Suddenly, Chloe turned and went back to Maria. Whispering so the men couldn't hear, she took her maid's hand and gave it a conspiratorial squeeze.

"Maria, please do not change the linens on my bed."

"*Sì*, Señora. I understand."

In the pink light of dawn, Emerson and Maria watched as the wagon grew smaller in the distance. It appeared to be nothing more than a worker driving a farm wagon past fields and groves on an early morning chore, for Jack and Chloe knew not to sit upright where they could be seen until Rodrigo told them it was safe to do so.

In the bed of the wagon they lay in silence, looking up at the fading stars, each wondering how this would end. Jack remembered lying on the deck of the *Sinecure* at daybreak looking at the same sky and feeling completely at peace. How hateful by comparison this morning was, except for one important difference: this morning he was not alone. This morning his hand held the hand of another person, the person his heart loved dearly. He would not have chosen this, but now that he had it, his life would be empty without it. And apparently empty was how it was to be.

At last Rodrigo stopped the wagon and told them they could safely disembark; they had gone past any area where they could be seen from houses or fields and were now in a secluded, forested area where the trail widened into a turnaround and went no farther into the brush. Jack climbed down over the wheel and helped Chloe to drop to the ground beside him. They walked to the front of the wagon, thanked Rodrigo, and said goodbye.

"Vaya con Dios, Madam. Vaya con Dios, Captain." He clucked to the horse and they disappeared around the bend, leaving Jack and Chloe very small and very alone at the edge of the forest.

While waiting for Rodrigo to return with the empty wagon,

Emerson and Maria performed their chores in grim silence. He carefully burned all of his notes and maps that might lead the soldiers to the fugitives and he made certain that every scrap remaining from their preparations was either put in its proper place or destroyed. Then he scanned the rooms again and again for any detail, however minute, that would be out of the ordinary.

Maria tidied Chloe's room with the same care, except that she made up the bed without changing the linens, as she had been instructed. Maria knew why the Señora felt that way. She could not seem to stop crying when she thought about her poor mistress. Chloe could very well die an awful death somewhere between Port Royal and Montego Bay and, even if she lived to return home, her heart would be broken beyond repair as she lay in this empty bed where she had at last found love. Maria wondered if perhaps God, in His wisdom, might let her die out of mercy.

She knew that Captain Bellamie, also, was in for a great deal of sadness when he found himself without Chloe. She could read him as easily as she could her mistress and she saw that his heart belonged to the Señora. She knew that Chloe had fallen in love with him the night he collapsed on her floor; it had taken him a little longer, but then, he had had to heal a bit before he could feel anything but pain and weakness.

The conversation that she had had with him the night Chloe bathed him had been revealing. Had she perceived him as an opportunistic cad taking advantage of the Señora's innocence for his own pleasure, she'd have taken a stand and interfered with their relationship in any and every way, but such was not the case. Chloe was still going to be hurt, but not because of any cruelty or disingenuousness on Jack's part and furthermore, he would be hurting, too.

Something odd had certainly happened between those two while she and Rodrigo were at market the previous day. She had fully expected to arrive home and find them exhausted from prolonged lovemaking and bonded more firmly than ever. The latter appeared to have happened, but the Captain bore marks of a vicious attack that could only have come from the Señora, marks that simply could not be explained away as violent lovemaking. She couldn't imagine the Captain attempting to force her mistress and even less probable was the idea of Chloe's resisting.

Whatever had happened, it apparently had not diminished their devotion to one another, so Maria guessed it was immaterial. She just hoped that whatever it had been, the problem had been resolved and they wouldn't fight like that on their journey.

Rodrigo drove the wagon into the barn lot, unharnessed the horse, turned it out into the paddock and went inside. Emerson was waiting for him at the kitchen table with his Irish whiskey, a bottle of wine for Maria and some brandy for himself. Maria brought three glasses and sat down with the men.

In silence they each poured their drink, then lifted their glasses and touched them together as Emerson spoke for them all.

"To Madam and Captain Bellamie. May their lives be spared."

Chloe and Jack had waited in the clearing until the sound of the wagon was swallowed up in the little noises of the natural world around them. Then she looked at him with the unspoken question: now what?

He checked his compass and unfolded a map, then pointed northwest. "That way."

The rainforest was dense and she followed in his footsteps as he sought to find a path. She had never been in a place such as this and, in truth, neither had he. The pirates often put ashore on one of the thousands of tiny uninhabited islands in the Caribbean to hunt game, pick fresh fruit, and build big, roaring fires for cooking their prey, but those beaches weren't choked with trees and vines, and he was surrounded by raucous, fierce comrades with a ship riding at anchor within sight of their party. Here, the jungle seemed a living creature sucking them into its great, green maw.

He shook his head to stop such fantastic thoughts before they robbed him of his nerve. Just at that moment Chloe screamed and he nearly jumped out of his boots. Turning back to her, he found her holding her arm as a large, red welt began swelling just past her elbow.

"Something stung me! Jack, it *hurts!*"

He scratched in the detritus of the forest floor until he had come up with enough cool mud to slather on the bump. Chloe watched him with big, frightened eyes and he felt as if he were looking after a timid child. He patted the mud onto her arm, declared it to be "all fixed," kissed her damp forehead and started back to the task at hand.

He tried to appear jaunty, but he worried about her. What if the thing that stung her had struck a fatal blow? What kind of creature was it? Could it have laid eggs in her arm so quickly, eggs that might hatch in there and—? He all but slapped himself to put a stop to such thoughts. Less than an hour into their trek and he was on the verge of falling apart.

He started singing. "Dum dum, dum dum, their rights maintain, and their united pleasures reign, while Bacchus' treasures crown the board, dum dum, dum dum, they both afford." Chloe, not realizing that he was singing to calm his own panic, concluded that he was eager to be at sea and away from her. She hoped that the creature that had stung her had poisoned her and she would die in his arms on this miserable trail. Then he'd be sorry.

The torpor of midday had settled over the Caruthers household. The three servants had completed their duties to the moment and were taking a much-needed siesta after having been up all night. The merciful alcohol had blunted their fear and grief and allowed them to rest.

Suddenly Beowulf roared out his warning and instantly all three were awake, hearts pounding, as the sounds of horses mingled with the dog's alarm. Emerson was on his feet with his frock coat straightened and his butler face on before the knock came.

This time it was Lieutenant Ambrose. "We are emissaries of the fort under orders from Commodore Rothwell to search these premises for the fugitive pirate Jack Bellamie."

"I am sorry, Sir, but Lady Caruthers has gone out for the day. Would you care to return another time?"

"Please step aside, Sir. We do not require your permission nor that of Lady Caruthers. Elgin! Your men to the barns. Cooper, check the outbuildings. The rest of you, follow me." At that, Ambrose and several men brushed past the butler and began searching throughout the house. Emerson waited until all were inside, then quietly closed the door and went about his business as if nothing had happened. He actually looked bored.

A scream from upstairs signaled him that Maria's room had been entered. He prayed that she would behave as he had instructed. She did not need to remain calm as long as she played her part. He held his breath.

Soon he heard a lot of Spanish from her and shouts of frustration from the soldiers as she went into her act. Finally, they gave up trying to interrogate her as she simply could not get their questions straight and appeared too panicked to try. He had to squelch a smile.

In the barn, Rodrigo first had to control Beowulf or the soldiers were going to shoot the animal. His act was different from Maria's and he played it to the hilt. He kept bowing obsequiously and apologizing, stumbling around trying to stay out of their way and be helpful and, of course, completely mucking up all verbal communication with them.

The soldiers were crudely insulting to him, but he behaved as a properly debased serf, wearing an ingratiating smile and appearing to take it as his due. If it weren't for his need to protect his mistress, he'd have gladly driven pitchforks through their icy hearts.

They searched every pile of straw, every grain barrel; they even poked around for trapdoors. They opened his cupboard and threw his personal belongings into the middle of the room. They threatened him. He all but genuflected. He kept his hands clasped tightly together to keep himself from lunging at the nearest one and snapping his neck.

At last, after tearing up the barns, haymows, and outbuildings, they left him and his dog.

He looked at Beowulf. "*Sì*, I would feed their livers to you for dinner!"

In the house, Maria had been reduced to hysterical sobs as the soldiers emptied cupboards and closets. They ignored her and went from room to room doing their mischief. Nothing valuable was broken, but the mess would keep the staff busy for days to come.

Having had no luck questioning the Cubans, they settled on grilling Emerson. They may as well have tried to intimidate the newel post.

No, he hadn't seen anything unusual. Yes, he was certain that Lady Caruthers would have told him if she had seen anything unusual. No, the rest of the staff would not keep such things secret from himself or Lady Caruthers if they had seen anything unusual. No, Lady Caruthers had not told him where she was going. Yes, she had left in a carriage with friends. No, she did not plan to return for several days. Yes, she did that often.

Emerson managed to give the impression that he was politely giving them time better spent elsewhere.

At last, Ambrose promised to remain "vigilant" in the area and departed after extracting a promise that the soldiers would be notified the moment anything unusual was seen by any of the household. As they cantered away, Emerson, Maria and Rodrigo began the lengthy task of restoring the estate to order.

13—Green Hell

The two fugitives were off to an inauspicious start. Jack's confidence was almost non-existent. Chloe was in pain from her sting and was angry with Jack, thinking him eager to be away from her. They were making very poor progress in the trackless rainforest and neither felt inclined to communicate with the other.

Worse, he thought that his heart was working too hard for the amount of effort he was exerting. If he were thinking clearly he'd have known that it was due to blood loss and elevated anxiety. Chloe's arm still hurt, her legs were aching and her feet, unaccustomed to wearing Maria's gardening boots, were beginning to blister. Out of foolish pride, neither would admit that there were problems and so, on they struggled in the steamy wilderness.

Jack was getting breathless and becoming quite worried, but Chloe herself was breathing so hard she didn't hear him panting in front of her. Suddenly, he tripped and went sprawling and Chloe, following so closely and not paying attention, fell on top of him, bruising them both. They lay where they fell, gasping and despairing.

"Chloe, Lass, ye need to get off me and let me breathe."

She glared darkly at him and pulled herself up, sitting down a few feet away.

Mother of God, she's angry with me! What have I done now? "Who was it insisted on makin' this trip with me, hm? I don't recall twistin' yer arm."

The fight was on. "Well, forgive me to hell and back if I can't get you to your destination fast enough! Odious though it may be, we're stuck with each other for the next two weeks, so please try not to make your disgust for me so damned obvious."

"What? Where did that ridiculous idea come from?"

"Oh, don't play innocent with me, Captain Bellamie. You

couldn't hold off on your little shanty until we were through even the first day?"

"Hold off on my what? God's wounds, Woman! I can't sing one of the few songs I know to try and lighten me mind in this green hell? What mysterious and arcane meaning do ye perceive behind 'Down Among the Dead Men'?"

"Did you think I wouldn't know that you were singing out of longing to be at sea and away from me? Or maybe you did it deliberately to put me in my place."

Jack didn't need this on top of everything else, but he could see that she was beyond reason and therefore it fell to him to bring the situation under control. He sat down on a nearby rock and lowered both his pride and his voice.

"Chloe, I'm a pirate. Shanties and forebitters are the only songs I know. I was singing to calm myself and help my thoughts to focus. I'm not doing as well as I had hoped, physically, and I've not been able to catch my second wind, nor even my first."

She looked at him warily, wanting to trust, but uncertain that she dare.

"As far as wanting to be at sea, I'll not deny it. Every day I spend on land is one day too many. But that doesn't mean that I want away from you, Chloe. Surely, ye can understand being of two minds when love is at cross-purposes? I'm unhappy away from the sea and I'll be unhappy away from you. My skies are forever clouded now."

"Do you wish you had never known me?"

"In some ways, yes. I'll never be as happy and carefree as I was before. But, Chloe, I truly love ye and that's something I never understood until now. No man should live out his life without knowing such love."

She hung her head, but didn't speak.

"Chloe, it grieves me that ye don't trust me. It is possible to be both a pirate and a decent man and I have not, will not lie to ye. I love ye, Chloe Caruthers. Believe that."

She went to him and laid her head in his lap. She didn't cry; she just stared into the tangled glade before them and sighed.

"I'm sorry, Jack. I do trust you, and God knows I love you more than life itself. I'm not doing well, either, and I'm afraid for us. I'm afraid we won't make it to Montego Bay."

At this point, they began comparing and cataloging their myriad aches and pains, until it became a jolly game of one-upmanship and they were able to laugh at their predicament. The spat had cleared the air of the awful tension that had been with them since they had climbed into the wagon that morning. They promised to be open, honest, and patient with each other about problems and the need to rest.

Finally working as a team, they devised a plan for the remainder of the day with modest goals that would not overtax them and crush their confidence. They vowed to pay closer heed to Emerson's caveats, beginning with drinking water and resting.

To begin with, it was midday and time to rest anyway, so their first goal was easily and pleasantly met. His pack held a light blanket that he spread on an even spot from which she had removed the stones and twigs.

Then they stretched out beside each other and were quickly asleep.

After their siesta, they treated their pains as much as possible and set out to conclude their first day on the run. Jack had made a minor adjustment in their direction which took them out of the thickest of the forest, making for easier travel, often allowing them to walk abreast and converse. The heat and humidity had abated somewhat and, with spirits considerably lifted, they covered more ground than they had expected to, considering their more sensible pace.

At last it was time to look for a place to make camp for the night. Recalling Emerson's advice, they sought a sheltered, secluded spot away from any likely human or animal pathway and preferably near water. Freshwater streams were fairly abundant in the area and they soon located a choice site beside a small brook.

In the fading light they gathered fuel for a fire, which was not a necessity, but were yielding to mankind's universal instinct that, no matter how empty the wilderness or how meager one's provisions, a small fire at evening means home. The operative word was "small," as Emerson had warned them that Europeans were inordinately inclined to build large, smoky fires, a beacon to enemies for miles.

As they settled in for the night, watching the embers die and listening to the music of the brook and the night creatures, they felt that their first day hadn't been so bad. Cuddling, they decided to make love, but fell asleep before it went beyond the talking stage.

Chloe awoke from her first night on the ground and took stock of her surroundings. First, she checked to be sure that Jack was all right; then she took note of the comforting sounds around her, especially the little brook. Disentangling herself from his arms, she put on her boots and made her way downstream to have some privacy.

Her sleep had seemed deep and restful, but she felt clammy and stiff and her feet didn't fit her boots as well as yesterday. She didn't want to move on, just wanted to curl up with Jack and stay put for a while.

She washed herself and tried to get in the mood to travel. Breakfast would help. Oh, how she missed Maria's tray with the freshly brewed tea and the sumptuous scones.

Returning to Jack, she found him still asleep and decided to join him, but as soon as she lay down he awoke.

"Yer up mighty early, Ducks. Eager to hit the trail?"

"God, no, Jack. I'd rather stay here awhile."

"Not advisable, Darling. We have miles to cover today, if ye recall. How did ye sleep, this first night under the trees?"

"Oh, soundly, thank you." Then, remembering their pact of honesty from the day before, she went on, "But Jack, I really don't feel very well."

The first thing he did was to check the sting on her arm; it appeared much improved. "How are ye ailin', Ducks? Guts or muscles?"

"Muscles, I guess. I rather hurt all over."

Jack stretched and winced. "That's two of us, then. I don't suppose ye be havin' pain in the stitches in yer side, are ye?"

"Very well, Captain. You win the pain game this morning. Let's eat."

So they breakfasted on salt pork, hardtack, and nuts, and then broke camp.

The next few days were relatively uneventful for the travelers, with nothing more alarming than a run-in with a large bird that wanted Jack's hair for its nest. He slashed madly at the thing with his cutlass as Chloe convulsed with laughter. Then he grumped about his favorite tricorne having been lost in the escape from Rothwell. He swore to put a Gypsy curse on any mortal who found his hat and wore it as his own. She figured he was all talk. *Gypsy curse.*

By evening of the fourth day, their rations were gone and they were going to have to start procuring food. Chloe assembled the hooks and line that Rodrigo had provided while Jack caught some insects to use as bait. But the stream they were fishing refused to yield up its bounty and even stole one of their precious hooks.

They had been trying to keep the hills and forests to their right and the fields and groves to their left while staying far enough in the trees to avoid being seen by ranchers, but the pain of their empty bellies finally drove them into the cultivated areas despite the danger. Using great stealth, they were able to fill their packs with sweet potatoes, mangoes, and corn before retreating to the safety of the jungle.

It was a blessing in more ways than one that they had gotten a decent meal that evening because the next morning would require all the strength they could muster.

14—Captured!

Morning of the fifth day found them optimistic. They were becoming hardened to the rigors of the hike and were full of self-congratulation over their successful raid the evening before. Furthermore, Chloe had discovered that she very much enjoyed romance in the natural setting, identifying with beasts in rut and liking it. Jack never ceased to be amazed at her capacity for such activities and felt himself the luckiest man in the Caribbean—up to three times per day. The expenditure of energy required for erotic pursuits had to be weighed against that required for travel, but their logic was that they were not on a stringent deadline and soon enough they would no longer have each other to pleasure.

After a hearty breakfast on their purloined bounty, they made love, dressed and set out again. The weather was cooperating by being more temperate, so much so that, at night, they actually needed the fire and they covered themselves with the skirt Maria had packed for Chloe to wear when they were back in civilization.

About an hour into the day's journey, they were passing through a cane field when they heard a terrible, grunting growl and a rumble of hooves followed by a wild boar bursting from the cane and charging at them in slavering fury. Chloe froze in horror as Jack drew his pistol and fired at the beast, but his shot went wide and the animal continued to bear down on her. Too late she tried to dive out of the way, although Jack had drawn the second pistol and this time the bullet found its mark.

The injured and enraged tusker turned and charged at Jack who held his ground with sword at the ready, the tip of the blade pointing downward. At the last moment, he stepped aside as nimbly as a matador and plunged the blade into the boar's neck, severing its spinal cord and stopping its murderous charge.

He ran to the injured Chloe just as shouts rang from across

the field. The shots had alerted the rancher who was now galloping toward them with his own weapon drawn. Calling on the superhuman strength of desperation, Jack picked her up and ran with her into the woods until he had gone into an area so wild and overgrown that a horse could not enter.

He heard the rancher shouting and cursing in what sounded like a mixture of Spanish and Arawak. Then, to his horror, he heard the man dismount and make straight for them, following her blood trail.

Hoping to draw their pursuer away from her, Jack started toward the rancher armed with nothing but a dagger; his sword was still in the boar and he had not had time to reload.

Time seemed to slow to a crawl as Jack ran headlong into almost certain death. His thoughts were clear and unrushed. He thought about what an ignominious end this would be for a pirate captain, how his crew would never know what had become of him, what an unspeakable death lay ahead for Chloe without him to protect her. He thought about how lucky they both had been to have found their love for each other and what a tragic waste this would be after such a short time together. He saw the man raise his weapon and take aim at him and he heard the hammer drawn back.

The shot rang in his ears and he had the irrational thought that he wasn't supposed to have heard the shot that killed him. A second later the rancher fell over, his musket firing harmlessly into the air. Jack stood transfixed, watching gouts of blood ebb away as the dying man's heart ceased beating.

He turned sharply and saw Chloe leaning against a tree, still holding her pistol in both hands at eye level, just as he had taught her. He ran to her, expecting her to go to pieces at having taken a life, but she kept her pistol aimed at the prostrate form until Jack took it from her and tried to embrace her. She would not take her eyes off the new corpse and she didn't seem at all remorseful.

Still expecting her to dissolve in tears, he held her and stroked her hair. "Chloe, my Darling Chloe, ye saved my life once more."

"The poxy bastard son of a mangy whore! I wish I could do it again!"

Jack was speechless. Where had she learned such language?

Suddenly Jack had too many urgent things to do in a short space of time and he hardly knew where to begin. He needed to tend to Chloe's wounds, hide the rancher's body, retrieve his sword, reload all three pistols, and get out of the area before someone else came after them.

He decided to take care of the weapons first, as being unarmed even briefly was pure folly. He reloaded the pistols, gave one to Chloe, and returned to the cane field for his sword, whereupon he found the rancher's horse calmly cropping grass beside the rutted road. He took the reins and led it into the woods, out of sight of the road, and tied it to a tree.

Returning to Chloe, he found her in great physical pain, but still with no regrets for having killed the rancher. He cleaned the blood off her leg where the boar's tusk had slashed it and found the wound to be deep, but the bone was not broken. He bandaged it as best he could before dragging the body up into the crags on the side of the hill. With a little Bellamie luck, scavengers would make short work of it before searchers could find it and begin a hunt for the killer.

As he passed near Chloe with his grim burden, she spat at the corpse and chucked stones at it. He was starting to wonder if she had lost her mind.

"He's dead, Ducks. He ain't gonna get any deader."

"He was going to hurt you. I'll never let them hurt you again. Never!"

The gruesome chore behind him, he helped Chloe to where the horse was tied and put her on the saddle, adjusting the stirrups so that she could steady herself as he led it through the woods along, but still out of sight of, the road.

As the impact of the morning's events sank in and the enormous effort took its toll on him, he felt his knees buckle and he knew that he had no more strength even to walk. He swung himself up behind Chloe and rested his chin on her shoulder as he guided their mount through the trees.

He lost track of how long he and Chloe had been on the horse; he was dozing part of the time, not truly navigating, but trusting the animal to follow the easiest path. Twice that path had led them back onto the road, not a safe place to be riding the mount of a murdered man. He would rally sufficiently to rein the horse back into the safety of the forest; then he'd nod off on her shoulder again.

For her part, Chloe was mostly leaning backward into Jack, their tendencies to collapse in opposite directions keeping each other upright. She was moaning softly, indicating that she was in pain, and he was aware that her face felt too hot against his. He knew that her wound was going septic; boars' tusks were said to be nearly as toxic as a snakebite. He had not cleaned it properly when he was hurrying to get them out of danger and now she was in trouble.

But so was he. The warm stickiness on his side told him that he had torn his stitches and he couldn't spare any blood, however little. He was so very, very tired and they were both going to die because of it. A voice in his head screamed, "Move! Move! Do something!" but his body would not respond.

The horse stopped in a swale to drink from a rill. When it lowered its head, the riders lost their balance, slid over its side, and fell to the ground where they stayed, unable to rise. He wanted to go to the animal and unsaddle it before it wandered off, his early upbringing telling him to protect the well being of a horse, but he could demand no more from his limbs.

The swale was damp and fetid; insects crawled and flew onto them, but they could do nothing but endure the discomfort. He was unsure whether Chloe was still conscious, but then she moaned again and he lifted his head to see her face.

Her eyes were open and she looked up at him. "Jack…"

"I'm sorry, Chloe. I'm so sorry." Then he had to lie back again, feeling the heat from her fever damning him for failing her. If only his first shot hadn't missed, if only he had taken the time to look after her injury before reloading or hiding the body or fleeing, or… if only he weren't so very weak himself.

Eventually, he was dimly aware that the sun was getting low. He could feel Chloe breathing, so she was still alive, but he didn't know how bad off she might be by now.

He was thinking he might be able to muster enough strength to drag them to higher, drier ground, when suddenly a shadow fell across him. He turned his head and saw five very large men looking down on the hapless pair with unmasked curiosity. They were armed with knives, spears and muskets, and two were carrying some sort of dead animal, the results, no doubt, of a successful hunt.

The men's skin was glabrous, blue-black and shiny. Their tall bodies were muscular and their hair was cropped close to their heads. *Maroons*!

The apparent leader of the hunting party stepped closer to Jack and poked him with the blunt end of a spear, speaking in a language that he recognized as being African, possibly Mandingo.

He had to think fast. If this awakened Chloe, she could exclaim something in English and their fate would be sealed. She might be asleep, awake, or unconscious, but he took a chance, hoping that if she were sentient enough to hear him, she would know to keep quiet. He began explaining their predicament in Romany, being as verbose as possible to clue her and confuse the Maroons.

The latter, at least, seemed to work. The men looked at each other quizzically and back to Jack, who was prattling on and on. They had never heard this language and so they could not place these two white people into any of the most hated categories.

They spoke among themselves and then seized him, dragging him away from Chloe. When they saw the blood on his side and how wobbly he was, they held him upright between two of them, while a third went to her. Jack realized that he had not been this frightened when the hangman slipped the noose around his neck four years before.

The man lifted Chloe, not roughly, turning her toward the others. To Jack's profound relief, he saw that she was awake. Her eyes, too bright with fever, met his own and he silently willed her to hold on and do not speak. He thought he saw her understand his admonition; at least she remained mute.

One of the men took their weapons. As abhorrent as it was to Jack to be disarmed, he realized that they weren't significantly more vulnerable than they had been before, considering that they were so sick, lost, and outnumbered.

He continued with a stream of Romany, pointing to Chloe's mangled leg and making grunting sounds, holding his extended index fingers at his mouth like boar tusks. The Maroons appeared to understand what he was talking about.

They exchanged some words among themselves, said something to Jack, and began hauling him along with them in the direction of the hills. Frantic, he looked behind him and saw one of the men put Chloe over his shoulder and follow them.

The journey into the hills was exquisitely miserable for Jack. The ground was rough and he struggled to keep his footing. He was terrified for their safety once they arrived at their destination, he felt acutely his failure to protect Chloe and could think of no possibility of both of them escaping. Even if he could get away, he could not leave her. He had no difficulty envisioning the remainder of his life and seeing that every minute would be a seething hell for him if he abandoned her.

He couldn't stop stumbling. His arms hurt from the men holding him upright and making him keep pace and he felt like a child among those towering hulks. He remembered hearing that Maroons were cannibals and they liked to rape white women. They knew unique methods of torture that would plunge a man into madness before dying. He longed to call to Chloe just to hear her voice, but didn't dare. Would they rape her in front of him? Torture and kill him in front of her? Without warning, he vomited. His captors paused until he stopped retching, then on they went.

After what felt like an eternity, they came to a small village of thatched huts. Fires burned in front of some of the huts and children and dogs scurried around as women in colorful skirts and shawls went about domestic duties, some with baskets balanced on their heads, others carrying jugs of water, cooking, or nursing infants.

At the sight of the men with their strange captives, the whole village seemed to erupt in chatter and excitement. Young and old swarmed around them with dogs barking wildly and children shrieking. Jack feared he would humiliate himself out of terror. He gagged again and his tongue didn't seem to fit back into his mouth properly. He was so parched that every breath was painful.

Through all of the noisy chattering, one woman emerged from the crowd, which parted to let her through. She was nearly as tall as the hunters, was decorated with more beads and feathers than Jack had ever seen on one person, and wore a kind of headdress that appeared to be made of pure silver.

She walked first to Chloe and said something to the man carrying her, who then put her on the ground in front of the woman. Jack concluded that the woman must be the queen or some kind of high priestess and it appeared that she held their fate in her hands.

The priestess knelt and looked intently at Chloe, who seemed to be awake, if not alert. Jack prayed she would keep enough wits to remain silent. The priestess looked at the wound and said something to the man who had carried Chloe. He picked her up again and took her through the curious crowd out of Jack's sight.

Before he could panic over losing sight of Chloe, the priestess came to him and loomed over him, looking intently at his hair—the fuses, the shark teeth—and at his earrings; she leaned down to stare at, not into, his eyes. She lifted the tail of his long, red sash and spread it to its full width, fluttered the fringe, then dropped it. She took his hands in hers and studied them, first the backs, then the palms, paying special attention to his many rings. She tugged at his short beard as if she expected it to come off. She said something to one of the hunters, inflected as a question, and his brief answer seemed to trigger her next move.

In front of the whole village, she suddenly grabbed Jack's crotch, causing him to inhale sharply and jump backward. His next thought proved to be the breaking point and he passed out on the dusty street.

Weightless. He was weightless, floating, drifting in warm, golden light. His braided locks wafted gracefully in and out of his field of vision. He lifted his hand and saw that the skin glowed with a soft luminescence and he knew that the luminescence was life itself, his life, one with all living. He sensed the fragrance of roses, heard ethereal music and required absolutely nothing; all was perfect.

Above him, two tiny points of light gradually grew larger as they came toward him until he saw that they were angels, cherubs with iridescent wings and nacreous faces. They hovered over him with beatific smiles and he felt loved, more loved than any mortal could comprehend, more loved than any mortal could bear. They drew closer to him and each placed a kiss on his cheek, then they floated away until they were once again mere points of light and were gone.

He knew that he had been granted a blessing beyond price.

Then he was falling, falling back into his corporeal frame. He cried out to stop, but could make no sound and a moment later he felt the uncomfortable confinement of his body enveloping him. He didn't want to open his eyes, didn't want to re-enter this imperfect world.

The smell of smoke assailed his nostrils and he heard a voice softly speaking unfamiliar words. With almost unbearable dismay he remembered where he was. What had they done to him while he was in his dream state? He had to know, yet was terrified to find out. He snaked his trembling hand down over his belly and, hesitating, sick with dread, felt between his legs.

Still there! Everything was still there. His relief was so intense that tears streamed from his closed eyes even as he laughed.

Only now could he dare to look at his surroundings. He was lying on a straw pallet on the ground in a circular room, a hut. Smoke from a little fire in the center drifted upward through an opening in the roof that admitted daylight; whether it was the day after their capture, the next day, or a week later, he had no way of knowing.

Captured! Chloe! Looking frantically about in the dim light, he spied her lying on a similar mat about six feet away. She appeared to be sleeping peacefully, appeared unharmed. Never had any human being been so dear to him; never had he been so overjoyed to see anyone.

On her injured leg there appeared to be a mass of large, wet leaves layered over the wound. However puzzling, it seemed to indicate that someone had attempted treatment. Surely, cruel, rapacious cannibals wouldn't bother trying to heal a victim, *would they?*

He remembered his own wound. Lifting his head, he could see a similar stack of wet leaves pressed against his side, which, coincidentally, was no longer hurting. Cautiously lifting the poultice, he peered underneath and had to blink to be certain he wasn't hallucinating: the blood was gone, the stitches were gone, and the injury looked to be closed and healing. *How long have I been asleep?*

Sighing, he lay back. For the moment, at least, all seemed to be well with Chloe and himself. A great calm came over him and his thou*ghts could project beyond the immediate.*

What if, he mused, *what if the Maroons had taken my manhood? Far better to be dead! I would no longer be me, no longer the Captain, no longer a man. Chloe wouldn't love me anymore. Worse, she'd pity me!* He shook his head. *Stop this! It didn't happen. Stop dwelling on it.*

But the near miss caused him to reflect on his life and the uses to which he had put his "Personal Treasures:" basic functions, fun and games. He smiled, remembering. *What fun. What games.* He had always regarded such pleasure as a providential gift to mitigate somewhat the pain and misery that is the natural inheritance of mortal man. The thought of losing them reminded him that he had never used them for their intended purpose, a man's best hope for a kind of immortality. The realization filled him with an ineffable sadness.

He looked at his sleeping Chloe. *If we live through this, I'm going to marry ye as soon as possible and raise a family with ye. I want to look into the eyes of our children and see the future in infinity.*

He smiled his snowy smile. *Ah, what children they will be. With your fire and my spirit, they will never be dominated. Your parents and my parents—all taken too soon—their lines will live on, stronger and smarter.* His eyes focused somewhere far away.

Reality, as it is wont to do, intervened in his reverie, grinding his beautiful thoughts into bitter dust. His world and Chloe's did not intersect. He must sail, must practice the only trade he ever knew. She was bound by *noblesse oblige*, would not abandon those whose lives depended upon her station, would never allow her precious offspring to be reared aboard a pirate ship; she would not be the Chloe he loved if she did. They could not remain together without sacrificing their personhood and, further, they would become beggars, as they could earn no living except in their respective worlds.

No, there would be no marriage with Chloe, no children, no continuity, no dotage. He had never felt so lonely.

He closed his eyes, trying to find the balance that was his before this ill-fated return to Port Royal, which now seemed a lifetime ago. His experiences of recent weeks had changed him, yes, but they didn't preclude his returning to the life he once had. He inhaled deeply, remembering the exultation that surged through him as he watched the prow of the *Sinecure* rise and fall, parting the onrushing waves.

A small sound brought him back to the present and he looked up into the face of a woman of indeterminate age, a face unlined, but wise and gentle. She removed the leafy poultice from his side, spoke to him in the African tongue he had heard before, then handed him a small gourd bowl and helped him to sit up, urging him to drink from the bowl. He sniffed the contents suspiciously; it had an earthy aroma, like a newly tilled garden, not unpleasant, but not tantalizing, either.

The first sip seemed rather bitter, but then he found that he actually wanted to take some more. Whatever it was, it was warm and comforting and he was painfully empty. He reasoned that they wouldn't go to all the trouble of treating his injury, then turn around and poison him. He thanked her with a little bow, as was his style, and also in Romany.

He found himself thinking in Romany after using it only so briefly with his captors. It surprised him that after all those years of putting out of mind that first decade of his life, it came back as if no time had passed. He realized that he still grieved for his parents and sisters, nearly as acutely as at first. Perhaps it was due to being too long on land; such thoughts rarely troubled him at sea. But which was his reality? *Yekka buliasa nashti beshes pe done grastende.* (With one behind you cannot sit on two horses.)

The woman lifted her eyebrows and made a motion with her hand, indicating Chloe, seemingly a question. Jack knew better than to give such an obviously Anglo name as hers, so he pointed to her, then, touching his fingers to his chest and opening his hand toward her again, indicating possession, he said *"Manishie"* (wife), followed by "Viollca" as her name. He knew the woman couldn't completely understand, but he was making an effort to bridge the language gap.

The woman smiled, nodded, and repeated, *"Manishie.* Viollca."

Encouraged by this small success and by the restorative effects of his meal, he started to go to Chloe, but was stopped by the woman's outstretched arm. She held up her hand, palm outward as "Hold." The old fear clutched at his heart.

He watched as the woman picked up a sliver of wood from near the fire and put one end into the flames until it flared brightly. Then she withdrew it and blew on it, leaving the tip a glowing ember streaming white smoke.

Protecting the ember with her cupped hand as one would a candle, she went to Chloe and trailed the smoke over her face. When she inhaled it, she breathed more quickly and her eyes fluttered open.

Jack feared she would speak before she could remember their situation, so he sprang from his pallet calling, "Viollca! Viollca!" He rushed to embrace her before he could be stopped and, with his lips very close to her ear, whispered, "Shhh." Then he drew back to look at her saying "Viollca! Viollca!" with still more passion, but ordering her with his eyes to keep quiet and play along.

She understood and wordlessly flung herself into his arms. The woman allowed their little reunion for a moment, then said something and gently pushed him away. She removed the leaves from Chloe's leg, revealing a clean, healing wound. There was no sign of infection and it dawned on him that Chloe had not been feverish when he held her. He wondered if he might still be dreaming or even be dead, as none of this made sense to him.

The woman presented a bowl of the earthy soup to Chloe, who looked to Jack for a sign. He nodded assent and, as had he, she sipped first and then drank deeply, after which the woman took the empty bowls and went out of the hut, leaving them alone. They held each other closely, partly because they were so grateful to be alive and together, but also in order to whisper safely.

"Yer doin' great, Ducks. Just keep playin' mute till we're out of here."

"Jack, what's going on?"

"They seem to like us; at least they've doctored us both back to health. I'm trying to guess why we haven't been killed. I can't be sure, but I know the language is one reason."

"What's 'Manishie Viollca'?"

"Viollca's yer Rom name, Ducks. My grandmother's name. Good name. And I told her yer my 'Manishie.' That's 'wife.'"

"You think she understood that?"

"When ye speak sincerely and back it up with gestures, the meaning gets across. Shh! Someone's comin'."

He was cuddling her, holding her head against his shoulder and murmuring softly to her in Romany when the woman who had been tending them re-entered the hut accompanied by the priestess and two other women. He looked up at them calmly, still holding his "*Manishie* Viollca" protectively and talking to her.

The priestess strode to them and parted them, but not harshly. She pushed him down onto his back and looked closely at his injured side; she touched the scar lightly and then pressed on it. He was concerned, but so far it hadn't hurt. She turned and spoke to the others who nodded in agreement.

Then she went to Chloe and performed the same examination on her wound. Chloe's eyes were round with apprehension, but she, too, was not harmed.

The priestess cupped Chloe's chin in her hand and studied her face intently. Chloe was trembling with fear that her eyes would reveal what she had so carefully hidden. The woman then spoke to her, calling her "*Manishie* Viollca," and clearly telling her something important, but what?

Then the four women abruptly left the hut.

Jack was able to tell the approximate time of day by watching a patch of sunlight creep across the floor of the hut. He was more comfortable now that he knew which direction was north and how much daylight remained, even though he had no immediate need for such knowledge. To have come through an experience wherein all control was taken from him, just being able to orient himself in time and space seemed like a taste of freedom.

He remembered his compass and wondered where his belongings were. His cutlass, like an extension of his right arm and the pistol that he had owned since his earliest years in the Trade were such a part of him he felt they couldn't be replaced.

While he mulled over these concerns, he absently stroked Chloe's hair as she lay with her head in his lap, contented and at peace in the moment.

Whatever had been done for them, the frightening weakness was gone; in fact, they seemed to have regained most of their usual strength. If he suspected that they were in danger, he could now attempt an escape for them both. *Cross that bridge when ye come to it, Jack.* But he preferred to have a plan, just in case.

Furthermore, their packs were nowhere in sight, not that the contents were of much value to the Maroons, but Emerson and Rodrigo had cleverly sewn two dozen gold sovereigns into the reinforced leather supports and straps of each. Coin of the realm would be of little use in the jungle or the broad coastal plain, but once back in civilization it could mean the difference between life and death. The few loose coins they carried in the pockets of their vests were for quick bribes or necessities as might present in the less inhabited regions. If they were to escape or be set free, they would need the hidden resources of those packs. There was still plenty to worry about.

Despite the kind treatment they had received thus far from their captors, he wasn't convinced that all was truly well for them here. It was possible that they were being healed in order to be proper human sacrifices to some heathen god. That practice was far less common among the African tribes than among those native to the New World, but it wasn't unheard of, and he could neither rest easily nor tell Chloe his concerns. And what tribute might the Maroons exact from them if they did elect to free them? If all of their belongings were taken, it was unlikely that they would live to see Montego Bay.

The flap at the entrance was pulled back and two women entered with bowls of food and drink, placed them beside the captives, and left. There was a kind of corn meal mush, some sort of squash, and strips of meat dark with smoke. All in all, it was tasty enough and they ate well. The drink seemed to be goat's milk with herbs and crushed fruit in it and was actually quite delicious.

By the time the empty bowls were removed, night had fallen and the noisy life of the village had given way to the quieter sounds of the forest. Jack and Chloe lay in an embrace, whispering and listening for footsteps outside the door. Nothing stirred.

The rising moon shed sufficient light that human eyes, once acclimated to the gloom, could see fairly well in the meager illumination that filtered through the smoke hole in the hut. The lovers, realizing that they were alone for the night, wanted to celebrate their newly regained health and strength with the act they had despaired of ever again performing.

Slowly, they undressed each other and reveled in the sight of their beloved lying close in health and love and desire. Side by side and face to face, they came together in a union that was both physical and spiritual.

Had another been asleep in the hut with them that person would not have known what was happening, so silent was their joining; yet neither had ever experienced such intensity, such transcendent ecstasy, as if their very souls had merged into one, a single essence that was at long last complete.

Afterward, they slept the dreamless sleep of the blest, still in the embrace that had taken them to the realm of the celestial.

Thus they were found in the early light when the priestess and her handmaids entered the hut. The initial shock and embarrassment at being seen naked in the position of an amorous embrace was quickly dispelled by the benign countenance of the priestess. Besides, were they to separate, they would reveal more than if they remained as they were.

The women placed on the ground near them bowls of food for breakfast, jugs of fresh water, and—wonder of wonders— their belongings! Jack poured out his gratitude, *"Nais tuke! Nais tuke! Nais tuke!"* (Thank you! Thank you! Thank you!)

When the women departed, he hugged Chloe fiercely. "They're not going to kill us! They're setting us free. We're going to be set free!"

Only then did she realize that he had had his doubts.

They washed and dressed, ate breakfast, and strapped on their packs and weapons. An inspection of the returned articles indicated that not one item was missing, not even the loose coins. He whispered to her that this might be a test.

"They know we have these coins, so we'll offer them to them before we leave. Do whatever I do. Give them anything they ask for, except yer little fur patch; that's mine."

He laughed out loud at the disconcerted look on her face. As much as he loved the lusty, gutsy woman he had discovered, he had missed the sport of shocking her ladylike modesty.

A little later, the priestess and her handmaids came into the hut and, finding their guests ready to depart, motioned for them to follow her outside. Hand in hand they walked through the village behind her, followed by her entourage. The crowd surged around them, but at a respectful distance and more subdued this time.

At the far end of the village where the trail led into the forest stood the same hunters who had brought them up that very trail—how long ago? The priestess stopped before the men and appeared to be instructing them. The hunters nodded their understanding and assent and then she turned to the captives.

She spoke to them in tones that implied a kind of formal farewell. Then she stepped nearer to Chloe and swept her thumb across Chloe's forehead and each cheekbone.

Chloe had no idea what this meant, although she was certain it was some sort of benediction, and she wished to thank the woman, but dared not speak. Recalling what Jack often did, she placed her palms together and bowed to the woman in the universal sign of gratitude and respect.

Jack turned to the priestess and addressed her first, then, in a sweeping gesture, all of the assembled multitude, bowing and saying, *"Nais tuke. Nais tuke. Nais tuke."* He reached into the pocket of his vest and drew out all the coins. Bowing again to the priestess and offering them in his open hands, he said, *"Ashlen devlese."* (May you remain with God.)

Chloe followed suit, bowing and offering her coins. The priestess took all of Jack's, spread them across her palm, chose one, and handed the rest back to him. She closed Chloe's hands around her coins, taking none of them, but speaking to her and calling her *"Manishie* Viollca."

She signaled to the hunters who then flanked the captives and began walking them toward the trail into the forest. Just before they moved beyond sight of the village, Chloe turned and looked over her shoulder at the strange and powerful woman who had saved them and who had blessed her in ways she could not yet understand.

15—Chloe's Prayer

The hunters led them back to the swale where they been found after falling from the rancher's horse. They bowed their gratitude to each hunter in turn, Jack incanting *"Nais tuke"* but, when he got to the apparent leader, the man pointed to the compass hanging from Jack's belt. His meaning was clear: give it to me.

Jack's heart sank, but he removed the instrument without hesitation and handed it to the man. This could end badly after all, if these large, armed men chose to strip them of their possessions now that they were beyond the authority of the priestess. They could even be hurt or killed if the men were sufficiently disobedient.

However, the compass was all that was taken, likely, Jack reasoned, because it could be explained in the village as a gratuity, whereas the packs and weapons would clearly have been stolen.

The men departed, leaving the two free to resume their journey. They stood in silence a short while before moving on and even then walked for more than an hour before speaking. They wanted to be well out of earshot before they dared.

At last, mentally returning from Romany to English, Jack focused on the journey ahead.

"It's going to be more difficult without the compass, but I've navigated by the heavens before and I can do it again. Don't be worried, Ducks." He wasn't quite that certain, being on land, but he wasn't going to tell her that.

It had been so long since Chloe had spoken above a whisper, when she started to speak her voice cracked and she put her hand to her throat and tried again.

"Urrkkk—I have perfect faith in you, Captain. I'm not worried," she rasped.

"Care to sing us a little song, there, Nightingale?"

"Very amusing. I can still yell at you, I'm certain."

"Yell all ye want, Ducks. Just don't bite me again." It was the first time he had mentioned it.

"Jack!"

"There! By the Powers, ye can yell."

She grabbed a leafy twig and began swatting him with it as he covered his head.

"No hitting! I'm innocent, I tell ye!"

Giddy with joy as the reality of their deliverance sank in, they laughed until they were doubled over.

In the kitchen of the Caruthers mansion, Maria cleared the table of their breakfast and carved another mark into the jamb of the door that her mistress and the Captain had passed through on the morning they left. This morning marked the completion of one more day, now fifteen altogether.

As apprehensive as she had been until now, she knew that the days and weeks ahead would be worse as the time approached to expect the Señora's return. It would be difficult not to despair each day that her mistress did not appear. She had kept a candle burning continuously on the little altar in her room for the safety of the two. At what point would she have to light candles for their souls? At what point would hope be gone?

Emerson had been their rock these two weeks, giving them ideas of approximately where the two would likely be each day, reminding them that delays must be expected and that the absolute earliest their mistress could return would be twelve to fifteen days, assuming the trek went flawlessly, that she was able to book passage immediately upon arrival in Montego Bay, and that the ship sailed nonstop in favorable winds around the western tip of the island and on to Port Royal. He never failed to remind them that such good fortune was grossly improbable and that, even so, Madam and Captain Bellamie would be in no hurry to make their final separation regardless of when they arrived in Montego Bay.

As midday approached, the sojourners were faced with

the decision of whether to rest, as was usual, or to keep moving and make up some lost time. Neither felt at all tired; in fact they were so mentally and physically refreshed sleep seemed pointless to them. Further, clouds had obscured the burning sun and a light breeze cooled them. Stopping to nap would be a waste of time.

It was decided, however, to pause and eat some of the fruit and dried fish their captors had given them for their journey, so they searched for a likely spot for a picnic.

Their mood had been almost childlike, so carefree after the series of misfortunes from which they had emerged virtually unscathed, but when they had selected the place to eat their midday meal, Chloe suddenly grew serious. She took Jack's hand and knelt on the ground; he did the same, wondering what this was about.

She folded her hands in her lap and bowed her head, so he did, too, watching her out of the corner of his eye. He now knew what she was doing, but it seemed odd to him, as she had never shown a religious bent. On the other hand, she was always surprising him, so why should this be different?

She closed her eyes and breathed deeply before speaking. As she intoned her prayer she gave thanks for their lives and health having been spared thus far on this perilous journey and especially for their release from captivity. She invoked a blessing on the people of the village for being so charitable toward them and she implored God's continued protection until they could arrive safely at their destinations and there find that all was well.

What she said next touched Jack to the heart. "I give Thee thanks, Lord God, for bringing this good man, Jack Bellamie, into my life to teach me the depth and breadth of human devotion and love. Please bless him with a long, happy, and prosperous life and keep him safely in Your care until You receive him at the last day. Let the certainty of my unending love for him bring him only happiness and not grief in our parting. And, please, *please* give me the strength to endure my life without him in a spirit of gratitude for having had him at all."

After a long pause, "Amen."

"Bater." (Amen.) Beyond that, he couldn't speak.

16—Tales Beneath the Rock

By evening, they were pleased with the
distance they had covered this first day back
on the trail. The weather had been nearly perfect, neither too
bright nor too dim, neither too hot nor too cool, and always that
light, caressing breeze. It made for excellent traveling conditions,
except that Jack needed to see the sun to guide them and the
ever-thickening cloud cover was making that increasingly
difficult. He said nothing about it to Chloe and hoped that it would
clear overnight so that the next day they could proceed with more
confidence.

But by morning the sky was a thick, leaden gray and they
could hear the rumble of thunder in the distance. Emerson had
warned them that, once they had crossed the approximate axis
of the island, they would encounter considerably more rainfall
and some rather intense storms. Apparently, this would be the
first.

They hurriedly broke camp and set off in search of shelter,
winding their way up into the foothills in search of caves or
abandoned mines. The wind was picking up dramatically, so they
took the first thing they came upon, a shallow overhang on a
steep slope.

Tearing small branches off nearby trees for brooms, they
quickly swept the shelter of debris and small creatures, and then
hunkered down behind a boulder as the fury of the storm drove
sprays of rain under the overhang.

It was unfortunate that the storm broke so early as the hard,
steady rain that followed robbed them of yet another day of travel
and they had to ration their food, being unable to forage or fish in
such weather. Nevertheless, sitting under the sheltering rock with

no interruptions or duties was not an unpleasant way to spend one of the few days left to them.

It gave them a chance for leisurely conversation they hadn't had for quite a while. The first topic was speculation as to why the Maroons had spared them, even helped them. Chloe wondered if all that had been said about the former slaves was wrong.

"No, not wrong. The Maroons' hatred of the English and Spanish, while the stuff of legends, is unfortunately very real. We saved ourselves, Darling, by carefully concealing our Anglo background."

"Well, that accounts for the language question, but you look rather Spanish and I'm the proverbial map of England."

"Ah, but try to see us from the Maroons' point of view. In the middle of Hell's soggy dooryard they stumble upon two pitiful half-dead creatures who seem to be as cast out from polite society as they themselves: an obvious female (look at yer hips and breasts, Ducks), unadorned, dressed as a man, apparently having come out second best in a scuffle with a boar, and mute in the bargain. Then there's the male, decked to his pearly teeth in jewelry and rings, wearing a fancy sash and complete with a stitched up and bleeding gunshot wound in his scrawny side." (He conveniently omitted the part about the priestess checking him to be certain of his gender; that fainting-in-the-street business was better left unsaid.)

"Your stitches were bleeding?"

"Aye. Must've torn 'em carryin' ye away from that rancher."

"The bastard." Apparently Chloe wasn't going to have any delayed guilt over having slain the man who was going to harm her Jack.

"Then the male starts spoutin' some gibberish language they've never heard before, certainly nothing associated with any known European nation. We're lucky we weren't kept as amusing oddities for the kiddies to poke with sticks."

"Do you think your being a pirate helped?"

"They didn't smoke me fer a pirate, Ducks, or our noggins would be decoratin' their ballroom this moment."

"They hate pirates?"

"Aye. Not all pirates are decent men, Chloe. Quite a few make a tidy sum transporting slaves to augment their more respectable pursuits of pillagin' and plunderin'."

"How awful! Did you ever have to do that?"

He looked at her sharply. "How can ye ask that?"

"Well, you've been a pirate since you were eleven years old. I'm sure you weren't always the Captain."

"Aye, Lass. And therein hangs a tale. On yer balcony the night I told ye about my parents, I mentioned Korsakov, my first captain and mentor in the Sweet Trade. Well, I served under him on the *Archangel* until I was sixteen and ye couldn't have asked for a better teacher. I loved the *Archangel* and regarded Korsakov as a father.

"By then I had proven meself in many a fight and had demonstrated a talent for working high up in the rigging; I was a respected member of the crew. Furthermore, I had survived some narrow escapes in battles and storms and figured the situation would last the rest of my life. The simple-minded optimism of youth.

"One day we attacked and bested a brigantine in the South China Sea and took on several of her crew including her bo's'n, man by name of Morelock. Well, ol' Morelock, he started fillin' Korsakov's head with tales of unimagined treasure to be had off the Gold Coast and nothin' would do but we set sail fer western Africa. Struggled our way 'round the Cape, nearly foundered three times in storms like ye never want to see. She was barely afloat. That was when I realized that I was actually mortal like everyone else.

"We were lucky to find a cay where we could careen and make repairs, but all that unproductive time just whipped Korsakov's greed into a frenzy. He and Morelock started talkin' how they could make quick swag carryin' two-legged cargo to the New World. At first I thought they meant passengers and that made no sense on a corsair, so I paid closer attention and learned they were talkin' about convertin' the *Archangel* into a slaver. I was sickened at the thought of it.

"What saved the *Archangel* and Ol' Blackjack was that Korsakov's frenzy to get rich grew so fast that by the time our ship was ready to sail again, he and Morelock had decided that the brig was too small for big-thinking entrepreneurs such as themselves and proceeded to make their first order of business the capture of galleons, behemoths, to fill to the gunwales with breathing bounty. Notice I said 'behemoths,' more than one. He and Morelock wanted one apiece to start their own fleet.

"Some of our crew didn't like this one bit, meself included. Some were even talkin' mutiny. We were passin' on easy marks that could have filled our hold with booty, but our illustrious captain would hunt only 'whales.' When we took our first galleon (ye should have seen that fight!) there was a great stir amongst the crew as to who would serve where. It finally ended in a vote that placed Korsakov as captain of the galleon with Morelock as his first mate, to become captain of the next one.

"Our own first mate, a good man named Claremont, became our captain and his crew included the like-minded from our original bunch and several from the galleon, those who wanted no part of the slave trade.

"Korsakov and Morelock figured the *Archangel* was not likely to win another fight such as we had just seen and they simply let us go so they could concentrate on their sea-going empire. Those of us on the *Archangel* went 'On the Account' and glad to do it, to be self-respectin' buccaneers once more.

"We sailed into the Caribbean huntin' Spanish gold and had a very happy and productive year as Brethren of the Coast. All was goin' well until we were caught in a storm off Haiti and were bilged upon our own anchor. Claremont ordered her run aground to keep her off the bottom and, once again, the *Archangel* was hauled out for repairs."

"Do you know if she's still in service?"

"Aye, I do fer a fact. More on that later.

"I was too bound to the sea to spend another long spell at a careening cay, so I took my share of the booty and started ship-hoppin'. Anything that flew the black flag was fine with me. The first was the barque out of Port-au-Prince what gave me the decorations on me back."

Chloe watched him, fascinated, as he talked. He was telling the story as much to himself as to her, reliving it, his speech sliding deeper into the style of the pirates. She could see the light in his eyes and, for the first time, understood his love for the sea. She was both happy and sad to understand it.

"It was the experience of signin' on with first one crew then another what gave me my insight into the whole colorful panorama of pirates. I saw decent men, Chloe, God-fearin' men what wouldn't say 'damn' to a snake, and I saw sadistic bastards what used the black flag to cover their blood-lust. That's the whole point behind piracy, Ducks. A pirate is completely free."

"But it's a hard life, isn't it, being at odds with all nations?"

"Aye, but freedom never comes cheap. Pirating in the Caribbean is generally easier than in some of the other seas because of the many little islands, mostly good weather, and abundant rich prey. I've no desire to go back to the places I'd been before returning here. Any pirate what needs more than that is gettin' greedy."

"Did you ever cross paths with Korsakov again?"

"Aye. Did I ever! And it cost me the *Sinecure*. Several years later I was on a brigantine in the North Atlantic stalkin' merchantmen when we came upon a pitiful sight indeed. A beautiful brig was dead in the water with her masts shot off and her rudderpost busted. We figured whoever had bested her had picked her over, but we put about just the same to see what might be left fer us.

"When she saw us strike the Union Jack and run up the black flag, damned if she didn't do the same! So, our scavenger mission became a rescue and no shots were fired by either vessel.

"As we drew closer, I saw it was my old friend Claremont and the *Archangel*. Well, it was a happy day, indeed, fer Ol' Blackjack to be reunited with his mates and his favorite ship. Turns out the *Archangel* had won that battle after all, sendin' the navy ship what beset her to th' bottomless depths of the Atlantic.

"The two crews spent the remainder of the day givin' proper sendoffs to the mates who'd perished in the battle, then went below and soaked up enough Kill Devil to float ol' Korsakov's galleon. Ugly ships, galleons. Big and hard to steer.

"When we had sobered up sufficiently, we made what repairs we could at sea and escorted her to Okracoke where we could do it right. Less than a month later, she was under sail again and Ol' Blackjack was her new first mate, the previous having been one of the guests of honor at the funerals that first day.

"I had three wonderful years on the *Archangel* with no further serious damages to her and only a few to meself until one morning. We was chasin' another brig what seemed to be heavy in the water, we figured with a hold full of something. Turned out not to be booty. It were artillery and she were a pirate hunter.

"We spent as much time maneuvering to avoid her firepower as loosing our own, but our ship was nimble and fast and our crew seasoned and keen.

"We took no serious hits ourselves and finally got off a lucky shot with a sixteen-pounder what pierced her hull and sent her down. But when the smoke cleared, poor Claremont lay bleeding to death on the deck. Splinter from a yard had gone right through 'is chest.

"We buried our dead, and I tell ye, Chloe, me 'eart near broke to see Captain Claremont slip beneath the waves. When the funerals was done, the crew took a vote and Ol' Blackjack became Captain Blackjack Bellamie, then we all got roarin' drunk.

"Me first act as Captain of the *Archangel* , after soberin' up somewhat, was to set sail fer the Caribbean, never to leave again. I figured the ol' girl needed a fresh start and a change of luck, so I had 'er hauled out and restored stem to stern and painted glossy black with a wide, white stripe. Then I put black and white striped sails on 'er and re-christened 'er and the *Sinecure* was born.

"We prospered there and had very little trouble from the crowned heads, nothin' we couldn't handle. Our reputation grew as a force to be reckoned with, which meant we took a lot of prey what just gave up without a fight. That's why pirates try to appear so terrifyin'; bein' feared saves us a lot o' trouble. Just the same, the next pirate ye come across—other'n yers truly, o' course—assume all the bad stuff is true until ye know otherwise."

Chloe was spellbound. She was being given a glimpse into a fascinating shadow world she could never know.

"Anyhow, one fine evenin' me and the crew was havin' some shore time in Tortuga when, who should clap me on me shoulder but me old friend Korsakov. Down on 'is luck 'e was, Morelock having stole 'is ship, that fine galleon, right out from under 'is arse—sorry.

"Well I figured, let bygones be bygones. Just because I don't agree with the man's philosophy don't make 'im an enemy. He were a good sailor and I figured I owed 'im a lot from the early days.

"The first mate I'd 'ad from the beginning 'ad left just that mornin' to sail back to the North Atlantic. Seems 'e were homesick fer Scotland. So, it 'appened I was in the market, as it were. Took Korsakov on as me new first mate and off we went.

"Everything was fine till we got wind of an emperor's ransom in jewels that had been collected by the late Rodney Loud and was reported to be stowed on a certain obscure, uninhabitable island off the coast of the Carolinas. The source of this rumor had a bad reputation fer lyin', so I couldn't see botherin' to leave the Caribbean on a fool's errand when rich prey were so plentiful right here.

"I trusted me crew, never 'ad reason not to and, since Korsakov was one of 'em now, I trusted him. Incredibly naive of me. His obsession with massive riches hadn't flagged since 'is days with Morelock, and 'e were goin' about poisonin' the minds o' the crew behind me back; got 'em greedy as 'imself before I realized what be goin' on.

"But by the time I discovered 'is perfidy, a mutiny were brewin'. Me and sixteen o' me loyal men was set adrift in a skiff t' die. Last laugh was on the mutineers, though: the jewels was long since found and purloined by the French! But it still took two long years to get me ship back and kill Korsakov. Ye've probably 'eard about all that, livin' near Port Royal."

"I think the question is, why were *you* in Port Royal this time with Rothwell so keen to hang you?"

"Same reason as when I left the *Archangel* the first time: too bored to stay on land fer a prolonged careening. The *Sinecure* needed major keel repairs and re-masted, but the necessary materials were proving difficult to obtain, so I left her in Vestal Cay in the care o' me quartermaster and boarded a frigate to work as an ordinary seaman fer a couple months just to have something to do. Told me crew I'd rejoin 'em in three months.

"Shoulda jumped ship before we made fer Port Royal, or at least stayed aboard and not gone ashore when we did. But I was 'oping to see me old friend and shipmate, Daniel Everson, and was wantin' fer some quality rum. That was where the marines recognized me, outside a tavern. I 'adn't been ashore one hour."

He looked at her and re-thought his words.

"No, I'm wrong. I should have done exactly what I did." And he kissed her to make his point.

The morning's activities of breaking camp, finding shelter, and enjoying prolonged conversation had omitted breakfast. The conclusion of Jack's story had brought them back to the present, which meant empty bellies. Their meager provisions were enough for one fairly decent meal, but if they were to eat later in the day, they would have to ration carefully. It wasn't pleasant, but they had done it before and were not especially uncomfortable. Yet.

For a while, their discourse consisted of subdividing the food, anticipating the contingencies of an extended stay under the rock and, such as it was, eating.

After dining on their small allotment, they settled back into entertaining each other with their life stories. Jack had wanted to broach the subject of Chloe's marriage and pregnancy to get the story directly from her so he could stop worrying that he would inadvertently refer to it and betray Maria's confidence.

"Chloe, Ducks, ye've 'eard all about Ol' Blackjack's life from birth right up to today, mostly, but ye've told me nothin' about yerself. Where were ye born?"

"In London, Jack. There was nothing remarkable about my early life. I also was one of three, having an older and a younger brother. Our father, Lord Benjamin Smyth III, was a Member of Parliament; our mother, Lady Penelope Finch-Smyth, was actually in the line of succession for the throne, if you care to count downward about thirty notches."

"Ah, so yer royalty!"

"Hardly. I received the usual education for a young lady of my social class, music, art, language, comportment and, of course, plenty of 'never do this' and 'never do that'."

"'Never do' what, f'r instance?"

"Well, 'never raise your voice,' 'never have an opinion about anything more important than the weather,' 'never ride astraddle,'—"

"'Never ride astraddle'? Why on earth not?"

"Oh, my dear Jack, it is most unladylike, unthinkable. When I was ten years old, I worshipped my older brother, Ben, Benjamin Smyth IV. He was fourteen and I thought he was Galahad incarnate. He had a hunter he called Raven and I never tired of watching them going over the jumps on our estate. They seemed as one being flying in graceful arcs. Made me think of Pegasus.

"One day I told Ben that I envied him because he could do that and he said we could get a teacher for me so that I could, too. But I had no desire to learn to jump if I had to use a sidesaddle and dress as if I were going to church. I wanted the freedom Ben had.

"My brother was always tenderhearted toward me, could deny me nothing, so, one day while Father was in town and Mother was having guests for tea, he took me to a part of our lands obscured from the house by a stand of trees and put me on Raven's back. He adjusted the irons to my short legs and placed the reins properly in my hands, instructed me in the rudiments of guiding the animal, and then he led us around a bit so I could become accustomed to balancing in the saddle.

"When he was satisfied that I could start, stop and turn, he released the bridle and let me guide Raven at a sedate walk. I did rather well and he allowed me advance to a jog, telling me how to post in rhythm with the horse. At last, he dared urge us into an easy canter and I could have touched heaven with my fingertips."

Jack was riveted, knowing firsthand the boundless freedom and joy to be found on horseback. He smiled, picturing little Chloe cantering for the first time.

"What we did next was insane. It's only by the grace of God I wasn't killed.

"Cantering quickly grew too tame for me and I urged the horse into a headlong gallop. Ben was frightened, screaming at me to haul back and, frankly, I was terrified; but that only added to the intense excitement that was like ice and fire in my chest.

"Blessedly, Raven was a quiet cold blood and he responded to my signals when I finally brought him around to Ben and halted. At that age, I didn't realize how easily I could have become the animal's hostage. In our youthful exuberance, Ben and I quickly recovered from the fright and I was able to persuade him to let me go over a jump.

"He insisted on demonstrating the procedure first, which meant my having to dismount for a time. After the breathtaking height of the horse, I felt as if I were one foot tall. I hated it, never wanted to be on the ground again."

"Now ye know how I feel about a ship."

She looked at him, pondering this, remembering. "Yes. Yes— Now I understand. I do understand."

Their eyes met as this unexpected commonality bound them ever more closely and the immense gulf between their worlds diminished to a degree.

"Ben went over the low jumps, shouting back instructions for me to observe as he did so. Soon, I was sure I could do it as well as he and begged to be allowed to try.

"So, I was boosted back onto my lofty perch and began my approach. Walk… trot… canter… circle toward the jump, not too fast—then—shift forward in the irons and lean low over the horse's neck, fists pressed onto either side of his mane and, all at once, the thunder of hooves under me ceased, his neck rose upward toward me and we were flying!"

She paused, closing her eyes, her breath coming faster. Then she came back to earth.

"Landing was not quite so graceful, as I sat back too abruptly and threw off Raven's timing somewhat. However, I was too small to be much of a bother and he was a mature, well-trained mount, so I wobbled, but didn't fall. I rode over to Ben to receive my well-deserved congratulations from my proud teacher. I was so excited, so exhilarated, I could scarcely breathe!"

Jack tacitly reflected that he had seen her that way more than once, but didn't want to interrupt the story.

"I was just ready to begin the second jump when we heard a lot of shouting coming from the trees. Our gardener had spotted us and was stricken to have witnessed such a horrible sight. I was hauled off the saddle and marched toward my waiting nanny who was livid and giving me to understand that I was in terrible trouble. As she dragged me, squalling and protesting, to the house, she shouted back to Ben that he was going to be punished, too. That really broke my heart.

"I was sent to my room to await sentencing. It was evening before I was summoned before my parents, who made me feel like the family's Great Disgrace and cursed me with no pie for a month and extra grammar and history to study. I would have considered it worth the price, but poor Ben was soundly thrashed for his part in the debacle and I could scarcely bear that.

"Ben's crime was that he could have gotten me killed and, of course, that was actually so. My felony was explained to me in private by my nanny who told me in very blunt terms that any activity which causes a young lady to open her legs, her 'limbs,' is always inappropriate, vulgar, common, and evil." Here, she just sighed.

"So, you never went over a jump again?"

"No. Never rode astraddle again, until after the boar hurt me."

The two sat in silence awhile, each pondering the unfortunate outcome to what was likely Chloe's happiest childhood moment. Jack pitied her and found that he actually felt fortunate to have had the life he had had. At least he had lived.

He wanted her to continue. "So, how did you meet your husband?"

"He was a colleague of my father's, a bit older than I, but from a good family, well-connected. He asked permission to call on me and my father granted it."

"You weren't consulted?"

"Why would I be? My parents always knew what was best for me. Saved me from the fires of Hell for riding like a man, didn't they?

"Lord Caruthers was very proper and polite and kind toward me and, in due time, he asked for my hand. On this, I was consulted, but I knew better than to refuse."

"Did you love him?"

"Love was not the question. It was a smart match and it was my duty to accept a smart match and take my place in society as a young matron. I was somewhat eager to be married, as most young ladies are, because it is your one moment of glory with church bells chiming for you, people bringing gifts, the house bedecked with flowers, a lovely gown you wear but once.

"Then, too, there's the prospect of being the lady of your own household, watching your children grow…" She trailed off and Jack knew that he must tread lightly at this point, let her tell it herself. But he had to ask what she would never volunteer.

"And the bridal night? Was that happily anticipated, too?"

She paused, looked down, and sighed. "No, it wasn't. It was the dark cloud in front of the silver lining. Girls of my station were told very little about what to expect, mostly to simply endure it, as it was the husband's right and privilege. I can't say what I was expecting, as I had so little information.

"The older women made it sound awful, a woman's burden, like the monthly curse and childbirth. As they bade me farewell when leaving the festivities, they patted my hand, shed a tear, and told me to be brave. But young ladies my age had heard something of romance and I, at least, hoped that the women were wrong, that it would be pleasurable."

"Was it?"

"God, no, Jack. It hurt, terribly. It was humiliating, even in the dark, and there was so much—mess—blood and all."

He wanted to put his arm around her, but sensed this was not the time; he waited.

"My husband was a decent man; he didn't enjoy hurting me. He apologized, thanked me before he left my room and—"

"Hold up , there! He left your room? On your wedding night?"

"Of course. Husbands and wives in our social stratum do not sleep together. That would be as unseemly as riding astraddle." She blushed at the inadvertent double *entendre*. "He had his room and I had mine. When he wanted—that—he simply came into my room, did it, and went back to his own."

Jack hated to pry, but he was fascinated by this ludicrous approach to love. "So, was he in your room every night? I would have been."

"Hardly. Perhaps once or twice a month. I was always glad when it was over, as then I could have a respite."

With the questions he asked he eventually came to understand what a minimal role sex had played in the Caruthers' lives. He had never heard of a man seeming to derive so little pleasure from intercourse. But then, if the husband cared for and respected his wife and truly believed that he was doing something terrible to her, well, it certainly wouldn't be much fun for a decent man.

"Had you never heard of a couple enjoying each other? I mean, not your parents, or anybody?"

"Are you mad? Wherever would I have been exposed to such a thing? My parents' home was as arid as my own. Had it not been for my younger brother's appearance on the scene, I would have assumed there were no further intimacies between them after my conception. Even so, I wouldn't allow such thoughts into my head."

His family experience had been diametrically opposite.

"My sisters and I were accustomed to hearing our parents making love from the time we were born. It was simply part of family life for us, something we expected for ourselves when we reached adulthood and marriage."

"*Ewww.* Wasn't it awful? Why weren't they more discreet?"

"There were five of us living in a wagon no larger than your dressing room, Ducks. Discretion was impossible. They were modest, I mean, we saw nothing, but there was no way to hide the sounds. In fact, ours wasn't the only wagon we could hear. Isolation simply isn't possible in a caravan."

She was trying hard not to be horrified. "How did that make you feel? I mean, how would that affect an innocent child?"

"It affected me as being normal and natural and a sign that my parents loved each other. That made me feel safe. We children were happy and secure.

"When my sisters learned how babies are started, they would sometimes giggle secretly the next day, hoping that we would soon have another brother or sister. That was a happy thought, too."

This proved to be the catalyst and, finally, she began to tell him about the baby.

"Unfortunately, I was raised to believe that the only purpose of marital intimacy was to produce children or to keep an energetic husband from straying. I did eventually become pregnant after we moved to Jamaica. But the child, a little girl, was born too soon and didn't live."

Now he could put his arm around her. It was the first effective consolation for the death of her baby that she could remember. She turned her head to his chest but didn't cry, merely waited until she was more composed, feeling safe against him. He let her proceed at her own pace.

"It changes a woman, Jack, to lose a child. I was different after that."

"In what way?"

"I very much needed to be touched, to be held. Even though the sex act was not enjoyable for me, I found myself missing it."

"Missing it? He stopped?"

"Yes. He must have assumed that I would not want to risk another pregnancy, so he never returned to my room. But he was wrong. I wanted more than ever to have children after that."

"Let me guess. The two of you dared not speak of such things."

"You guess correctly."

He added his other arm to the embrace, his heart aching at her lonely, empty life. He kissed her forehead and then looked gravely into her eyes.

"Ye'd 'ave been a wonderful mother, Chloe. If the kiddies didn't obey, ye could always bite 'em into submission."

"Jack!"

"Yer yellin' again, Ducks."

But she was grateful for his effort to lighten the mood. They wrestled and played and kissed and felt happiness return in doing so.

Eventually, the remainder of her story was told, the deaths of her family and then her husband. She expressed genuine regret that her husband would never know the joy she had found. A good man, a decent man, his life had been as sere as her own and for the same ridiculous reasons. She prayed he would be compensated in Heaven.

She poured out her bitterness that she had not been permitted to say goodbye to any of her loved ones. Most of all, she missed Ben. At this point she did cry and it was all he could do not to join her, remembering his own losses.

"Jack, when we part in Montego Bay, I *will* say goodbye to you. Thus, you will not die without my having said it."

He was glad she had accepted that they must part, but this was a most depressing twist.

17—A Strange Proposal

The principal framework of their stories having been shared, they whiled away the hours of enforced inactivity by filling in sections with details and anecdotes, learning more about each other and, naturally, growing still closer in understanding. At one point Jack told her, in all sincerity, that she had the makings of a pirate, her courage and natural rebellion having been covered with only a thin veneer of civility. She took that for the compliment it was intended.

He teased her about how her very proper, highbrow London English would sound aboard a pirate ship, imitating her remarkably well, though exaggerating somewhat.

"Oh, if you would be so kind, my *deah* man, do weigh the anchah, *do*. Theah's a good boy. Thenk you so *veddy* much, indeed. And, by the by, pleazz cawz the black flegg to ascend. Oh, you ah so *veddy* kind." Chloe was helpless with laughter.

She learned that "Jack Bellamie" was an English name that he had borne since his days at the orphanage and that his real name, his Rom name, was Jacobo Petulengro. She said it several times to get it to roll off her tongue as it did his.

He tried to teach her how to recognize types of ships by their rigging, but she soon decided that it was far too complicated and not really necessary to know. So, they started singing songs, each learning new ones from the other. The bawdy pirate shanties shocked and delighted her; of course, that hardly surprised him.

But then she grew serious. "Jack, the day I, um, bit you, you spoke poetry to me in bed and then sang a song, all in Romany. What was that?"

"It was a child's poem my mother used to recite to me at bedtime. It's about the birds and the horses and the little children sleeping well because they are loved. Something to that effect. It's the only poem I remember in that language, but it always soothed me at night and I wanted to soothe you. The song was a lullaby, saying to not be afraid, the wind is your blanket, the stars your candle. Like that." His eyes had grown misty and he had to stop talking.

"Jack. You can never know how much I love you."

A whisper, "No, I think I do."

The day had been quite entertaining and had strengthened their bond as nothing else could. In fact, somewhere during their lengthy dialogue, it hit Jack that this woman was his *friend*, his *best* friend.

He had never had a truly close friendship in his life, always hiding away part of himself, dissembling, guarding and not daring to trust. As much as he enjoyed the camaraderie of other men, he would never dream of sharing his secrets with them as he had with Chloe and, until he got to know her, he had never regarded a woman as anything but a superficial amusement, certainly not a friend.

He realized that this was the true basis of love. He would kill for her, die for her, yes, but he would do as much for his ship, his crew, even a stranger if the situation called for it. Yet, he would never share his grief with them, let them see his tears, let them know him. *Astonishing!*

At evening, they ate their few remaining morsels and prepared to sleep, hoping that tomorrow they could travel and obtain food. As the light faded, they spread their blanket on the rocky floor and settled down to rest. Oddly, neither initiated lovemaking and they simply snuggled together in anticipation of sleep.

However, the combination of hard, uneven stone under them, their deprived stomachs wanting more food, and the fact that they had expended very little physical energy during the day made sleep nearly impossible. In addition, the darkness under that rock was impenetrable. Hour after hour, it remained like an executioner's hood, black and smothering, commanding the eyes to remain open and attempt to conquer it.

For what seemed half the night, Jack lay holding Chloe and thinking, thinking, unable to turn off the futile cycle of thoughts. He kept recalling the strange, otherworldly dream/hallucination in the hut, the blessing of the angels, and his thoughts about marrying her and having a family.

His mind could not resolve the dilemma of wanting to make her his wife and live together as a couple, as parents, yet also longing to be at sea at the helm of the *Sinecure*, chasing prey and shouting among his fellows. No matter which of the two scenarios he entertained, the other called to him.

He could not go on without resolving this! There had to be a middle ground. Actually, there would be but for Rothwell's personal vendetta against him. He would not hesitate to marry her and be away at sea for a while, return home, then back to the ship. Sailors had done it since ancient times and he was certain Chloe loved him enough to commit to such a life. But she would be a widow again almost immediately if he tried it. Rothwell was the linchpin. If he could kill Rothwell...

No, that was virtually impossible and attempting to do so would only make him the prime target of still more authorities, if he survived in the first place. He was unable to endure this irresolution.

Then, he had a most logical thought. *This is not about just you, Bellamie. The question clearly involves the choices of two people. It isn't your decision; it's yours and hers.*

He touched her hand. "Chloe? Darling, are ye asleep?"

"No, I haven't been able to drop off. So uncomfortable."

"Do we have a piece of candle left? I need to talk to ye and I can't see ye." It was never this dark on a ship.

The tiny light made the cave more comfortable and they sat up. He took her hands in his.

"Chloe, my mind is troubled, so troubled I can endure it no longer."

She frowned her question and waited for him to continue.

"We both know that we cannot be together and we both accept that, don't we?"

"We do, Jack. Why bring this up now?"

"Hear me out, Ducks. I have to ask ye something no man should ever have to ask the woman he loves. Chloe…" This was harder than he expected. He was suddenly afraid of sounding foolish.

"Chloe, I'm askin' ye to be my wife. I know we have to be apart, but I want to marry ye anyway. It's not fair to you and it's not fair to me, but I want ye to say yes if ye love me enough to have it like this."

He saw her eyes well with tears and he had the crushing thought that he had hurt her yet again. But, she was also smiling.

"Yes, Jack! Yes, I'll marry you, even if we never see each other again. I'd rather live my life alone as Mrs. Jack Bellamie than live it alone as Chloe Caruthers. Yes, yes, I'll be your wife!"

He felt a weight lifted from his shoulders. As lovers do in such circumstances, they kissed and laughed and beamed at each other and made silly plans for details of the ceremony. He vowed that if he could ever, ever come home without making her a widow again, he would surely let nothing stop him. They both noticed that he referred to being with her as "home," but neither mentioned it. The statement's spontaneity bespoke its sincerity.

This monumental decision settled to the satisfaction of both, they suddenly wanted very much to make love, which they did, and then slept quite well.

The day spent sheltering under the rock had been unproductive insofar as putting miles behind them on their physical journey, but it had resulted in more "ground" being covered between them than in all the time since they first met. What they had gleaned about each other and what they had discovered about themselves as a result, many couples never achieve in a lifetime of cohabitation. They were instinctively cramming years of togetherness into a few precious weeks.

They had both grown up. Jack was now much more than the man-child hiding from himself and others by playing pirate; Chloe was no longer a soulless marionette whose strings were pulled by an invisible, but omnipresent, aristocracy.

Surprisingly, having shed their protective armor, each felt stronger, freer, and even safer. They discovered that they liked themselves, that underneath the shell of the persona was an individual of surpassing depth and hidden strength.

But—could this metamorphosis endure when they were back in their respective *milieus* and away from the symbiosis of their union?

18—Eden

The day dawned gray and misty, but the rain had stopped and the clouds began thinning and breaking up in the west. Gloriously, they could actually determine which way was west. That was all they needed to attack the trail once again.

The first order of the day had to be food. They were now without any kind of comestibles and would soon become weak if they didn't eat. More than anything, they were craving protein; meat or fish would be a delight.

But the storm had the streams running swift and full, too turbid to catch anything on a hook, and Jack was wondering if he could remember how Emerson had described making a deadfall trap for catching small game. Certainly, it would be easy enough to shoot something, but gunshots could be heard and they didn't wish to go through that again. Attempting to chase down an animal to cut its throat with a dagger or sword would be too great a gamble, likely a futile waste of precious energy.

While he was pondering these unpromising options, he glimpsed movement from the corner of his eye. A turtle was making for the nearest water at top speed. He walked over to it and crushed its shell with a large rock, then proceeded to carve it up for roasting while Chloe searched for tinder and firewood.

That was the next problem; everything was wet. She branched out, looking under rocks and in hollow trees, moving out of sight of Jack. So focused was she on her mission that she neglected to mark her trail for return. When she finally had an armload of dry twigs, bark, and moss, she started back and realized she had no idea which way that might be.

At first, she was not unduly concerned. She walked around a bit, expecting at any moment to discover a familiar sight, but her surroundings became ever stranger and she was unable to return even to the spot where she had first realized she was lost.

She had left her pack with Jack and it held her powder and shot and her pistol, so now she couldn't fire a signal shot or defend herself from danger. He had warned her to keep such supplies on her person, in her vest pocket, and she had intended to, but…

She panicked and began to scream for him, but she could hear her voice being muted and swallowed up by the heavy air and thick, sodden vegetation. She started to run and then realized that she could be running toward him or away from him. Yet, standing still was unbearable.

She began to sob hysterically, crying for Jack as a child would for its mother.

He was so hungry the raw turtle meat was starting to look good. *Where is she?* He was a little irritated; it couldn't take that long to locate dry materials, surely. His belly was hurting and the tasteless foam of emptiness kept coming up into his mouth.

"Chloe! Bring what ye have. We'll eat it raw if we have to. Just hurry! Chloe? Chloe! Where'd ye go? Answer, woman!" Silence. His heart gave a little thump of fear.

He started in the direction he thought he had last seen her go, but he really hadn't been paying attention. He called and called for her, each time pausing to wait for a response. Nothing.

He began to search in a kind of impromptu grid, much as he guided the *Sinecure* when seeking prey in a given section of ocean but, without navigation instruments, he was forced to constantly mark his trail to avoid becoming lost himself.

Now he, too, was fighting panic. It were as if Chloe had been plucked from the face of the earth. The fear and the hunger were making him lightheaded and he was close to losing control and plunging madly into the wilderness to find her. A shred of reason still remaining, he returned to the spot where he had killed the turtle to retrieve their effects and begin searching for her in a more rational manner.

He shouldered both packs and, unwilling to abandon that beautiful turtle meat, crammed it into his pockets. Despite the ache in his gut he couldn't have swallowed anything at that moment, but he hoped that very soon he and Chloe would be dining together.

The sun climbed into the sky, burning off the mists and clouds, making the air steamy and uncomfortable. Jack was sweating and clammy but hardly noticed.

He had called until he was hoarse and his throat hurt. With each passing minute his hope was fading, he was weakening and becoming nauseated. His legs were rubbery and his hands trembled, although how much was from fear and how much from starvation would be difficult to say. Worse, his mind was becoming sluggish, his thoughts fuzzy and indistinct.

Chloe could not simply sit still and hope he would find her. She kept running about, changing direction and, like Jack, becoming hoarse from calling out. Blinded by tears and plunging through some low trees, she hit her head on a branch and dropped like a stone, sliding and rolling downward, finally coming to rest against a fallen log. There she lay, seeing stars and unable to rise. She was aware of a continuous rushing, roaring sound and assumed it was death bearing down on her.

As the morning wore on she still could not stand, although her head began to clear somewhat. She was just so defeated and she could still hear that sound. She was going to die here without ever seeing Jack again, without getting to marry him, all because of a stupid turtle. She wept bitterly.

He rested on a rock and tried to order his thoughts. His voice was nearly gone and he was quaking. Furthermore, he was now as lost as was Chloe. His peripheral vision was becoming white and he knew he would lose consciousness soon if he didn't do something, so he bent over with his head between his knees to bring the blood back to his brain.

That seemed to work as a stopgap measure and allowed him time to think about what he may do to save himself. He needed food and he needed it immediately, so he pulled out the turtle meat and stuffed a chunk into his mouth.

It must have had some sort of flavor, but he was aware only of texture. He chewed no more than necessary to force it down his throat, repeated the action with another piece, and then a third. He was not eating for pleasure; he was eating to save his life. Blood ran down his chin, soaking his beard and onto his shirt. He looked like a madman or one near death from internal hemorrhage.

He was about to start on the fourth piece when his poor, abused stomach rebelled. After being too empty for too long, it was suddenly receiving large, un-masticated wads of raw, bloody meat and it reacted with a cramp that dropped him off the rock.

He curled into a ball on the ground hoping the first pain was the last, but a second one caused him to writhe and cry in misery. He knew that letting the food come up would ease the cramps, but he wasn't going to do that and be hungry and weak again. He was fighting his own body and the outcome was far from certain.

Another cramp and he pounded his fists on the rock to counter the torture. The fourth was the worst yet and he sobbed and rolled in the dirt, but would not give up his meal.

The next two were milder. He had won. He lay panting and tentatively relaxing various rigid muscles.

At last he was pain-free and breathing normally. As he rested, he could feel the precious nutrients enriching his blood, could feel some strength returning, some hope returning.

Death, if that's what that sound was, didn't seem to be getting any closer, so she carefully moved a little, checking for broken bones or massive blood loss. Everything appeared intact. That wasn't necessarily good news to Chloe. If she were going to die here, she'd rather it be quick.

Just as she was about to try standing, she heard a shot, then another and another. Had someone hurt Jack? Was he dead or was he injured and needing her? If they were coming for her next, she was helpless to defend herself. Would they kill her outright or rape and abuse her first? She held her breath, listening.

Before she could drive herself half mad with these thoughts, she heard another shot and, again, a second and third. Now she understood! It was Jack signaling her by firing all three of the pistols, pausing to reload, and firing again.

She stood and began struggling up the slope toward the sound. She tried to scream to answer him, but her overstressed voice refused to respond, giving out only a forced squeak as in nightmares. She clapped her hands and threw stones and twigs, anything to make noise.

Three more shots, closer this time. She was frantic to answer him, but could produce nothing, until she suddenly thought of Ben. Could she still whistle as he had taught her? Two fingers in the mouth, after all these years, remember how to do it. Now!

Jack heard the shrill note just as he was ready to fire a fourth volley. He had never heard her make such a noise, but it had to be Chloe. It had to be! He ran toward the sound and heard it repeat.

Moments later, he emerged from the thicket just as she clambered to the top of the slope down which she had fallen. They started to run to each other when he halted abruptly and shouted, "Stop! Don't move!"

Eager to be back with him, she ignored his warning and rushed on. His eyes widened as he saw that she wasn't heeding him and, with the last of his voice, he croaked out, "*Now*, Chloe!"

She stopped immediately and in an instant saw the reason: a large snake lay between them, now much closer to herself than to Jack, thanks to her failure to hold up when he told her. She froze, staring with abject horror as the serpent raised its head and fixed its lidless gaze on her. She heard, but did not register, the singing, metallic scrape of a sword being unsheathed.

As the snake tensed for the strike, Jack covered the distance between them in three great strides, his weapon already descending as he slid to a stop. The forward motion of the snake's strike and the lateral slash of Jack's sword, both faster than the eye could see, collided in mid-air not six inches from Chloe's arm, severing the beast's head and lofting it airborne to land with a thud some ten feet away.

Chloe fainted.

They were whispering again, but not by choice, as the morning's panic had badly strained both voices. Having mostly recovered from their harrowing experience, they planned that, after dining, they'd head back toward the less wild path they had been following before becoming lost. With much more caution this time, they gathered fuel for a fire.

After cooking and eating the rest of the turtle meat, they smothered the little fire and prepared to get under way. For the first time since charging through the trees to kill the snake, Jack had a moment when his ears were not filled with the sounds of their whispered conversation, noisy footfalls, or other incidental clatter of their activities. He halted, listening.

"Chloe. Hear that? What is it?"

"I don't know. I heard it when I fell down the bank."

Unable to contain his curiosity, he started toward the sound; she followed him closely, fearful of becoming separated again.

The foliage seemed to be getting thicker, lusher, and even more fragrant as they drew closer to the strange noise. He stopped and spread aside some enormous plants. She heard him gasp and ran to his side.

Before them lay a spectacle of superlative beauty: a silver-white waterfall cascading with feathery mists onto smooth boulders before bubbling away as a stream hidden under a canopy of green that occluded the sun. Oversized ferns, trailing vines, and fragrant blossoms of every hue flanked the cataract as rays of sunlight turned the spray into evanescent rainbows. The air itself, emanating from the paradise, was exquisitely sweet, cool, clean.

Awestruck, they neither moved nor spoke for some minutes; eventually, Jack whispered two words.

"It's Eden."

So irresistible was their discovery, they agreed to sacrifice yet another day of travel in order to partake of such splendor, the likes of which neither could hope to see ever again.

Confident of their privacy in this secluded paradise, they decided to first move downstream to the shallow rapids and wash their clothes, all of their clothes, including the blanket. There was no denying that they were both rather gamy, their travels and adventures having afforded only minimal opportunities for personal hygiene.

Once the laundry was finished and draped on sunny shrubs to dry, the two moved upstream to deeper, calmer water to scrub themselves and each other. Naked as newborns, they were completely uninhibited in this perfect and concealed Shangri-La. To Jack, it elicited memories of bathing in the river with the other children of his caravan; Chloe had no experience with which to compare it, but chalked it up to yet another incredible adventure, compliments of Captain Blackjack Bellamie.

With the work portion of the frolic completed and their bodies squeaky clean, the remainder of the day was reserved for fun. With the ease of a dolphin, Jack swam to the bottom of the pool at the base of the falls, scouting for safe places to dive. He surfaced, shaking the water from his head, his braids swirling about, then crawled up onto a large rock and launched himself in a facile arc precisely into the area he intended, parting the water like a blade with scarcely a ripple disturbed.

Again and again he performed this maneuver as Chloe watched in breathless admiration, drinking in the beauty of his body. Lithe as a cat and lean as a whippet with his great, black mane sailing as he flew, the sight was arousing her. Seeing him poised on the rock with all of his charms bared to her, she cast him as the very essence of the natural male animal; he was her bull, her ram, her lion, her stallion!

Engrossed in his aquatic recreation, he didn't notice her approaching his rock until he emerged from the pool once more and came face to face with her.

Her eyes were fever-bright, her cheeks flushed, and her lips parted in an inviting, flirtatious smile. She sidled toward him.

"Jack, that's so wonderful," she breathed. "I love watching you dive."

"Why, thank ye, Ducks. I could show ye how, if ye like."

"Maybe later." She was rubbing herself against him in a totally unmistakable manner.

He caught on immediately, of course, and responded with the natural physiological reaction, but decided to play with her a bit. Remembering how he had loved seeing her beg the night before their "big day," he wasn't about to pass up another such opportunity. Unconcerned that his erection gave him away, he played innocent.

"What is it ye be wantin', Chloe, Lass? I'm not a mind reader, ye know."

Taking his hand, she led him off the rock to a soft, mossy spot where lying down would be comfortable. He followed meekly enough, but remained standing.

"What? Point to what ye want, Ducks. No, point, don't grab. It's not polite to grab."

"Please, Jack. Pleeease!"

Oh, he loved this! "'Please' what, Girl? Yer not makin' yerself clear to Ol' Blackjack."

"You know what I want. You know. Let's, Jack. Let's, right here, right now. You want it, too; that's obvious."

"Want what? Ow! Easy on the merchandise, Darling. I don't want to misread yer signals, Ducks. Spell it out fer Ol' Blackjack, hm?"

She placed his hand where he couldn't possibly mistake her condition, but he kept grinning vacuously at her, his milk-white teeth flashing, taunting her. He didn't withdraw his hand, but moved it just enough to make her gasp. But he still refused to hold her or lie down.

The benefit of growing up with brothers served her well for the second time that morning; she hooked her heel behind his knee and shoved at the same time, toppling him onto his back. Advantage: Chloe.

Before he could recover from the surprise, she was on him, taking him.

He was, of course, unable and unwilling to resist any further, it requiring all of his fortitude just to hold until she had climaxed. Feebly, he wheezed out, "Help! Help!"

When she had dismounted and collapsed at his side, he brought her hand to his lips as he usually did after loving her, but this time he whispered, "No pie fer a month," before falling asleep.

After their satisfying romp in the moss, they recovered and went back into the water. Jack resumed diving, his pleasure multiplied knowing that she was watching, enraptured.

Finally, he swam over to her, urging her to join him; she was still standing on the bottom in chest-deep water.

"I can't swim, Jack. I never learned."

"What? I suppose that was unladylike, too."

"Rah-ther."

"Well, c'mon, then, Lass. This is the day."

He proved to be a patient and effective teacher and soon she was euphoric, moving through the pool with the confidence of a bird in flight, even diving down and daring to open her eyes to partake of the lovely aquamarine secrets of the stream. They met and kissed and fondled each other underwater, they raced (Jack won), they competed to retrieve a coin tossed to the bottom (he let her win), but she never quite mustered the courage to dive off the rock. Rome wasn't built in a day, she reasoned.

Eventually they required rest and, as reluctantly as children brought in for a nap, they left the water. Their craving for protein having been satisfied by the turtle, they enjoyed replenishing their energy with the fruit that was growing, varied and abundant, nearby. While they were gathering the edibles, Jack saw something that he decided to keep as a surprise for Chloe until after they had rested.

Their hunger sated, their thirst slaked, their lust appeased, their bodies cooled by the water and warmed by the sun, they stretched out like basking lizards on the smooth rocks and were soon asleep.

She opened her eyes, her restful slumber rapidly dissolving, and looked for Jack. He was sitting beside her, watching her, his knees drawn up to his chin and his arms draped around them. He gave her a little smile, closing his eyes and then opening them very slowly, not parting his lips, a lazy and sensuous expression that she hadn't seen before.

"Would ye like to see a magic place, Ducks?"

"More magic than this?"

He didn't answer, just extended his hand to help her rise, and then led her along the bank to the side of the falls. When they were so close they could almost touch the falling torrent, he stepped up onto a ledge and helped her to join him. Moving a little to the right, he drew her alongside and she saw what he was talking about: the ledge extended behind the falls, a deep sill behind a curtain of water.

In reverent silence they walked slowly along the ledge, aware that they were among the blessed few who would ever have such an experience. The noise of the cascade made talking impossible, but words were trivial in the face of such majesty. Engulfed in the cacophony of the falls, the silence between the lovers held more meaning than poetry or rings of gold.

It was possible to traverse the entire width of the cataract hidden on the secret sill, the deep seclusion of which was both erotic and awe-inspiring. Such a setting turns love between a man and a woman into a sacrament. They worshipped each other, slowly kissing and caressing every aspect of their beloved's body, as mist from the falls disguised the tears of inexpressibly profound emotion.

They made love but once in that pristine grotto, but in the otherworldly realm in which they dwelt, the beginning and the end of the act were impossible to discern.

Eventually emerging from their hidden cathedral, they swam and played until the shadows began to lengthen. The water seemed perfect to Jack, just cool enough and, at first, it had seemed so to Chloe, but she had become rather withdrawn toward the end of their day, telling him she was getting cold and complaining that her nipples were aching. He urged her to get out of the pool and get dressed, as their clothes were now dry.

Only with great reluctance did he join her, and not until he had dived a half dozen times more. Tepid, salty seawater was never as bracing and restorative as this!

Once dressed, they packed their gear and walked away from their Eden, never to return. They would make camp someplace higher and drier this night and not awaken to the lovely song of the falls, for if they did not take this precaution, this holy place would surely rob them of yet another day, and another after that.

19—The Pendulum

It had been a day filled with nearly every factor to induce deep, restful slumber: panic and resolution, euphoria, recreation, and passion satisfied. The weary, fulfilled travelers made camp, had a light meal and were asleep almost immediately upon lying down.

As dawn colored the eastern sky, they awakened refreshed and ready to get back to the business of covering ground. Jack stretched and looked over at Chloe, who smiled sleepily at him and opened her arms for a good morning embrace. Remembering yesterday's fun, he figured it would be nice to begin this day with making love, just to get the trek off to the best possible start, so he commenced the now-familiar kissing and stroking that never failed to ignite her like gunpowder.

She seemed to be enjoying the attention and was responding in kind, but there was something lacking; he thought he just needed to do more and he intensified his efforts. She was smiling and returning his kisses but, by now, he knew her body nearly as well as his own and he knew she was not getting lusty.

Puzzled, he paused and looked at her. "Is something wrong between us, Ducks?"

"No. Of course not. Why would you ask me that?"

"Yer not warmin' up to Ol' Blackjack like ye usually do."

"No, I want you, Jack, I really do. Let's go ahead."

"Chloe, ye don't have to appease me. It's all right if ye aren't in the mood right now, but be honest with me."

"Jack, I'm in the mood, I truly am. Here, let's do it." She tried to slither under him, to welcome him into her. He touched her.

"Ye can say 'Yes' all ye want, Ducks, but I know what it means when yer like this: yer not ready."

She became shrill. "How dare you, Jack Bellamie! I kiss you and embrace you and *spread my legs for you* and tell you 'yes,' and you won't take me because, in your expert opinion, I'm 'not ready'! I think it's you who have the problem!"

"Chloe, it's sheer folly to even hint that I'm not—that I *wasn't*—aroused. I'm a man; my desire is obvious to the casual observer."

"Then, why didn't you take what was offered? I would have warmed up once we got started."

"Because, Darling, getting 'started' would have been unpleasant for ye. Please don't be angry with me because I refuse to rape ye."

"Rape me? How is it rape when I agree in every possible way?"

"Ye didn't agree in the most important way, Ducks. I've no desire to take ye if yer only humorin' me."

She was angry with him, but it was because she was far angrier with herself and she was aghast that her own body had betrayed her. In her mind and in her heart she had wanted him totally, but her anatomy had remained unresponsive nonetheless. That was frightening. Someday very soon she would ache for him and he wouldn't be there, would never be there again.

He was getting dressed to begin the trip and, when he turned back toward her, she was face down, weeping silently into her hands. He was moved by her anguish, but he was also nonplussed why something so sweet and simple should be blown out of all proportion. He knelt beside her and patted her shoulder.

"Chloe, it isn't important. There'll be other times, Ducks. Let's just get ready to go."

She whirled on him. "Maybe it isn't important to you, Jack, but it is to me! Do you have any idea how humiliating it is to be rejected by the man you're going to marry?"

He felt his patience starting to break. "Chloe, dammit, I didn't reject ye just because I didn't rape ye. I'm not going to take the blame for this dispute when I tried to do the right thing!"

She fairly spat at him. "Oh, of course, the ever-perfect

Captain Bellamie couldn't possibly be wrong—" But here her rage gave out and she dissolved in great, heaving sobs.

Poor Jack was at a loss. He tentatively started to go to her to touch her, to hold her, but drew back, afraid of her fury. She might even bite him again. But while he was debating his next move, she rose and stumbled into his arms, nearly hysterical.

He held her close, glad to know what she was wanting from him at the moment, at least. She was babbling something about loving him so much and being sorry and not knowing what was wrong with her. *Well, that's two of us,* he mused.

"It's all right, Ducks. It's all right. This, too, shall pass. Now, dry yer tears and let's get movin'."

She accepted his kiss and squeezed him tightly. He thought that perhaps the storm had passed until she said, "All this could have been avoided if you had just taken me when I told you to."

For a split second, he imagined how satisfying it would be to slap her.

Defeated, he sat down and put his head in his hands.

"Chloe, I don't know what's gotten into ye, but yer puttin' me through hell. Will ye please just accept that I consider it rape if yer not aroused? I don't know why that makes me a bad man."

"I didn't say you're a bad man, Jack."

"I know that some pirates enjoy rape, hell, some husbands apparently did—do—but I don't. You don't know how much I loathe the whole idea of—that. Let's please change the subject and get on the road. Please?"

Now, it was her turn to be puzzled, but he was standing and shouldering his pack, so the discussion was closed.

They walked in silence more than an hour before pausing briefly to breakfast on some fruit. During their meal, the tension of the morning's disagreement hung in the air between them, but they remained polite to each other; nevertheless, they talked very little.

When they sat down to eat, Jack chivalrously handed her the choicest pieces first and she thanked him. But after just a couple of bites, she gagged and complained that she was sick to death of fruit, that she would be ill if she didn't soon get some tea and something baked with real flour. He would have helped if he possibly could have but, since he couldn't, he felt accused once more.

He kept quiet, hoping to avoid another row. Sometimes Chloe seemed a stranger to him. At least she, too, was miserable when they were on the outs, so she wasn't picking squabbles for sport.

She sat with her head down and looking away from him. Neither said anything, until Jack suggested they get going.

She took that moment to start it again. "It wouldn't have been rape."

"Chloe!" He caught himself before he added fuel to the flames.

"Well, it wouldn't have."

"Very well. Fine. All right. Whatever ye say. Let's get going."

"Don't patronize me, Jack."

"I'm not patronizing ye. I just want to drop this damnable subject and never bring it up again! Is that clear enough to understand?"

"Oh, very clear, Captain. Subject closed. By all means, let's 'get going.'"

She couldn't know how upsetting this was for him. He kept his face dispassionate, shouldered his pack and moved off ahead of her.

He knew he should probably tell her why this subject affected him so and he certainly trusted her to understand, but he didn't feel up to talking about it. Maybe he'd tell her before they parted. Maybe not.

The terrain had leveled considerably and the forests were giving way to acres of cultivated fields. The advantage was a better selection of food to steal, but the disadvantage was being so much more exposed, both to being caught and to the elements. Also, as Emerson had predicted, they knew they would encounter more rainfall and they had no ready means of shelter.

They trudged on in silence until midday when Jack suggested
catching some fish at a small stream they were crossing. Their
skills might have improved or perhaps they were simply lucky,
but they soon had three nice fish to cook for lunch. Even starting
a fire was easier, as they had learned to carry some dry tinder
with them. He worried about the smoke, though, in such open
country, but luckily a small breeze dissipated it this time.

After a satisfying meal of fish and sweet potatoes, they were
soon back on their way. Ten words had not been spoken between
them.

Their pace was better in this flatter country, but they often
had to struggle through tall crops with no discernable path and
only the sky to guide them. It could be rather claustrophobic.

Chloe was following about three paces behind Jack in a
canebrake as it wasn't productive to make two paths, but that
kept her feeling isolated from him and, with no conversation and
little to see, she plodded along, staring at his back and thinking.

She replayed in her mind the whole scenario that had brought
her to this juncture. She recalled her fear of losing him when he
was so sick, his gentleness in teaching her about passion, his
humor, his courage, his breathtaking beauty diving from that
rock. Every memory filled her with love for this colorful pirate;
even the times she had been angry with him, it was her
overwhelming love that drove the tempest.

Now they were worlds apart at three paces and she wasn't
sure who was at fault. He had certainly taken the high road, but
she had meant every word when her body had revolted. How
could this be? She didn't feel well at all; perhaps she was taking
a fever.

A silent hour dragged on, then two. Bored, she began
mentally undressing him, could hear his ragged breathing as he
labored to make them both happy; she inhaled deeply, her eyes
closed, remembering the smell of his skin.

Suddenly, she was seized with such desire she had to have
him—immediately! She called to him and, when he turned, she
rushed at him and threw her arms around him, kissing him with

such frenzy she nearly toppled them both. Before he could free his mouth to protest, she was practically growling.

"Now, Jack! I want you now! Hurry! Hurry!"

She was trying to undress them both, struggling with their belts and packs. He was looking at her with genuine alarm, thinking she had surely gone mad.

"Chloe! What are ye doing? God's wounds, Woman! Stop! Calm down!"

"Now, Jack! Hurry! Please!"

He had his hands full trying to calm her and keep them both clothed until he could make sense of this. He held her at arm's length and it took some force to do so.

"Jack! I'm ready now! I really am! I neeeed you! Now!"

"All right. All right, Chloe. We will. Just settle down and give me a chance to change tack. All right?" He knew she wasn't equivocating this time.

The stifling heat and humidity in the canebrake, the muddy ground between the stalks, the lack of a single square meter of even surface—it would be difficult to imagine a less inviting bed. But Chloe's wild heat made him as indifferent to the discomfort as she and he was soon ready.

It wasn't until afterward that they realized they were probably going to have bruises. She was dreamy-eyed with fulfillment and relief that her responses were back to normal. He was happy himself, for the moment, but he would not have termed it "normal."

Back on the hike, Chloe felt as if all the misery of the morning were over and would not return. She felt like singing. Jack was truly concerned about her, although he had sense enough not to mention it. His fears would soon be compounded.

They were traversing a citrus grove, enjoying the openness and fresher air, when, suddenly, she called out, "Oh, no! Oh, no, no, no! Oh, Jack, look!"

She was kneeling, looking at something on the ground and, by the time he got to her, she was already in tears.

A tiny baby bird lay on its back, its little beak open, dead, no doubt fallen from the nest.

"Oh, it's just a baby. Poor little thing never had a chance to live. Oh, its poor, poor mother." She was weeping copiously.

He was actually afraid now. "Chloe? Sweetheart? It's all right, Ducks. It doesn't feel any pain now. Don't cry," he crooned, petting her.

"But, look at it, Jack. It's a jack! A little baby jack! Oh, no! Oh, nooo!"

Only an ornithologist could have determined the species of the bare little hatchling, but to Chloe it was a jackdaw and that was that. She was inconsolable.

"Chloe, Dearest, it's nature that does this. Not all baby birds survive. But for every little dead jackdaw, there are many more, maybe hundreds more, that live and fly and are happy and make more baby jacks. Its mother won't grieve long. They have very short memories."

"How would you know? You're not a jack—well, I mean, not that kind. She might be wanting to die herself now."

"Ducks, they have short memories because their lives are short. Wherever she is, ye can be certain she has other babies to tend and that keeps her busy."

She wanted to give it a proper burial. He was afraid not to humor her, so he made a little shroud out of a bandage Maria had provided and dug a small hole in the shade with the point of his dagger. They interred the little mite and Chloe cried rivers as they patted the tiny mound of earth into place.

She wanted to put rocks over it to keep out scavengers. Jack dutifully fetched some and didn't mention worms. She wanted to make a little cross; he found twigs and tied them together with some of the fishing line. Then there were the flowers. But when she wanted to sing a hymn, he drew the line.

She was about to take offense at his callousness, but he explained that he was too choked up and it might scare the other birds, anyway. He just knelt beside her there at the wee grave and held her and tried to comfort her.

And he worried. He really, really worried.

The sad business of the bird's funeral behind them, they resumed their journey. He kept closer to her, casting wary glances at her, anticipating another outburst of some sort. She walked quietly on, eyes downcast, subdued.

Fortunately, they were making better time despite the stops for Chloe's problems. Jack wanted to cover as many miles as possible that day, fearing his only hope for saving her sanity was to get her back to civilization as quickly as possible.

She now seemed malleable to his leadership, even until time to make camp. He had expected another crisis with every step, but no more manifested. However, her dispirited sobriety was eerily unnatural and nearly unnerved him. He was loath to provoke her, but found her emotional outbursts almost easier to bear than this.

When he suggested a spot to spend the night, she nodded in agreement and began mechanically performing her usual tasks for bedding them down. She kept her eyes averted and he sensed that he was shut out of her little world.

He built a fire, then he handed her some food and began to eat also. She absently took a few bites, staring into the flames, her eyes unfocussed.

As she was paying him no heed, he took time to study her objectively. The change that had come over her appearance had happened gradually and as a result of the hardships of their journey, so he hadn't noticed it until now. He had been seeing her through the eyes of love as still the soft, creamy, silky creature he had fallen for back at the estate.

But the woman before him would not have been deemed attractive, save by a mariner very long at sea. She was gaunt and burned from the sun and wind. Her hair that had wafted over his face like a fragrant cloud as they made love was now coarse and dull, tied up with care for nothing but keeping it out of her eyes as she walked. Her clothes were torn, stained and too large on her frame. Her hands, curled loosely in her lap as she knelt by the fire, had been so milky white with dainty nails like small, pink seashells on her fingertips, but now looked like the claws of an unfortunate bird of prey: rough, scraped and cut, ragged, grimy and bruised.

His heart ached seeing her like this. She could be home in her mansion this moment, in a silk gown, sipping wine on the veranda after a delicious meal, becoming drowsy as her maid turned down the counterpane on her great scented feather bed upstairs. But this poor, bedraggled creature had done this for him; because of her undying love for him, she had chosen this sorry plight for herself and he knew that, given the opportunity to reverse her choice, she would do it again.

No one had ever loved him unconditionally—loved him at all—until Chloe. He didn't deserve it; he was a criminal, sly and dangerous. Although he would never deliberately hurt her, she was in serious physical and mental decline because of him. The enormity of her sacrifice nearly overwhelmed him.

At that moment, he loved her even more than when her feminine charms set his loins afire. He looked at those poor, damaged hands, hands that had nursed him with a mother's tenderness as he lay suspended between life and death, hands that had caressed his body as if it were an object of worship. He took those dear hands in his own and held them to his lips in a prolonged kiss.

Chloe merely looked at him as he did so, looked at him with no life in her eyes, only a resigned sadness. His own eyes welled with tears and he drew her into his arms as his heart fairly burst with a new ardor: fiercely paternal devotion. She was so small and innocent and hurt and he wanted—needed—to protect her, must protect her.

For once he ran his hands over her body not for eroticism, but to assess the changes in her health. He easily felt every rib, every vertebra. Worse, when he caressed her bottom, he found that the soft, plump, womanly mounds he had adored were gone, vanished while he was not paying attention.

Only her breasts remained full. He cupped one and started to kiss it, but she shrank back from his touch, not in anger, but in pain. He was horrified to have hurt her.

"I'm sorry, Sweetheart. I'm so sorry. I was too rough with ye."

"No, it's all right, Jack. You didn't mean it."

She suddenly appeared too frail for sex. He needed to embrace her and, to him, she was still beautiful, but he couldn't imagine intruding into that fragile body. She was content just to lie in his arms, enjoying the different way he was holding her, feeling safe and protected. He stroked her hair, feeling its roughness and loving her all the more. She spoke and her voice was calm but serious.

"Jack, please be truthful. Tell me, do you think I'm losing my mind?"

He had never lied to her, never intended to lie to her. But how was he to answer this?

"My Dearest Friend, I think this journey has taken too much from ye. I'm certain ye'll be fine again when we get to civilization, with good food and a warm bath and a soft bed to rest in. I'll get ye a new dress and a hat, too. We'll drink tea and eat scones in bed all day. And I'll make ye my wife; I'll do that first."

She said nothing, just snuggled a little closer, listening to his heartbeat and his breathing, enjoying the same ecstasy those sounds had given her when he was still unconscious from his wound. He went on, his warm, resonant, masculine voice deepening her comfort.

"I think we have only two more days' travel left, maybe three, four at the most, then we'll be in Montego Bay and I can take proper care of ye."

"Then I have to give you up."

"Chloe, don't say that. We'll stay a while there. We'll go to a nice hostelry and get the best meals and drink wine and enjoy our honeymoon. We have the money to do these things for ourselves and we'll have earned the right. We already have, well, you have."

"And then I have to give you up."

"Please, Chloe, please don't do this to me, to both of us. Try not to think past the honeymoon. Think how very much I love ye. We're so tired tonight, let's not take on the woes of the future until it gets here."

She said no more and merciful sleep soothed their troubled minds.

20—Dancing on the Strand

The morning appeared promising enough; at least the weather was fair and Chloe remained subdued but rational. Still, Jack found himself being very solicitous about her and bracing for an emotional tempest with every breath. He had resolved not to spar with her when she became overwrought again; in the first place, it was futile to argue with an unbalanced person and in the second, his pity and concern would preclude anger from this point. He kept a wary eye on her, hoping to head off the next crisis before it could get out of hand.

They were making progress when, in early afternoon, Jack suddenly halted, putting out his hand to stop her, too. She watched him, bemused, as he lifted his chin and sniffed the air like a hound picking up a trail. After a moment, he turned to her, a look of pure delight setting his face aglow.

"Chloe, Ducks, d'ye smell that? It's the sea! We've made the northern shore."

As she tried in vain to pick up the scent, he ran to a nearby tree and scurried up, as agile as a marmoset. At the top, he parted the branches and leaned out perilously far in hopes of glimpsing his long lost home. His whoop of joy told her he had seen it.

He all but jumped from the tree, so great was his excitement. Grabbing her by the shoulders, he tried to make her understand the importance of this discovery.

"We made it Chloe, Lass! We can't get lost now. The fact that we've made the shore on only the seventh full day of travel means we veered from the northwest and have come out well east of Montego Bay. All we do now is keep the ocean on our starboard and we'll walk right to our destination."

They hugged and literally danced with relief that this one danger was finally past. Then they made straight for the beach and waded in, splashing and laughing, but all the while wasting no time, moving westward. Other than small detours around natural jetties and other minor obstacles, they walked in the foaming edge of the surf.

The freedom of movement, the renewed hope, and the blessed breeze filled them with a sense of deliverance that propelled them onward as nothing before. Jack felt as if his very blood were singing with the rhythm of the waves. How he had missed the sea! He would never leave it again. He skipped and danced across the sand and had to quell the urge to break into a joyous, headlong run, just to free muscles that had been cramped for too long in the stifling confines of land.

At one point, as he twirled in abandon, flinging his braids around his head and enjoying the invigorating sting as they slapped his cheeks, he glimpsed Chloe, plodding diligently behind him, considerably less euphoric than he.

He danced back to her, caught her in his arms and swung her around, lifting her into the air. After a moment, she caught his mood and she laughed—the first time he had heard that lovely sound since Eden.

He set her lightly back onto the ground and took her hand and, as if by prior agreement, they broke into that headlong run. Naturally, he could easily outdistance her, so, after she started to become winded, he dropped her hand and all but flew ahead of her down the strand.

When he was finally forced to stop and catch his breath, he was well in front of her. Turning to watch her approach, he leaned forward, his hands on his thighs, and gasped in pure pleasure, feeling his lungs pumping out the stagnant air of the inland forests and fields and replacing it with the life-affirming perfume of the ocean. There he waited until she caught up with him whereupon he swept her into a lush embrace and kissed her, at first almost roughly, then gliding into the tenderness that she remembered from that first transcendent moment by the harpsichord.

At last they settled into a consistent, brisk, walking pace, often holding hands and talking and laughing. Except for her appearance, Chloe seemed almost normal again.

She was beginning to notice something about Jack that she had not seen before, although everyone else who knew him had: his gait was a sailor's rolling sway, as if he were drunk or on board ship. She didn't realize how much of his life had been spent in both conditions simultaneously.

His speech was also changing subtly, becoming more benignly arrogant, punctuated with cocky facial expressions, mocking, sneering, showing more teeth.

Although none of it was directed negatively at her, she wasn't sure she liked this new Jack. She missed the gentle, doe-eyed swain who had wooed her and won her. She was seeing him in his element now, just as he had seen her as the refined gentlewoman in hers. *Now that he doesn't need me, will he still love me?* She nevertheless maintained her outward equanimity and he had no idea such doubts were vexing her.

Although they had no estimate of how far they were from Montego Bay, it wasn't so important now and, as often happens when a worry loses its hold, the cause for that worry resolves itself. They put more miles behind them that day than any so far.

Making camp on the beach seemed more like a holiday than a necessity. They caught enough little crustaceans to have a sumptuous feast not experienced for longer than either could remember and having salt eased the craving that had been with them since they were released from the Maroons.

Although Jack had decided not to approach her for coitus after that last disaster and then seeing her as so frail, her improved appetite and color along with the major upturn in their circumstances made him rethink that decision. Besides, he really wanted her here by the fire, by the sea. Nevertheless, he approached cautiously, prepared to change course at the slightest hint of trouble.

He needn't have worried; her ardor was as genuine and her satisfaction as great as his.

But as he was falling asleep he heard a tiny sound, barely detectable under the voice of the surf; she was crying, very softly. Normally, he would take her in his arms at the first sign of tears, but something about this told him she didn't want him to know, that this sorrow was intensely personal and he mustn't intrude. He could only hope that it wasn't the start of a new problem for her, and for him.

The second day of their trek over the sand was as successful as the first. Jack estimated that they may have covered as many as fifteen miles or even more each day. In this open place they had more hours of daylight to travel and even walked on into the darkness hours for a while, as the moon and stars shed enough light to see tolerably well.

Chloe showed no further sign of her secret melancholy from the night before, although he surreptitiously watched her for clues.

The second night on the beach was nearly as pleasant as the first, at least in the beginning, and although he listened carefully, he did not hear her crying this time, another relief for him. However, sometime after midnight clouds rolled in, obscuring the moon; the wind came in from the north and picked up, whipping the surf.

The travelers slept on in blissful ignorance until they were rudely awakened by the sudden squall. They sat up and pulled the blanket from under themselves, trying to use it as shelter. But shelter was not to be had and the blanket quickly became sodden and heavy, worse than outright exposure. They sat huddled together in the drenching storm and so they remained through the long hours until daylight, soaked to the skin and miserable, but there was no remedy for it.

21—Close Enough for A Pirate

Morning. Still pouring. Philosophically, they knew that wet was wet whether moving or sitting, so they trudged off westward once more. Jack hoped this change of luck was only the weather; that, they could handle. But, as if a premonition, his concern was realized when they came upon an area of rugged terrain where some uplands drained to the sea, requiring a considerable detour and taking them back inland.

They slogged on, eventually finding a wagon road, muddy, but traversable. They had been on the move about two hours when the rain stopped, leaving the air thick and heavy, a condition they had hoped not to encounter again.

Morosely pushing onward and not being vigilant, they rounded a bend and nearly crashed into the back of a large farm wagon stopped in the road. Two black men were placing melons from the adjacent field into the already full bed, while a third was climbing onto the driver's seat to take the reins of the team. The shock momentarily paralyzed all five people. Jack was first to recover.

"Whoa, Mates." He put his hands in the air; Chloe did likewise. She wondered why he was speaking English to these men and if that meant she could, too. She'd wait, just to be sure.

The driver looked evenly at Jack. "Why 'Whoa', Mon? It be *you* wi' de weapons."

"My wife and I mean ye no harm. We be long afoot, having been run off our small holding near the Rio Minho."

"Your land be took?"

"Aye, and all our goods, save what ye now see."

The men had no difficulty believing this story from obviously down-and-out vagrants such as these.

"Where ye bound, Mon?"

"Montego Bay, my Good Man. My wife has kin there who will take us in for a while. Can ye tell us how far we've to go?"

"Two day, less, on your feet; one day on dis."

"Am I to take that as an offer to ride, then?"

"It be your choice, Mon. D' Bay be our destination, too."

Delighted at this turn of events, Jack gave his gracious bow of gratitude to the driver, boosted Chloe over the tailgate onto the melons and then joined the two pickers along the rails. The driver clucked to the mules and they moved forward, the feel of wheels rolling under them and locomotion achieved by other than their own muscles a delicious luxury.

The final leg of their journey was nearly completed. As the sun hovered red above the western horizon, they saw the buildings and ships of Montego Bay ahead in the distance. The driver stopped the mules at a fork in the road about half a mile from the town and told his passengers that the wagon would be going left and that the shortest distance to the main district would be the right, so Jack and Chloe disembarked, bowed and thanked their kind hosts and set out on foot for the final brief trek.

From the pickers they had learned the present calendar date and were finally able to deduce that they had been ten days in the Maroon village. That gave them an idea how much time they could spend in Montego Bay without Jack's risking not getting back to the *Sinecure* before she sailed. They had at least a week.

Shortly, they stood among the buildings at the outer perimeter of their destination. Jack felt that they should be happier, but neither looked particularly glad. Chloe had been mostly silent all day on the wagon, watching the scenery falling away behind them and thinking that it was somehow appropriate, as their adventure was ebbing away into history, too.

"We made it, Chloe, Ducks. We beat the odds."

"Now what?"

"We need to find a proper inn, we need baths, we need decent clothes, we need a parson; all these things are better found in the daylight. Would ye be up to one more night on the ground with Ol' Blackjack?"

"Of course. Of course."

In a secluded bend in the beach they made camp for the final time.

As he rolled off her, she informed him, in her most prim, clipped English, "Very well, Captain. That was the last until we are married."

"What? No wakeup romp on our last morning as wanderers?"

"Indeed not, Captain. I refuse to fornicate on my wedding day."

"I suppose ye think that'll qualify ye as a virgin in our bridal bed."

"Close enough for a pirate, Good Sir."

Thus, the final day closed with a laugh and a kiss.

22—One

Before they left the safety of their campsite, they took their daggers and released the forty-eight gold sovereigns from the straps of the packs, putting them into the pockets of their vests along with the assorted coins already there. Chloe donned the skirt that had served as their coverlet at night. It felt odd and cumbersome after the freedom of breeches. Another burden for a woman.

They abandoned the disreputable-looking blanket in the brush along the strand and Chloe hid her pistol and dagger in her pack that was no longer stuffed with her skirt. Among civilized people, it was more acceptable for Jack, being a man, to keep his weaponry displayed as before, of course. She felt a pang of resentment, then reminded herself that he didn't make society's rules; in fact, as a buccaneer, he would readily support her dressing any way she liked, draping herself with swords and arms and riding astraddle any damned time she wished.

As prepared as they could make themselves on the trail, they walked boldly into town, her hand on his arm as proper as royalty. But Montego Bay was a typical West Indies port town, so the odd and downright bizarre were commonplace. No one gave them a second look.

Breakfast. Tea and scones. Cow butter and honey. Leisure dining under a shade tree watching the ships going and coming. No Oriental potentate ever enjoyed greater luxury.

After their meal they shopped for Chloe's wedding dress. She wouldn't consider anything that wouldn't be perfectly acceptable on the street or in a shop. Being rather reclusive, she had no yen for affectation, preferring comfort and tasteful simplicity. He would agree to anything she chose; she was the bride.

Her selection was champagne-colored and sprinkled with tiny embroidered roses, with delicate white eyelet lace at the collar and cuffs and down the bodice. At the cobbler's they found proper shoes to replace Maria's grubby boots and at the milliner's she chose a lacy hat with a champagne silk ribbon.

Then she bought a satin sleeping gown and peignoir, pale cream with sky blue ribbons. She blushed as shyly as a young girl when the shopkeeper wrapped it for her as Jack looked on.

Next they bought new breeches and a shirt for Jack. He stubbornly held onto that sorry sash, though, refusing to so much as look at a new one. Said it had "character." She remarked that *he* was the character.

While at the tailor's, as Chloe was trying on dresses, Jack had inquired of the proprietor where they could find the nearest Anglican church and he learned that the vicar's name was Pelham. Carrying their bundles now that the clothing issue was settled, they followed the tailor's directions and came upon a fairly large stone parish house on a quiet street away from the center of town.

The doors were standing open, admitting the meager breeze, so they went in. Once their eyes had adjusted to the dim light, they saw a lovely chapel of some size, with polished woodwork and rich tapestries. It appeared to be a good source of loot, but he had forbidden his men to sack religious establishments, ostensibly out of respect for a higher power but, actually, because his spooky Gypsy upbringing made him afraid of incurring a jinx of some sort. Best to leave such matters be.

He didn't tell her that he had never legitimately been in a church before. At the orphanage, the requisite religious services were provided in the assembly hall so that the unpleasant-looking children would not upset local parishioners by attending their fine establishment. He hoped he wouldn't make some great *faux pas* and embarrass her, so, just as she had followed his lead on the trail when dealing with potential danger, he would follow hers here, if in doubt.

A voice came from the doors behind them.

"May I be of service?"

"Um, we, my fiancée and I, that is, we're looking for Reverend Pelham."

"You're looking at him. How may I help you?"

"We wish to be married, um, today. Here. If that's acceptable."

"What time today? Surely not this minute."

"No, we have business and we need to, um, get ready— for the wedding, that is. How about this evening around six?"

"That will be acceptable. I must conduct a brief interview first, so, we can do that now or you may wait until before the service."

Jack looked at her; she was clearly leaving it up to him.

He wanted that part over with. "Let's do it now, then."

So, the two followed Reverend Pelham into the vicar's office and sat nervously awaiting their interrogation.

"Groom. Name?"

"Jack Bellamie." Apprehensively, he watched for a flicker of recognition of that infamous name, but the vicar, looking bored, merely scratched away with his quill in a large book.

"Occupation?"

"Sailor. Sea captain." That was common enough in Montego Bay.

"Age?"

"Thirty-two."

"Place of birth?"

"Newcastle, England."

"Bride. Name?"

"Chloe Smyth Caruthers." She prayed he wouldn't recognize the name of the late lieutenant governor.

"Occupation?"

"Widow."

"Age?"

"Thirty-one."

"Place of birth?"

"London, England."

"Are either of you presently wed to any living person, anywhere?"

Two negatives.

"Is there one or more diagnosed cases of mental deficiency or insanity in the immediate family of either of you?"

Again, two negatives.

"Do you both enter into this union of your own free will and without duress or coercion from any person?"

Two affirmatives.

"Go tend to your business and be back here at six. Will you have witnesses?"

"No. Does that matter?" Jack didn't like the judiciary sound of this.

"Doesn't matter. My good wife and the church clerk will suffice."

"Oh, and um, Reverend? Can you direct us to a comfortable inn for tonight? Someplace safe and respectable."

"There's the Oak Tree just west of town; provides good food and other amenities, but it's rather dear."

"That's all right. We'll manage."

They made straight for the Oak Tree.

Jack requested their best room for a week, explaining that they would be wed that evening and that they wanted privacy. He asked if there were bath facilities and learned that, for a price, one could have a bath in a full-sized copper tub with servants assisting and all linens, lotions and soaps provided; he paid for two.

They went to their room. It was large and airy with double French doors to a balcony overlooking a distant vista of the sea. A basket of lavender on the dressing table lightly scented the air. The floor had a fine oval carpet and the walls sported gleaming sconces. The bed was truly opulent, high and soft, with many pillows and bolsters, topped with a ruffled canopy with sheer drapes furled on the posts. They looked at each other. They could read each other's minds: in a few hours...

Jack escorted his bride-to-be downstairs to the salon where her bath was waiting. He instructed the maids to do anything for her that she wished, as she would be his bride tonight. She blushed deeply, he glowed with pride, and the maids exchanged knowing glances. He kissed her cheek and said he had some things to do and to tell the menservants that he would be back for his own bath later.

It seemed a shame to pay for things that could so easily be filched. He wished he hadn't promised her that he wouldn't steal as long as they were together. What did she expect from a pirate? Well, he would keep his word to her, but it still seemed wasteful.

He went to the bazaar near the waterfront where ships from all over the world unloaded wares of every description for quick sale. He browsed slowly, making sure to miss nothing, weighing his choices. It was amusing to watch the proprietors watching him. He just didn't look honest. He discovered that it was a new and enjoyable experience to confound them by simply being innocent.

He bought a beautiful hand-carved teakwood box with a depiction of a hunter going over a hedgerow and then some very costly mint candies to fill it. He bought a small vial of scented oil from Arabia. He bought himself a new ring.

But he wanted something special for his wife, something she would always have with her, to remind her of her absent husband and their wedding day. After a thorough search, he found it.

Lastly he located a flower vendor with the best selection, conferred with the proprietor, made a note of the location and returned to the Oak Tree.

Chloe looked at herself in the large mirror in their room. Scrubbed to a shine, her scented skin fairly glowed, yet the ravages of their journey were still evident. The makeup the maids had applied helped some, but did not completely disguise the affects of sun and wind. Her fingernails, while clean now, were so short most were broken down to the quick. She feared it made her hands look stubby.

The dress was lovely on her, disguising her emaciation and accenting her remaining femininity. She moved, turning this way and that, hearing the soft rustle of the new fabric.

Her hair was not yet dry, but it smelled like the lavender on the dressing table and it was soft and shiny once more. She combed it again, feeling the comb slide without resistance through the silky strands. She tried the hat. Perfect! She approved of this attractive woman as a bride worthy of Captain Blackjack Bellamie.

Just then, there was a knock at the door. When she opened it, a servant bowed to her and said, "Madam, Captain Bellamie has arrived and is about to begin his bath. He requests his clothes."

"Oh. Of course. Here." She handed him the bundle.

She closed the door and sat down at the dressing table. She had nothing to do but wait and reflect. She replayed the whole story, from the moment Jack's dagger touched her throat to this, sitting in her wedding dress, about to become his wife. Everything that had transpired in her entire existence, taken as a whole, was but a grain of sand on the beach that had become her life in the space of one month.

Which day had been the greatest? The day she realized he would survive? The night she bathed him? The first kiss? The first time he made love to her (the day she bit him)? The night he proposed under the rock? Eden? Today? Impossible to choose.

And which would be the worst? It was coming up. Stop it! Don't think about it. He said not to think about it. Crying would spoil her face. Focus on tonight. *In this very bed, Jack will belong to you alone.* She felt as if she had never had him before, the excitement was so great. She was becoming flushed and her breath was getting short. *This won't do, Chloe Smyth Caruthers. Get a grip on yourself.*

She checked the time on the longcase clock beside the

door. Four o'clock. She stared at the weights and listened to confirm that the clock was still running. *Yes, it's four o'clock.*

Jack had it easy: his time had been filled throughout the day. *This is torture. Hurry, clock. Hurry, hurry! No. Don't wish it away. Every second ticks off one second closer to losing him.* Tears brimmed. *Stop it!*

The mental jousting was still plaguing her when there was another knock. Same servant.

"Madam, Captain Bellamie requests the pleasure of your company in the dining hall."

He rose from his chair when she swept regally into the room. His breath caught in his throat at the sight of her; she was radiant, more beautiful than anything he had ever seen, and all his. He had a memory flash of the two cherubs kissing him; he was beginning to understand their blessing.

She was no less smitten at the sight of her love, glorious in his fine clothes, as clean and well-favored as a gentleman, yet still the eccentric rogue, the braided, sloe-eyed pirate captain. She felt faint and might have swooned had he not taken her in his arms at that moment. He guided her into her chair, not across from his, but beside it where he could touch her.

A waiter set two glasses of wine before them.

They lifted their glasses and touched them together. Jack intoned the toast.

"To a blessed union and undying love."

After a memorable repast of roast duck, sautéed vegetables and fresh bread, Jack gave her the gifts he had purchased for her, all save one. She took them up to their room and, when she returned, it was time to walk to the church.

The evening air was sweeter as the sea breeze blew away the day's heat. As they passed a certain corner, Jack told her to stop. He walked over to the flower vendor he had conferred with earlier and bought a perfect bouquet for a bride in a champagne wedding dress with tiny embroidered roses.

He handed Chloe the bouquet with a deep, sweeping bow. People were watching the touching scene and smiling at the unmistakable tableau unfolding there on the street, but he didn't notice. He offered his arm to her and they marched off to their wedding.

On the steps of the church, he paused and turned to her.

"Chloe, I have something for ye, a memento of our wedding." He reached into his vest pocket and brought out a small purple velvet pouch.

She looked at him questioningly and opened the drawstring with trembling hands. Out slid a dainty silver chain. Strung onto it was a small silver anchor surrounded by a pilot wheel.

"Chloe, I'll be forever anchored to ye and, if I'm so blest, I will steer for home, to my *ves'tacha* (beloved) *Manishie* Chloe."

Reverend Pelham was accustomed to the occasional strange couple appearing for the marriage rite; this was another one. He and his wife exchanged a look.

The bride spoke and carried herself like an aristocrat, yet she looked as if she'd been laboring in the fields a long time. The groom was cleaned up and properly dressed now, but the reverend knew a pirate when he saw one.

Furthermore, he was used to weeping brides; more did than didn't, and this one was no exception. But a teary-eyed groom was rare, especially one who was clearly a pirate (captain, he claimed) and who stood through the proceedings with a silly lopsided grin showing a lot of white teeth while the tears ran unchecked down his cheeks.

Oh, yes, he and the missus would remember this wedding for quite a while.

The ceremony took only a few minutes, there being no pomp and circumstance to complicate it. The vows were read and said, as the two never took their eyes off each other.

"I now pronounce that you are man and wife before God. Let not man put asunder what God hath joined together. Captain Bellamie, you may kiss your bride."

She emerged from behind the screen, smiling shyly, and approached the bed, her peignoir flowing around her. He was speechless. This vision was real and she belonged to him. He had not stolen her nor paid for her nor bartered for her; she had given herself freely out of her incomprehensible love for him.

Their union had begun amid blood and injury, lawlessness and flight. It had been tested in pain, starvation, privation, fear, and exhaustion. Yet, it had prevailed, even thrived, and had now brought them to this joyous estate. Their marriage was consummated in comfort, safety and legality.

As he held his bride in his arms before falling asleep, he murmured, *"Corthu. Corthu."* (One being, joined.)

23—I Own A Harpsichord!

Maria carved the mark into the doorjamb: twenty-two days gone. Despite what Emerson said, this was too long. She was ever on edge during the day, listening for the sound of a carriage approaching the house. At night she stared into the darkness, listening to the whisperings of her soul: alive or dead? But she could sense nothing. She feared her intuition was overwhelmed by her relentless anxiety.

Two days prior, she had begun a Novena to Saint Christopher and she was still lighting the candles for their safe return.

Visitors to the Caruthers house were a rarity, yet, in the past three weeks, there had been four such callers for Emerson to manage, two social calls, one request for charitable contributions and a follow-up visit from Lieutenant Ambrose. With his usual aplomb, the butler had turned them away, twice telling them, "Madam is out," and twice, "Madam is presently indisposed." No one seemed to question his explanations and they left without delay, but it unnerved Maria.

When at the bazaar, the servants listened carefully to any local gossip, trying to discern whether suspicions had been raised about either of the fugitives. They heard nothing, the excitement of the Captain's earlier escape having grown stale without further news.

Just as he had promised, they had tea and scones in bed this first day as man and wife. For once, there was not one thing for which they had to rise and dress; every minute of every hour, their only duty was to revel in each other.

Finally, in the cool of early evening, the lovers emerged from their plush nest to stroll arm in arm along the streets of the town, enjoying the luxury of aimless wandering. Their cloud of bliss seemed impenetrable until Jack made a stupid mistake.

As they ambled along, making small talk, a tall, stunning redhead emerged from a doorway and glided past them in a cloud of French perfume. Instinctively, he swiveled his torso to gawk at her; too late, he realized his error. For a brief second, he dared hope that Chloe hadn't seen it, but when he turned back to her she was ghostly white. She turned on her heel and headed straight for the Oak Tree.

She would burn in hell before she let him see her cry, but she would see him do so before this was settled. Her pace was so fast she was practically running; he scampered after her, calling her name and apologizing profusely. She refused to acknowledge his presence.

In the hostel, she ran up the stairs to their room; he took them two at a time to beat her to the top. In the hall, she sped ahead and they arrived at their door at the same time. Only now did she speak.

"Please make other sleeping arrangements for yourself tonight, Captain."

"Chloe, please, it meant nothing, it was just a reflex. I don't want her, I want you."

She wouldn't waste any more breath on this scoundrel of a husband and she needed to get away from him to vent her rage and pain. She pushed past him, opened the door, slipped inside and shut it in his face.

"Chloe, open this door! I'm yer husband, dammit! Open! *Now*, Chloe!"

This time "now" didn't work; this time he had really botched things. To make matters worse, a dignified couple was passing by and gave him a disdainful look, wondering what crass thing he had done to be evicted from his marriage bed. He smiled lamely at them.

"Little game the wife and I like to play."

They turned up their noses and went on, buying none of it.

He pounded on the door. No response. He tried calm reason.

"Chloe, Darling, please let me in so we can talk about this like adults. Please. I can make it up to ye, just let me in."

The little click told him she had latched the door. Why hadn't he thought to simply open it himself before she did that?

"By the Powers, I'll break it down! Is that what ye want?"

Silence. He threw his weight against it once, to show her he meant business. Nothing. He really didn't want to break down the door and get them tossed out into the street.

"Very well, Mrs. Bellamie. If that's the way ye want it, I'll be taking my leave, wandering around Montego Bay, scorned and lonely."

Still no response. He stomped around, making ever-softer footfalls to make her think he was going. The door stayed shut.

Chloe listened to him clamoring to be let in and threw herself onto the bed, pulling the pillows over her head to shut out the sound of his voice and to muffle her own screams and sobs. Her poor mind kept replaying that horrible moment when her beloved had turned away from her to look at another woman. Everything was ruined, simply ruined!

Out of ideas, the penitent pirate sat down on the floor and leaned against the barrier that separated him from his wife.

Time dragged on for the estranged pair. Eventually light faded to dark and the inn became quiet. Jack lolled against the door, occasionally turning his head to place his ear against the wood; he heard nothing. He was certain she was crying, after all, she cried over little dead birds, but it bothered him that she was so quiet in the wake of something this awful. For once, he actually wanted her to cry. If she weren't crying, maybe she didn't love him anymore. He hated killing anything and now he'd killed her love for him, his greatest treasure.

It occurred to him that she might be amenable to a gift, but he had spent his own money on his wedding gifts to her and now had only her gold sovereigns. That would likely do more harm than good, buying a lady an apology gift with her own money. He could steal it; that was his own source of income. But no, breaking a promise to her at this time probably wasn't a good idea, either.

He was exhausted from the unresolved stress, and the ocean breeze sighing through the window at the end of the hall lulled him into a melancholy slumber.

The ringing of the bell was out of place in this paradise they had named Eden. Who was so rude as to ring a ship's bell and intrude upon the privacy of a happy couple? She looked at Jack, naked and splendid on the rock, poised to dive. Had he heard it?

Alas, he had. He relaxed his posture and turned, walking away from the rock, away from her. She ran to catch him, but he was moving up the gangway onto the ship, fully clothed now, walking toward that damnable bell. She called to him, but he didn't seem to hear, the bell drowning out her feeble voice.

She tried to scream but made no sound as the sails were unfurled and caught the wind, filling and billowing, to carry him away forever. She flung herself at the ship, trying to grab and hang onto it.

The spasm of flinging herself at the ship woke her, but the bell was still ringing, farther away now. Had it taken Jack?

Panting from the exertion of the nightmare, she sat up. The sound of the bell was coming from the harbor, drifting in on the wind through the open French doors.

The misery of what had happened flooded over her and, with the lingering anguish of the dream, she ached with emptiness.

The clock showed 3:30. Where could he have gone? He had admitted to her that he drank a great deal of rum when not with her; perhaps he had gone to a tavern and gotten drunk, maybe picked up a whore, maybe went in search of that redhead! What if he had found a ship bound for the Bahamas and was already gone? Or he could have been hurt in a fight, beaten and robbed. It wasn't out of the question that the authorities could have caught him. He might be dead!

She rushed to the door. She was going to go find him, no matter the danger to herself in this rough port city. She yanked open the door and tripped over him as he fell inside.

He shook his head trying to clear it and make sense of the situation. She was sprawled across him, moaning and rubbing her forehead where she had hit the doorjamb.

He recovered first and grabbed her before she could bolt. She gave no resistance though, merely wriggling to get her arms around him.

They crawled back into bed and snuggled together without a word having been spoken. There would be time to talk tomorrow.

He awoke slowly, realizing that it was morning, although the gray, stormy skies kept the room dim. Chloe still slept, so he quietly left to get food for them; this would be an excellent day to stay inside, to rest and to resolve yesterday's unpleasantness.

They had spent their second night of marriage fully clothed and, until nearly morning, apart. What a sad commentary on a union that had but one week to exist!

When he returned, she was still asleep. He undressed himself and began gently removing her clothing. This awakened her, somewhat, but she allowed him to finish and then turned over and went back to sleep. He curled around her and nodded off.

They eventually ate breakfast in late morning. She was quiet, but didn't seem angry any longer. After the meal, he tried to hold her but she gently resisted.

"Jack, let's talk about what happened yesterday."

He hated this sort of thing, feared it might get out of hand, but knew they had to get it behind them before they could resume their honeymoon.

The conversation was civil, adult and rational but, ultimately, it was the ancient impasse between the male and female psyches. Neither could fully grasp the other point of view but, out of respect for each other, they agreed to be more understanding. Then the compromise was sealed with lovemaking and all was well once more.

Later, when he told her that he would have bought her a gift but had only her money, she floored him with a revelation he had not once considered.

"Jack, you're my husband now. Everything that is mine is also yours."

He had to think about this. He had never owned anything but his few personal belongings, had always regarded the wealth of others as something to be taken and squandered. Never once had he thought about what it would be like to be on the other side.

"I own a mansion?"

"Yes, my Love. A mansion and an estate and a lot of money and jewels, horses, stables, furniture, artwork."

He was awestruck.

"A harpsichord. I own a harpsichord!"

She found this amusing. "That, too, my Darling. You own a harpsichord."

"And servants."

"And servants."

"I don't like that."

"Jack, they're servants, not slaves. They are free, but in my—our—employ. It is their occupation and they take pride in their work. Emerson is the fourth generation of his line to perform this vital service. I respect them and care for them like family and I feel certain that it is mutual."

He remembered his lengthy talk with Maria. It had been clear that every word Chloe had just said was true. Maria had even demonstrated a thinly-concealed suspicious attitude toward him until she was convinced he cared for the Señora and would not harm her.

Now, it was Chloe's turn.

"I own a ship."

"Not so, Ducks. Ye don't own a ship, because I don't own a ship. The *Sinecure* is mine only so long as the crew keeps me as their captain. To pirates, a ship is a tool of the trade. They can switch from one to another as easily as changing their hat."

"So, the ship isn't owned, it is merely used."

"Aye."

"But you love the *Sinecure*; you devoted yourself to getting her back from Korsakov."

"That I do and that I did. My love for her is that she was my early home as the *Archangel*, and my first and only command. I was driven to bring Korsakov to justice for the unholy thing he did to the *Sinecure* and me. Some pirates think I'm daft for loving a ship, but piracy attracts all kinds. That's the kind I am."

She suddenly saw him as vulnerable, even though a fierce pirate captain. His heart could be broken by that ship.

When she was so distraught over his having to leave her, he had tried to tell her how he felt at the helm of the *Sinecure*, but she didn't want to hear it. Now she did.

She watched and listened for over an hour as he waxed rhapsodic about his ship, regaling her with fascinating tales (some of which were surely embellished) of his many exciting exploits, dangers and triumphs. He would never have a more riveted or adoring audience.

What a brave, clever husband she had! She hung onto every word, trying to commit it all to memory for the time when he was no longer there to tell her. Where she had once regarded the *Sinecure* as a hated rival, she now loved the vessel because he did.

Jack loved to talk and Chloe loved to listen and this reciprocity drew them still closer. Neither would ever find another to fill this role so well. Their day involved short conversations and long stories interspersed with bouts of playful, ferocious and tender love.

They had been together only a month and yet had so many things to reminisce about. During talk of their Maroon captivity, Chloe asked him why their captors had refused to take their coins.

"What good is coin of the realm to a Maroon? The priestess kept one as a memento of our visit, no doubt to be displayed as a pretty bauble."

"Then why did we offer them?"

"Because the Maroons know that, in our world, those coins are vital. Our offer was a sacrifice, the ultimate gratitude."

"You knew she wouldn't take them."

"Aye. I knew she wouldn't take them."

"When she did that thing with her thumb as we were leaving, and the words she spoke to me the night before—what do you think that was?"

"I can't imagine, although I've thought about it ever since. I think she was speaking some form of the Mandingo tongue; if I come across any Mandingos, I intend to try to find out. This much I know: she liked ye, Chloe, saw ye as somehow special. I think it's one reason we were spared."

"How is it we were there ten days with no recall save the first and last?"

"That's difficult to say, but I think we were under the influence of some sort of alchemy. We might have been asleep or in a kind of trance or we might have been awake but were given something to expunge our memory. The Maroon tribes know a lot of what's called 'Black Magic,' but it's mostly the skilled use of herbs and concoctions."

"Jack, I had a strange dream while there, as if I were not in my body any longer."

"Chloe! Did ye see two angels?"

"Yes, I did. They kissed me and I was utterly happy."

"I had the same dream! Then I had to come back into my body and I didn't want to."

"The same with me. What was it, Jack?"

"I can't begin to say, but I have to believe someday we'll know."

Neither could explain how, but they knew this shared experience bound them in some powerful, mystical way.

24—The Birth of Blackjack

In the pensive silence that followed this startling conclusion to their conversation, each was aware that they had only a few more days to share such things and then all chances would be gone; anything not said must remain unsaid forever after.

Chloe felt she owed him an apology, although he would not agree.

"Jack?"

"Aye?"

"The day that I was so emotional, the day I made you bury the little bird... I'm sorry for what I put you through. You were a saint, so patient with me. Please accept my gratitude and my apology."

"Chloe, Lass. Ye owe me neither thanks nor apology. Ye couldn't help it. I was very worried about ye."

"I don't know what came over me, Jack, but it hurts me that I burdened you." Here she giggled. "You were so generous to promptly accommodate my excessive needs that day."

"Aye, and I still have the scars to show fer it."

That turn led to some playful wrestling, but it also caused her to open a subject he had resolved to let lie unless she brought it up.

"Jack. The whole problem began with our disagreement over what constitutes rape. You became quite upset over the subject. Why does it affect you so?"

He sighed.

"Because, Ducks, I know firsthand what it's like to be raped."

She could not speak. She knew he wasn't meaning the aggressive sex play she had used with him, knew it didn't involve a woman at all. It took her a few moments to realize exactly what he was saying; she never knew such things occurred, could occur. It got worse.

"I was but a child, Chloe, too small to know what was happening until it happened."

He moved closer to her in the bed, his head near her shoulder; he didn't want her to look at him as he was telling this, but he wanted her to comfort him. He had never told it to a soul and knew the words would come hard. She held him in her arms, protecting him.

He had been barely twelve years of age, still in his first year on the *Archangel* . The crew had put ashore in a tiny port, a pirate haunt in Haiti. Little Jack had been to such places before and enjoyed watching his shipmates drink, gamble, and carouse as they never could on board the ship. He usually stayed around them until they melted away with various whores, then he would either sleep near the dock until daybreak or return to the ship, if he found a boat going that way.

Sometimes the pirates tried to get him to drink or even go with one of the prostitutes (who always made a fuss over him and embarrassed him), but his first experience with rum had made him violently ill and he had no idea what to do with a woman. Happy just to be a pirate (now promoted from Cabin Boy to Powder Monkey), he was in no hurry to shed the remainder of his childhood.

Captain Korsakov and Swain, the quartermaster, protected their game little shipmate from overeager pirates who wished to relive their own puberty vicariously. Still small enough to pass for ten or even nine, Jack was, nevertheless, useful to the ship's operations without further pretense of adulthood.

On this fateful evening, the crew was still going strong in the tavern when Jack went outside to relieve himself. Before he could refasten his breeches, he was violently seized and dragged into a narrow passageway between two buildings. His abductor was a huge, red-haired man with bad teeth and a dirty, red beard and wearing a bicorne with a shrunken head attached. Jack was mortally afraid, thinking the man intended to kill him.

The poor child had no idea what hell actually lay in store for him.

The brute laughed at the boy's frantic struggles, Jack being no more effective than a kitten against the churlish pirate. He was slammed face down over a large crate and held easily with one hand while the man stripped off the unfastened breeches with the other.

He couldn't understand why the man was removing his pants to kill him, but something primordial told him this would be worse than anything he could possibly imagine.

A moment later he knew, as his innocence was shattered and his screams were swallowed up in the cacophony of the tavern.

He came to sometime before dawn, lying in his own vomit on the filthy stones of the passageway, bleeding and in awful pain. He was afraid to move for fear his tormentor was nearby and would rape him again, but when he found that he was alone, he reached and pulled up his breeches, lest his mates find him thus. He heard someone crying piteously and wondered who else had been hurt by that terrible man, then realized that it was he who was weeping.

He crawled over to a rain barrel and hid behind it. There he sniffled and quietly cried and wiped his nose on his sleeve and tried to make himself as small and invisible as possible. He wanted his mother more than he ever had in all his life, for no one on earth could help or comfort him.

Morning light found his shipmates wending their way back to the *Archangel* in various stages of hangover. They were weighing anchor when one pirate asked if anyone had seen Jack come aboard. At first no one was alarmed, but when it became apparent the boy was missing, Swain shouted "Drop anchor!" and the boat was lowered with several pirates to go back and look for him.

They searched and called and asked if he had been seen, all in vain, until one man heard a tiny, pitiful sound coming from behind the rain barrel. The jaded old pirates took one look at him, his breeches soaked with blood, his little face red and swollen from crying, and they knew what had happened. To a man, they had murder in their hearts and lusted to rip the guts out of the beast who had done this.

Upon questioning Jack, they knew from his description that the culprit was one "Red" Skinner, a coldhearted bastard from the *Vengeance Star*. They spread out to find him while Lars Johanssen, the *Archangel*'s cook and part-time surgeon, stayed with Jack, trying in vain to get close enough to the child to touch him.

Jack was like a wild, injured animal; he knew no friend. Johanssen was very disturbed by the mental state of their youngest crewmember and feared the boy would be permanently disordered by the experience. He kept speaking softly to Jack, trying to calm him, telling him everything would be all right, but the look of horror in the child's large, dark eyes did not abate.

Eventually, the rest of the pirates returned with the hapless Skinner in tow, prepared to "comfort" their ravaged little shipmate the only way they knew how: to administer justice before the victim's eyes.

The trial was swift and sure; Swain asked Jack if this were the man who hurt him, Jack nodded, and the sentence was carried out. The pirates tore into the monster with the fury of a tropical hurricane, punching and kicking and delivering every form of attack. When the man went down under the flurry of blows, they drove their boots into his crotch with all the hatred in their hearts. Each time he passed out, they threw water from the rain barrel on him to revive him for more of the same.

They beat him to death as Jack watched.

The pirates returned to the ship after spitting and urinating on the corpse, each in turn. Jack was swept along between Swain and Johanssen, twitching and squirming to avoid being touched. The moment he was aboard, his only thought was to flee the stares of the crew and be alone, so he bolted down the ladder into the hold and didn't stop until he was far behind the casks and crates, as hidden as he could possibly be.

The crew were busy getting the ship underway and were grateful to be occupied to keep their minds off Jack, but the usual mirth and optimism associated with making way were gone, the men performing their duties with grim efficiency and a minimum of chatter.

Each was hoping someone would go to the wee mite and bring him out of seclusion, get him back to normal, but none knew how. The consensus was that Johanssen would be the best suited, but he knew this was too big for any of them.

A night passed and Jack remained in the hold. The crew were getting worried. When Korsakov demanded that Johanssen do something before the pall over the crew began causing problems, Johanssen had only one suggestion. His older sister, Lizbet, was just two day's sail from their present location, on a small island where she lived alone in a cottage, having raised several children, including four of her own. She would know how to treat a physically and emotionally injured boy. Swain ordered their course set for that island at once.

No one had been able to lure Jack out of the dank hold of the *Archangel*, nor could he be induced to talk. Johanssen brought food and fresh water and left them within reach twice each day, but when he returned he found only the smallest amount gone; he just took away the old and left fresh, hoping Jack would develop an appetite.

The whole crew was relieved to have arrived at Johannsen's sister's island, as the presence of such a vexing and unsolvable problem in the hold was putting them all on edge. Furthermore, they needed to take some swag soon, but few felt up for a good fight with that kind of sadness aboard.

They dropped anchor and Swain and Johanssen went below to get Jack, not knowing how he would react to being physically removed from the ship. He still would not respond to verbal requests, so they took hold of his skinny little arms to drag him out. He didn't resist, but allowed them to move him along as he kept his head down, looking at no one.

Johanssen was telling him that his sister wanted a strong young man to help her with her farm for a couple weeks, that she needed Jack and would be very grateful for his assistance and then they would come back for him.

Jack said nothing. He didn't believe him, figured he was so ruined they were going to maroon him. He had vowed to himself that they would not see him cry and he was fighting hard to keep that vow, but his little heart was breaking to think that his mates would betray and abandon him just because that terrible thing had been done to him.

There were five of them in the ship's boat: Swain, Johanssen, Layton, Constant, and Jack. When they put ashore, he could see a cottage with a curl of smoke rising from the chimney. Dogs and guinea fowl in the fenced yard sent up a racket, bringing a woman out of the door carrying a broom and looking for the cause of the disturbance.

Johanssen and Constant leapt out of the boat first, Constant tying the craft to a piling as Johanssen ran up the path toward the woman, who appeared delighted to see him. Swain and Layton helped Jack out of the boat and proceeded slowly toward the cottage with him.

Johanssen seemed to be talking very fast to his sister, telling her why they were there, no doubt. But when the rest of them approached, Jack saw her peer past her brother to look directly at him, whereupon she slapped Johanssen hard on his upper arm, and Jack heard her say, "Lars! He's just a baby! What's d' matter wi' ye!"

He was mortified. Apparently Johannsen's sister considered him too puny to be of any help to her. He felt so worthless and was so embarrassed.

Johanssen rubbed his smarting arm and introduced Jack.

"This is Lizbet. She'll be good to ye as long as ye mind her. Be a good lad and we'll be back fer ye in a couple weeks."

Lizbet was already in charge. "Make it no sooner dan FOUR weeks, ye worthless bunch o' heathens." But she kissed her brother on the cheek and told him not to worry and please be careful.

Jack was terrified. He didn't know what to make of this tall female with the gray hair and strong hands. He didn't want to be on land with a perfect stranger; he wanted to be a pirate like he was before that demon turned his world to ashes.

As he stood watching his mates return to the boat and then wave back to him as they rowed away, he felt Lizbet's hand on his shoulder and was surprised to find that it was the first touch he had not resented since his mother's death two years before.

"Come along, Li'l Jack, let's get ye settled in. First, we have to clean ye up some. I wouldn't let ye sleep in d' sty d' way ye are."

He followed her obediently around to the back of the house where a broad veranda of brick and flagstone was roofed and deeply shaded with fragrant vines. A small table and three chairs stood to one side, a large rocking chair was in the center, and a rope hammock spanned the other end. A single step led into the back of the cottage and a narrow walkway wound from the edge of the veranda to a small building, perhaps a smokehouse, beside which was situated a bricked well with a sloped roof and a wooden crank.

Lizbet left him standing on the little walkway while she went into the smokehouse and emerged with a metal washtub, which she placed beside the rocking chair on the veranda. Jack saw all of this, but still managed to keep his head down and not speak.

She dropped the bucket into the well, drew it up full and poured the water into the tub, then repeated the action twice more, leaving the final bucketful sitting beside the tub. Next, she plucked a cake of soap from beside the door.

"Come, Li'l Jack, get out of dose filthy clothes and let's get ye in dere."

As terrible as his clothing was, blood dried on his breeches, dirt and vomit on his shirt, he didn't want to strip naked in front of a strange woman! Would these indignities never cease?

But she didn't wait for him to cooperate. She knelt beside him, unfastened his reeking shirt and removed it, then did the same with his pants. He was dangerously close to tears, finding himself helpless once more as a stranger took control of his body. To make matters worse this was outside, in full daylight, and his little penis, finding itself unencumbered, stood straight up.

He didn't think he could take any more humiliation and tried to twist his body to cover his shame. Lizbet saw this and spoke to him softly.

"Don't be embarrassed, Li'l Jack. Ol' Lizbet's raised many small boys, so ye don't have nothin' I've not seen before." She helped him into the water.

He started to sit in the tub, as would be normal, but it hurt him and he squirmed and wriggled to try to ease the pain. Lizbet knew immediately what was wrong.

"It hurts your little arse, don't it, Sweetheart? Here, just kneel in d' water. Dat's good."

Now he knew that Johanssen had told her what had happened. His emotions were ready to boil over, embarrassment, sadness, shame—and gratitude for her kindness. Tears were forcing their way out despite his firmest resolve.

She was washing his grimy, matted hair, scrubbing his scalp and his neck and it felt good, as if he were shedding something incriminating. She began washing his face. Now, with her being on his level, he finally looked at her. He saw eyes as softly gray as the smoke from her chimney, eyes that looked into his own with infinite compassion and understanding. It nearly undid him and he started to cry.

"It's all right, Li'l Jack. Ye just cry if ye need to. Ol' Lizbet won't tell yer mates. It's all right."

Still, he tried hard to maintain control, but his orphan's heart wanted to unleash the torrent of tears he'd been holding for too long.

When she stood him up to wash him "down there," he was flinching and gasping with pain and fear of pain. But she could not have been more gentle, talking to him, being so very careful with him, and soon enough the ordeal was over and she was pouring clean rinse water over him.

She wrapped him in a soft old linen sheet to dry him and also because he had no clean clothes to wear. He didn't know what to expect next, but what she did was exactly what the poor child needed. She picked him up, still swaddled in the sheet, and carried him to the rocking chair, sat down with him in her lap and cradled him in her arms. Then she just rocked him, gently patting his back and humming a lullaby. He had no more need to be strong.

He sobbed onto her breast, shaking, and clutching her blouse in his tiny fist. She let him cry himself out, cuddling him protectively, making it all right.

He spoke the first words since the morning after he was raped.

"Mama! Mama!"

"It's all right, Li'l Jack. Mama's here."

The first few weeks, he was privileged to be a small child again. Lizbet was with him every moment, nurturing him, gaining his trust, letting him sleep in her bed at night so he would feel safe. Although each day she had to do hurtful and embarrassing things to heal him, he came to rely on her gentleness and eventually dropped his guard completely.

He had never had an adult welcome him entirely into her world and expect nothing from him. She took him with her to do the chores around the little farm, telling him why each thing was important, sharing funny stories about her children or some of the livestock, letting him do some easy tasks and praising him mightily for his skill.

She took him to the two little graves on the hill behind the barn where her children who had died of the fever were buried. Every day she and Jack picked wildflowers and decorated the graves. Lizbet never cried or showed any weakness, but told him special things about the two and how grateful she was that four had survived.

In the evenings, she would sit in the rocker and sew, making new clothes for Jack while he played and splashed in the old washtub, staging mock sea battles with bits of kindling. Lizbet always acted as if he were the cleverest child she ever knew to do such things.

Soon, he had proper boy's clothes to wear instead of her old smocks, although those still made good nightshirts. His injury was mostly just a bad memory and he was a carefree little boy once more—that is, until the incident with the pigs.

Lizbet was drawing water for the animals when she heard a terrible racket and Jack came barreling around the corner of the smokehouse, crying and incoherent. She caught him as he leapt up into her arms, nearly wild, and carried him to the rocker and tried to soothe him, but he was some time calming down enough to tell her what had happened.

Reading between the lines of his story, she concluded that he had seen the boar mounting the sow and thought he was witnessing a repeat of his own attack. The porcine squealing and shrieking had confirmed his conviction that it was an act of violence.

Work came to a halt that afternoon as Lizbet was charged with explaining the facts of life to a motherless child who had experienced way too much of life already. Besides the basics, she had to help him understand the differences between what had happened to him and what was normal, natural reproduction.

Her heart ached to think what a heavy burden that little mind had to accept. Overwhelmed, he finally just hid his face between her arm and her side and stayed very quiet.

Eventually, much subdued, he was ready to resume helping her. She watched closely, but couldn't tell whether he was going to be all right until they were at the sty and he asked her if he'd get to see the babies before he left. After that, his mood lightened and, by evening, he was sailing his little ships on his washtub sea once more.

This wise surrogate mother knew that Jack needed the company of other children but, since there were none available, she took time to play games with him, guessing games and word games while they were working, hide-and-seek when they weren't. They never ran out of things to talk about and even had some "in" jokes that would be funny only to them.

They shared secrets like great pals. She told him she had accidentally broken Lars' favorite fishing rod when they were young, then threw it into the sea and convinced him a strange child had stolen it. Lars went raging and stomping around for three days, looking for the child that met her description. She never told him the truth and he still believed it. Little Jack vowed to keep her confidence and felt wonderfully smug to be privy to such important information.

In turn, he told her about his being a Gypsy. She was genuinely fascinated, asked him many things about the Roma life, and told him she thought Gypsies made wonderful, colorful pirates. He glowed to hear that.

Each day they went to the dock where they caught fish for the pan or played on the beach, building castles and ships and drawing in the sand. She taught him his letters and numbers that way and he thought it was just another game.

He had not been so healthy and happy since he was with his family and, even though he must have been a lot of work for Lizbet, she was in her glory having a child again. She told him he didn't have to go back to the *Archangel* if he didn't want to, that his home was with her if he chose. He gave that some thought; it was tempting to remain in this Elysian place, but he was bound to be a pirate, a *Gypsy* pirate, he winked.

She sagely accepted his decision and spent more time helping him to get back his macho self-confidence, so vital in a new pirate.

When his mates returned for him, Lizbet sent him into the house to get ready as she had instructed. While he was gone, she said a great deal to Lars in Norwegian, no doubt filling him in on Little Jack's progress and, from the sound of it, laying down the law about watching out for him in future.

When Jack emerged from the house, his mates were amazed. Before them stood a splendid young pirate, his shoulder-length black hair in braids, a yellow bandanna around his head, a gold (actually brass) hoop in one ear, and on his finger a ring of smoothed bamboo. He was wearing a voluminous white shirt, new breeches and a fine vest with pockets for important pirate-y things. A great green sash was tied around his tiny waist and held with an oversized belt (an old saddle cinch, cut down), and his right hand sported a muslin fencing glove.

She gave the pirates orders to get "Blackjack" some proper boots and a hat, then she handed him a bundle containing his belongings, including two additional outfits and a small parcel of ginger biscuits.

Lizbet's last act of generosity was to shake his hand solemnly and not call him "Little" Jack in front of his mates. With thanks and farewells all around, the pirates strode off toward the boat.

Jack's last act of childhood was to turn and run back to Lizbet for a final kiss. Then he caught up with the other pirates and climbed into the boat to go to his life as a buccaneer, waving farewell to his "Mama."

None of the crew ever mentioned what had happened to him that night, in Haiti, and none now remained who ever knew about it. He went back to being the "best powder monkey ever" and enjoyed his new (secretly Gypsy) pirate persona immensely.

Lars Johanssen was washed overboard in a terrible storm two years later. A year after that, Jack killed for the first time. During a raid, he came upon one of the crew raping a woman in a shed. Jack ran the man through with his sword, nearly skewering the poor woman in the process. Had proof existed to convict him he would have been executed, as one simply does not slay one's crewmates. But nothing was found to tie him to the death and the matter was forgotten—by all but Jack, who remembered, not with remorse, but with satisfaction.

Years later, when he had returned with the *Archangel* to the Caribbean as her new captain, he sailed back to Lizbet's island and went alone up to the little farm. The cottage had fallen in and vines and scrub had overgrown the veranda and pens. He walked up the hill and used his sword to slash away the weeds from around the little graves and found only two crosses still; wherever she was, she was not buried with her children.

He picked two bunches of wildflowers, placed them on the graves and returned to his ship.

25—One, Breached

The top of his head was wet where Chloe's tears had flowed during the affecting story. His voice had remained soft but steady, as he had come to terms with the intense emotions of the experience years ago, but he could feel her heart beating fast and hard and knew that she was stricken to hear it. He would not have told her had the ending not been so positive and had it not been such a key to understanding the Jack she now held in her arms. He wanted her to truly know him; no one else did or would.

Of all living, she alone knew about his Roma heritage and now she alone knew how he had come to be the unique Blackjack Bellamie. By placing his true self in her heart and mind, he would feel less like a brief spark snuffed out when his life ended in a noose or in the arms of his mistress, the sea. Chloe's love for him gave him a kind of immortality and he wanted to be certain she loved the real Jack and not merely his carefully crafted image.

When the narrative had ended both remained as they were, for any movement or words would have broken the poignant spell.

He felt pleasantly empty, as after stowing bounty safely in a hidden place and preparing to sail his lightened ship before the wind once more. She was awash with the multitudinous hues of a woman's love for her man, including fervent maternal tenderness. She would never meet the intrepid Lizbet, but she loved her dearly for salvaging this treasure and preserving him for her.

Their time together was growing short. Soon, Chloe would be bound for home so that Jack could be assured of returning to the *Sinecure* before it was too late. His crew would keep to the

Code and depart with him or without him. But naturally, he would not leave Montego Bay until he had seen his wife safely aboard the ship that would carry her back to Port Royal.

The past few days had been spent quietly communing, verbally and otherwise, sealing and affirming their unity. By their fifth day as husband and wife, they barely spoke above a whisper as the enormity of what was upon them pervaded their waking hours, for as tragic as it is to lose a lover, they were each losing their best friend as well.

At last it was time to go to the harbor and determine what vessels would be sailing for Port Royal within the next few days. Jack took charge as the protective husband, wanting to assure his spouse's safety and comfort. As Chloe looked on, he conferred with the harbormaster and learned that the *Cagway* was a sound ship with a respected captain and would likely make port the next day to sail with the evening tide on the following as her regular run between the two cities.

So now they knew the name of the ship that would separate them. "Cagway" could have been the title of a vengeful god for the dreadful awe the name engendered in the two.

They enjoyed few laughs those final days, but some mirth slipped through despite the depressing atmosphere. At one point, as they were discussing how they would cope with the absence of each other, Chloe touched her precious necklace Jack had given her at their wedding, saying, "Every day I'll remember the words you spoke as you gave me this and pray that the wheel may turn back to me. I only wish I had something so meaningful to give you for remembrance."

Without missing a beat, Jack raised his left arm, sliding back his shirtsleeve to show the scar like a double horseshoe where she had bitten him.

"By the Powers, Ducks, ye've done so with a gift I'll ever possess."

"Jack!"

"Yer yellin' again, Darling."

It was a relief to share a genuine laugh, but it was short-lived and sadness flowed back into the silence that followed.

The next day they walked to the harbor and saw the *Cagway*, a well-appointed brigantine, being unloaded of passengers and cargo from the southern coast. They stood in silence and watched; their final night as one was now imminent.

Neither had much appetite for their evening meal despite their having sprung for the best of everything in hopes of lifting their spirits. Nothing would comfort them, not even the most delectable dishes. They picked at their servings and drank a lot of wine and retired to their room.

As they lay in each other's arms, Chloe asked, "When did you first know that you loved me?"

He took his time answering, as he wanted to be truthful.

"The night ye bathed me, Chloe, I didn't sleep at all. Yer revelation about—yerself—was so unexpected I couldn't stop thinking about it and I debated with meself whether I wanted to continue courting ye, as I knew we would fall in love and I wasn't sure I wanted that responsibility. By morning, I had decided to proceed with ye, but I hadn't yet felt what I now know as love, had no idea how it really feels. Then ye played music for me and the deep affection that had been in my heart made itself known. I was already in love with ye when I kissed ye."

He then posed the same question.

"I've asked myself that a hundred times and I must admit that I was never *not* in love with you from the moment you came to me. I also didn't yet know that it was love but, in retrospect, I can tell you the very moment it began. When you fainted on my carpet while trying to threaten me I was so fascinated by you I took advantage of your insensibility to look closely at you. While I was doing so, you shed a single tear and my heart broke. That was when I fell in love."

"But, when did ye know?"

"The day you made love to me for the first time, when I had turned from you and was sitting by the upstairs window. It hit me like a lightning strike as you knelt beside me, trying to talk sense into me. At that moment, I realized that it had been there all along."

These were important revelations to take away with them.

They began playing "what if," enjoying speculation about their life together. Chloe vowed she would bear him many children and that they'd all look like him and so would their grandchildren. He insisted on half of them looking like their mother. Furthermore, he would buy her the best hunter-jumper in the New World and she could ride astraddle over jumps every day, except when she was too pregnant to get into the saddle. The mental picture made them laugh and then they cried, grieving for their children and grandchildren and being together through the years.

They tried to stay awake all night to wring every moment from the few remaining hours, but around 2:00 they fell into an exhausted sleep and later awoke to a bright Caribbean morning. The day lay ahead of them, as the evening tide would be around 7:00, but they had no desire to leave the quietude of their room.

By now, almost everything had been said and words had become superfluous. Throughout the day, they rested in each other's arms and looked into each other's eyes and each read volumes there. The tragedy that was upon them negated any erotic feelings until about an hour before time to depart for the harbor. As sad as that last intimacy in Chloe's great feather bed had been, they would have rejoiced exceedingly to have that opportunity once more and be anticipating several weeks together.

Afterward, they dressed in silence, gathered their belongings and quit their bridal chamber. No condemned ever walked to the gallows with more lugubrious step than did they along that last avenue to the harbor.

Jack approached the captain of the *Cagway* and explained that his bride would be a passenger to Port Royal and that her welfare was of paramount importance. The captain assured him that the crew were more than able to provide her with a safe and pleasant passage. Jack paid the fare and stood holding her hand, unwilling to release her until the final moment.

The last of the outbound cargo was aboard and the crew were preparing to make way. The newlyweds stood near the gangway wrapped in a tight embrace. There were no tears, no words, for no outward manifestation of grief could adequately express what they were enduring. They simply clung to each other.

As the last call to board went out, Chloe whispered, as she had vowed she would, "Goodbye, Jack. Goodbye, my beloved husband."

She turned from him and walked up the gangway. He couldn't swallow. At the rail, she stood watching him, her face impassive except for the horrific anguish in her eyes; his countenance was the same. The crowds swirled around them and no one noticed the heartrending drama taking place on the dock.

Lines were thrown off and the wind caught the sails as the anchor chain rattled the severing of Chloe's connection to Montego Bay. The vessel glided silently from the harbor while the lovers watched each other grow smaller. Neither moved, frozen in a kind of shock, staring, not even daring to blink, lest a fraction of a second of this final sight be lost.

The ship hove to starboard, making her way into open water, abruptly bringing the aft castle between the two and occluding their view of each other. Chloe collapsed to the deck.

His heart lurched as the turn of the ship took his love from his sight, but he continued to stare through a blur as the creamy sails grew ever smaller. Then he turned away, unable to watch the ship disappear.

After a time, he turned back to an empty horizon and felt as though his chest were laid open to an icy wind.

PART
TWO

26—No More Scones

Yellow sunshine streamed into the kitchen, but it held no cheer for Maria. The Señora's words to her that terrible day rang in her head: I'll be back within the month. That was no longer possible. She carved the thirty-second mark into the doorjamb, not even trying to stem the tide of tears. Her novena was completed, the month was completed, the time of hope was completed. Tonight she would light candles and pray for their immortal souls.

Rodrigo had given up trying to appear optimistic around her. Emerson staunchly maintained that a safe return was still possible, but now did so only in response to her despairing remarks. He no longer volunteered encouragement. In his heart, he, too, was concerned that Chloe had not yet returned and the quiet hours of darkness found him formulating plans to deal with the servants' situation without her. He would take charge, of course, but there were no easy answers.

Rodrigo saw it before they heard it and he ran into the house, wide-eyed.

"Maria! Emerson! Carriage!"

Maria heard the shouting and hurried downstairs; Emerson came from the parlor.

"What is this, Rodrigo? Why the shouting?"

Just then, he heard it himself. Adjusting his attire, he strode to the door as the other two watched discreetly from a window, hope and fear gripping their hearts.

The carriage halted under the portico; the footman placed the step and opened the door. A flounce of champagne-colored skirt appeared, then a daintily shod foot, and Chloe stepped out into the brilliant sun. Mayhem erupted behind Emerson.

"Welcome home, Madam. How very good to see you." The butler bowed and took her valise. From his demeanor, one would have thought that she had been away for only a few nights.

Once inside, however, she saw her staff struggling to maintain propriety in the face of almost unbearable joy. Maria clearly wanted to embrace her mistress and, frankly, Chloe wanted that, too. She reached out her arms to her devoted maid.

She had no taste for formality now; she went into the kitchen as they all followed, all talking to her at once, asking questions. She sat down at the big table where meals were prepared and the staff ate, the table where she and Jack had received their packs and instructions more than a month before.

"Please, sit. Sit." They obeyed and waited eagerly for her to speak.

"To answer your questions, yes, I am well and yes, the Captain is well, also. I assume he had no difficulty boarding a ship for the Bahamas, but he saw to it that I was safely bound for home before securing his own passage. I pray he has no difficulty, as his journey will necessarily be longer than was my own." Her voice was unusually soft, even for her.

She paused and swallowed. "Captain Bellamie and I give each of you our most heartfelt gratitude, as we would have surely died on this venture had it not been for your extraordinary preparations. We literally owe you our lives."

She paused again. The servants were silent now, studying her and seeing that she was not as they remembered her. The lovely dress, so pristine and new (this being only the second time it had been worn) contrasted sharply with her physical appearance. She looked as though she had had a difficult journey, naturally, but rest and comfort would remedy that. No, it was her face, her eyes, which betrayed a tragic void that seemed to go to her very soul.

She gazed into the distance for several minutes and then said, more softly still, "Captain Bellamie and I were married October the second."

The ecstasy at the erstwhile Caruthers household was short-lived. After Chloe's revelation that she and Jack were wed, she said she didn't wish to talk anymore, that she just wanted to sleep.

Maria had helped her upstairs and watched with a breaking heart as she walked to the balcony and remained looking down at it for a long time, then slowly turned back to the room and stood passively while Maria removed the champagne dress with the tiny roses. She wanted it hung up in plain view of her bed. That was unusual for the ever-tidy Señora.

She refused offers of food, of tea, of a bath, of wine or brandy. She was far, far beyond solace in any form.

She climbed into the great feather bed and turned face down, inhaling the scent of her husband from the sheets and pillows. When Maria asked if there were anything she could bring her, Chloe did not respond.

Throughout the day and evening, she remained in her bed, saying nothing, not even crying. When Maria approached, Chloe merely waved her away.

She eventually turned onto her back and stared dry-eyed at the ceiling, her hand on the necklace she had been wearing when she arrived. Maria concluded that it was a gift from the Captain, but dared not ask.

That night, Emerson and Rodrigo slept better than they had in recent memory, the specter of the loss of their mistress now past. But they didn't see what Maria was seeing.

All night, the faithful servant slept little and then only lightly, keeping vigil at Señora Bellamie's door. She would have welcomed the sound of weeping, as that would help cleanse and heal the poor bride's shattered heart, but the eerie silence continued.

Maria returned to the kitchen carrying the tray she had taken upstairs not ten minutes earlier. Emerson and Rodrigo looked up from their breakfasts, aware that something was amiss. She placed the tray on the table in front of them and turned back the towel. The food was untouched.

"The Señora would not eat. She said to never bring her scones ever again."

All three were familiar with Chloe's fondness for scones and tea in the morning. Now they knew that something was very wrong with their mistress and that their troubles were far from ended just because she had returned.

27—Hobson's Choice

Wouldn't that be ironic? Chloe's first husband had died in a storm off the coast of Cuba and now her second husband was in grave danger of meeting the same end. In the darkness and chaos he clung to a rope and prayed the chock would hold on the windlass around which it was turned. The order to take in sail had come too late as the squall swept down on the barque, seemingly from nowhere, and now they were being blown off course. Jack knew these waters well, knew that the ship was perilously close to shoals, but the storm was in control of their fate.

A wave broke over the deck before he could prepare himself and he strangled on the smothering brine. When his head was out of the water once more, he gasped and spat, trying to quell the reflex before he was submerged again, but before he could recover, the ship lurched and rolled to larboard, slamming him against the deck.

He was fighting to get away from the rigging before she went down when he realized they weren't sinking. They had run aground. He crawled upward in the dark over lines and yards until he was clinging to the upper portion of the steeply canted mainmast above all but the worst of the swells.

Over the howling of the tempest, he heard shouts from other survivors below and in the tangle of rope and sail. He didn't have to tell the sailors to get as far upward as possible, but he kept shouting, "Here! Up here!" as one after another followed his voice to the relative safety of the masts. In the darkness he grappled for those who were growing too weak from their desperate struggle. With a rope wound around his left hand to secure himself, he leaned down again and again, hauling up a shipmate by the hand, the shirt, even a mass of long hair, until there were no more to help.

The storm was abating, but morning light was still a long time away.

Jack was never one to envy the dead. He could not imagine any physical or mental distress great enough to make him regret drawing breath, but the next two days would bring him as close to that inclination as he would ever care to come.

The early hours of daylight after the storm naturally brought a mix of joy and sadness to the twenty-plus mariners clinging to the mangled rigging. Relief at having been spared was tempered by the loss of their ship and their crewmates and by the terrifying helplessness of the stranded.

The ship lay on her side, shallowly submerged and visible through the clear water. Wreckage drifted around them along with the macabre spectacle of the dead bobbing near the surface. However, they didn't have to endure the sight of the bodies for long, as the calm sea suddenly appeared to grow blades, the gray dorsal fins racing in and out, churning the water and staining it crimson. The air was filled with the sounds of the thrashing of sharks and the crunching of bone.

One sailor, overcome by the display, fainted and fell from his perch on a yard into the sea below and was quickly devoured. Those who had not already secured themselves to their place of safety were suddenly moved to lash themselves onto the rigging by any means available. The night before, after helping the others, Jack had tied himself to the mast with a piece of sail and prayed the wreck would not slip off its precarious footing and haul him under with it.

Eventually, their provender consumed, the sharks vanished below the mocking calm of the Caribbean. Nothing of the hapless vessel showed above the surface but the masts with yards and spars, some lines and ruined sails and the "lucky" few who had survived.

All was quiet except for the occasional *basso profundo* groan of the ship settling onto the shoal that had destroyed her. The tropical sun traced its agonizingly slow course across the firmament, roasting the men from above and below as the water reflected its rays with little diminution. Those who could reach bits of sail tried to shield themselves from the merciless incandescence; those less fortunate felt their flesh being seared and blistered.

Jack had pulled the back of his shirt collar over his head and lay on the mast with his face turned to the west during the morning and to the east after noon. He tried to keep his hands in his shadow and was grateful that his boots and breeches covered his legs, as any exposed flesh would be cooked. Nevertheless, the heat penetrated all clothing and coverings and was exquisitely painful.

Most of the men, Jack included, had swallowed seawater while struggling to survive the storm and now their thirst was becoming maddening. Neither a morsel of food nor a drop of fresh water was to be had. Everything remained in the hold of the ship, so talk inevitably came around to someone diving into the wreck and retrieving precious supplies. The conversation itself gave comfort, allowing the helpless men to feel as if they had some control over their situation, but no one wanted to join their comrades in the bellies of sharks to perform a fool's errand.

The sailors grew quiet as the realization sank in that they had no options. The silence continued through the remainder of the daybreak and into the blessed relief of evening.

Jack dozed as the scorching heat of the sun dissipated. However, his muscles were cramping with the need to stretch and move, and the thirst was making each breath painful. He tried to tense and relax his back, his legs and arms, his belly, but to little avail.

While still on their trek, he had recognized that he was more fortunate than Chloe in that he would be busy nearly every waking hour, keeping him from dwelling on their separation and grieving. She, on the other hand, had nothing but a terrible leisure, which he didn't covet. He hoped that her prayer for strength that day in the forest would be answered.

Now, he, too, had nothing to do but think. His initial musings were that he had been a fool to remain three more days in Montego

Bay after Chloe left. He hadn't intended to linger, but he had been away from rum for so long and he was so miserable without his wife that he had made no effort to avoid lying dead drunk in the streets until a brief rainstorm had sobered him sufficiently to regain some self-control.

Thus he found himself on this ill-fated barque headed for the Bahamas with time running out to return to the *Sinecure*. If he were to die here, Chloe would never know what had happened to him for, even if others survived to tell the tale, he was known to them as Jack da Silva.

Surely he would live through this, after all, he was actually Captain Blackjack Bellamie. He had come through worse than this. But he wasn't immortal; one day his luck would fail and he would be gone. *Not yet, not this time. Please!*

The sun rose in a cloudless sky and another day of torture began for the men in the rigging. One appeared to have died overnight, his lifeless body dangling above the sea by the rope he had tied to a spar. *Must've been injured in the storm; too soon to die of this quite yet.* Jack tried not to look at him.

As the day dragged on, he would hear a sailor cursing or another weeping, a third praying, all punctuated with silence. One man became hysterical, screaming that they were going to die, that he was going to drink seawater and get it over with. Some of his mates nearby tried to reason with him and apparently succeeded in hushing him, at least.

Jack was in misery. Every inch of him raged with pain and dehydration; he knew he would be sweating from the agony if only he had sufficient fluid in his body to produce it. By evening he was thinking that perhaps the ones who died in the storm were the lucky ones. Even the one eaten alive by the sharks was no longer suffering.

He mentally slapped himself. *Bellamie, ye hypocrite! Ye told Chloe that as long as ye can take one more breath, there is hope, and now yer envyin' the dead.* He deliberately filled his lungs and exhaled slowly, savoring the blessing of breathing.

Dawn of the third day. Two more deaths overnight, two more gruesome reminders of their own fate hanging in the rigging. No one spoke; other than the occasional soft moan, it was as quiet as if they had all died.

Jack drifted in and out of consciousness. While awake, he longed for Chloe, thinking how she would care for him in his present state, give him sweet cool water, bathe his baking skin, devote every moment to comforting him. In his fevered dreams, he was on the *Sinecure*, but her deck kept dissolving beneath his feet, forcing him to leap from board to board to avoid falling into an abyss.

He jerked awake, panting, both legs in cramps from jumping in his dream. Then, calming somewhat, he thought about the two angels who had kissed him while he was out of his body in the Maroon village. Where were they now? Waiting to take him away for good? He could no longer remember the euphoria of their kisses. He slid out of the real world again.

They were back in the hut in the village. The Maroon priestess cupped Chloe's chin and spoke to her, first in the Mandingo tongue, then in English, translating: Love your husband, *Manishie* Viollca, for tonight—

A shout slammed through his brain, obliterating the dream. Now fully awake, he heard it again.

"Sail, ho!"

Everyone was twisting to follow the pointing finger of the shouter. Blinded by the sun, Jack shielded his eyes, but couldn't yet discern anything. He was about to conclude that the man was hallucinating when he saw it in the distance to the northwest.

Then he thought that he himself was seeing things, for a second ship was sailing behind the first and rapidly catching up. He couldn't make out flags or markings, but he knew from a lifetime of experience that they were about to witness pirates taking prey. He kept his mouth shut, his heart nearly bursting with excitement.

The two ships drew nearer to the wreck, the corsair closing

rapidly on the East Indiaman as it dawned on the sailors around Jack what was happening before their eyes. They began to scream and curse the pirates, wasting still more precious energy cheering for the victims. Jack kept his silence. He needed to know the identity of the predator before he could ascertain whether he and his fellow survivors were in danger. Some pirates were worse than Satan himself; others would be a welcome sight indeed.

He was desperate to identify that ship. He heard the cry, "There it is! There's the black flag!" and he felt a little better; at least the buccaneers weren't running up the red one. No Quarter Given would be the worst sign imaginable right now.

Squinting didn't help; he could see that the flag was black, but he couldn't make out the markings. *Don't let it be Low! Please, not Low!* He found a tiny hole in the trailing end of the piece of sail that was holding him onto the mast; he tugged it around until he could hold it in front of his face and peer through it.

On the black field, he could make out a skeletal devil stabbing a heart. *Teach*! It was Edward Teach and the *Queen Anne's Revenge*. Thank God and all the angels it wasn't that sadist, Low! They could still come out of this alive and free if they would listen to him and follow his orders, to a man.

Just then he saw a flash of light from the *QAR* and moments later heard the boom of cannon fire. The men around him roared encouragement to the East Indiaman, urging her to blow the filthy pirates out of the water.

He didn't take offence (no one was supposed to love pirates, anyway), and he knew better than to try to reason with them yet. They wouldn't listen to him and furthermore, the sounds of the battle were coming nonstop now.

He wished he could see more details of the confrontation. It appeared the East Indiaman was putting up a good fight, clearly trying to sink the *QAR*, while the *QAR* was trying to defeat the East Indiaman without sinking her. This was the unfair advantage that prey held over pirates: sinking the plunderee was self-defeating to the plunderer. *No one ever said making a living would be easy.*

At last the two ships were alongside each other and he knew that the East Indiaman was being boarded. Now the hand-to-hand fighting would begin. He longed to be there, his right arm ached to wield a sword once more. He didn't realize that his teeth were bared and his eyes were round with exhilaration, just watching and imagining. The pain of thirst and hunger was forgotten as he fought vicariously alongside his brethren.

The sounds of combat, the shouts and clanks and pops drifted across the water to the captive audience. After an hour or less, the colors were struck on the East Indiaman and the huzzahs of the pirates rang over the ocean. Jack's shipmates groaned and cursed. Some vented their rage and frustration by waxing eloquent describing unique and sadistic tortures for the pirates. He allowed them to vent their spleen and didn't speak until they were silent once more.

"Gentlemen, has it not occurred to ye that there are now two perfectly sound ships within signaling distance, either one of which represents rescue to the likes of us?"

"Aye. But what's to be gained, as they're both in the hands of murderous pirates?"

"In the first place, not all pirates would be interested in slaying a score of down-on-their-luck, but nevertheless experienced, sailors such as ourselves. In the second place, that ship is the *Queen Anne's Revenge*, captained by none other than Edward Teach, himself."

"Teach!"

"Blackbeard!"

"God have mercy, we're doomed."

"Listen to me! We need not be numbered among said captain's victims, but ye must follow what I tell ye to the letter. Do ye understand?"

"Why should we listen to you, da Silva? How is it ye know so much about pirates?"

"Because my name is not Jack da Silva. My name is Jack Bellamie, Captain Blackjack Bellamie. Ring a bell?"

The men were all talking at once, expressing amazement, recalling tales, both true and fabled, of the exploits of the man before them. Jack grinned, his teeth flashing in the burning sun. At last, they quieted and their bo's'n addressed him.

"So, how is it that Captain Blackjack Bellamie proposes to save us, single-handedly, from the wrath of Edward Teach?"

"Captain Teach will be in a singularly expansive mood for the next day or so, having scored such a lucrative victory as we have just witnessed. Therefore, calming his customary bloodlust should be relatively easy—if—and ye'd best pay close attention here, Gentlemen—if—ye follow my lead and corroborate everything I tell my esteemed colleague, no matter how outlandish it may sound or how spurious ye know it to be."

"We can do that, sure."

"Aye."

That would be easy enough; just let this pirate captain talk to that pirate captain, agree with everything he said and they were as good as saved.

"Oh, and one more thing, Gentlemen, and I cannot overstate the importance of this: when Captain Teach cordially invites ye to turn pirate and sail with him, ye'd best acquiesce with gusto."

"No!"

"Never!"

"I'll never turn pirate!"

"Very well. It's yer own funeral."

"Why?"

"Ye'll be given just two options, Gentlemen: turn pirate and turn with a will or be put to death in some unusual and entertaining way. But it's entirely yer choice, o' course." Sometimes being a buccaneer was almost too much fun!

The sailors were suddenly keen on piracy. That settled, they needed to get their future hosts' attention before the light faded and the pirates got blind drunk.

28—The Scorpion

Both ships were now anchored about half a mile from the wreck. The pirates in the launch had already started their post-battle binge, but nevertheless skillfully maneuvered close to the rigging to take the surviving mariners aboard. Behaving professionally, Jack oversaw their safe entry into the boat and was last to take his place. No sooner had he set foot in it than one of the younger pirates recognized him.

"Mother of Mercy! It's Captain Blackjack Bellamie or me rum was tainted."

"Aye! That I be. And is this little Fielding I see before me?"

"Aye, Cap'n. Last I heard o' ye, the *Sinecure* was terrorizin' the whole of th' Spanish Main and makin' th' King's men cry fer their mamas."

Jack laughed in genuine mirth to hear how his reputation had grown in the Sweet Trade. The sailors watched the boisterous reunion with wide eyes and with a marked pallor underneath their sunburns.

"That we were and that we do, young Master Fielding, but me ship's been hauled out nigh three months now and it's time to go On the Account, that is, if yer worthy captain has left any booty t' be taken."

"There's some, Cap'n, there's some. Cap'n Teach will be powerful glad t' see ye again, I'd wager."

"I'll be proud t' shake 'is 'and fer a masterful dispatch of that East Indiaman. 'Twer a sight t' see. Right, ye scurvy dogs?"

The pirates-to-be readily agreed, afraid not to.

Not revealing his trepidation to hear the answer, Jack inquired as to the disposition of the defeated vessel's crew. Teach was known to kill them all when resistance was encountered, a practice Jack deplored as fiercely as rape.

"Oh, we killed the captain and officers, but Cap'n Teach is keepin' most o' the crew t' man the ship. She's gonna sail under 'is colors now." Teach was renowned for aspiring to admiralty.

" 'Most' o' the crew? What about the rest?"

"Oh, you know, Cap'n. The ones what resisted went t' Davy Jones' Locker."

It sickened Jack to hear of Teach's disregard for human life, but he knew the lesson wasn't lost on his shipmates from the wreck.

Blackbeard was in an ebullient mood and, seeing that his long-time colleague had witnessed his latest success, he became downright effusive. After the initial greetings and exchange of friendly insults, he asked Jack why he was stranded in the rigging of a wrecked ship with a bunch of non-piratical-looking seamen.

His piercing gaze at the terrified men was worse than their burns and dehydration. Nevertheless, Jack was in control, as usual, when lies and rodomontade are the order of the day.

"Ah, Cap'n Teach, these men have put their lives on the line fer Yers Truly, so desirous are they o' turnin' pirate. Ye see, me *Sinecure*'s been hauled out fer nigh on to three months now so a goodly portion o' me men have set sail with other crews, and who's t' blame 'em?

"Well, I hitched a ride on their fine barque out o' Montego Bay in hopes o' gettin' back to Vestal Cay and me ship, when, lo, I sees their captain cheatin' and abusin' 'is sailors at every turn. Pumped up in 'is pride was 'Is Lordship, and no ordinary seaman could please 'im.

"After a couple days o' this, I took their bo's'n, that fine gentleman right there, I took 'im aside an' told 'im that I be a pirate captain and that brethren in th' Trade would never be subjected t' such as that. Well, he began talkin' to 'is mates and soon enough there were a mutiny brewin'.

"Half the crew sided with their pompous ass of a captain, half of 'em sided with me. Predictably, a battle ensued and our side prevailed.

"We marooned the survivors, includin' their humiliated officers and took over the ship. We was headin' t' Vestal Cay when we was caught in a squall and foundered on the shoals. Thus, we was just hangin' around when yer fine flag appeared and gladdened our weary eyes."

Physically, Teach was twice the man Jack was, towering over him and outweighing him by half again; but mentally, he was no match for the cunning and manipulative Gypsy. He draped his arm about the smaller man's shoulders and steered him toward his cabin, calling back to his first mate for rum.

"What about me men, Cap'n? They be in need of food and drink, not to mention some medical attention."

"Yer right, Jack! Where's me manners? Le Sage. See to it that Jack's crew gets what they need."

Much relieved, Jack relaxed in Teach's cabin, enjoying his hospitality and talking shop. He could see that the other captain's lust to command a fleet was becoming an obsession and he shivered at the reminder of Korsakov. Despite the apparent camaraderie, he knew not to trust Teach and worried that the man might even try to commandeer the *Sinecure* for his growing flotilla.

Nevertheless, the *Queen Anne's Revenge* would be the quickest way back to his ship and his fabrication would have secured the gratitude and service of the sailors from the barque. Without question, the *Sinecure* would be needing men when he arrived and these would be valuable indeed.

All in all, Jack was feeling rather smug over his handling of the events, and was just sinking into the warm oblivion of rum when Teach dropped a bomb.

"So Jack, what do ye think o' yer new rival? Have ye seen 'er? I 'ear she's as fine-lookin' a pirate captain as ye'll ever see, present company excluded, o' course."

Jack had been immersed in escaping from Rothwell and falling in love and so was out of the loop of pirate gossip. He didn't allow his surprise to show, though. He studied his fingernails.

"Oh, I don't know, Edward. Sounds t' me like a lot o' bilge. Can't recall ever seein' 'er, though. What's the name o' 'er ship again? The D—, no, it were the M—? Damn, me memory's failin'!"

"The *Chimera*. Flies a black flag with a red whiptail scorpion and an hourglass. I 'ear she's been workin' the South China Sea and the Indian Ocean most o' 'er life. She ain't a kid."

"I 'eard she goes by 'Dreadwitch.' That true, ye think?" Jack was playing Teach like a harpsichord—well, like Chloe would play a harpsichord.

"'Dreadwitch'! Now, I've 'eard everything! No, one o' me crew got within sight o' 'er in Tortuga and 'eard 'er called Scorpion, hence the flag. Last name o' Scarpia."

"Scorpion Scarpia. Rings a bell. I figure it's 'er gender what gives 'er such renown, though. Fleur caused quite a stir when she got 'er first command."

"Don't sell the Scorpion short, Jack. She sacked two towns on the isthmus and escaped from Panama with 'er whole crew just one hour before they was all t' hang."

"So I 'eard. Well, it'll be interesting t' cross paths with 'er one day. She go fer men, I wonder, or is she like Fleur?"

"She ain't like Fleur, although what she does enjoy remains t' be discovered."

Here the two captains laughed uproariously and lasciviously, speculating wildly about what diversions or perversions the Scorpion might be agreeable to.

29—Many A Truth...

The Caribbean was glassy-calm, cerulean blending to violet where it met the cloudless sky. In the little cove, a mild breeze from the sea kissed the verdant foliage, picking up the myriad scents of fruits and flowers, and then wafted back toward the shore with its fragrant bounty. Just beyond the northernmost spit a ship rode quietly at anchor, her striped sails furled, her glossy hull gleaming like obsidian in the golden sunshine.

High in the rigging, Jack was making his third inspection, examining every knot and block with assiduous care. He wore only breeches and his bandanna, preferring to work barefoot in the rigging and to be shirtless when performing manual labor in a safe place. In settings not inhabited exclusively by pirates he was obliged to wear a shirt so that his scars and tattoo would not reveal his identity prematurely.

On the deck, Reed, his first mate, was ticking off items on a list as Lemon Eye Lopez, the quartermaster, with the help of another pirate, was folding the large black flag.

Intense activity roiled throughout the ship as the sparse crew prepared to make way in a few hours. The twenty additional seamen from the lost barque were a welcome addition, as the long delay during which the *Sinecure* had been hauled out had seen her crew reduced by more than half as men sailed on other ships, some with intentions of returning, some not.

It was all part of a pirate's life and Jack bore them no ill will for their choices. However, taking on more hands would be a priority in the immediate future if the crew were to maintain their accustomed lifestyle wherein many sailors make light work for all.

He completed his aerial inspection, working his way

downward and finishing with a final check of the sheets and shrouds. Seeing that all was made fast, he went down into the hold to confirm that the supplies were stowed to suit him. He paused, inhaling the sweet smell of pitch and new wood from the massive repairs on the keel and ribs. Soon enough that would be replaced with the fulsome essence of bilge, but it was all heady perfume to Jack.

Reed followed him into the captain's cabin as they conversed about the final preparations and initial headings. Jack made some marks on a chart on his desk and looked over the Ship's Articles, then settled into a chair, tipping up a tankard of rum.

The conversation flagged and Reed looked steadily at his captain.

"Jack, the whole Caribbean knows ye got that hole in yer side from our friend Rothwell, but no one can figure how ye escaped from under their noses. C'mon, Cap'n, give us a hint."

"I already told ye, I ran up into the 'ills where I was captured by twelve dusky maidens who nursed me back to 'ealth and kept me as their passion slave until I escaped through an abandoned silver mine."

Reed sighed. "I know. That's the same daft tale ye've told ever since ye got back three days ago. Ye know ye can tell me the truth and I'll not spread it."

"That is the truth. I don't know why no one believes me when I tell these things."

"Oh, please. Remember the squids that wove their tentacles into a net—"

"And caught enough fish to feed the whole crew."

"Give it up, Jack. Everyone knows it were a school of mackerel ye sailed into what saved ye. But just between us, truthfully, how'd ye escape Port Royal while wounded so severely?"

"Truthfully? I fled into the interior, was rescued by a beautiful, rich, high-toned English lady and doctored by 'erself and the staff at 'er mansion, then the two of us hiked across Jamaica, was captured by Maroons but charmed our way out of it, then rode a melon wagon into Montego Bay and got married."

"All right, Jack, I give up. If ye don't want to tell me, why don't ye just say so?"

"Because there's no sport in that, Mate."

"But what about that bite scar on yer arm? That's new, isn't it? What'd ye do, try to sweet-talk the wrong whore?"

"She's not a—well, actually, I did that to meself while makin' love to the nubile daughter of a lieutenant in the Royal Navy. She was doin' something so pleasurable I bit meself to avoid screamin' and alertin' her father who was sippin' brandy in the next room."

"Why do I try?"

"Because, Mate, I just might tell ye the truth sometime. Ye never know."

"I'll not hold my breath."

Jack chuckled to himself and drained the tankard.

30—An Omen of June

The dynamic in the household had shifted dramatically. Despite the similarity in the ages of the four, Emerson had become the *pater familias*, Maria the nurturing mother, and Rodrigo the cajoling uncle. Chloe, having abdicated any semblance of dominion, was now the frail and often obstinate invalid child around whom the functions of the others revolved.

She would not eat except for Emerson's most strenuous urging, would not get dressed, undressed, or bathed unless Maria did it for her, refused to leave her room but for Rodrigo's pleading and in his company.

She was emotional about the strangest things. She refused to play the harpsichord and insisted the door to the parlor be kept closed at all times and she would not set foot on the balcony or the veranda at night. It took Maria and Emerson days to persuade her to allow Maria to change the bed linens; she acceded only when Emerson suggested she keep the dirty ones in the bed with her, rolled into an elongated pillow she could hold in her arms. She refused to eat scones, but kept and treasured a long black hair she had found on the floor. From the texture, Maria suspected that it was likely her own, but wisely let her mistress enjoy the unspoken fantasy that it had come from the Captain.

She refused to wear any of her own clothing except for the old skirt she had taken with her on the trek and Maria's plain work smocks, which hung on her small frame, accentuating her emaciation. She wore no jewelry save the necklace which she never removed, used no makeup, and kept her hair in a long braid down her back day and night. The only time she had behaved as the Mistress of the Manor had been when Rodrigo was going to fetch the doctor for her. She had drawn herself up into her most imperious stance and adamantly forbade it. It was to prove a wise move in retrospect.

Left to her own devices, she would have remained in her bed and slowly died of a broken heart, but her staff would not allow it. All three were in her room every day doing something, anything, to keep her from giving up.

Her initial apathy had lifted enough that she would quarrel with them, resist their ministrations, albeit feebly, and even weep a little, but she wouldn't unleash the swelling torrent of tears that would bring emotional catharsis. She remained locked within her grief and the others both dreaded and welcomed the day when the dam would finally break.

Except for the announcement of her marriage that first day, she had made no further verbal reference to Captain Bellamie; likewise, none had been spoken in her presence by her staff. She subconsciously regarded his name as too sacred to speak aloud, and the servants were apprehensive about the effect it might have were they to do so.

Thus, the Bellamie household remained in a tenuous equilibrium that would prevail through the weeks following Chloe's return.

It was well past midnight. Captain Blackjack Bellamie lay stretched out on the deck of his beloved ship, his fingers locked behind his head, watching the stars through the rigging, a sight that never failed to calm his deepest soul. His heartbeat merged into the rhythm of the smooth back and forth sweep of the mastheads and he felt his connection to the great cosmic scheme that lay beyond mortal comprehension.

This was a perfect night for his contemplative meditation, moonless, cloudless, uncounted legions of stars giving nearly as much light as a full moon. *What's out there?* Is that where the ones who have gone on now dwell? Were his parents looking back at him this very moment? Was Lizbet? And his sisters, were they up there or still here on Earth?

He felt the familiar calm and the familiar melancholy, but

there was a new sadness now. All the losses he had known were especially keen tonight and he knew that this new one, like the rest, would never leave.

Emerson, Maria, and Rodrigo sat at the kitchen table finishing their evening meal. At first, their conversation was about the usual mundane concerns of domestic life and then, naturally, it turned to the subject of their unfortunate mistress.

Emerson gave his usual report on her nonexistent appetite and Rodrigo said that she had become sick once again during their morning stroll.

Maria had tidings she had prayed she would not have to divulge, but now she owed it to the men to include them in this latest crisis.

"The Señora has still more difficulty ahead. She has been home for more than a month now and I have seen nothing."

The men looked blank for a moment, then Emerson understood.

"Oh. Oh, dear. Are you sure?"

"*Sí*, she could not have hidden it from me."

Rodrigo hadn't caught on. "Hidden what from you, Maria? What have you not seen? What should you see?"

"Maria is Madam's personal attendant, Rodrigo. Think about it. What should she have noticed within the past lunar month?"

He didn't have to think for long.

"Oh. *Oh!*"

Nothing was said for several moments while each let the weight of the situation sink in.

"Maria, has there been any discussion with Madam about this?"

"No, but I have tried, without speaking too boldly, of course. She does not seem to understand."

"Are you saying that she refuses to take your hints and address the subject?"

"She seems unaware of her condition."

"You bathe her. Is it becoming apparent yet?"

"No, it is much too soon."

On the subject of the timetable, they calculated, based on Maria's recollection of Chloe's cycle, that the child would be due around middle to late June.

Emerson was concerned for her ability to carry a pregnancy to term in her present state.

"She is barely able to sustain her own life. Unless she begins taking nourishment soon, she will lose this child and likely die herself."

"If the Señora loses another child, especially the Captain's child, she will surely die of grief."

That night, Maria lit candles on her altar once more and began a novena to the Blessed Virgin.

31—Judge and Jury

Jack stared through the glass at the distant ship, scarcely able to believe his luck. Barely one day out and they had come upon an unescorted merchantman apparently on a northeast bearing. The wind was in the *Sinecure*'s favor and she was sleeker, faster, and more maneuverable than ever, thanks to her recent overhaul. The chase would be a short one.

All of the meager crew were engaged in trimming for the pursuit and preparing for battle. The black flag with the three stars and upturned crescent moon was run up early on, the element of surprise being unnecessary as there would be no question in the minds of the merchantman's crew as to the intent and purpose of this black and white vessel rapidly closing on them.

The prey ship kept trying to both outrun the pirates in defense and turn for loosing a broadside in offense, effectively achieving neither objective.

Nevertheless, she fired the first volley as soon as she was within range of the onrushing *Sinecure* and the battle was engaged.

Now, it was the corsair that was angling to present a more difficult target and still unleash a cannonade. The roar was deafening and the air was thick with smoke as the early moments of battle saw a nearly even score between the two vessels. Danger notwithstanding, the *Sinecure* surged on, Jack having full confidence that they would prevail and board their quarry.

His instincts proved correct for, although the merchantman had the *Sinecure* outgunned, her artillery was not being utilized to its full advantage, some cannon apparently being delayed in the reloading, others remaining unfired altogether.

Still she was not an easy mark. Two shots had penetrated the *Sinecure*'s shiny hull through the white stripe above the gun deck, one had torn through the mainsail, and a fourth shattered the larboard rail and scuppers, ripping across the deck and killing a pirate, the momentum hurling his body into the sea on the starboard. As soon as they were within striking distance, Jack called for chain shot and the victim's mainmast crashed to the deck, taking down several unfortunate sailors and throwing the remainder into chaos.

Seizing the advantage, Jack urged the *Sinecure* onward and soon they were alongside and the grapnels were thrown.

Normally, Jack considered victory to be assured once the other vessel was boarded. The innate savagery, multiple battle skills and willingness to fight dirty gave the buccaneers the edge over even seasoned soldiers. However, their greatest asset was often their sheer, overwhelming numbers, pirate crews typically being much more thickly manned than those of comparably sized vessels.

Unfortunately, the *Sinecure* was still seriously understaffed, in Jack's opinion, and he worried that the combat would go against them. Nevertheless, this was how a pirate captain increased his crew, so the chance had to be taken.

Incredibly, the resistance from the merchantman proved ineffectual at best and her colors were struck within minutes.

Formally confronting her captain, Jack accepted the hilt of his sword and took charge of the vessel, a barquentine named the *Leaping Hart*.

It quickly became apparent why the skirmish had gone so easily to the pirates. The seamen were pitifully few in number and their captain was a mere stripling who stared at Jack with wide, terror-filled eyes. Jack pressed his advantage.

"Do ye have a name, Captain?"

"Y-Yarborough, Sir."

"Well, Captain Yarborough, would ye be so kind as to tell me where be the real captain of this vessel and the remainder of 'is crew?"

Jack suspected the answer and he was going to make this pup squirm in front of his men.

"G-gone, Sir."

Quick as a cobra strike, the tip of Jack's sword was touching the youth's quivering Adam's apple.

"Do ye know who I am, Mr. Yarborough?"

"N-no, S-Sir."

"I am Jack Bellamie, Captain Blackjack Bellamie. Name ring a bell?"

The shaveling blanched and tears sprang to his eyes, while his crew shrank back until stopped by the swords and cocked pistols of the pirates. Jack continued, his fearsome black gaze fixed on the quaking youth.

"Clearly, ye've 'eard of me, *Boy*, so I assume ye know my feelings on mutineers. Do ye? Do ye know 'ow I feel about mutinous *dogs*?" As he spoke, he was advancing menacingly, driving Yarborough backwards step by step to avoid that sword. "Well, speak up, Mutineer Yarborough! Do ye know?"

The youth's mouth worked, but no words would issue forth. Jack's lips were drawn back into a snarl, his teeth flashing like marble fangs, and he appeared to be a split second from impaling the kid.

"Pl—, pl—se, pl,—" Yarborough stammered, beginning to sob.

Jack lowered his sword and gave an exaggerated eye roll.

"All right, all right. Stop blubberin'." Then, to the pirates, "Lock these scabrous mutineers in the brig—on this ship. Then unload all 'er cargo and scuttle 'er."

The vanquished sailors sent up a wail and some of the pirates, the ones who had sailed with Jack before, gasped. Reed went to Jack's side as the hapless prisoners were escorted below. His face showed concern.

"Jack? Do ye know what yer doing? This isn't like ye."

"Are ye disputing my authority, Mr. Reed?"

"No, Sir, Cap'n. But, to condemn the lot of 'em to death. Isn't that too cruel for the famous Captain Blackjack Bellamie?"

"Who is the Captain, here? Leave me be!" He turned on his heel and strode over to where Lemon Eye was orchestrating the stowage of the booty.

The *Leaping Hart* was laden with silver, mahogany, and tea; there was even Oriental porcelain and silk. Unloading her took a while and Jack made sure he was visibly in charge as the captives watched and listened.

As the hold began to empty out, he drew up a chair near the small brig where the mariners were packed too tightly to sit. He settled, rocking the chair onto its back legs, and lazily cocked his boots up onto one of the cross bars of the cell. He sighed contentedly and pared a fingernail with his dagger. The frantic seamen watched in sickening fear, saying nothing.

After a long, agonizing time, Jack spoke, never taking his eyes off his task of personal grooming.

"Well, Gentlemen, I've changed me mind. Seems a shame to scuttle such a fine vessel as this." Here a few sailors expressed relief, but he ignored them and went on. "So, me crew's gonna pick 'er clean, then set 'er adrift."

A timid voice asked, "What about us?"

"What about ye?"

"What are you going to do with us?"

"It appears to me yer exactly where mutineers should be, so I ain't doin' nothin' wi' ye."

Several of the men began to keen and cry; they begged him to kill them on the spot.

"Since we're on the subject o' lingerin' deaths, suppose ye tell me what ye did wi' yer captain and crewmates. Marooned 'em, did ye?"

"Nay, Cap'n Bellamie. We di'n't maroon 'em. They was all killed fair 'n square in a pitched battle."

"'Pitched battle,' ye say. With who, I wonder?"

At this, an uncomfortable silence ensued until Jack spoke again.

"Could it be the battle was with the miserable dogs I see before me? And what, pray tell, was yer reason for riskin' condemnation t' th' fires of Hell?"

At this, the cell erupted as all the men tried to talk at once, their voices strident with rage and anguish, telling tales of torture, sadism and tyranny that would do Edward Low proud. The story was similar to the fiction Jack had used on Teach, only much more savage and, sadly, this one was true.

He listened, his face expressionless, but his guts were in knots. This was an impasse for him; he despised mutineers, but he also loathed heartless officials of any stripe. As much as he needed more crew, mutineers were very poor candidates, so he would pass them over.

He had never intended to scuttle the ship nor set it adrift with the men in it. The terrifying scenarios were his contribution to their penalty for mutiny. His actual plan, after throwing a scare into them, was to release them from the brig, give them sufficient food and water to get them to the nearest port—Nassau—and no farther, and let the authorities deal with them, as their crime would be obvious. After all, no one would believe that pirates had taken the cargo and then set half the crew free with provisions.

He was only half listening to the clamoring sailors, thinking ahead to packing them off to Nassau, when he heard something that struck deeply.

It seems that the father of young Yarborough had been an ordinary seaman with the same crew, this being the first voyage the two would work together. The plight of the men had been steadily worsening when the vicious captain had ordered the elder Yarborough flayed for breaking a china serving bowl. In his agony, the man had begged his son to kill him, which the heart-broken boy did.

The flash of his pistol ignited the fulminating rebellion that then raged for two days. When it was over, none of the officers remained and many sailors on both sides were dead. Yarborough was made captain, certainly not because of any skill or experience, but as a kind of nominal reward for his courage in the uprising and his terrible ordeal; besides, none other was significantly more qualified. They were sailing aimlessly, having no idea where to go or what to do when they were spotted by the *Sinecure*.

Although he didn't indicate that he had heard, Jack had taken the tale to heart. He amended his plan, but didn't intend to make it easy on them; they were, after all, mutineers. He stood and stretched.

"Well, Boys, I can't hang around chewin' th' fat all day, so I'll be takin' leave o' ye." He ambled out and ascended the ladder to the deck as the poor captives begged for mercy, thinking they were about to be set adrift to die a long, horrible death.

As Jack crossed the plank to the *Sinecure*, his men began preparing to make way. One pirate asked, "Ready to scuttle 'er, Cap'n?"

"No. She's not to be scuttled. Leave the anchors and grapnels in place 'till tomorrow." He entered his cabin as his crew looked after him in confusion.

32—How to Win Crew (and Influence Sailors)

Jack was the only man on either vessel who knew what was about to happen. He could have easily and safely shared the information with Lemon Eye, with Reed, even with the entire crew of the *Sinecure*. But, having once been the victim of a mutiny himself, he would trust no one ever again—except Chloe, of course.

He had secured the loyalty of the twenty sailors with whom he had been shipwrecked by throwing a scare into them—a very real danger, to be sure, in that case—and then saving them in a grand gesture of magnanimity and subterfuge.

He would do the same with the poor wretches agonizing in the hold of the *Leaping Hart*, but now the terror would have to come from himself. He was sickened to think of the misery he was inflicting on them, but it had to be done if he were to avoid another mutiny for, to Jack's mind, a mutineer was like a sheep-killing dog: after the first violation, another was almost certain.

His crew were now drunk as lords, reveling in the time-honored victory celebration of buccaneers. Lemon Eye, once more Jack's equal in command now that the battle was over, retained sufficient sobriety to prevent damage to the ship or the disobedience of standing orders, in this case, the order to do nothing to the *Leaping Hart*.

He was lucid enough to realize that what he saw on the jib boom was not a good sign.

"Jack! Jack! Come down off o' there, Man! Are ye daft?"

His captain appeared not to have heard him. He knew that Jack was never completely sober while aboard the ship and likely had had an extra quaff or two of Kill Devil this night. He was surely in no condition to be balancing astride that narrow timber, his lithe body swaying with the gentle rocking of the anchored ship, staring at the rising and falling horizon.

Lemon Eye could usually tell when Jack was in his "Daft Captain Blackjack" mode and rarely was alarmed that the craziness would extend to endangering the ship, the crew or Jack, himself. He and others who knew the Captain (as much as Jack allowed any of them to know him) saw that the man's apparent lunacy was employed as a means to an end and could be terminated as abruptly as it began.

But this present aberration could not have been for anyone's benefit; it was only by accident that he had looked toward the bowsprit and glimpsed, despite the darkness, a small figure riding as far forward as it was possible to go and still be on the ship. One false move and Jack could have fallen into the water and no one would have known to fish him out. Lemon Eye surveyed the situation, debating whether to attempt climbing out to drag his captain to safety.

He started up onto the prow and realized that he was already dizzy; trying to physically pull the man away from peril would likely kill them both. He could think of no crewmember who was less rum-impaired than himself at the moment, so enlisting aid was impossible. He had no choice but to persuade the Captain to return to the security of the deck.

"Cap'n! Ye can't stay out there on that boom, Man. Ye'll kill yerself and leave me wi' this daft crew o' your'n t' run. C'mon, Jack. Come back in."

Jack ignored him. He had heard him, but he ignored him. Lemon Eye worried too much for a pirate, even a quartermaster, he concluded.

He needed to be alone with his thoughts and this was the only place he could be assured no one would follow him. His captain's cabin, typical of those on other pirate ships, was not a private refuge, but was open to all the crew as a kind of lounge. It was, this night, at capacity.

He was irked that he had been seen.

Lemon Eye wasn't letting up. Jack needed to deal with the heavy load of secrets he was carrying and now it was obvious that solitude could not be had on his ship. Every time he would begin following an orderly sequence of thoughts, Lemon Eye's annoying braying shattered his concentration.

Irritated, he whirled to shout to his quartermaster to "bloody shut up," but the action threw him off balance and he fell off the boom into the sea.

Mayhem soon erupted on the *Sinecure* as Lemon Eye tried to rouse the rum-soaked pirates to save their captain, but despite a sincere desire to help, none could muster the physical coordination necessary to accomplish the task. Lemon Eye got a rope into the water, but couldn't haul up the sodden Jack by himself.

Frantic, he tried to wrap the line around a windlass, but fumbled and watched in horror as the end flew from his hands, shot across the rail and over the side.

Jack knew what was going on and that he would have to save himself.

His hands could find no purchase on the slippery sides of the *Sinecure* and he knew that his stamina was not infinite. Furthermore, he remembered with horror the sharks at the wreck site. He swam the short distance to the *Leaping Hart* and searched for something, anything to cling to. He proceeded aft, feeling his way along the length of the vessel, unable to see well in the dark below the convex side of the ship.

At last, he caught the splintered edge of a hole torn by one of the *Sinecure*'s cannonballs. Desperate, he grabbed onto it although it cut into his hands, the blood streaming down his wet arms and dripping into the sea. He absolutely had to get out of the water now, as the sharks would arrive any second.

Ignoring the pain, he pulled his body upward until he could put one foot into the same ragged opening as his hands. Momentarily safe from the sharks or drowning, he had to decide what to do next, as his three-point attachment would not be long sustainable. To his right and upward he could see an open gun port several feet away. Knowing that there would be no second chance, he tensed every ounce of strength into his one leg and launched himself toward the port, uncoiling like a spring.

He caught the edge of the opening, but just barely. At first holding on with only his fingers, he forced his ravaged hands inward to get a surer grip, eventually hauling himself up until he was hanging into the port from the waist. The rest was easy.

Collapsing alongside the cannon, he gasped for breath and shuddered to realize how close he had come to destruction. His hands, still being somewhat numb, would eventually hurt much worse than they did at the moment and he'd probably have a sore leg for a few days, but that kind of pain was inconsequential and fleeting. The agonizing helplessness in the watery darkness, anticipating that first searing bite as a chunk was torn away from himself, followed by the awareness that he was being eaten alive— no physical discomfort could compare with that kind of psychological agony.

Yet he had deliberately inflicted such hell on these unfortunate crewmen, prolonging their suffering for hours and threatening them with a far more protracted and painful demise than that which he had just escaped. He would not wait for morning to enact his plan.

He felt his way along the bulkhead trying to ascertain where the ladder to the hold might be. The darkness was nearly as bad as that he and Chloe had endured under the rock.

In brig below, the captives remained silent, listening to the noises Jack was making as he drew nearer. Had he not been cognizant of the situation, he'd have known of the prisoners' presence despite the silence and darkness by the unmistakable smell of fear. He usually enjoyed that aroma because it meant he had unnerved an opponent, but tonight it made him rather queasy.

His lifelong experience with ships served him well, and he soon found his way into the pitch-black hold.

Poor Yarborough, still trying to play the leader, called out in a trembling voice, "Who goes there? Identify yourself!"

Jack smiled to himself. The kid might actually have the makings of a captain after all.

"It's Captain Bellamie, so show some respect."

"Captain! Why've you come back? Are you going to execute us?"

"I've come to have a word wi' ye. Where's a candle in this place?"

"Over by the ladder, on a hogshead to the left. We can talk in the dark, though." Yarborough was eager to get on with this unexpected development.

"There'll be no talkin' unless I can see yer eyes. Ye can't hide yer souls from the likes o' Captain Blackjack Bellamie, so don't even think o' lyin' t' me."

He fumbled about, eventually locating the candle and flint and lighting the wick. Ever the conscientious mariner, he carefully replaced the chimney and carried the welcome item to the cell.

He paced slowly back and forth, resplendent in his wet, disheveled and blood-soaked ferocity, holding the light to study the faces of the men who looked at him with pleading eyes.

"Gentlemen, I am Captain. Black. Jack. Bellamie. *The* Captain Blackjack Bellamie. I take what I want and I spare no one. I strike no bargain save the benefit be my own. *Capiche?*"

They looked at him as if they were seeing Lucifer incarnate.

"Ergo, I wish ye t' tell me, what would ye give me in exchange fer yer lives?"

"Anything, Captain! Anything! Name it, it's yours!"

He gave a sardonic laugh.

"Gentlemen, don't insult my intelligence. I have already taken every material thing ye had. Now, think carefully and answer honestly. What have ye that I could possibly value sufficiently t' set ye free?"

The silence was electric, but it didn't last long.

"Ourselves, Captain! All we have left are our lives and our allegiance."

"Am I to take it that yer offerin' to serve me as loyal, dedicated pirates who will remain steadfast in fealty in the face of surpassing peril, even unto death?"

"Aye, Sir! Aye! We give you our solemn word!"

Jack fixed his intimidating black eyes on each of the sailors, one by one.

"So say ye all?"

The chorus of affirmatives left no doubt. He allowed the noise to fade to silence for effect, appearing to debate within his mind whether to take them or to revert to his original horrific plan. When he was certain that he had won their total commitment and had made them sweat a little more, he spoke.

"Very well, Gentlemen. I accept yer offer. As I have saved each one o' ye from an unspeakable death, each one o' ye, to a man, owes 'is life t' me. From this moment forward, it's pirates ye be, buccaneers, corsairs, Brethren o' th' Coast. Yer crewmates on th' *Sinecure* will be yer teachers whilst ye go On the Account. But mark my words and mark them well: at the merest hint of disloyalty, yer life is forfeit, and it will not be a quick nor a painless death."

Now that he had effectively broken their spirits and secured their unswerving devotion, he could allow the natural progression of life in the Sweet Trade to awaken in them the autonomy that sets a pirate apart from all other men.

33—The Dam Bursts

The rider of the magnificent charger cantering toward the manor was every inch the polished gentleman, from the top of his gold-braided tricorne to his gleaming boots. Handsome, tall and trim, he sat his mount with practiced ease, his spine erect yet pliant as he moved in synchrony with the horse. His attire, while expensive and elegant, belied the loftiness of his station, for this was a social call. He carried a bouquet of roses.

Dismounting under the portico, he was met at the door by the butler who, while impeccably proper and respectful, nevertheless would not admit the suitor into the mansion.

"Madam is indisposed today and cannot entertain guests."

"Is there a more suitable time that I might plan to call?"

"It would not be for me to say, except that Madam is unlikely to welcome callers at any time in the near future."

"Very well. Would you be so kind, then, as to give her these flowers and tell her that with them I send my warmest regards?"

"Of course. Good day to you, Sir." He bowed slightly, went inside and closed the door.

Once inside, he studied the beautiful gift with which he had been entrusted. Starting for the back hall, he paused at the stairs.

"Maria. Please come down here. I require your assistance."

After discussing the event, the two proceeded through the kitchen and out the door with trepidation bordering on dread. Whatever was about to transpire would not be good.

Chloe and Rodrigo approached from the path around the garden, she holding onto his arm and looking wan and fragile, he walking slowly to accommodate her. As the four met on the veranda, Emerson offered the roses to his mistress who took them, looking puzzled.

"You had a visitor, Madam, but I sent him away. However, he left you this bouquet with his warmest regards."

"Pray, who would be so bold?"

Maria squelched the instinct to cross herself as Emerson struck the spark.

"It was Commodore Rothwell, Madam."

Chloe's eyes widened and she went even paler than she had been. Several seconds passed as she fitted together the elements of the incident. The man who, virtually single-handedly, was responsible for her permanent separation from her beloved husband, the man who had grievously wounded her beloved husband, the man who fervently wanted to kill her beloved husband, this man—the man who was the reason she was suffering the unrelenting torments of Hell—this man was trying to court her!

Her nostrils flared as she filled her lungs for the outburst.

"Rothwell! Wretched, bastard Rothwell!"

Her hands grasped and wrenched the bouquet, driving thorns into her tender flesh, the pain welcome in her state of inexpressible rage. She hurled the mangled roses to the ground with an energy the servants could scarcely believe she possessed and then she spun around and took off at a run down the trail behind the barns. Alarmed, the three gave pursuit.

Catching her was easy; calming her was like trying to saddle a lioness. She lashed out at them with her arms and legs, screaming, all but foaming at the mouth like a rabid animal. Her bony little fist connected with Rodrigo's eye causing him to retreat to determine if the damage could be permanent. All the while she was screaming at them.

"Damn you! Leave me alone! Let go! Let go of me! Let me die! LET ME DIE!"

The sobs that tore from her wracked her whole body as she sagged onto the dusty path. She sounded as if she were turning herself inside out, each exhalation commencing with a guttural scream and continuing until her chest was depleted of air, followed by a rasping, agonized inhalation to begin the sequence once more. Thus she continued for what seemed an eternity to her servants.

Emerson had grabbed her in a bear hug from behind, catching her hands in his to prevent any further injury to the other two. He had sunk to the ground with her, still holding her weakening hands, but now to impart strength and comfort rather than restraint. Maria tried to touch her, to attempt to soothe her, but Chloe shook her head furiously and the sorrowing maid backed away.

Their mistress, her energy now spent, would have been lying on the road were it not for Emerson's embrace. She drooped in his arms, limp.

As the initial fury of the storm settled into seemingly endless weeping, he softly told Maria to go look after Rodrigo, that he would remain with Madam.

Alone with his pitiful mistress, he continued in the paternal role into which he had been thrust after her return. He merely held her, saying nothing, gently patting her arm and rocking her. He had resolved not to speak until she chose to, knowing that she should be allowed to work through her own stages of healing.

The tableau of Chloe and her devoted butler sitting in the middle of the path had not changed for more than an hour. She was no longer crying, just staring straight ahead and seeing nothing. Utterly spent, she was content to lean back against Emerson's chest and let him pat and rock her.

Now the only sounds were the hum and whir of busy insects and the symphony of birdcall. Chloe finally spoke, softly and calmly.

"Please let me go, Emerson. I can no longer endure this grief."

He didn't let go. "Madam, you must. Captain Bellamie would never forgive himself if he knew that his love had cost you your life."

"Captain Bellamie will never know. We will never see each

other again. Emerson, this pain has to end. Please allow me to do what I must."

"I cannot permit you to harm yourself, Madam. You are needed and loved by your staff, but, more importantly, your innocent child, Captain Bellamie's child, must be given the opportunity to live."

She turned to look at him as if he had gone mad.

"Madam, I know that deep in your heart, you must be aware that you are with child."

Her eyes went off focus as her thoughts turned inward and he saw that he was correct. The knowledge was there all along, but had been buried.

"You may never see your husband again, but part of him lives in you now, so you are never without him. In a few months, you will hold his child in your arms. Is that not reason enough to endure and prevail?"

She clasped her arms across her belly, aching to hold her Little One, Jack's baby. She shed quiet tears, tears no longer of rage and bitterness, but of beautiful, almost unbearable, tenderness.

34—East Meets West

The first weeks of her return to sailing had been remarkably fruitful for the *Sinecure*. Her hold was filled with booty and her crew was skilled and eager, with two-thirds of their numbers still on the honeymoon of slavish devotion to their captain. Secretly, Jack was eager for the day when they were past this and thinking like normal pirates, but all things come in good time; they were still new to the Trade.

With so much prosperity below decks, there was little reason to continue working until the loot had been properly squandered on a good time, so Lemon Eye set the ship on a course for Tortuga. The veteran pirates were filling the heads of the novices with visions of extreme pleasures and extreme perils to be encountered in the notorious port. They were not exaggerating.

Jack had not been on a shore-side carousal since before meeting and marrying Chloe. He knew this day would come, but he had not dwelt on the subject long enough to settle his mind on a course of action—or inaction, as the case might be. He lay on his bunk staring into the darkness and grudgingly facing a question having two mutually exclusive answers.

Tomorrow they would make port around sunset, just as the evening bacchanals would be commencing. His loins warmed with remembrance of times past in the pirate haven. It was now nearly two months since he had held Chloe in his arms. He needed to feel a feminine form against his flesh once more.

Yer a married man, Bellamie. Ye know what that means. No one dragged ye t' the altar. His eyes misted to recall the sweetness and passion of that day. *If ye could ask 'er, she'd quickly aver that yer t' remain faithful.* He remembered his amazement at her love for him, how he was compelled to bare his soul to her so that she would know and love the real Jack. He remembered the spectacular and unfeigned ardor. *Mother of God, how I miss her!*

Then his counter-conscience weighed in. *That's all well and good, but this was a unique marriage t' start with. We knew we'd have t' remain apart f'rever. A man like me can't face a life of celibacy. I'm not a bleedin' monk!* Surely Chloe, in her infinite love for him, would understand—wouldn't she? *Understand! She'd bite me damned arm off!*

What's sauce fer the goose be sauce fer the gander. If that be valid reasoning, then it's just as acceptable fer her t' take a lover. That thought enraged him, arousing lust for murder.

Now what, Bellamie? That answers it, does it not? When the boot is on the other foot, it's completely out o' th' question.

That's different. It's different fer women and men.

His two sides were squared off now.

Different? How?

A man does it fer physical pleasure. A woman does it fer love.

Like the whores?

Whores do it fer money. That has no place in this argument.

Would yer faithful wife agree wi' that?

She doesn't have to agree or disagree. She'll never know.

"I'm a pirate and a decent man, Chloe. I'm a pirate and a decent man, Chloe." Yer a pirate and damned liar!

There are lots o' married pirates who use whores.

There are lots who don't.

But they get t' go home t' their wives. Besides, if I suddenly stop usin' whores, th' crew might think that I'm no longer a man. Or they might suspect I'm married and that could endanger Chloe. Or—

So, yer intendin' t' perform the act in front of 'em, then?

Of course not! This is goin' nowhere. I want t' stop now.

Hypocrite! Ye made a big production t' Chloe, complete with a graphic demonstration, of 'ow a man manages without 'is woman. Now yer sayin' there's no relief except in the arms of a whore.

Go away! I want t' go t' sleep.

Good luck with that.

Had he possessed none of his senses save one he'd have known he was in Tortuga. The sights or sounds alone would have revealed it, yet nothing is so evocative as smell. The olfactory *pasticcio* of rum, unwashed bodies, gunpowder, and sex plunged him back into his mindset, begun years before, of unbridled revelry. He swaggered and reeled amid the joyous mayhem, his captain's coat flaring behind him like a stallion's tail as he scouted the taverns for clues as to where to begin his evening's binge.

Despite his cocksure demeanor, he nevertheless was at odds with himself on a number of dichotomies.

For one thing, some of his crew had already split off, knowing in advance where to find a preferred whore or favorite drink, but most followed their captain like a retinue as he swayed through the streets, secretly pleasing him to be seen as their liege and displeasing him for the same reason. For another, he couldn't decide whether to go where he would meet up with women he'd used before, enjoying the titillation of remembered pleasures, or seek out new bawds with the attendant thrill of novelty.

More importantly, he still had not resolved whether, having settled upon a strumpet for the evening, he would actually consummate the deal (for which his body was burning) or go to her room for the appearance of things and drink himself senseless before he could perform. That was a weasel's way out, he knew, but he had had no luck devising a better plan.

At length, he swept into a fairly unfamiliar waterfront tavern, secured a tankard of rum and made his way to a table. His ever-present shadows followed suit, Yarborough sitting beside him and watching closely, trying to copy his captain's every move.

This pup needs a bawd, Jack thought. He started looking around for a whore to take the kid off his hands.

Shortly, a buxom wench sidled over to Jack and began pushing her breasts against him, leering suggestively. He pulled her onto his lap and cupped his hand to her ear, whispering, whereupon she burst into a fit of giggles and coyly mock-slapped at him.

"No! Yer lyin'. Truly?"

"Truly. Here."

He dropped some coins into her hand. She dismounted and bounced over to Yarborough, running her fingers through his golden curls and down over his bared chest. He went crimson and choked on his swallow of rum while the pirates around them guffawed, drowning out his stammered protests. He looked to his hero for guidance, but Jack just stared straight ahead, implacably pulling long, satisfying draughts from the tankard. The whore caught the youth by his arm and dragged him through the back door to the hoots and cheers of the patrons. Jack breathed a sigh of relief.

Almost immediately his lap was filled with another of the professional women. She began wantonly putting her hands in his shirt, pinching his nipples, flicking her tongue on his neck, biting his earlobe. She reeked of sweat, cheap perfume, and other men's lust. From years of conditioned response, he felt himself stir to arousal even as he remembered the intoxicating fragrance of his wife, the lavender and her sweet clean skin suffused with her erotic musk that was for him alone.

Nevertheless, he was no longer thinking rationally, the rum and desire pre-empting reason and memory. He buried his face in her ample bosom and began pawing at her, kneading her soft flesh.

A small voice in his brain cried, "Stop! Remember your promises. Remember Chloe. You promised! You promised!"

He paused in his activities to take a swig of rum, hoping to still the annoying voice. As he lowered the tankard, he abruptly froze, his eyes locked onto the dark eyes of a woman across the room. His breath caught in his throat and he rose from the chair, letting the forgotten prostitute slide unceremoniously to the floor. As if in a trance, he walked toward the stranger who was similarly riveted on him.

Clearly, she was not a whore. Her clothes were plain, rather drab in fact, but they were the garb of a seasoned pirate: breeches, shirt, vest, boots, and a large belt and shoulder belt carrying a cutlass, a dagger, and two pistols. She was slight of build and darkened from years before the mast. She wore a large gold hoop in each earlobe and sported a mass of wild, black hair held out of her eyes with a faded blue bandanna. She watched Jack's approach with a fierce, unblinking gaze.

When they were face to face, they exchanged words unheard by the noisy, milling crowd and no one noticed them depart together.

The *Sinecure* was to remain at Tortuga for another day and night, there being no necessity to curtail the crew's recreation prematurely. The hold was still nearly full of swag and the men were loath to return to work until they were sated with all the charms the port had to offer. Therefore, Jack's absence went unnoticed until the morning of departure.

Lemon Eye Lopez, despite his own pounding skull, was manfully directing the bleary-eyed, hung-over pirates as they prepared to make way. It was Reed who first realized their captain was missing.

"Lemon Eye, where be Jack?"

"Don't you know?"

"No. He ain't in his cabin, nor th' hold, nor th' riggin'."

The call went out across the decks, but none had seen the man since they had first arrived. Yarborough, bedraggled but with high color, looked stricken.

They were about to lower the launch to return to shore, when a shout went up that a boat was approaching.

Actually, it was not one boat, but two, each filled with pirates whom the crew recognized as having been in the taverns and brothels they themselves had frequented of late. The newcomers were remarkable only for the inordinate number of Orientals among them. In the prow of the lead boat was Captain Bellamie and beside him a female pirate with the unmistakable bearing of authority.

As the boats approached the *Sinecure*, Jack shouted that all were to come aboard.

His puzzled crew looked on with astonishment; surely, even

Jack Bellamie could not wish to add so many at one time. When the last pirate had come aboard, Jack and the woman ascended to the quarterdeck, looking down on the two throngs assembled in the waist.

The crews eyed each other suspiciously and no one talked except to his own shipmates. When the murmuring had died down, Jack spoke.

"Gentlemen, we have here gathered upon the deck of the *Sinecure* the crew of said ship and that of the schooner *Chimera*. I am Blackjack Bellamie, captain of this ship—"

"And I am Scorpion Scarpia, captain of the *Chimera*," the woman finished in a clear, strong voice. When the murmuring had quieted once more, Jack continued.

"From this day, these two vessels and their crews will operate in tandem, working as a team both in taking prey and in fending off the undesired advances of John Law."

The Scorpion took her turn as the announcements alternated between the two captains.

"The crews will be full equals in all dealings and no one shall violate the terms of the Code."

"I will retain Mr. Lopez as my quartermaster and Mr. Reed as first mate."

"And I will retain Mr. Somers as my quartermaster and Mr. Chang as first mate."

At last one of Jack's men found his voice.

"Hold up, there. Where be the profit fer us?"

And another. "If both ships be equal, then all plunder must be divided amongst two crews, so each man receives but half a share!"

Shouting above the chorus of irritable agreement, the Scorpion explained.

"Aye, 'tis true the plunder must needs be divided amongst a greater number, but because each ship is the other's full complement in strengths, more plunder shall be taken, and the advantage of greater defense afforded."

As the crowd mulled over these words, Jack went on.

"Both the *Sinecure* and the *Chimera* are fast, far faster

than any other known in these waters, and their riggings, square for the *Sinecure* and fore-and-aft for the *Chimera*, give such a team great agility in any wind. The *Chimera* is shallower on the draft, but the *Sinecure* is more heavily armed. The opportunities for stalking prey, using the element of surprise and double raking when necessary lend us advantages neither would enjoy alone."

"Any man who wishes to disembark from this crew or my own is free to do so now or at any time in future. Likewise, any who wish to join the crew of the other vessel need only sign that ship's Articles with no questions asked. In shore-side assemblies, you are but one crew."

The men were still skeptical.

"And which o' ye be the commodore, Cap'n Scarpia? Who be admiral o' this fleet and which the flagship?"

"Neither!" Jack bellowed. "Neither captain holds sway over the other's crew and neither ship is the flagship. The *Sinecure* flies my flag and the *Chimera* flies Captain Scarpia's."

"But what about disputes?"

"Aye, and negotiations?"

"If we be but one crew when ashore, who be our captain then?"

And so it went. With a few exceptions, the men of the two crews reluctantly agreed to remain and provisionally accept the new arrangement save that, to a man, they refused to accept the absolute equality of the captains; the captains refused to accept otherwise. Finally, Jack and the Scorpion were forced to concede that, in certain circumstances, one person must speak for the entire team. They declined to make that decision and the men held such refusal to be a case in point.

A vote by the crews would be futile, as each would elect their own captain and nothing would be accomplished. So, in frustration, the captains agreed to a coin toss and, at first, that seemed to set well with the men, until one of Scarpia's crew yelled that it should be decided by contest, not mere chance.

As one, the assembled multitude roared, "Aye!"

35—The Duel

The terms of the contest were settled and the two ships made way with the tide, departing from Tortuga and bound for an agreed-upon island where this important activity could be conducted without interruption from outsiders.

Both crews had been warned by their quartermasters to keep to the Code and refrain from gambling while aboard ship. This was not exactly draconian, as each was unanimous in the certainty that their captain would prevail, although it was tempting to wager on how long the match would go on before the victor was crowned. The real betting would come when all were gathered ashore. Jack and the Scorpion hoped grudges would not be the result. The guidance of the Code existed for good reasons.

The last traces of sunset colored the western horizon as the ships dropped anchor and all personnel piled into the boats to row ashore.

Despite the serious purpose of their conference, being pirates, they set to creating the proper atmosphere of decadence before commencing with the business at hand. An enormous bonfire was built on the beach and rum was consumed in earnest, although most of the men were quite drunk well before the first sail was reefed. The two captains likewise joined the revelry, drinking, swaggering, and swearing as befit their station.

At length, it was time for the contest to begin. The pirates formed a semicircle with the fire as the focus at a safe distance and Jack and the Scorpion facing off in the middle. The noisy celebrants hushed as every eye went to the combatants.

In a flash, both swords were unsheathed and the two blades touched, each sliding tauntingly along the other as neither contender blinked. With their eyes locked on each other, the two circled, sidestepping and leaning slightly forward.

Abruptly, the Scorpion lunged at Jack who artfully dodged while slashing at her. Blocking with her blade near the hilt, she pushed forward, driving him back to keep his balance. Disengaging, he struck low and she blocked again, this time leaping backward and sideways to attack from a new angle. He saw it coming and was ready for her.

Over and over the blades clashed, the ringing of steel on steel unceasing as sparks from the fire ascended to join the stars before winking out. The pirates made few comments at first, but became more voluble as the duel gained ferocity.

The contest was not supposed to result in either captain being killed or maimed, just the besting of one combatant by the other, but neither was accustomed to sport fencing and their skills were long honed by the savage experience of battles to the death. As the contest wore on, they became more heated and more aggressive and, before long, Jack had drawn blood; soon after, so did the Scorpion. If any of the men had suspected that the apparent bond between the two would dilute their bloodlust in a fight, such suspicions were quickly dispelled.

They looked like two fearsome beasts, their wild manes flying, their clenched teeth bared and flashing in the firelight, blood staining their sweat-soaked clothes, nostrils flared, every sinew taut. The crews no longer saw a man and a woman; they saw two virtuosi, two superb practitioners of their craft turning in a monumental performance on a stage of sand.

The fight grew wilder still. They were moving, covering more ground, dancing, leaping, running. At one point they hurtled toward the crowd, which parted in a hurry before those slashing blades.

They fought up into the scrub above the tide line. They leapt onto boulders to gain a superior stance or elude a thrust. They parried around trees. They locked blades and pushed away, grimacing. The white of their opponent's teeth and eyes and the silver flash of the blades carried the battle away from the light of the flames, through saw grass and brush, back down to the strand beyond the fire, to the edge of the surf and up the beach again. The pirates followed at a safe distance, unwilling to miss the split second that could come at any time and decide the victory.

On and on they fought, their chests heaving with exertion. Drops of perspiration flew from their bodies, sparkling in the firelight. The Scorpion was bleeding from her shoulder and forearm; Jack was cut on his thigh and down the length of his upper left arm. Again and again one would appear to have the other at bay, only to be suddenly on the defensive once more.

Eventually, the men could see that neither sword was being held as high as before. Apparently, the victory would go to the one possessing that tiny extra portion of stamina that the other lacked. The pirates were feeling the exhaustion themselves as the relentless tension took its toll.

The slashing slowed, as did the traveling, but obviously a concession was out of the question. Still going at each other, the two captains at last crossed swords in a final clash, sliding together to lock at the hilts, nose to nose and there, for a long moment, they stayed so posed, unmoving, like a statue. Then as one, they lowered their weapons, dropped them to the sand, and collapsed gasping into each other's arms.

The pirates sent up a deafening roar of cheers and curses, releasing the pent-up energy engendered by the spectacle. None had bet on a draw, so no gold changed hands. Furthermore, to their great consternation, the issue was still undecided.

Jack and the Scorpion, seeming to have lost interest in the proceedings, sheathed their weapons and turned and walked toward the water, seeking a brief swim to refresh themselves and wash away the blood and sweat.

The quartermasters took charge of keeping order and settling the matter once and for all.

After their swim, the pair was seen walking slowly down the beach, beyond the light and noise, to sit close together at the edge of the water, conversing quietly; so they remained for nearly two hours before returning to the group. Deliberately or not, they sent a clear message that they could not care less about the outcome.

Upon rejoining the others, they learned that Lemon Eye had held two straws in his fist and Somers had drawn the short one, so Jack was the "Lead Captain." He merely shrugged, lifted his tankard to the Scorpion who clanked hers against it, and then he drank himself into oblivion by the crackling fire.

36—A Blessing Revealed

In the weeks following her crisis, Chloe had calmed considerably and the four became, once more, the peaceful household that had existed before the arrival of the Captain. The air of sadness caused by her grieving for her husband was tempered by the happy anticipation of the birth of their child, as mistress and servants turned to making preparations for the infant's arrival.

Her appetite had not returned, but she was sufficiently self-disciplined to take nourishment for the sake of the baby. She continued her daily walks with Rodrigo, although now it was not to silence his incessant urgings but to increase her strength for the gravid months ahead. In her bath each day, she critically surveyed her belly, watching for outward signs of the little one's presence, noting with tender joy each added centimeter. But she still cried every night.

She feared so many things. Far worse than never seeing her husband again was the dread that she would one day learn of his capture and execution or of his death in battle or at sea. Additionally, if she were to lose his baby, there would be no reason under heaven to continue her own life.

And how would she explain to the good people of the region the presence of a swarthy little newborn? To claim Rodrigo as the father would invite awful scandal and besides, Maria would never allow it. To refuse to name the father would lead to dangerous speculation that might well connect her with the disappearance of the Captain. To allow Maria and Rodrigo to claim the baby as their own was unthinkable.

She wanted the child to know its heritage, to bear Jack's name, to wear its legitimacy like a crown, but none of these things would be possible in the present situation. She considered moving the household to another island or to the Colonies, but there was no place in the Empire that the widow of a lieutenant governor would not draw attention with a baby born so many years after her husband's demise.

The most important consideration, by far, was the delivery of a healthy, full-term infant, so she pushed the other weighty matters from her mind several times a day to concentrate on her own physical and mental health. However, in her absence, her staff discussed such matters at length, but could devise no acceptable answers.

Precious time was running out. Chloe had succeeded in avoiding all visitors since Lieutenant Howard had questioned her during the initial canvass back in September. Now the Christmas season was upon them and social intercourse among those connected with the government would increase apace until after the governor's New Year's ball. Even a known recluse such as herself could not remain in hiding without raising questions. Emerson urged her to accept a few visitors while she still looked normal in her regular clothing. She very reluctantly agreed.

The mansion was decorated for the season and the servants engaged in the attendant interactions and shopping while in town or at the bazaar. It was a relief for them to truthfully answer inquiries as to their mistress' health by saying that she was well and happily anticipating the holidays. Each week they returned home with messages of greeting and good wishes and, despite herself, Chloe was warmed by the thoughtfulness of her neighbors and acquaintances.

One Friday about a week before Christmas, Maria and Rodrigo returned from market with a package that had been delivered by post ship from an unknown sender and source. The address, crudely scrawled on the small, rough box, read: Deliver to Mrs. Chloe C. Mistresse of Carutheres Mannor in Porte Royall in Jamaca.

The servants gathered at the large table in the kitchen to watch her open this exciting and mysterious parcel. Inside was a bundle wrapped in faded sailcloth and tied with twine. All four were breathless as she untied it. Under the coarse material was a royal purple silk scarf cradling a small, delicately carved Pernambuco figure of a jackdaw in flight. In its beak was a diamond.

Tears spilled down her cheeks as she grasped the meaning of this most precious gift: her beloved was alive! He was alive and he loved her and he was thinking about her and he wanted her to know it. He had made contact with her!

Closing her eyes, she sank slowly to the bench, clasping the treasure to her bosom and whispering, "Jack... Jack," with almost holy reverence.

Her three friends were nearly as moved as she. They sat, not taking their eyes from her face. When at last she looked at them, smiling through her tears, she breathed, "He is alive. My husband lives."

Then she rose, still holding the little wooden bird to her heart, and glided into the hall and toward the stairs.

Maria followed as Chloe went into her room and placed the priceless token on the table beside her bed along with the teakwood box and the vial of perfume.

She waited discreetly at the door as Chloe, unaware of her presence, stroked the satin-smooth wing feathers with her fingertip and whispered, "Jack, my Dearest. We are to be blest with a child, the product of our love. Male or female, this child will know every good and praiseworthy thing about you. So long as I live, you will live in our child's heart. I will devote every moment of my life to loving and nurturing and protecting this precious part of you..."

Maria silently exited and closed the door.

That night, Chloe slept deeply and, in her dreams, awoke in the hut of the Maroons. The priestess cupped Chloe's chin and looked intently into her eyes, then spoke, first in Mandingo, then in English, translating: Love your husband, *Manishie* Viollca, for this night you will conceive.

37—Greater Love Hath No Man

The *Sinecure* and the *Chimera* had polished to perfection their new skills of hunting in tandem. The crews and captains of both vessels had found an unexpected exhilaration in a perfectly executed team chase and capture. Working like wolves in a pack, each knew the role to be played in any given situation, whether the best strategy would be simple pursuit, entrapment, double raking, or ambush. After the first few engagements, their tactics had become flawless and the Scorpion's promise of increased takings and greater protection had been fulfilled beyond each pirate's fondest hopes.

The crews were well populated and the holds were filled with swag, so work was light and the rewards were great. Furthermore, their increasing focus on the Spanish ships returning from the New World had often taken them below the equator, out of the Caribbean (despite Jack's vow) and ever southward along the coast of South America. Consequently, they had slipped beyond the hottest light of scrutiny from the Royal Navy, even as their stock had risen exponentially among the Brethren of the Coast.

However, no rover was entirely safe from the British Crown. One evening the little fleet was anchored in a sheltered cove along the coast of Portuguese Brazil celebrating a particularly satisfying and lucrative victory. The pirates were ashore, drinking rum and roasting newly-killed meat and generally howling and raging as much as possible without the comforts of civilization (read: whores) until such time as they could make port someplace more accommodating. In their overconfidence, no one had posted a watch.

In the darkness beyond the cove a single large man-of-war moved cautiously toward the two corsairs. The captain watched the celebration through his glass, trying to gauge the number of buccaneers and ascertain the identity of the vessels at anchor. Taking on two heavily armed pirate ships single-handedly would normally be a foolhardy venture for a lone hunter, but catching the crews ashore and away from their artillery could result in a double capture that would make a captain's career.

He could scarcely believe that there was no watch aboard either ship, but surely, if there were, the alarm would have been sounded by now. Drawing closer, he could see that it was a brig and a schooner, although it was impossible to determine the color of the brig's furled sails in the darkness. Nevertheless, he was almost certain it was Bellamie and Scarpia. If so, his reputation would be set for life.

He conferred with his officers. Attacking the pirates on land would work only if the soldiers could silently and with reasonable safety infiltrate the dark and treacherous jungles surrounding the noisy melee, use the element of surprise, and block the escape routes into the forest or to the boats. Even so, the soldiers were outnumbered by nearly four to one in what would then have to be close combat with skilled, well-armed, and savage opponents.

Attacking from the beach would result in a few initial pirate deaths and then the soldiers would be killed like fish in a barrel. Also, he didn't like to think about the fate of any of his men taken alive by the cutthroats.

A barrage of cannon fire from the man-of-war directly into the party would yield an easy victory, but would kill a great many pirates, quite likely including one or both of the captains. He wanted as many prisoners as possible and he positively lusted to see Bellamie and Scarpia brought to justice in a British court of law even as glory was heaped upon his own head.

No, he must lure the miscreants back to their vessels and begin the attack before they could load, maneuver and fire. Additionally, one of the ships must be kept seaworthy to be manned by his forces as a prison ship for transporting the large number of captives. They would spare the *Sinecure*, it being the one of greater legend.

The plan now in place, the man-of-war moved silently abeam of the *Chimera*.

Yarborough's devotion to Jack had not flagged, although he had matured considerably and showed every promise of becoming a pirate to be reckoned with. To his captain's (usually) unspoken consternation, he was never far from the older man's side and had succeeded in emulating Jack's walk and gestures, to the endless entertainment of the veteran buccaneers in both crews. Yarborough didn't care; he knew quality when he saw it.

The appellation "Junior Jack" had pleased the youth, but the name hadn't stuck. The gawky Yarborough was nearly a foot taller than his idol and looked nothing like him; besides, the connotation was far too benign for the pirates' tastes. Some of the suggested replacements had been so vulgar that it had become a game among the crews to top the latest with one still more salacious.

Yarborough didn't seem to notice. He was too focused on polishing his persona to pay any attention. Jack called him "Yarborough" or "Pestilence" or "Bleedin' poxy reeking scurvy bilge rat," depending upon how far the boy had tried his patience.

The Scorpion found the youth's attachment to Jack charming and felt rather maternal toward the kid herself, although she was careful not to show it. She always called him by his given name: Thomas.

It was Thomas Yarborough who saw the muzzle flash before the roar of the first shot reached the beach. A second later the assembled multitude knew that the *Chimera* was under attack and assumed the *Sinecure* was, too. Like a great swarm of enraged hornets, they poured into the boats and pulled for the ships.

The *Chimera* was already in trouble. The first shot had taken down her mainmast, toppling it into her foremast and snapping it, also. The second had shattered her rudderpost, a third had pierced her hull at the stern and she was fast taking on water.

The pirates who boarded her found themselves in chaos in the darkness, the deck littered with broken yards and spars, torn sails, ropes and blocks everywhere, hatches covered with debris barring access to the gun deck. Several were killed in the continuous shelling and several more fell into the sea as she abruptly turned bow up to begin her death plunge.

The survivors swam back to the boats and started for the *Sinecure*. In their terror and desperation, most didn't look back to witness the upturned prow of their beautiful vessel slip downward and vanish beneath the black surface of the Atlantic.

However, the delay before the *Sinecure* was attacked had been invaluable to the pirates. After the initial shock, they realized that the man-of-war had singled out the *Chimera* for fast destruction and that gave them time to weigh anchor and drop canvas on the *Sinecure* and begin to move her into position, not merely to defend, but to attack.

That the naval captain was deliberately trying to spare the brig allowed Jack to go on the offensive. The skilled rovers had only to aim their always-loaded cannons and touch off the spark and the battle was engaged.

Jack sailed his ship directly at the man-of-war, neither vessel yet in position to unleash a broadside. He wanted to board and board quickly, knowing that the pirates' advantage lay in hand-to-hand combat. The ones in the boats from the *Chimera* saw what was happening and made for the enemy straightaway, determined not to lose their remaining ship and be captured. Furthermore, the lust for vengeance was now a fire in their blood.

The *Sinecure* charged so close to the naval vessel as to nearly ram her. Both ships opened fire before the *Sinecure* was fully alongside and pirates were swinging onto the man-of-war before the grapnels had been thrown. Sharpshooters in the rigging of the enemy ship had little luck picking targets amid the swirling mass of pirates in the darkness and smoke and more than one met his end when a furious buccaneer climbed high enough to get a good shot at the sniper silhouetted against the lighter sails. On the decks below, swords clashed and pistols cracked, and men shouted, cursed and screamed.

Immediately upon boarding, some pirates ran down into the gun decks to kill the artillerymen and silence the cannons before the *Sinecure* also was lost. The men fought back savagely and blood mixed with spilled powder, making the boards slippery despite the sand sprinkled about to prevent such difficulties. Meanwhile, the guns of the *Sinecure* continued their fusillade unabated and the man-of-war began taking serious damage.

Nearly insane with fury, Jack charged up the ladder to the quarterdeck after the hated captain. With no time to reload his pistols, he sought to engage the man with swords and advanced on him so rapidly he nearly drove him over the railing.

Barely having time to unsheathe his weapon, the captain of the warship backpedaled away from Jack's flashing blade, but Jack was not interested in toying with his enemy or humiliating him. He wanted to kill him as quickly and efficiently as possible and then go after his officers. This wasn't the exciting game of taking prey; this was war. In his mind's eye, Jack saw something flying from the mast of his own ship that he had never actually seen there: the red flag of No Quarter Given.

The captain sensed from descriptions he had heard that this madman was the infamous pirate whose capture could make his career for him, but this wasn't at all how he had envisioned it. Desperately fending off the aggressive drive of his adversary, he struggled to get his left hand on his pistol. The honor he had dreamed of now paled in the face of keeping his life and he was more than ready to kill Bellamie at the first opportunity. At last he had the weapon in hand, bringing it downward to level at the pirate's head as the hammer was drawn back.

Jack's eyes widened as he realized that he was a fraction of a second from death.

Then a great, crushing blackness ended his senses.

The sounds of battle had ceased only to be replaced by scraping, thumping and splashing. His head throbbed with a ferocity that rang each heartbeat in his ears.

Pain! Heartbeats! I'm still alive!

He forced open his unwilling eyes and waited for them to focus. A welcome face swam into his field of vision.

"Jack? Are you awake?"

"Aye. Where am I?"

"On the *Sinecure*. You had us quite worried, Ducks."

"What happened?"

"You hit your head on a belaying pin when you fell. You've been unconscious for several hours."

"The ship!"

"It's all right, Ducks. The warship has been sunk. It's over now."

"Oh, God. Your *Chimera*. I'm so sorry."

"It was only a ship, Ducks. I'll get another. Meantime, I'm just a member of your crew."

He would never understand how other pirate captains could be so cavalier about their vessels. He actually envied them. Loving something—or someone—so much was a kind of bondage.

"How about the men?"

"Not good, Jack. We've lost nearly half our numbers, mostly from my crew."

"Who?"

"Oh, Jack, I've lost Chang. He was my mentor when I started sailing the eastern hemisphere and is the only first mate I've ever had." She looked away and fought back tears. "But you've lost Lemon Eye, and poor Deevers is mortally wounded. I doubt he'll survive to midday. We've lost both our surgeons, although we've captured one from the navy, and both cooks are gone and all but one carpenter."

"Reed!"

"He's wounded but he'll live, as will Somers."

"Why so many deaths when we've obviously prevailed?"

"The soldiers scuttled their ship while many of our crew

were still aboard, willing to sacrifice their own to kill pirates."

Jack felt the helpless fury of wanting to punish those who were past feeling pain.

"Any prisoners other than the surgeon?"

"Eight midshipmen. Four ordinary seamen. All others perished."

"The captain?"

"Dead."

"Who?"

"I did."

Just then the whole vessel shuddered as a great thud and rumble were followed by an enormous splash. Jack tried to rise to look out a window, but fell back, dizzy.

"What's going on? And why are we listing?"

"We sustained a lot of damage, Jack. We have to jettison everything possible to lighten and stabilize her until we can make Topgallant Cay and careen. Somers is acting quartermaster, if you don't object."

"No. No, not at all. Good man, Somers." Jack was relieved to have such a capable person making decisions.

"Back to the captain. When did you kill him? How? Ran him through? Why didn't he kill me when he had the chance?"

"I shot him, Jack, right after Thomas threw you to the deck as he fired. That's how you hit your head."

Her next words broke Jack's heart.

"Thomas took the bullet meant for you, Darling. He laid down his life to save yours."

38—A Daughter's Ace

The holidays were now a distant memory, albeit a rather more pleasant memory than the four at the Bellamie household would have imagined under the circumstances. Jack's unexpected gift to Chloe had been precisely the catalyst required to allow her, and by extension, her staff, to embrace the joy of celebration and the happy anticipation of new life among themselves.

The month of April was nearly upon them and Chloe's condition was abundantly apparent no matter her style of clothing. Her natural reclusiveness once more served her well and none but her three servants had any idea what was happening with her. Emerson's advice to her to accept visitors during the holidays before she began to "show" proved wise, as no one now questioned her situation, several having so recently seen her alive and well.

She was taking excellent care of her health for the baby's sake and had regained most of her appetite, although scones were still out of the question. Actually, as pregnant women are wont to be, she was possessed of unusual cravings. She wanted mangoes nearly three meals per day and couldn't get her fill of goat cheese.

Blessedly the morning sickness had at last subsided and she was gaining strength despite her ungainly appearance as evidenced by the duration and pace of her daily walks with Rodrigo.

Nevertheless, for all of the positive aspects of her condition, certain problems, large problems, persisted. None of the four had expressed any workable suggestion as to how to explain the presence of the baby. Chloe still cried for Jack nearly every night and wept to Maria one evening that his face was fading from her memory. With no portraits of her husband to remind her, she feared she would lose him for a second time as he slipped away from her recollection. Maria told her that she would see him in the face of their child to the end of her days. Chloe prayed the baby would be a near copy of its handsome father.

Once again, Emerson could see that the resolution of the situation fell to him. Once again, he burned midnight oil, pondering the possibilities and pitfalls of each speculative course of action, organizing his thoughts in as objective a manner as he could with the information he had at hand.

When he had at last settled on a plan, he realized that he must keep it from Chloe until it had come to fruition, for if it were to fail, it would fail due to events which would tear her apart were she to learn of them. He and Maria and Rodrigo would remain mum to her about it, would carefully protect their mistress from such a calamity.

A week later, on his Thursday recreation day, he rose before the sun as usual, mounted Zeus as usual, and cantered off as usual. But once beyond sight of the house, he changed direction and galloped toward town.

The young carpenter opened the doors at the back of the shop to allow the sawdust-laden air to escape into the alley. Just then he observed a horseman approaching, a nattily dressed middle-aged man of regal bearing astride a large gray hunter. Assuming this was a customer, he paused by the doors until the man had halted beside him and dismounted.

"Yes, Sir, needing a good carpenter, are you?"

"Are you Mr. Daniel Everson, the proprietor of this establishment?"

"At your service, Mr.—?"

"Bentley. Emerson Bentley. I am the butler at the Be—, at the Caruthers mansion. May we speak in private?"

Puzzled, the pirate-turned-tradesman invited his visitor into the small room that served as his office and closed the door.

The heat of midday had rendered the mansion and its grounds nearly devoid of activity when the lovely young woman swept into the drawing room and over to the older man, planting a kiss on his cheek and making him smile despite the interruption of his reading.

"Jenny, Darling! What brings you here this time of day? Shouldn't you be resting?"

"Oh, Father, you coddle me so. I'm pregnant, not consumptive." She patted her barely rounded belly.

"Jenny! That word! Please observe some decorum."

"Father, I don't have time for a dispute with you over my manners. I need to speak with you about an urgent matter concerning Jack."

"The pirate? Damnation, Child! Can we never put that sordid episode behind us?"

"Father, may I remind you that your first grandchild is coming as a direct result of the matchmaking efforts of that pirate?"

"I know, Jenny. I know." He sighed. "What has Bellamie done this time?"

"It seems he has gotten Chloe Caruthers pregnant." Jenny just loved shocking her father.

"Jenny, that word again—*what?*"

"Listen, Father. This is important. Her butler paid a visit to the shop this morning and told Daniel that, when the Captain went missing last fall after Uncle wounded him, he escaped to the Caruthers mansion. Lady Caruthers took him in and nursed him back to health. Then—"

"Lady Caruthers! How dare she? That is tantamount to treason! Well now, of course, she must be placed under arrest."

"She most certainly will not be arrested, Father! Please hear me out. Her butler told my husband that Jack and Lady Caruthers fled across the island to Montego Bay to escape Uncle's men, and there they were married in October. He left to return to his ship and she sailed back to Port Royal, not yet knowing that she was carrying his child."

"Another Bellamie. Why is God torturing me?"

"Father, please. Anyway, Jack does not know that he is to

become a father and his wife is pining away at this time when a woman most needs her husband."

"Why are you burdening me with this, Jenny?"

"Because you're the Governor. You are the only person short of the King who can remedy this situation."

"Jenny, your fidelity to your reprehensible friend is indeed touching, but I feel no compulsion to protect that criminal while he enjoys a happy reunion with his treasonous wife and his misbegotten offspring. He should be everlastingly grateful that he still draws breath, much less leads the life of an honest man. No, I'm afraid I must refuse."

Jenny fully expected this reaction and was prepared for it. She suddenly clasped her arms across her middle and bent forward with a little cry of pain. The governor sprang to her side.

"Jenny! Darling! What's the matter? Are you all right?"

"Oh. Oh, Father," she panted. "I mustn't become so upset. It's bad for the baby. Oh, dear, I don't think I can endure knowing that poor Mrs. Bellamie will have hers without a husband or loving parents to comfort her, that her poor little innocent child will never know its father, that—oh! oh! *ow!*"

"All right! All right, Jenny. I'll do it, just please calm down. Take a deep breath, Dear. I'll send for the doctor." He reached to pull the cord to summon the butler, but she placed her hand on his arm, stopping him.

"No, not yet. Oh, I'm feeling better already. Now, let's talk about what we must do to unite that little family."

"Well, it isn't too difficult to figure out. I'll have to issue a Letter of Marque and Reprisal to Bellamie and all who sail under his flag. Then he can return in safety."

"That is not enough, Father, and you know it. That buys him safety only while at sea. He must receive a full pardon from the Crown or else the charges will hang over his head. He can be arrested and executed for past offenses the moment he disembarks."

"Oh, that won't happen once he's a privateer."

"Without a formal writ from you as an agent of the Crown,

it *will* happen! Uncle can't wait to get his hands on Jack and he'll be within his rights to do so unless you officially call him off."

The governor sighed.

"That is true, Jenny. Commodore Rothwell keeps Bellamie's old hat on his desk, waiting to reunite it with its owner on the scaffold. This is going to sit very hard with him."

"That is unfortunate, Father, but completely beside the point. You must make Uncle understand that he is to order all of his men to leave Jack alone when he arrives. Uncle is military through and through. He'll obey a command no matter how distasteful."

"Of course, Jenny. What else? Bequeath part of my estate to Bellamie's child? Rename the island in his honor?"

"Sarcasm doesn't suit you, Father. You must cover every eventuality including granting irrefutable immunity from prosecution to Mrs. Bellamie and all her staff and to anyone else who might have helped Jack escape."

His own child's role in another escape was never far from Governor Hunter's mind.

"Why don't I just appoint him lieutenant governor while I'm at it?"

"Capital idea, Father! I knew you'd come around."

"Sarcasm doesn't suit you much better, my Dear. Drawing up these documents will not be difficult, nor will curbing Commodore Rothwell after the initial shock, but how do we get word to Bellamie? Any navy ship that approaches his vessel will be attacked forthwith, as will a merchantman."

"Daniel and I have already discussed this. The only type of ship that can safely hail a corsair, besides another corsair naturally, would be an industry vessel, a whaler or a collier, a turtler, perhaps. You prepare the documents and Daniel can locate Jack and deliver them to him in safety, since he is known and respected by the pirates."

"Jenny? Are you sure? He would be gone several weeks and there is no guarantee of safety."

"I am not so far along in my pregnancy as is Mrs. Bellamie. I can spare my husband for a few weeks at this time. True, his safety is not guaranteed, but there is no real and present danger. In fact, more than anyone else, Daniel can discharge this duty with impunity. It would be patently wrong of us not to correct this injustice."

"It's not an injustice, it's—oh, what's the use. Have your husband meet with me tomorrow evening and I will have the documents signed and ready for him."

He accepted her always-welcome kiss on his cheek and then remained staring at the door after she had exited. He knew that he had been gulled, but there was no undoing it now.

39—Topgallant Cay

Jack was having difficulty resisting the urge to wallow in self-pity. The brief but glorious time of sailing with the *Chimera* and her crew was over. Two fine ships and more than three hundred good men and true from both sides of the battle now lay in watery graves near Portuguese Brazil. His beloved *Sinecure* was so badly wounded she required all the skill her crew possessed to keep her afloat until they could reach Topgallant Cay. His head hurt most of the time and he longed for Chloe's tender ministrations.

Somers had his hands full with a decimated crew, a dispirited captain, and a damaged ship, but his skill and dedication were equal to the task. The Scorpion lent her strength and advice where useful while being careful not to overreach, being captain no longer.

The lump on Jack's head was shrinking by the day, but she worried about his state of mind. It was unnatural for him to be depressed. She knew he blamed himself for not posting a watch that night, but she was as guilty as he and, for that matter, so were Somers and Lemon Eye. It was tragic, but it was over now and life must go on.

Somers entered the cabin where Jack slumped, staring out at the sea; the Scorpion stood beside him, rubbing his shoulder.

"Cap'n, I've ordered another fotheringsail on the starboard breach. That should get us to Topgallant if we don't run into bad weather."

Jack didn't respond. The Scorpion asked if he had heard Somers.

"Aye. I heard. That's good, Somers. Do whatever is necessary."

"I intend to, Cap'n." Somers gave Jack a strange look. He was the quartermaster; he didn't require the captain's permission to make these decisions. He was merely informing him of their progress. Jack hadn't moved and Somers resisted the urge to ask him to repeat what he had just been told.

Emerson dismounted and handed the reins to Rodrigo, who looked at him questioningly. The butler gave an almost imperceptible nod and made certain that Rodrigo saw the slim leather portfolio he carried under his coat, then he strode toward the house to wash up for dinner. Maria was setting the table for four.

Chloe arrived in the kitchen shortly thereafter and sat down. As usual, she enjoyed the ambience of the meal with her friends and didn't notice their uncharacteristic and barely-concealed impatience. When she was at last safely ensconced in her room, Maria hurried back to the kitchen where Emerson and Rodrigo waited.

"Please tell us, Emerson. Did the carpenter have news this time?"

"He did indeed. His good wife has secured all necessary seals and signatures and he is soon to depart carrying the full pardon and the Letter of Marque for Captain Bellamie. He gave me this document, which exonerates Madam and each of us for our roles in aiding and abetting the Captain. We cannot yet show this to Madam, of course, but we can rest secure in the knowledge that all of us are safe from prosecution for these crimes henceforth. If all goes well and Mr. Everson succeeds in bringing the Captain home, we can then show them to Madam and alleviate yet another worry for her."

Maria clasped her hands and gave a heartfelt prayer of gratitude, to which the others echoed, "Amen."

Now that the time had come to bid him farewell, Jenny sorely regretted having allowed her husband to embark on this errand. She stood under the portico of the governor's mansion and fluttered a handkerchief at the departing coach, then covered her face and wept as her father tried to console her.

Remembering that she had been instrumental in bringing this situation about, she forced herself to regain her composure, lest her father begin to gloat.

It was some comfort to her to know that three people at the Bellamie estate were praying for his safe return, just as she, and she would have loved to go there and visit and talk with them about the two fathers-to-be out there somewhere on the vast ocean. But the butler had warned Daniel that Mrs. Bellamie must not know, lest the mission fail for some terrible reason and she then be devastated.

So Jenny had to remain at the fort, witnessing Rothwell's black moods and enduring others' myriad subtle and not-so-subtle hints to reveal what she knew about the sudden and mysterious absolution her father had granted the notorious pirate captain. She had never felt so alone.

Topgallant Cay held a full complement of ships in various stages of repair. Four pirate vessels and an errant whaler, which had wandered too far south in search of the Common Cachalot, lay at anchor or hauled out on the sandbar. The tiny cove had room for no more. Jack's heart sank as he handed the telescope to Somers.

"Cap'n, it doesn't look promising, but two, maybe three of 'em appear to be at least minimally seaworthy. The *Sinecure* is unlikely to remain afloat another night, so I'm going to take the launch and inquire if one could mercifully put about and let us in to careen. You should join us, if you're feeling up to it."

"Aye, I'll go along. I'm still the captain of this ship."

No one disputes that, thought Somers.

"I'll go, too. Sometimes a woman can be more persuasive when dealing with men." The Scorpion was trying to sound nonchalant. Actually, she was unwilling to leave Jack's side with him in his present, lingering melancholy. All they needed to compound their already awful luck would be for him to pick a fight with a colleague.

So, the boat was put in and quickly filled with pirates eager to escape the gloom of their battered ship. Jack, Reed, Somers and the Scorpion automatically put on their most confident airs, instinctively seeking to avoid tarnishing their gleaming reputation in the Trade. By the time the launch was docked, its occupants were in full swagger.

Boasting of how they had taken their damages in a pitched battle with three warships, all of which were sunk, the *Sinecure*'s officers set the tone for the behavior of the rest of the crew and soon pirates and whale men were swarming around them, clamoring for details of the exciting yarn.

"First things first, ye scurvy dogs. Me *Sinecure* needs t' careen and do it quick-like, so's I'll be askin' fer a volunteer t' kindly give 'er berth," Jack slurred. It felt strange to "talk pirate." He had stopped doing so, reverting to more polished English, the same day he took up with the Scorpion. She never talked that way. Ever.

The crew of the whaler, already grateful to pirates in general for letting them make repairs in safety and then treating them as equals, were now overjoyed to meet a captain of such renown. They couldn't wait to defer to Jack and were honored to move aside for the *Sinecure*. The necessary arrangements were made and the sorry brig limped into the safety of the cove as all personnel made ready to abandon her and haul her out.

Jack and the Scorpion sat close together under a canopy of woven palms and watched the men working to repair their ship. Despite the extensive damage, it would not take more than two weeks to put her right once more. The structure of the vessel, the masts and keel and ribs, was sound and the necessary materials were readily at hand, unlike the near-rebuilding that had kept her so long at Vestal Cay.

Nevertheless, he stared morosely at the activity and said little. The Scorpion watched him for a long time; he didn't seem aware of it.

"Jack, Darling, are you feeling unwell? Your bump is completely gone except for some discoloration."

"I'm fine. I'm fine. You worry too much."

"No, I don't. You haven't been the same since the battle. Jack, you've been a pirate too long to let these things get to you. The *Sinecure* is going to be as good as new. Don't despair so."

"I'm not despairing. I know she'll be right again. But the *Sinecure* and I, we're both getting older and it isn't fun anymore. We've seen too many battles, too much death, too much destruction, too many days sitting ashore while my ship is hauled out."

"In the first place, you were having great fun less than a month ago when we were preying in tandem and in the second place, if you didn't insist upon using just one ship throughout your whole life, you'd spend more days at sea and not brood so much over an inanimate object."

"Leave me be. Just leave me be." He bent forward and lowered his forehead onto his arms, which were folded across his knees.

She leaned over to place a kiss on his head.

"I'll leave you be, Darling, but have faith. Your luck is sure to improve. Believe that."

Taking their cue from the buccaneers, the men on the now-repaired whaler concluded that their northward itinerary could spare a day or so of unbridled revelry before returning to the grim duty of work. On the advice of their benefactors, they set a course for Tortuga.

40—Outrage!

Daniel Everson hadn't been in a waterfront tavern since his pirate days sailing with Jack Bellamie nearly five years before and he felt out of place now, despite his favorite sword at his side and Jack's beat-up old black tricorne on his head. The noises, the stench, the fights made him wonder how any man could be entertained by such debasement. The prostitutes, seeing his youthful, clean and handsome appearance, flocked around him, interfering with his ability to move from one place to another to listen for conversations that would tell him which ship would be bound for the Windward Passage.

Four hours of defending himself against the unwanted advances of whores and challenges of drunken sailors had produced no leads that wouldn't be foolhardy to follow. He debated putting aboard anything eastbound and trying another port, but he knew the setting would be similar and the prospects no better.

The stress of the day, from having to leave his darling wife, to the hypervigilance in the taverns and the frustration of not finding a proper ship, had worn him down. He could feel himself becoming discouraged despite knowing that the right opportunity would surely present itself within a day or so.

He could have gotten a room at one of the inns, but he wanted to conserve his funds in the event his mission proved overlong. Still, he wanted to get away from the din and frenetic activity, so he wandered down to the boatyards and looked around.

Spying an overturned skiff, he crawled under it and promptly fell asleep.

Dawn had not yet colored the eastern sky when he awoke with a start, hearing strange voices nearby, and he sat up too quickly, hitting his head on the seat of the skiff. Momentarily dazed, he lay back and began mentally putting the pieces together, realizing where he was and why.

That done, he listened to what the voices were saying. Two men were discussing the best places for catching turtles and the proximity of good markets for their take. He heard one say something about sailing with the tide and heading for Cape Rose. Immediately alert, he scurried from under the skiff and approached them.

Indeed, they were the bo's'n and coxswain of a turtler and indeed, they were bound for Cape Rose and the Windward Passage. Daniel inquired if they could use another hand and was told to report to Captain Martens on an old lapstrake schooner they identified as the *Felicity*. He lit out in search of breakfast and a launch to take him to his ship.

Daniel found life aboard the turtler harder than expected due to the age of the ship, the nature of the work, and the paucity of crewmen, but the camaraderie of the men made the hours fly. He found them to be a cross between pirates and law-abiding mariners in that they were relatively free of strict rules so long as the vessel was not endangered and the payload was obtained and properly secured.

From experience, he knew that pirates and turtle men often caroused together in ports no honest sailor would approach, so he requested being dropped at Tortuga since they were heading that way. The captain saw no reason not to, providing the work was done to his satisfaction.

There was no cause to dissemble before these men, so Daniel let it be known from the beginning that he was on the trail of his friend, Captain Blackjack Bellamie, and the *Sinecure*. They had been at sea only two days when another sailor, overhearing his conversation with a shipmate, dropped a bomb that nearly made Daniel call off his mission of mercy.

"Sure an' yer prob'ly headin' in the wrong direction there, Sonny. Ol' Blackjack Bellamie and his lover been workin' the South Atlantic fer some months now. Ye should find yerself a ship bound that way, not Tortuga."

Daniel felt himself go pale, but surely he had heard wrong.

"Jack Bellamie and who, did you say?"

"His lover, the one they call the Scorpion or Captain Scarpia. Her ship's the *Chimera* and they been workin' as a team and really tearin' up the Spanish trade, from what I hear tell."

Sudden nausea almost overwhelmed him. So, Jack was not a decent man, after all. How could he have misjudged his former captain so? Had he been so immature that his judgment was colored by it? *Fool! Fool!*

He only dimly heard the ensuing discussion among the mates of how pretty the Scorpion was, in a wild, animalistic sort of way, how she had preyed on ships in the eastern hemisphere for years before coming to the Caribbean, how the two were now inseparable. As is standard among mariners, several relayed horrific tales from an "unimpeachable" source, tales that had the Scorpion eating human flesh, commanding a crew of fanatically devoted Chinamen, and copulating with Jack in front of both crews and their hostages. Daniel turned away, sickened to his heart.

He had never hated any human being as he now hated Jack Bellamie. At least Korsakov had not pretended to be anything but a vicious, bloodthirsty rogue. He felt personally betrayed by his former friend's perfidy and would have resigned his charge at the first opportunity, but the former Mrs. Caruthers (he couldn't bear to think of the poor soul as "Mrs. Bellamie" now) deserved better. He resolved that he and Jenny and Governor Hunter would plot with Mr. Bentley to keep such terrible news from her as long as possible.

Over and over, he rehearsed the scenario when he would finally make contact with the bilge rat, what he would say, how he would remain aloof and unemotional, deliver his news and quit forever the *Sinecure* and her black-hearted captain.

He prayed that Jack and this "Scorpion" person had not sunk into such depravity that they would kill the messenger. Jack would likely spare him out of respect for his allegiance to Jack during the mutiny, but the Scorpion might go berserk and have her Chinamen do something horrible to him, especially if Jack had not already told her that he had a wife ashore. Now fear was joining outrage. He sorely regretted having started this quest.

He whipped the tricorne from his head and ruffled his hair with his fingers, as though trying to rid himself of a pestilence.

His duties on the *Felicity* had become dreary and exhausting and, by the time they put into Tortuga, he was grimly set on completing this mission and returning home as quickly as possible. The debauchery of the place made no impression on him now, as he could imagine nothing more debased than Jack's behavior. Indeed, a drunken tryst with a whore would be mild compared to the infidelity of heart and soul that Bellamie was now exhibiting. He went from tavern to pub seeking information and, at every turn, heard more stories about the two captains and their unholy union.

At last he came upon the crew of a whaler that had actually been with the renowned *Sinecure* recently at Topgallant Cay. The men were eager to relate their experiences with the notorious captain and had information that was first-hand and up-to-date. Daniel bought them a round of drinks and settled in to listen.

He gleaned the important information that the *Chimera* had been sunk and that the Scorpion was now sailing with Jack on the *Sinecure*. He also learned that the *Sinecure* had been damaged in a fight and was being repaired when the whaler left, that Captain Bellamie had said he was done with the South Atlantic and was returning to the Caribbean. In fact, they had overheard Jack and the Scorpion hatching plans to prey on merchantmen sailing from Jamaica to Britain in the waters between the Caymanas and Cuba.

Daniel's search was now much narrower. It would be easy to find any number of corsairs or turtlers bound for the same area and few would refuse to take him aboard or fear crossing paths with the *Sinecure*.

By midnight he had secured passage on the pirate ship *Proteus*, which would set sail at noon. He returned to the harbor to find a secluded spot to spend the night.

41—A Strained Reunion

As do honest men, pirates possess varying degrees of ambition. The captain of the *Proteus*, one Albert "Looter" Ferrell, and his crew were motivated, not by riches, but by the freedom and relative ease of a life lived beyond the rules of polite society. To them, swag was merely a means to an end. Never before had Daniel been aboard a ship whereon all enterprise was geared toward the least amount of effort.

The ship itself, an aged clinker-built barquentine, showed myriad signs of benign neglect. Everywhere was slapdash patching: sails, yards, windlasses, futtocks, strakes. Even the cannons were dull and had areas of rusty patina. He didn't want to imagine the condition of the hull below the surface. Ferrell's own flag, a reclining skeleton holding an hourglass, bespoke lassitude.

Able to neither deny his lifelong work ethic nor endure boredom, Daniel turned to performing any duty for which he possessed a modicum of competence while the pirates looked on in a kind of bemused contempt. Occasionally, he would give them a look intended to shame them into joining him, but he still had a lot to learn about this crew. He worked alone.

On the second day out, someone spotted a ship dead ahead and apparently sailing unescorted on a northeast bearing. Closer scrutiny revealed her to be an East Indiaman riding low in the water. The hold of the *Proteus* being empty, Daniel felt they would surely pluck so ripe a plum that seemed to have been sent by providence.

As Ferrell stood on the quarterdeck staring through the glass at the prize, someone shouted, "Run up the black flag, Cap'n?"

To Daniel's astonishment, Ferrell drawled, "Nay. Just put

about and give her berth." And that's exactly what they did, with not so much as a muttered protest from the crew.

In retrospect, he concluded that it was probably a blessing for himself, as such a beat-up old tub as the *Proteus* was unlikely to best a well-armed East Indiaman.

After a week, he had given up trying to correct the ship's problems single-handedly and, like his hosts, performed only the most essential tasks and then only when directed by the quartermaster. He spent a lot of time—too much time—staring out at the sea and fretting over his former friend's infidelity.

He mentally rehearsed speeches designed to wither Jack and, if not bring him to heartfelt penance, at least diminish his enjoyment of his inamorata. He envisioned seeing hurt and shame and regret in Jack's eyes as his words stung like hornets. But then he would remind himself that he really didn't know the pirate at all, had sorely misjudged and overrated him. He just might be forced to pay the highest price for his vituperation and Jenny would bear their child as a widow.

Three more times Ferrell passed up opportunities to take an easy mark. His crew seemed perfectly content with those decisions, but Daniel was nearly beside himself. Jack had told him once, "You're a born pirate, Boy," and so it must be, as he was beginning to wonder how much longer he could endure sailing with these great slugs. If it weren't for his intense hatred of Jack, he would keep to the original plan, put aboard the *Sinecure* when they found her and return to civilization in the relative sanity of a working privateer vessel. But he figured the less time spent in Jack's company the better, so he was stuck with Ferrell's holiday camp.

He leaned on the railing as they slowly cruised under a minimum of sail, watching the water throwing small rooster tails as it rolled past a crude wooden slab nailed haphazardly across a breach in a strake at the waterline. He wondered if the *Proteus* could catch a leaky rowboat manned by a sickly grandmother.

When he looked up at the horizon again, he saw something in the distance. Apparently no one else was bothering to watch.

"Sail! Sail off the larboard stern!"

The quartermaster, irritated at being roused from his nap, called, "All hands, as you were," and pulled his bicorne over his eyes again. Frantic, Daniel ran to the captain.

"Cap'n Ferrell, if we don't put about, she'll pass abeam of us and we'll lose her!"

"Son, we don't want her."

"Why not? You're pirates! Don't you want to take prey and earn a living?"

"If we wished to earn a living, we'd all be carpenters."

Just then their argument was interrupted by a shout.

"Cap'n she's giving chase!"

"Drop sail and run up the Union Jack, then."

The false colors were raised, the decrepit ship gave a small surge as wind caught the sails, and the pirates showed interest in another ship for the first time. Daniel saw the captain's body suddenly go tense as he stood watching their pursuer through the glass.

"Hold up! Strike the Union Jack and run up the black flag!"

Daniel caught his breath, thinking that they were going to do battle after all when a shout from the waist put that idea to rest.

"Man the guns, Cap'n?"

"Nay. She's a black brig sportin' striped sails. We've found Bellamie."

Daniel was surprised to feel more trepidation at this news than had a battle been imminent.

From a distance, it appeared an easy mark. Jack, Reed, Somers and the Scorpion took turns with the glass, watching the antics of the pathetic barquentine before them. When they saw the Union Jack, they concluded that it was some down-on-their-luck work crew hardly worth the chase. Jack was considering calling it off to search for bigger game, when he suddenly lowered the glass, scowling.

"God help us. It's Ferrell."

"What's he needin' now, I wonder?" Reed looked as disgusted as his captain.

The Scorpion and Somers were puzzled.

"Ferrell? Who's that?"

"How do you know he needs something?"

With a sigh, Jack explained. "Ferrell's a long-time pirate in these waters. No competition for us, by the way. Goes by the nickname 'Looter,' but anyone who's run across him knows him as 'Moocher.' His ship's always ready to fall apart, his crew are as lazy and trifling as he, and they never have adequate supplies because obtaining such might require work. In truth, they're more scavenger than pirate. Ferrell prefers to tail other corsairs and pick over their leavings like a jackal. Had the same crew for years because they all have the same attitude and no other captain would want 'em."

Somers was ready to put distance between the two ships and get on with things, but Jack disagreed.

"Let's see what they're desperate for this time. I won't run off and leave any of the Brethren to suffer hunger or thirst if I can help it. But they're not getting anything that isn't necessary."

Before hearing the disheartening news about Jack and the Scorpion, Daniel had envisioned a happy reunion with his old friend, standing on the railing of whatever ship brought them together, waving Jack's black tricorne and making jokes about chasing him all over the Caribbean to return it. Now, he stood in the waist of the *Proteus* watching the exchange of coarse, piratical greetings between the two crews as she hove to and wishing the next few hours were over.

There was a bit of a melee as some pirates from each ship boarded the other to greet old acquaintances and lavish friendly insults on each other. Somers and the Scorpion made themselves scarce, leaving the more experienced Jack to deal with Ferrell. They didn't notice an obvious landsman following that captain across the plank to the *Sinecure*.

The greeting between the two captains was cut short when Jack spied Daniel. "Moocher" took the opportunity to catch up with Reed, draping his arm across the first mate's shoulders preparatory to currying favor.

However, the joy that glowed in Jack's countenance at seeing Daniel was not returned and Jack knew something was amiss. Before he could ask, Daniel spoke with icy control.

"May we go someplace private to talk, Captain Bellamie?"

Looking puzzled, Jack nevertheless jauntily invited him into his cabin before it could fill up with crewmen.

"And how is the fair Jenny? Heard you married. Is that why you've been conspicuously absent from the Trade all this time?"

Daniel remained silent, his face an unreadable mask.

Jack closed the door and tried again.

"So, let's hear it, Boy. Indeed, how is the lovely Jenny? Tell it now, did you really get married?"

"Yes, we are married and she is as well as can be expected under the circumstances."

"Circumstances? What circumstances?"

"We are expecting our first child."

Still trying to be lighthearted and flailing his hands about, Jack fairly sang, "Ah! So the boy is a man after all! You're going to be a father."

"So are you."

This stopped Jack in mid-flail.

"What?"

"Your wife is pregnant. The child is due in June."

Ashen, Jack went to the door, his ebony gaze fixed on Daniel as if he were afraid this apparition might vanish were he to blink. He pushed open the door and, never taking his eyes off the younger man, he shouted for his first mate.

"Reed! Mr. Reed!"

"Aye, Cap'n?"

"Send the Scorpion in here, please."

Daniel's composure failed at the mention of that name.

"No! Leave your paramour out of this discussion—"

"My paramour? Is that—"

"I have no desire to meet her nor so much as lay eyes on her. Please let us conclude this conversation alone."

"Well, you're going to meet her, like it or not. Ah, there she is! Tshaya, this is my old friend and carpenter from before the mutiny, Daniel Everson. Daniel, I'm pleased to introduce my sister, Tshaya Petulengro Jamison Scarpia, better known as the Scorpion."

Daniel, of course, was speechless and, barring her appearance, Tshaya was as charming, gracious and polished as a lady of the Queen's court, compounding his astonishment. Jack was nearly incoherent with laughter, part of which was an hysterical reaction to the news about Chloe.

"Tshaya (hahaha). Tshaya (fmmmpff), young Dan here tells me (hahaha), he has wonderful news about my—oh (hehehehe)—my wife, and he thought you were my lover!" At this point, he gave up attempting to talk, doubling over and staggering to a chair into which he fell, helpless.

"Your lover?" Tshaya turned to Daniel who was still mute but looking a little miffed. "His lover? Wherever did you get such an idea?"

Daniel found his voice as Jack guffawed in the background.

"Well, all the pirates in Tortuga and Port Royal said... Well, how was I to know?"

That instantly shut off Jack's merriment.

"Port Royal! Damn their eyes! Pirates gossip worse than old women. What if it gets back to Chloe? Prepare to set sail for Jamaica! I'm going to clear this up if I have to sink every ship in the Trade."

His sister was alarmed at his rash declaration.

"Jack, no! You can't go back to Jamaica. You don't stand a chance!"

This was Daniel's cue to perform the second part of his mission. He produced a portfolio from inside his vest.

"Not anymore, Miss, Mrs., uh, Scor—, um, Tshaya. My wife is the governor's daughter and, when we learned that Jack was about to become a father, she—"

"A father! Jack you're going to be a father! I'm going to be an aunt!"

At this, chaos broke out in the captain's cabin. All three were talking, loudly, at once. Jack was vowing to brave the entire British Empire, France and Spain to be at Chloe's side, Tshaya was rhapsodizing over her niece- or nephew-to-be, and Daniel was trying to shout above the din that Jack was a free man and could return to his wife in safety with the papers he had brought.

Hearing the ruckus, Somers and Reed came running with Ferrell plodding behind, irked that he had been interrupted mid-plea. As soon as they burst through the door, Tshaya was trying to hug them both.

"Jack's having a baby! Jack's having a baby!"

Reed just stood, gaping, while the ever-droll Somers cast a lingering look up and down the Captain's frame, coming to rest on his nearly concave midsection.

"I never would have guessed."

"Not me, you jackass! My wife."

"Yer *married*?" Reed was incredulous.

"Aye, and about to become a father it seems."

"I thought we were friends. Why didn't ye tell me?"

"I did tell ye, but ye wouldn't believe me."

Reed's mouth worked as he thought back, trying to ascertain when such information had been revealed. Then it hit him.

"The English lady! The one who helped ye escape. Ye went to Montego Bay on a melon wagon and got married there."

"Aye. The English lady on the melon wagon."

"Ye made it sound like a lie."

"That was your interpretation."

Somers was nearly as surprised as Reed. He studied Jack, frowning.

"You told no one. Not your quartermaster, not even your old friend and first mate. What's the matter with you, Bellamie?"

"In the first place I did tell someone. I told my sister." (It was not a secret that Tshaya was his sister, but, being less than outrageous gossip, that information hadn't yet made its way through the pirate grapevine.) "In the second place, if such information ever got back to the government, my wife and her good servants would be in serious, nay deadly, peril, and in the third place, I didn't want a bunch of scurvy seadogs feeling sorry for poor, lonely Jack! *Capiche?*"

"Well it does help explain your foul mood of late."

"My foul mood! I'll have you know, Mr. Somers—"

"Gentlemen! Gentlemen." Daniel stepped between the two. "If we can put aside these differences for a moment, I have important documents that will change everything."

He opened the portfolio and spread the papers on the table.

"As I was saying, my wife is the governor's daughter and, when we heard that Mrs. Bellamie was with child—"

"How did you hear? Who knows about this?" Jack was suddenly frightened for Chloe's safety if such information had leaked beyond the four at the estate. So, Daniel had to start at the beginning, with Emerson's first visit to the carpenter's shop, the exoneration of Chloe and her staff, the full pardon for Jack and then the Letter of Marque.

Each new revelation was met with questions and a general feeling of optimism and relief at the answers until Daniel showed them the Letter. This was met with silence as the pirates took in the meaning. Somers was first to speak.

"Privateers. We'll be privateers. This isn't good, Jack. If the men wished to work for the government, they'd have joined the navy. This isn't good."

"It's good in that it removes one of the largest threats to our enterprises," Tshaya opined. "We spend as much time and powder and effort avoiding the King's men as we do taking prey. This could free us considerably."

"Free us from taking English ships, including East Indiamen!"

"It seems to me we've done quite well in recent months taking nothing but Spanish ships. England isn't the only nation to sail the waters of the New World, you know."

"No, but she's the largest, richest and most powerful."

"All the more reason to take prey under her approval and protection!"

Jack could endure no more of their bickering.

"Please! Please. Let's keep our heads here. This is a momentous decision, to be sure, and each man will have to weigh the pros and cons and then opt according to his own best interests. For me, there is no choice whatsoever. My duty is to be with my wife and child and now I can do so while still practicing my craft. The *Sinecure* and I are henceforth privateers and that much is settled. The men will naturally have their free will in the matter. Some may stay with me, some may leave."

"Some may mutiny!"

"Mr. Somers, that is enough," Tshaya commanded, reverting to her former authority. "After we have gotten the *Proteus* on her way, we'll call a general meeting and inform the men, then take a vote. I'm sure many will want to leave, as the spoils of privateering are considerably less for the crew, but others will welcome a respite from the shadow of the noose."

Jack added, "Aye, the spoils are less if disbursed according to the terms of the Letter, but as captain, I will assure that each man gets an equal share in the same proportion as before. There should be little diminution in their take."

Somers was not impressed. "Sure, you'll keep the proportions as is, but those proportions will be disbursed only after the Crown has taken its cut."

He had him there. Jack had no answer to that and the outcome would simply have to wait until they could vote. He didn't reveal his inner terror that he could be facing another mutiny. He suddenly needed more rum.

Despite the numbing effects of Kill Devil, Jack could not relax, his imagination running away with gory scenes of mayhem and mutinous disaster. Neither Reed nor Daniel, not even Tshaya could calm him and Somers didn't even try.

Ferrell was in no hurry to leave as his crew were partaking fully of the *Sinecure*'s hospitality. Since both crews were dead drunk, the ships remained together through the night, but by morning Jack urged Somers to get the men back onto their proper vessel so they could make way. Ferrell was "a little short" on water, flour, nails, and oakum, so Jack gave him a goodly amount of each and made his apologies that he couldn't visit longer.

"Unless ye wish to join us on our next raid... Going to be a rough one. Probably entail a long chase and a longer fight, but yer welcome to share in the fun."

Ferrell had no intention of expending that much energy, so he rounded up his droopy pirates and made a fast getaway, well, fast for the *Proteus*.

Jack, Reed, Somers, Tshaya, and Daniel decided to head for Jamaica straightaway, remain mum about the Letter and not hold the vote until shortly before they were due to arrive, reasoning that a mutiny was not as likely near a port where a man could jump ship and pursue other options. Nevertheless, Jack was a wreck and was making the others the same. Somers urged the ship at full sail to put an end to all the angst as swiftly as possible.

Jack was beginning to understand Chloe's mood swings on their flight across the island. He felt euphoria at the prospect of seeing his wife again and having a family, then terror at a possible mutiny, followed by sadness and regret for the death and pain he had caused in his career, and all within the space of an hour's time. *Of course, she was that way because she was pregnant*, he reasoned. *Come to think of it, I'm this way because she's pregnant*. The thought was amusing to him and brought him a little equanimity that was most welcome.

The nerve-wracking secret was not revealed to the crew of the *Sinecure* until they were a little more than a day out of Port Royal. At the gathering, Jack made the announcements with his usual unassailable air of confidence and authority that belied the fear in his heart. Although he wasn't resolutely determined to keep his family a guarded secret, he nevertheless instinctively refrained from revealing such intimate details to the crew, giving his reasons for the sudden change in status as "pressing personal matters ashore" and dismissing the attendant questions with a wave of his hand.

He did not need nor wish to open himself to anyone but Chloe—and Tshaya, of course. After all, she had helped their mama change his nappies, so there was little to hide from her. Oh yes, there was also Mirella, their older sister who now lived near Charles Town on the Ashley, Tshaya said. Mirella had done all that and more, ordering her little brother about and tattling at the least infraction, smirking when he got his fanny spanked. *Damn women! How'd I end up with three of 'em bossing me around? Bet the baby will be a girl, too. She'll be making me dance before she can talk.*

The meeting was a lengthy affair as the pirates had many questions and most of the answers led to debates of varying duration. Tshaya and Reed were helping field the queries and clearly showing their loyalty to Jack. Somers was playing his cards close to his vest, cagily waiting to see the outcome before committing himself. He was devoted to Tshaya, but loathed the whole concept of privateering, considering it to be a form of prostitution no self-respecting buccaneer would consider.

Eventually the discussions wound down as the pirates finally possessed sufficient information to make their decisions. Jack was somewhat more confident since there had been no hint of the dreaded mutiny and all hands seemed agreeable to bringing the *Sinecure* safely into port no matter their choice. He called for a vote.

In his fretting, he had not taken into account the fact that the majority of his crew was comprised of rookies who had not yet gotten the hang of the piratical ideal of putting one's self first. He was their captain and this was their ship and their allegiance remained with him. Several more were long-time associates of Tshaya and Somers and respected their opinion sufficiently to follow them, not realizing that Somers was waiting to see the men's decisions before making his own. In short, Jack lost fewer than thirty men and the grumbling was minimal. He was greatly relieved, but angry with himself for having put himself through so much unnecessary misery.

That night, Jack slept deeply and, in his dreams, awoke with Chloe in the hut of the Maroons. The priestess cupped Chloe's chin and looked intently into her eyes. She spoke to her, first in Mandingo, then in English, translating: Love your husband, *Manishie* Viollca, for this night you will conceive.

42—One, Once More

Chloe sat at the window in the upstairs hall, the same window where she sat the day she realized that she was in love with Jack. She could no longer safely negotiate the stairs with her belly incongruously huge on her delicate frame, so her world was reduced to her room, the balcony and the upstairs hall. The resulting solitude and the unrelenting physical discomfort had eroded her earlier happiness and plunged her deeply into grief from which not even the impending birth could lift her.

Unable to remain long in any posture, she slowly heaved her bulk into a standing position and arched her spine, pressing both hands into the small of her back, trying to ease the strain. She wandered over to the gallery and looked down just in time to see Emerson stride to the door as voices were heard outside. Fearing to be seen in her present state, she hurried (as best she could) back to her secluded sitting area and eased herself onto the damask bench in the classic backward-leaning posture of late pregnancy.

Emerson would get rid of the intruders in short order. She turned away from the hall and resumed looking down at the unchanging garden below.

Her thoughts were far away from this mansion, this estate, far out to sea on a black ship with a white stripe and black and white sails. Her eyes weren't seeing the verdant garden; her ears weren't hearing the whispered voices and quiet footsteps on the stairs until a soft noise close by caused her to turn her head.

A second later, the universe ceased to exist except for the brimming dark eyes of her husband.

PART
THREE

43—Emerson, Tshaya, and Geoffrey

Maria and Tshaya were surprised that the shock of Jack's return, the introduction of a sister-in-law, and the abrupt release from all danger of prosecution had not sent Chloe into labor straightaway. Chloe herself had begun to think that she would never deliver; her body was as miserable as her heart was ecstatic.

Nevertheless, another week went by, then two, and May turned to June. Observing Chloe's exceptional girth relative to her stature, the other two women privately worried that if she carried the pregnancy to full term the infant would be too large to arrive without endangering both mother and child.

Jack was almost comical in his solicitousness. He waited on her, catered to her whims, fanned her, massaged her swollen feet, and sponged her with cool water a dozen times a day. She was unable to sleep more than an hour at a time and he matched his schedule to hers, waking with her through the night to rub her back and help her try to find a position that allowed her to rest. Maria was grateful for the help, being worn down from tending to her regular duties and assisting Chloe day and night.

Jack slept with Chloe, but sometimes his presence increased her discomfort and he would repair to the bedside cot Maria had used. Nevertheless, he was attuned to her every sound and was instantly alert when she so much as sighed heavily.

Tshaya was becoming concerned for his health, as he was looking haggard. She repeatedly offered to sleep on the cot and look after Chloe, allowing him to get a night's rest in the guest bedroom, but he wouldn't hear of it. He felt responsible for his wife's suffering.

With his focus so narrowed and his days and nights filled, the running of the ship by proxy fell to Tshaya. For the first week, the *Sinecure* lay at anchor, her crew getting into mischief ashore and accomplishing nothing for their new employers. In desperation, Tshaya and Emerson studied the terms of the Letter of Marque and concluded that Jack's physical presence aboard the ship was not required so long as he was the captain of record, the ship flew his flag and was commanded by his duly appointed subordinate. Tshaya handled the logistics of making Somers acting captain and gave him an agenda that ostensibly came from Jack but was, in fact, devised by herself and Emerson. The ship was to go out on short forays and return to Port Royal with full reports and any booty taken for the Crown. She assigned certain crewmen as couriers between the ship and the manor, freeing more of her time to help her brother and sister-in-law.

Nevertheless, she was often required to return to the ship to handle some minor crisis for her brother and she hated being driven in the dogcart by Rodrigo. Furthermore, it was compromising his duties at home to be gone so much. One morning she realized the courier was two days late and she prepared to leave for the harbor in a hurry. Rodrigo said he'd go hitch up the horse, but Tshaya stopped him.

"No, Rodrigo, that's a waste of your time and mine. I'll take that big gray hunter Emerson rides."

"No, Señora Scarpia, Zeus is too spirited. It would be dangerous."

"I'll go get him myself if you won't help. This is wasting time." She started for the barns.

"Please, Señora, no one rides Zeus but Emerson."

"Have you another swift horse?"

"No, but Bella is a gentle mare. I could—"

"This isn't a pleasure ride, Rodrigo! Where is Zeus?"

"In this first barn. But wait, Señora. If you insist, I will tack him up for you."

By now they were in the barn at Zeus' stall.

"I can't wait for a damned saddle! Hand me that bridle." She brushed past the stammering Rodrigo, swept a bridle from its hook and had her arm over Zeus' neck pulling the bit into his mouth before either horse or man realized what had happened. A moment later she had unlatched the stall door and was hurrying into the sunlight holding the reins below the bit, the confused Zeus jogging behind her.

Without so much as a pause, she swept to the animal's near side and, in one fluid motion, grasped his withers and swung onto his back as he leapt into a run. Rodrigo stood gaping, watching the pair rapidly growing smaller in the distance.

The stableman wasn't the only witness to the remarkable spectacle. In the dining hall, Emerson was adjusting the arrangement of a silver tea service when he heard the clatter of hooves and looked out the window. The sight that met his eyes made his breath catch in his throat: horse and rider moved as one being, the woman's long black hair and the horse's snowy tail standing straight out like ships' pennants as they vanished over the rise.

Jack was pleased that Tshaya and Somers were managing the affairs of the *Sinecure*, but he rarely thought much about it at this critical time. Despite his lack of rest, he never tired of being with Chloe and talking about the future—the future they had both despaired of having. This was his first time to be close to a pregnant woman and he could not get enough of feeling the baby move and kick. The two decided that the child would soon be a real handful if it were so active after being born. He often put his ear to her belly, but could make no sense of all the noises he was hearing, saying that it sounded to him like something was capsizing in there.

Her earlier moodiness and unpredictability had smoothed out into a kind of constant serenity despite the physical discomfort. Having Jack safe at her side and his child so full of life within her, she would not have traded her pain for the comfort of a cloud. She always had a smile for her husband even though she was now past being able to fill her lungs or her stomach. She was growing weaker and everyone in the household seemed to realize it except her and Jack.

As the Bellamie home was settling down for the evening, Emerson opened the library door intending to find something to read before bedtime, then he halted, startled. The room was occupied. Tshaya stood by a window, reading by the fading light. She looked up and smiled. He bowed slightly.

"I beg your pardon, Madam Scarpia. I didn't mean to intrude." He started to back out of the door.

"Nonsense, Emerson. Please don't leave on my account. It's just been such a long time since I've had access to a well-stocked library that I simply must indulge during the rare quiet moment."

"I understand, Madam. May I assist you in locating a preferred volume?"

"Emerson, please. Call me Tshaya. I'm neither your employer nor your senior."

"Very well, M—, Tshaya. If you wish."

"I wish. Please, let's not be so formal. My brother and I are rather uncomfortable with such protocols. Just consider me a friend and discourse with me as such."

"Very well, um, Tshaya. If we are to be friends, perhaps I could be so bold as to inquire where a pirate captain learned to handle horses so well?"

"Horses? Oh! You saw me on Zeus. I apologize for taking your mount without asking, but I had urgent business with the ship and required the swiftest in the stable. It was rude of me and I shan't do it again."

"Not at all, M—, Tshaya. Besides, he isn't my horse. All of them on this estate belong to Madam and I know that she would deny you nothing, especially for the good of the Captain's vessel. But you haven't answered my question."

"Oh. Well, I know that you are aware of our Roma heritage, my brother and I. Gypsy children are on horses before they can walk and become as attuned to horses as to each other. Of course, after my adoption by Lord and Lady Jamison, I did receive formal training in dressage and hunting."

"You are schooled in equitation?"

"I am. My sister, Mirella, and I had an excellent teacher in the Colonies."

Emerson was spellbound by this exotic beauty dressed as a pirate and speaking like a peer.

"Does your brother also ride so well?"

"He does, but without the formal training. I am one year older than Jack; Mirella is two years older than I. After we were orphaned, we were separated and I lost track of my brother and sister. Mirella was put to work as a milliner's assistant and I was less than a mile away from her, slaving away at the ovens of a baker, although we were unaware of each other's close proximity.

"Poor Jack was taken to a brutal orphanage until he was grown to a size sufficient for manual labor, but he eventually escaped and you have heard how we were so fortuitously reunited this year."

"Most astonishing, especially considering you had both become pirate captains."

"I myself shall be amazed by that to the end of my years. Perhaps it is an inherited tendency to live outside the law and rise to leadership."

"Perhaps. But you rejoined your sister at an early age, did you not?"

"It was wonderfully fortunate for us. Lord Jamison was eccentric, to put it gently, and had defied his parents and married an Italian woman, Teresa Scarpia, several years before, but their union had not been blessed with children. Lady Jamison was heartbroken by her empty nursery and sought to assuage her anguish with the lovely things that her husband could easily afford.

"Her particular fondness was hats. One day a few months after we Petulengros were separated, she visited the milliner's shop where Mirella was working. Well, Lady Jamison took one look at my sister and fell in love. She saw herself in Mirella's dark features and inquired as to her parentage. When she learned that the child was an orphan with no future except hard work, she promptly gave the milliner a small fortune to part with her and took her home."

"What did Lord Jamison say to that?"

"I'm told he nearly fainted, but soon realized that this was the fulfillment of his wife's longings, so he spared no expense getting my sister settled into her opulent life. But Mirella, while grateful to be adopted and adored by such generous people, realized that she held a trump card—"

"Trump card? You know about trump cards? Do you also play bridge?"

"As a matter of fact, I do, although not for many years now. I'm afraid I'd be a poor partner."

"It will return faster than you might imagine. But, do go on."

"Of course. Mirella refused to be happy for her new parents, thanking them for each proffered benefit, but weeping and unable to eat. Lady Jamison was frantic and when she asked the reason, my sister told her that she was unable to enjoy such luxury knowing that her sister and brother were suffering. It didn't take Lady Jamison long to inquire about town and locate me. I was taken forthwith to the Jamison estate and reunited with Mirella.

"But poor Jack. His name had already been changed for him and he was miles away in Portsmouth. I suspect the Jamisons didn't try too vigorously to locate him, as they didn't seem terribly keen on having a male child of Gypsy lineage. I don't know why that mattered to them, but it did.

"Eventually, Mirella and I had to give up on him. He was so small and had been so wild as they took him away, we feared he might have been killed shortly thereafter. We made a pact never to forget him and, years later, Mirella named her firstborn son after him. Somewhere in Virginia there is a tree with his name carved on it. We did that shortly after our arrival in the New World."

"If Scarpia was your foster mother's maiden name, how did it become your surname?"

"After our adoption, the family traveled quite a bit. We visited most of the countries on the continent at one time or other and frequently went to Italy to visit Mother's relatives. Mirella and I soon became fast friends with our new cousins, including a boy two years my junior, Vincenzo Scarpia.

"For years we were playmates and correspondents, then Mother's family moved to the Colonies to cultivate vineyards. I was 18. Two years later, Mother persuaded Father to move us there as well so that she could be closer to her relatives. Father was still estranged from his own parents, so he cheerfully packed us up and we set sail for the New World.

"We settled in Virginia, but were still rather far from the Scarpias. Traveling overland seemed worse to me than sailing the Atlantic, but I found myself willing to endure considerable hardships to be with Vincenzo. When I was 22, we were married.

"On our first anniversary, we decided to return to Italy and England for a visit. Five weeks out, our ship foundered and sank in a storm. Vincenzo drowned and I was barely alive, hanging onto some flotsam with a dozen other survivors, when we were rescued by a frigate that was bound for Iberia on some sort of clandestine mission.

"When we arrived at our destination, we found ourselves among pirates and privateers from Lisbon. I was still in shock from losing Vincenzo and just wanted to go home. Since one of the corsairs was bound for Okracoke, I put aboard disguised as a pirate. By the time my gender was discovered, I had made myself valuable to the functioning of the ship and little stir was made.

"The ship was the *Talon*. I didn't disembark at Okracoke, but stayed with her for several years, thoroughly learned the piratical crafts and grew to love life in the Sweet Trade. Eventually I went to the eastern hemisphere and became a captain. Went through several ships before returning to the Caribbean on the *Chimera* and there I found Jack."

"And it is our good fortune that circumstances ultimately brought you to this estate."

"Thank you, Emerson. The pleasure is mine, I assure you."

"I see you were reading Chaucer. Are you an admirer?"

"Oh, very much so. I never tire of *The Canterbury Tales*."

"Nor do I! Which is your favorite?"

"It's difficult to select just one, but I think perhaps 'The Wife of Bath's Tale.'"

"Ah, one of mine also, along with 'The Miller's Tale.'"

She held the book to her bosom, closed her eyes, and began to recite:

> Whan that Aprille with his shoures sote
> The droughte of Marche hath perced to the rote,
> And bathed every veyne in swich licour,
> Of which vertu engendred is the flour.

His voice soft with wonder, he joined her and they continued in unison:

> Whan Zephirus eek with his swete breeth
> Inspired hath in every holt and heeth
> The tendre croppes, and the yonge sonne
> Hath in the Ram his halfe cours y-ronne . . .

44—Say Goodbye

Maria and Tshaya helped Chloe into her voluminous sleeping gown as Jack prepared himself for bed in the dressing room. When she was settled, she asked Maria to leave the two of them alone.

Sensing something of import, Tshaya sat on the bed beside her sister-in-law and took her hand.

"What's on your mind, Darling?"

"Tshaya, please, before Jack comes back, I need you to promise me something."

"Anything, Dear. What is it?"

Chloe's eyes filled with tears, but her voice was steady.

"Please stay with Jack and help him to be a good father. Raise our child with him and keep Emerson and Maria and Rodrigo with you. They've been my family ever since I was widowed. Let them remain as such for my child."

"Chloe, I'll do anything you ask, but you're going to raise this baby with Jack, not I."

"Tshaya, I'm not going to make it through this. I've grown too weak. There was too much time in the beginning that I didn't take proper care of myself while I was immersed in grieving for my husband. I didn't even realize that I was pregnant until Emerson made me face it."

"No, Luv. You have great inner strength. You'll come through. I know you will."

"I won't. I've known it for weeks now and have hidden it from Jack. Let him be happy until the last, Tshaya. He's endured so much already. But I will give him a robust child and that will be my *magnum opus*, my greatest gift to the love of my life."

Now Tshaya was crying.

"Chloe. Chloe."

"Please bury me with this necklace. It was a wedding gift from Jack and I've never taken it off since that day. Now, we must compose ourselves before he returns."

"I give you my word. I will do all you have asked."

When Jack entered the room, his sister was fluffing a pillow for his wife and he detected none of the sadness from the moments before.

It was shortly before midnight on the eighth of June. Chloe had been especially restless since dinner and had at last fallen into a fitful sleep. Jack dozed on the cot beside the bed.

She opened her eyes and twisted her shoulders, frowning. Suddenly she gasped.

"Jack! Jack!"

"Wha', Ducks? What is it?"

She didn't answer, but she grabbed his wrist and he knew that her labor had begun. He roared, frantic to summon help.

"Maria! Tshaya! Come Quickly! *Now*! HURRY!"

Within seconds both women were in the bedroom as Chloe was seized with a violent contraction. Jack and Tshaya tried to comfort her while Maria ran to alert Emerson and Rodrigo.

Emerson was in the kitchen making preparations for the long night that lay ahead for the household when Tshaya rushed past him and out the door on the run. She arrived at the stables just as Rodrigo was climbing into the dogcart.

"I am going for the midwife, Señora Scarpia. Tell Señora Bellamie that help is coming."

"Rodrigo, listen to me. Not the midwife. Bring the doctor and for God's sake, hurry!"

His eyes widened as he caught the meaning behind her words. He shouted to the horse and they dashed into the night.

Chloe rested between the pains as best she could while Jack and Tshaya fussed over her and Maria made ready for the delivery. She tried to ease her husband's obvious anxiety by smiling and making little jokes about how eager the baby was to make an appearance, but then another contraction would start and she would writhe and scream and clutch at the blanket.

Her water broke just as Maria was tucking extra linens under her for that very purpose. Jack was shocked, as he didn't know that was a normal part of childbirth. Everything that was happening put him more on edge and his sister watched him with a mixture of pity and concern.

Emerson joined them to wait for Rodrigo's return and was invaluable in helping to keep a feeling of normality between the pains, conversing and asking questions designed to focus the others' thoughts on more pleasant things.

"Captain, Madam, have you decided upon a name for the child?"

"If it's a girl, we'll name her for Chloe's mother and mine."

"And if it's a boy, he'll be named for Jack's father and mine, which was also my brother's name."

"And those names will be...?"

"Penelope Darklis Lizbet Bellamie or Benjamin Veshengo Thomas Bellamie."

"Lizbet? Thomas?"

But just then Chloe had another contraction and the questions went unanswered.

Morning was a mere hint in the eastern sky as Emerson and Rodrigo sat on benches outside Chloe's room. From within they could hear her moaning and crying out in agony, now quiet for only brief periods and noticeably weaker. Neither man was conversant in obstetrics, but nonetheless each sensed that this was not going well. The occasional word overheard from the doctor or one of the others gave them little encouragement. Maria's trips past them to fetch things were hurried and she gave them only sparse information.

There had been an ugly scene when the doctor arrived and attempted to eject Jack from the room. Maria had tearfully begged the enraged captain to acquiesce for the sake of his wife, but Chloe herself was pleading for him to be allowed to remain. The doctor held his ground until Jack and Tshaya took him aside and explained why it was in his own best interests to get over it. One angry pirate was bad enough, but two...

At length the house was filled with the first lusty cries of a healthy newborn and Jack soon emerged with a tiny bundle in his arms, his face glowing.

"It's a girl. Penelope Darklis Lizbet Bellamie."

The other men rushed to peer at the wee, squalling thing, smiling and relieved. Emerson touched the baby's little fist and looked at the new father.

"How is Madam, Captain?"

Before he could answer, a guttural scream from the room made all three men blanch. Jack handed the baby to Emerson and ran back inside. Emerson held and patted the infant to calm her as her mother howled and wailed.

For more than twenty minutes, Chloe screamed, sounding less human with each outcry. Then, all was quiet.

The door opened and Tshaya walked out carrying a mewling, cooing baby in her arms, her face showing an expression of both amazement and pain.

"A boy. We have twins."

"And Madam? Is Madam all right?"

She burst into tears and Emerson was instantly at her side.

"No, Emerson. No, she's not all right. Not at all."

Holding little Penelope in one arm, he put the other around the woman's shoulders and eased her onto the bench beside him. Rodrigo put his face in his hands and wept.

A moment later the doctor came out of the room wiping his hands on a towel. All three rose.

"Doctor?"

"She is very low. It won't be long. Someone should locate a wet nurse."

The room was dim, the draperies drawn against the encroaching heat. A lamp burned on the little reading table. Jack lay beside his wife, watching her and holding her hand. Her eyes were closed and she was a ghastly ashen gray.

Her eyelids fluttered open. Her voice was nearly inaudible.

"Jack?"

"I'm here, Darling. I'm right here." He sat up and leaned close to her, still holding her hand.

"The babies?"

"They're fine, Love, just fine, strong and healthy. You did well, Sweetheart. You did very well."

"Jack?"

"Yes, Dearest?"

A long pause.

"Please say goodbye. You must tell me goodbye."

"No! I'll not say it. I won't give you up!"

She hadn't the strength to argue with him. Her eyes focused somewhere far away.

"Jack? Do you remember the dream we both had in the Maroon hut?"

"The one with the two cherubs. We have our two cherubs now, Chloe. We know the meaning now."

She smiled.

"Yes. Our two cherubs. Tell them I loved them."

She closed her eyes and sighed. Then she was still.

"Chloe! No! One more breath, Chloe! Just one more! *Now*, Chloe! One more breath! One more breath!"

Epilogue

The little island was the picture of tropical serenity, the blue-green Caribbean lapping at the shores and glittering in the morning sun. Three houses of moderate size and elegant style sat about 500 feet apart and well back from the beach and docks, surrounded by gardens and lawns. Behind the houses were barns and sheds of varying sizes and a large, oval ring of white board fence, all amid fields and paddocks. Livestock of various kinds were beginning their day in peace and plenty.

On the lawn of the easternmost dwelling a flamboyant peacock spread and rattled his tail as he strutted, herding his harem of peahens before him. A man in a farm wagon was guiding the horse out of the barnyard of the westernmost house and toward the groves beyond.

By a paddock behind the middle house, a blond-haired woman in breeches and riding habit was adjusting the saddle girth on a splendid black horse as a small child scurried about, chasing a yellow butterfly. An older girl of about six or seven was helping her mother by looking after her little sister, not allowing the younger child to stray too far.

On a low hill beyond the farms, a black-haired boy sat bareback on his dappled pony watching the horizon through a telescope, his little face serious as he concentrated his search in an arc of about 40 degrees. His bored mount shifted its weight and pawed the ground with a fore hoof, bobbed its head and snorted, eager to be off. The rider absently patted the animal's neck and murmured a calming word, then abruptly stopped his sweep with the glass and fixed it to one spot.

Suddenly, with a whoop of joy, he drove his bare heels into the pony's sides. In an instant, the two were hurdling down the hill toward the center house, past the tidy little cemetery with its two crosses and fresh wildflowers, the boy holding the reins with one hand and waving the telescope above his head with the other.

"Mama! Mama! He's back! Papa's here!"

"Are you certain, Ben? It could be any ship, you know."

"No, Mama! It's a black brig with a white stripe and black and white sails. It's Papa. It *is*!"

In her excitement, the woman carelessly dropped her hat onto the ground and didn't bother to retrieve it.

"Oh, Ben, how wonderful! Quick! Ride over and tell Tia Maria and Tio Rodrigo. Pen, run and tell Auntie Tshaya and Uncle Em while I put Raven away."

She hurriedly unsaddled and unbridled the horse before turning him into the enclosure, then grabbed the giggling little butterfly bandit and sped across the vine-covered veranda into the house, emerging through the front door moments later with her hair freshly combed. Holding her child's hand she rushed through the front dooryard and out the gate, scattering dogs and guinea fowl, then down the path to the beach.

Standing on the dock, the two waved and waved, the woman twirling a royal purple silk scarf and jumping up and down in order to be seen more easily from the approaching ship.

Before long, they saw their greeting returned by a slight, dark-haired man standing in the prow, wearing a captain's coat and waving a battered old black tricorne.